I0665136

# A GIFT OF SHADOWS

Also by Stephanie Stamm

*A GIFT OF WINGS*

# A GIFT OF SHADOWS

## THE LIGHT-BRINGER SERIES: BOOK TWO

## STEPHANIE STAMM

ZEKE & ME BOOKS
KALAMAZOO, MICHIGAN

This book is a work of fiction. Any references to historical events, real people, or real places are used fictitiously. All other names, characters, places, and incidents are the product of the author's imagination, and any resemblance to actual events, places, or persons, living or dead, is purely coincidental.

Published by Zeke & Me Books, December 2014

Copyright © 2014 by Stephanie Stamm
Cover by Ravven, www.ravven.com

All rights reserved. No part of this book may be reproduced, scanned, or distributed in any form or by any means without the prior written permission of the author.

ISBN 978-0-9883042-2-2

For Mom

# CHAPTER 1

The December wind slipped icy fingers beneath Lucky's collar. She snugged her scarf closer to her neck and stepped up her pace. As if she needed anything other than anticipation to speed her steps. For the first time in the two months since she had been Made Naphil, she had more to look forward to than a day in Zeke's basement.

She spent most of her waking hours in the brownstone's lower level—either in the gym, working with Malachi or Aidan to hone her more powerful Naphil body, or in Zeke's study, playing student or completing the work he assigned her as his assistant.

But not today.

Today she had a field trip to the training center.

She had to admit she was a little scared of how she would get there. Aidan, Kev, Zeke, and Malachi did it all the time, but she'd only practiced dematerializing in Zeke's house. That was disconcerting enough. Fading from one place and reforming on some other dimensional plane, or wherever the training center was, added a whole new level of discomfort. Still, it sounded better than getting squished through the Gates.

She reached Zeke's block to find Aidan standing in front of the brownstone waiting for her. He raised a hand when he saw her, and she responded in kind, a smile curving her lips. He looked so handsome, his golden curls bright against the upturned collar of his black leather jacket. When she reached him, he hooked an arm around her shoulders to pull her close and dipped his head down to hers.

"Good morning," he said, his breath warm against her cheek.

"Morning."

She tilted her face to receive his kiss. His lips clung to hers, and she pressed herself closer against him.

"So," he said, when he raised his head, "are you ready for an advanced lesson in dematerializing?"

She nodded. "Just please don't let me scatter my molecules so far I can't pull myself back together."

"No worries," he said, catching her hand in his and heading up the stairs to the door—which opened before they could ring the bell.

"Perfect timing," said Zeke. "I was on my way to the kitchen to make some tea when I saw you coming up the stairs."

He ushered them inside, closing the door behind them to shut out the cold. "Would you like some? Tea, I mean."

Aidan shook his head. "Sorry, we don't have time. We have to be at the training center in a few minutes."

"Thanks, though," Lucky added. "A cup of hot tea does sound pretty great."

Zeke gave her a warm smile. "Another time."

Aidan shrugged out of his leather jacket. Lucky dropped her backpack beside one of the living room's seldom-used chairs and draped her coat over it.

"Okay," Aidan said, stretching both hands toward her. "Take my hands. It can be pretty difficult to dematerialize to a place you've never been before, because you can't put an image of it in your mind. It helps if you're touching someone else who has been there."

"But we won't be touching anymore when we dematerialize. And what if our molecules get scrambled?"

Aidan laughed. "They won't get scrambled. And, yes, we will still be touching in a way. You know what it's like to summon and dismiss your wings, right? They always exist as energy. When you summon them, you convert that energy to matter. This is sort of the same thing. We're just adding movement. In the simplest of terms, when we dematerialize, we convert our entire bodies to energy, which relocates to our new location and reforms as matter. The energy that makes up our bodies will remember how to reform into our bodies, like the wings remember how to reform each time you summon them."

"Right. Nothing to it," Lucky responded. "Easy peasy."

Aidan grinned. "Ready?"

"I guess." Lucky put her hands into his.

"I'll get us to the training center. I've been there lots of times, and I've never materialized halfway through the wall. At least, not yet."

Lucky squinted at him, and his grin widened. "You concentrate on our linked hands—how they look, how they feel, the texture, the temperature, the tightness of the grip, as many details as possible. That should keep you with me."

Lucky raised her eyebrows. "Should?"

Aidan grinned again. "Will," he promised.

"Okay." She took a deep breath.

Aidan's hands tightened on hers, and she opened her senses so she could grasp every possible detail of her connection to him. With every sense at full volume, she could not only see their linked hands, but the places where their energetic fields overlapped. Her sense of touch was so heightened she could feel the tiny ridges on Aidan's skin. She could hear his pulse as well as her own, smell his scent mingling with hers. She could even detect a subtle change in her sense of taste, as if something of Aidan traveled through her fingertips, up her arms and all the way to her taste buds.

"Now," she breathed.

And then she was gone, and everywhere, and nowhere.

And then she was standing with Aidan again, the touch of his hands on hers filling her senses.

"Here we are," he said.

Lucky released his hands, flipped off the extra switches in her mental control room, and looked around her.

They stood outside a huge brick complex that looked like a cross between a factory and a school. It was surrounded by extensive grounds, marked off in the manner of athletic fields and littered with various types of equipment, all unfamiliar to Lucky. People spilled out one end of the main building, pulling on gear as they headed toward one of the marked off areas.

"That's my troop," Aidan said. He took one of her hands and led her toward an entrance at the side of the building. "Let's go find Kev. I'm late."

He pressed his palm against a panel in the doorframe, and the door clicked open.

"What's with the security panel?" Lucky asked.

"Additional protection. No one can materialize inside the buildings, and only the members of the Forces have security clearance. If our enemies manage to get through the wards surrounding the property, they still won't be able to get inside the center."

Stepping through the door behind Aidan, Lucky entered a large gymnasium. She didn't recognize any of the equipment organized into neat groupings in different areas, but she did recognize the young man jogging toward them.

Aidan gave Lucky's hand a quick squeeze. "See you later."

He waved to his brother as he ran past him and out the door on the room's far side.

"How was the trip?" Kev asked, coming to a halt beside her. His eyes crinkled at the corners when he smiled.

"Good," she said. "Quick. And I don't think I left a trail of misplaced molecules between here and Zeke's."

Kev chuckled. "But without a trail of molecular bread-crumbs, how will you get back?"

"Uh-oh. Maybe I'm stuck here." Lucky smiled at him.

"Then we might as well make use of the time. How about that tour I promised?"

Kev showed her the complex's various buildings and practice fields. In addition to multiple gyms with traditional strengthening and athletic training equipment, there were spaces designed for more types of specialized training than Lucky could have imagined. The troops seemed to be taught every type of combat technique known to human and angel, and the facility held all the gear and equipment they could need. There were rooms for solo and group workouts, state-of-the-art battle simulators, and multiple fields for drills and practices.

There were also a number of barracks, mostly empty, but ready for habitation should the need arise. Since the members of the Forces of the Fallen could dematerialize to and from the training center at will, they weren't required to live on site. But the barracks were available for quartering the troops should any extended conflict require round-the-clock training or centralized living.

"What do you think?" Kev asked as they strolled from the barracks back toward the complex's main building.

"It's amazing, kind of overwhelming."

"Wait 'til you see what's up next."

Lucky looked a question at him, but he offered no more information.

"Where is the training center located anyway?" she asked.

"Shift time and space infinitesimally in any direction, and you'll find another existential plane. This space is carved out of one of those. When the Forces first organized, Zeke and the other leaders of the Fallen decided the location of the training center should be as hidden and protected as possible. They feared staying on earth in our normal dimensional reality would pose too many dangers to the humans the

Fallen were sworn to protect. So they found this space, created the training center, and linked it to our dimension, restricting access to the Forces. That means no unwitting humans stumble into it, and it's virtually impossible for our enemies to find."

They had reached another door into the main building but on the opposite end from the entrance Lucky and Aidan had used. After Kev pressed his hand to the door's security panel, they stepped into a hallway. Kev led the way across the hall to another sealed door.

"Are you ready for this?" he asked.

"Since I don't know what's behind the door, I'm not sure how to be prepared," Lucky said. "But I guess I'm ready whenever you are."

Kev touched his palm to the security panel and then held the door open to usher her through. Lucky gasped. Lit cases filled with knives, swords, spears, laser-like weapons, and other items she couldn't begin to identify lined the walls. Free-standing cases stood at regular intervals down the room's center, each of those also filled with weapons. Kev pressed a button beneath one of the lit wall displays and a huge drawer, likewise filled, slid from the wall.

Lucky scanned the weapons gleaming in the bright light. Her gaze lingered on the swords with their elaborate hilts. She longed to feel the weight of one in her hand, even as her mind and stomach quailed at the idea of employing the deadly blades.

She walked slowly around the room, studying the cases and their contents. So many ways to die. For a moment, she imagined the cases filled not with weapons but lifeless bodies. When she had made a complete circuit of the room and returned to Kev's side, she gazed at him in silence.

"I know," he said. "I'm used to it, and it still gets to me. Every time."

She swallowed. "Will I learn how to use these?" she asked, her voice subdued.

"Some of them," Kev answered. "After your Gift manifests, you'll be brought back here to see which ones resonate with your particular Gift. You'll be taught to use those that call to you. And one or more of them will become yours."

Lucky took in the information in silence. She didn't like the idea of a weapon or weapons staking a claim on her.

"Your broadsword," she said. "It—called to you?"

Kev nodded. "And the shield."

"You don't know how to use the rest of these?"

"Oh, yes, I know how to use the others. I captained the Forces before Malachi. I learned how to use them all." Beneath Kev's matter-of-fact words Lucky sensed a depth of emotion she couldn't quite gauge. "But Pacifer and Aegis— the broadsword and shield—are mine. They're the only ones I can summon at will."

Lucky remembered Aidan fighting Luil in the grounds of the country club. "Like Aidan's sword and spear?"

"Yes. They belong to Aidan as Pacifer and Aegis belong to me."

"Do all the weapons have names?"

"Just the claimed ones. They're named during the Bonding, when the weapon and its owner are linked."

"The owner names it, like a pet?" Lucky grinned.

Kev shook his head, his face serious. "No. The name is revealed. It's forged in the link of the weapon and the owner. If someone else bore my broadsword, it would have a different name."

"Could someone else bear it?"

"Not as long as I live. Upon my death, provided the sword is not destroyed with me, it will once again be among the items available for Bonding."

Lucky shivered. She didn't want to think about the possibility of his death.

"I wonder when my Gift will show up," she said. "It's been over two months since the Making."

"It will manifest in its own time. I understand it's different for everyone." Kev gestured toward the door. "Ready to go? There's one more place I want to show you."

"What's your Gift?" Lucky asked when they were back outside, walking toward a smaller, windowless building set off from the others.

"Fire," Kev said.

"Show me?"

Kev shook his head.

Lucky was still curious, but she didn't push. "What's in there?" she asked, tilting her head in the direction of the building they approached.

"You'll see."

Neither of them spoke again until they reached their destination, but the silence wasn't riddled with tension or anticipation, and Lucky felt no need to fill it.

When they reached the doorway to the building, Kev stepped back indicating Lucky should open it. Glancing from Kev to the door, she saw that, unlike all the others they had passed through on the tour, this one had no security panel. With heightened curiosity, she pulled the door open and stepped inside, Kev behind her. As she looked around, her eyes widened, and her mouth dropped open.

They stood in a kind of hallway, roughly eight to ten feet wide, enclosing a central open-air courtyard, which could be seen through the panes of glass that formed the top part of the hallway's inner wall. In the center of each side of the inner wall, a door granted access to the rectangular courtyard. The hallway was floored with smooth, pale wood a couple of shades lighter than the panels that covered the lower halves of the outer walls. Potted plants and fountains decorated the corners of the room.

Lucky crossed to the inner wall to gaze out onto the courtyard. It had been designed for relaxation and meditation, with a curving walking path and a few individual-sized benches placed near pools of water, artfully positioned rocks, or pieces of metal sculpture. Trees and shade plants sur-rounded it all. She would never have thought to find such an oasis of peace in the midst of the training center, with its gyms and practice fields and weapons room.

"It's so peaceful," she whispered, turning back toward Kev.

"Yeah." He bent to remove his boots, and Lucky did the same, setting hers beside his next to the door. "Malachi is a very wise man."

"Malachi?"

Kev nodded. "This was his idea. We added it a few years ago. I'm glad he suggested it. I come here often."

Taking a step down the hallway, Kev held out his hand to her and, without thinking, Lucky put hers into it. After a couple of steps, she realized what she'd done and loosened her fingers from around his. Kev dropped her hand as if she'd stung him and clasped his hands together behind his back.

"Sorry," Lucky breathed.

"No need to be."

His breathing deepened, and she felt him slipping deeper into himself as they walked slowly around the hallway.

When they had walked three-quarters of the circuit, she moved to the door to the inner courtyard. Like the outer door, this one had no security panel. She opened the door and stepped into the courtyard.

She made her way to one of the benches and sat down. The bench she had chosen faced a small pool of water with a single rock resting inside it. An abstract metal sculpture stood a few inches away from the pool.

She studied the lines of the sculpture. Shaped from simple curves and interlocked forms, it somehow managed to convey both peacefulness and sensuality at the same time. Something about it made her want to touch it. She resisted the urge, but the piece drew her eyes back to it every time she looked away. After a few moments, she relaxed and allowed her gaze to caress the sculpture's lines and curves.

The warm sunlight shining into the courtyard provided a nice change from the cold back home in Chicago, and she relaxed in the heat. Her gaze softened on the sculpture, and soon her eyes drifted closed. Several minutes later, she felt a shadow fall across her and opened her eyes to look up at Kev.

"We'd better go," he said. "Aidan's drills have ended, and he'll be waiting for us."

Lucky noticed he'd tucked his hands into his jeans pockets. She wondered if he'd done so to keep from reaching for her hand again.

They had made it halfway back to the training center's main building when she spoke. "Thank you," she said. "I enjoyed the tour, and I'm glad you ended it with the meditation space. It's lovely."

"It was my pleasure," Kev said. His smile was as warm as the sunlight in the courtyard.

# CHAPTER 2

Laughter bubbled out of Lucky's throat when she bobbled the barrel roll for the third time.

"Let's do something else and come back to this later," she said, as she came to a hover next to Aidan.

He chuckled. "Okay. How about a vertical climb and a plummet? Those are all about strength and timing without so many subtle muscle shifts."

He explained how she should move her wings for the climb and performed the movements with her at a much reduced speed. Then he demonstrated the move, firing himself upward with such force that he was far above her in a matter of seconds.

"Your turn," he shouted.

Lucky took a deep breath, steadied herself, and drew her wings down and back with all the force she could muster. She didn't make it as far as Aidan, but she thought she reached a respectable height for her first try.

"Good job," Aidan said. "Again."

The height of her climbs increased with each attempt. When she shot to only a few yards short of Aidan, he suggested switching to plummets.

"The trick to the plummet is stopping exactly when you want to."

This time Aidan demonstrated the move first. Diving straight downward, he stopped inches short of the training center roof.

"See what I mean?" he asked when he returned to Lucky's side.

"Yeah. I don't think I want to get that close yet."

Aidan grinned. "I wouldn't recommend it."

He showed her how to position her wings and suggested she try a slow dive the first few times. Once she felt comfortable with that, he had her increase both her dive speed and distance.

Lucky offered a silent thanks for the extra space between her and the roof when she pulled up several yards beyond her designated stopping point. As with the climbs though, she improved with practice.

When Aidan called a halt, saying it was time to head back to Zeke's, she felt more than a little pleased with herself.

After making a sandwich in Zeke's well-stocked kitchen, Lucky logged a few hours of study time.

Then she changed into workout clothes and made her way to the basement gym for her combat lesson. There she found Malachi, not Aidan, sitting cross-legged at one end of the practice mat, his long braids tied at the nape of his neck.

"Aidan has been detained. I'm afraid you are stuck with me this afternoon," Malachi said, rising to his feet in what appeared to be one fluid movement.

"Okay." Lucky smiled at him. "Kev showed me your addition to the training center complex today. It's perfect. Gorgeous and peaceful."

Malachi inclined his head. "The original design had a certain void I thought needed filling."

"Kev said you're a very wise man. I agree."

"Wise enough, perhaps, to sense an attempt to delay the inevitable?" Malachi asked.

"How can you even think such a thing?" Lucky grinned, but her muscles tightened in nervous anticipation as the humor that lit Malachi's eyes took on a predatory cast.

Lucky's fears proved to be justified. Malachi was a far more formidable opponent than Aidan had been in the few hand-to-hand sessions she'd had with him. She had accused Aidan of taking it easy on her. She couldn't say the same of Malachi. By the end of the session, she was drenched with sweat, aching in muscles she hadn't even known she had, and much wiser about what to do and what not to do when grappling with a man over twice her size and with a lifetime's more experience. When Malachi finally relented and called it quits for the day, she collapsed on the mat, panting.

"Now that," she said between breaths, "was a workout."

"You enjoyed it?" Malachi asked, lowering himself to sit beside her. His breath didn't seem to have sped up at all.

Lucky groaned. "I don't know about 'enjoyed.' But I worked hard, and I learned a lot. You could give Aidan some lessons on training."

Malachi's eyebrows rose. "Aidan is usually quite good. Perhaps your relationship has clouded his judgment...?"

"Maybe." Her breathing restored to normal, Lucky pushed herself up to sitting. "When I accused him of taking it easy on me, he demonstrated why he had to hold back. But still, I think he could be tougher without being too tough. You got the balance right. You pushed me to my limits without overwhelming me."

"I'll talk to him. Maybe he will hear it differently coming from me."

"Thanks."

Lucky stood and stretched a bit to relieve some aches. They were already beginning to subside. Her newly Naphil body recovered much more quickly than her human one had. "I'd better get cleaned up. I don't have much time before my lesson with Zeke."

"He may not be available," said Malachi. He rose with his usual fluid grace. "I believe he is with Aidan."

Lucky frowned. "Well, I'll stop by the study anyway," she said. "Thanks for the session, Malachi."

She headed toward the door to the showers.

After she had showered and changed, Lucky went to Zeke's study as promised. A note taped to the door informed her the lesson had indeed been cancelled. Crumpling the note in her hand, she climbed the basement stairs. She retrieved her coat and backpack from where she'd left them in the living room and stepped out into the cold Chicago evening.

She was digging through her backpack for her phone—maybe Mo would want to get a pizza or something—when she felt a strange tingling against her breastbone. She pulled her scarf aside and drew the chain holding the Light-Bringer's Medallion and her locket from beneath her sweater. The locket glowed in the graying evening light.

A few moments later, a familiar flame-haired figure dressed in a stylish, long, dark coat and high-heeled boots, stepped out of the alley to her left.

"It's been a long time, my dear," Lilith said, falling into step beside her. "How is my granddaughter these days?"

Lucky ignored the question. "Have you found anything?" she asked. The last time she had talked to Lilith, the woman had promised to look for information about Josh's attackers. Lucky had almost given up hope of hearing from her.

Lilith smiled enigmatically. "Straight to the point, aren't we? No 'Why, I'm doing quite well, thank you, grandmother. How are you?' How are we going to form a relationship if you won't even pretend to have an interest?"

Lucky sighed. "I'm sorry—Lilith. I've still not quite adjusted to the idea of you as my grandmother."

"Understood. But I would very much like to get to know you, my dear. I hope you feel the same about me."

"I do," Lucky said, after a pause. She did want to get to know Lilith. She just didn't know if she could trust her.

"Good," said Lilith. "As it happens, I do have news. Is there someplace private where we could talk? I have something to show you."

They had almost reached Lucky's apartment building, and after a slight hesitation, she invited Lilith inside.

She was grateful only the cats greeted them. She didn't want Josh to hear what Lilith had to say—even if it did concern him. She didn't even want the two of them to meet yet. Lilith still felt too much like a stranger for Lucky to introduce her to her best fam.

After tossing her backpack and coat in her room, Lucky ushered Lilith into the dining room. Both her room and the living room seemed too intimate.

Lilith removed her coat and draped it over the back of one of the dining room chairs before sitting in the one beside it. The coat had hidden an equally stylish dress in a shade of purple so dark as to be almost black. The fabric looked like cashmere to Lucky, and she wanted to touch it to see if it felt as soft as it appeared.

Staring at the elegant woman across the table, with her scarlet hair and emerald eyes, Lucky found it no wonder she had a hard time believing Lilith was her grandmother. The woman didn't appear anywhere near old enough. Then again, Zeke didn't look his age either. And Lucky had been told Lilith was as ancient as the Cherub.

"Well?" Lucky prompted.

Lilith reached into the pocket of her coat and pulled out a small vial. "Would you bring me a glass of water please?"

Lucky did as requested. When she placed the water on the table, Lilith removed the stopper on the vial and tipped a few drops into the glass. The water thickened and turned red.

"That looks like the antidote Sambethe gave Josh to counteract the toxin," Lucky said.

"This is no antidote. This is the *toxin* that poisoned your cousin."

"What?" Lucky gasped.

"I know of very few places where the toxin can be obtained. Its distribution is forbidden. However, in our world, like yours, those with the will find a way. I asked someone to contact the likely sources and learned that someone placed a rather urgent order on the day of your cousin's attack. When my agent tracked down the buyer, he told her he had not purchased it for himself, but for a client from outside the Dark Realms. He did not know the client's name, but with some persuasion, he managed to provide a description. She was small, he said, and had long white hair."

"No," Lucky whispered.

Lilith again reached into her coat pocket. "I contacted him later, and he identified the woman in this picture."

Lucky stared at the picture, unblinking.

"No," she said again. "She wouldn't…"

"I showed him more than one picture, Lucky. He chose this one without hesitation."

"You're lying."

Lilith shook her head. "No, I am not. I know you don't trust me, Lucky, but I swear what I say is true. I promised to find out what I could for you, and this is what I found."

Lucky jerked to her feet, toppling her chair. She left it lying and walked across the room and back, her arms clasped about her stomach. She felt like she might throw up.

"Sambethe," she said. "Sambethe poisoned him?"

Then she remembered something that had happened the day before, something that had seemed insignificant at the time, and she stopped, her breath catching in her throat. "No," she whispered. "Please, no."

She had barged into Zeke's study without knocking, catching him mid-conversation with a miniature hologram Sambethe. He had hurriedly ended the conversation and deactivated the hologram, but Lucky had seen the fear she might have overheard something he'd rather she hadn't on all four of his rapidly shifting faces. She'd known he meant to conceal something from her, but she had never imagined…

Zeke knew. Sambethe had betrayed her, and *Zeke knew*. A hand over her mouth, she turned and ran down the hall to the bathroom.

She knelt next to the toilet, her body wracked by dry heaves and sobs. When she felt a cool hand on her forehead, she turned to find Lilith kneeling next to her, a damp wash-cloth in her other hand. Sitting back on her heels, Lucky took the cloth and wiped her face with shaking hands. Then she began to cry in earnest. She didn't resist when Lilith drew her into an embrace.

It took a while for the tears to subside, and they left in their wake the icy flame of an anger deeper than any Lucky had ever known. She had trusted them, and they had betrayed her. They had threatened the life, the soul, of one of the people she loved most in the world. Why? To force Lucky to go through the Making, so she could help the Fallen fight this Destroyer Sambethe kept talking about? But if she hadn't survived the Making, if she'd died, Josh would be worse than dead now. Sambethe had willfully gambled with both their lives.

Had Zeke known from the beginning?

And what about Aidan? And Malachi? And Kev?

"I trusted them," she said.

"I know you did," Lilith answered. "Perhaps you should give them a chance to explain?"

Lucky shook her head. "I can't go back there right now."

"Then come with me," Lilith said, pulling Lucky to her feet. "You can stay with me for a while. It will give us a chance to get to know one another."

"I can't leave Josh," Lucky began, but even as she spoke, she realized she couldn't stay. Her whole life was bound up with Zeke and the Fallen—her studies, her training, her job. The thought of being a part of any of it seemed unbearable. And Lilith offered her a way out.

"Okay," she said. "I'll come with you."

Lucky threw some clothes and a few books into a bag, along with the statue of Michael and the dragon, which she grabbed at the last minute. She made sure to dispose of the glass of Dark toxin Lilith had mixed, even throwing the rinsed glass into the garbage for good measure, and scribbled a new note to Josh on the white board:

*I'll be gone for a while. Don't worry.*

*Love,*

*L*

*P.S. Let Mo know.*

Then she rejoined Lilith in the dining room. The red-haired woman had already donned her coat. She held her hands out to Lucky. After positioning the long cross-body strap of her travel bag and settling her backpack straps over her shoulders, Lucky placed her hands into Lilith's.

"Close your eyes," Lilith said, "and concentrate on our linked hands."

Lucky closed her eyes and let Lilith carry her away into the Dark.

# CHAPTER 3

Lucky groped her way through a darkness more complete than any she had experienced in her entire life, city dweller that she was, and that included the preternatural darkness in which she'd swirled after being skewered on an angelic sword. Even that nearly tangible blackness had had pinpoints of light. This? Nothing.

Her hands encountered fabric, soft and thick like velvet. No sooner had her fingers found it than her feet tangled in it, and she stumbled forward, hoping she didn't pull what she assumed to be curtains from the wall as she did so.

She didn't fall far, and she landed against what felt like pillows through the heavy fabric. Regaining her balance, she felt for the curtain's edge and pulled it back. She wondered why it had even been drawn, given the scant amount of light seeking entry through the windowpane the drapery had hidden. Perhaps it was meant to provide privacy for the pillow-filled window seat.

Lucky couldn't tell what colors the pillows were—in the dim light, each appeared to be a different shade of gray—but she could see well enough to discern that the pillows came in multiple shapes and sizes, and as she ran her hands over them, she felt a like variety of textures. All were soft and cozy, offering an invitation she couldn't resist.

She boosted herself into the window seat, formed a nest of the pillows, and settled back to look out the window. Her room was on at least the third floor, perhaps the fourth. She had a fuzzy recollection of climbing many stairs, aided by Lilith, but she had no real sense of how many. The warm milk Lilith had insisted she drink to calm her and help her sleep must have contained something more than a little honey. She didn't know how long she'd slept, but she felt well-rested, and she didn't seem to have any lingering effects from whatever had been in the milk.

Avoiding the memory of how she came to be there, Lucky gazed down at the grounds of Lilith's home. Like the pillows on which she rested, everything was painted with the gray hues of weak moonlight. She looked into a garden, with symmetrical paths and what appeared to be Greek or Roman statues positioned at regular intervals. The paths all led toward a large, ornate formal reflecting pool and fountain on the garden's far edge. Beyond the fountain, a forest stretched to the horizon.

She wondered what time it was. No luminous digital display broke the darkness of the room. She supposed she could try to find her phone in the depths of her backpack, but who knew if it would function here. Was she in a realm beyond the range of satellites? Maybe time didn't even work the same way.

She burrowed deeper into the mass of pillows and let herself remember why she had come here. Sambethe had poisoned Josh. She had given him the toxin in the guise of a cure. Had she also planned the attack? Or had she merely taken advantage of it when it happened? In a way, it didn't matter; the outcome remained the same.

And what of Zeke? And Aidan? And the others? With the initial shock of discovery behind her, she couldn't believe they had helped Sambethe. Zeke and Aidan's determination to keep her from undergoing the Making—until it became clear she had no choice—had seemed genuine. Surely, neither could have known what Sambethe had planned at the time.

But since then? She knew Zeke had found out and had kept it from her. And his deliberate silence felt like a betrayal. He should have told her the moment he learned anything, even the moment he suspected.

She shifted against the pillows. She would have to talk to him sooner or later, but right now later seemed the better option. She didn't know how long she could stay with Lilith, but she got the feeling her new grandmother would let her remain as long as she wanted.

A tap on the door interrupted her thoughts. Before she could even acknowledge the knock, the door swung open, and a girl who appeared to be about her age stepped into the room.

"You're awake," the girl said, leaving the door open and strolling across to the window seat. "You like to rise with the moon?"

"Moon?" Lucky asked, feeling stupid.

Apparently the other girl thought she was stupid too. She pointed out the window toward the sky. "You like to get up early, to rise with the moon?" she asked, enunciating each word with care.

"Where I come from, getting up early means to rise with the sun—or, depending on the time of year, before the sun," Lucky said.

"Oh, right. You're from the human realm. Sorry. Things are a little different here. No sun, just the moon."

Lucky didn't think the girl sounded sorry. In fact, she sounded snide. Lucky studied her in the dim light. She was tall, with pale skin and dark hair. Her hair looked black—but what didn't in this light?—and was cut pixie short. She wore snug-fitting leather pants and a tank top—again probably black—that showed off her well-toned arms. A dark mark, like a tattoo or some sort of sigil, swirled across her neck, starting beneath her left jawbone and extending to her right collar bone, the edge disappearing under the strap of her tank.

The girl examined Lucky in return, and Lucky forced herself not to tug the hem of her over-large t-shirt lower on her bare legs. The t-shirt was one of Aidan's—black, with a white Icarus logo. He had lent it to her at some time or other, and she had shoved it into her bag without thinking. She had almost refused to put it on when she'd gotten ready for bed, but she hadn't brought anything else she wanted to sleep in, and she had been too tired to care much. She could imagine what she must look like to the other girl, with her bare legs and her long hair messy from sleep, partially buried in a nest of pillows. No wonder the girl looked at her as if she were beneath her notice.

"Grandmother sent me to ask you to join us for breakfast," the girl said, her tone making it clear the invitation did not come from her.

"Grandmother?" Lucky asked.

"Lilith," said the girl, as if stating the obvious.

"She's your grandmother too?"

The girl's lip curled. "Does that make you feel less special?"

Lucky opened her mouth and then closed it again. She had no response to that question. When her stomach growled, she offered instead, "Breakfast sounds good. Let me put on some clothes."

The girl started back toward the door. "I'll wait outside while you get changed."

"Thanks. I won't take long."

The girl—who, Lucky supposed, would be her cousin—shrugged, as if she couldn't care less, and stepped into the hall, closing the door behind her.

Lucky pulled on a pair of jeans and a long-sleeved tee—this one in her size—and shoved her feet into her favorite lime green Chuck Taylors. She had brought only those and the boots she had worn the night before. The sneakers weren't appropriate for Chicago winters, but their comfortable familiarity had called to her when she'd packed. Since she hadn't seen any snow in the dimly lit garden, she decided they'd do.

She had dragged a brush through her hair and was pulling it up into a ponytail when she heard another tap on the door.

"Come in," she said. "I'm almost ready."

"You don't have to dress in the dark," the black-haired girl said. *"Yehi 'or."*

Something like a torch flame appeared near Lucky and hovered, flickering, in the air a couple of feet above her head.

"How did you do that?" Lucky asked.

"It's a simple bit of magic. Anyone can do it."

"I can't."

"Everyone here can do it, even the humans. For a granddaughter of Lilith's, it should be no problem."

"But what do I do? I don't even know how to start."

The girl rolled her eyes. "Focus on where you want the light to appear. Then picture it there and say *'Yehi'or.'"*

Lucky stumbled over the words, and the girl repeated them. Lucky tried again.

"Better," the girl said. "Now picture it. Make it appear."

Focusing her attention on a spot in the middle of the room, Lucky spoke the words. A faint flame appeared and floated there.

*"Choshek,"* said the girl. The flame disappeared.

She looked at Lucky. "Do it again."

Lucky repeated the exercise. This time the flame burned a little brighter.

"That'll do," the girl said. "Focus again and say *'choshek'* to make it go away."

The flame went away on Lucky's first attempt.

"Good. Come on, or we're going to be late."

*"Choshek,"* Lucky said, focusing on the flame the girl had created. It disappeared as easily as the other.

*"Yeh—,"* she began when she stepped outside the door.

Before she could finish speaking the magic words, a series of torches appeared, lighting the hallway.

"You don't have to make your own torch in the public areas of the castle. Grandmother has spelled them to light when anyone is present."

Confirming her words, torches ignited before them and faded behind them as they walked down the hallway.

They were halfway down the first flight of stairs when the girl broke the silence. "Grandmother said you're called 'Lucky'?"

"It's my nickname. It's short for Lucinda."

"Whatever," the girl said, evidently uninterested in additional information. "I'm Branwen. My friends call me Bryn." After a tiny pause, she added, "*You* are not my friend."

Lucky resisted the urge to respond with her own "Whatever," and since she could think of nothing else to say instead, she remained silent.

Three flights of stairs took them to the main floor, and after a series of twists and turns down various hallways, Branwen said the dining room was straight ahead. Lucky hadn't seen much of the place the evening before—just the entryway, the stairs, and the small private kitchen in Lilith's personal apartments where she'd sat only long enough to drink the warmed milk—but from what she could gather, there was a lot to see. Maybe Lilith would give her a tour after breakfast—or Branwen. She'd prefer to have Lilith as an escort, but she'd settle for Branwen if necessary.

Lucky had assumed there would be just the three of them for breakfast, but, to her surprise, several other women milled about the dining room. Most wore long dresses that reminded Lucky of paintings from the middle ages or the garbs of women at a Renaissance Fair. She and Branwen were the notable exceptions.

Many flickering torch lights floated several feet above the huge table in the room's center, and more hovered near the walls, as if stemming from invisible sconces.

As she and Branwen entered the room, all eyes turned in their direction, and conversations stopped or dropped to whispered murmurs. Lilith, wearing a flowing gown of deep purple velvet, disengaged from one of the groups and stepped forward to take Lucky's hand and draw her toward the table.

"Everyone, this is my granddaughter Lucky, the daughter of my son Luil. Please introduce yourselves, welcome her to Nadach, and do what you can to make her stay with us as comfortable as possible."

Lilith's words seemed the cue to turn Lucky into a one-person receiving line. Each of the women—a few of them only girls, Lucky now saw—came to greet her before finding a seat at the table. By the time she took a seat as well, Lucky had heard far too many names to remember them all. She had managed to capture some of them, but that of the blonde girl seated next to her eluded her.

As Lucky scooted her chair closer to the table, the girl turned an excited face towards her, long hair spilling over her shoulders. "I'm so glad to get the chance to talk with you. I heard you have been Made Naphil," she said. "Is it true?"

"Alicia," came a sharp voice from across the table. "Do not trouble our lady's guest with impertinent questions."

"Of course not, Mother." Alicia turned back to Lucky, looking chastened. "My apologies, Miss. I meant no offense."

Lucky felt an immediate liking and sympathy for the girl. She was probably no more than a couple of years Lucky's junior, but her expression made her seem younger.

"It's okay. You don't need to apologize," Lucky said. "And I won't know who you're talking to if you call me 'Miss.' Call me Lucky. Please."

Alicia's face lightened. "Lucky. I like that. I'm Alicia."

"It's nice to meet you, Alicia." Lucky smiled at the girl.

"It's nice to meet you too," Alicia said. Casting a quick glance across the table at her mother, who was now engaged in conversation with another woman, she leaned closer to Lucky and asked in a low voice, "Is it true you have been Made Naphil?"

Lucky chuckled. "Yes, it's true."

Alicia's blue eyes widened. "I have never met a Made Naphil before. I have never met any Nephilim. The Fallen are not permitted to come here, so I see only Lilith, her family, and the others among the Bound."

"The Bound?"

Alicia waved her hand in a gesture that encompassed everyone at the table. "We are all Bound to Lilith. Some of their own choice, some because others Bound us. My mother, for example, Bound herself—and me—to Lilith many years ago."

"I still don't understand." Lucky frowned. "What do you mean your mother Bound you both to Lilith?"

"Well—," Alicia began, but she stopped speaking when a number of women entered the room from a side door, bearing bowls and platters and pitchers. They moved around the table filling glasses and cups and serving a variety of foods from the many dishes and bowls they carried.

Lucky accepted a little from each of the dishes, none of which looked like anything she would consider breakfast food. There were no scrambled eggs, and she didn't see a single pancake or slice of French toast or bacon among the offerings. But there were rolls, several kinds of vegetables—most of which she didn't recognize—a few different bean dishes, some small roast game hens, and grilled fish.

After everyone's plate had been filled and the serving women had retreated back to the kitchen, she turned to Alicia. "Do you always eat like this?" she asked.

The blonde girl laughed. "No. This is because of you. We always gather for breakfast, but we don't usually have this much food. Lilith wanted to celebrate your arrival. Dinner tonight will be even more of a feast—and everyone will be there."

"Everyone?"

"Yes. We are just the women who live in the main part of the castle with Lilith. Her sons and the single men live in A wing, and the couples and families live in B wing."

"Oh," Lucky said. She didn't know what she had expected when she agreed to accompany Lilith to her home, but she hadn't imagined her new grandmother lived in a kind of castle which seemed to house an entire village.

"I'll give you a tour of the central area of the castle after breakfast," Alicia promised. "And then we'll get Bryn to take us to the training field. We can watch her lessons."

The prospect of watching her rude cousin's training session didn't excite Lucky as much as it seemed to excite Alicia, but she did look forward to the tour and finding out more about life in Lilith's world, as well as the people who lived there. She would have to question Alicia again about those she called "the Bound."

Lucky didn't get a chance to ask Alicia anything more during breakfast, as the other women seated around them began drawing them into conversations. By the end of the meal, she had added a few more names to the list of those she remembered; she had learned that Alicia's mother, Morgan, did not seem nearly as welcoming as her daughter; and she had eaten enough that she decided she should skip lunch, especially since it sounded like dinner would be huge.

When Lucky rose and pushed her chair back under the table, Alicia touched her arm to get her attention.

"Wait here. I'll be right back," she said. Then she spun and ran across the room, her long, straight blonde hair flying out behind out. She caught up to Branwen as the taller, dark-haired girl reached the door.

Lucky couldn't hear their conversation, but she guessed Alicia asked Branwen to take the two of them with her to her training session. Her suspicions were confirmed when Branwen looked up and cast a less than friendly glance in her direction. She appeared to agree to Alicia's request, though, despite her evident aversion to Lucky. She nodded and smiled indulgently at the younger girl before she turned and left the room. Alicia's eyes sparkled with excitement as she half-ran, half-danced her way back to Lucky's side.

"Bryn said we could go with her to the training fields," she said. "We are to meet her at the entrance to the A wing at a quarter before the eleventh hour. That gives us plenty of time to tour the main area. It's big, but it's mostly living quarters. Are you ready?"

Lucky nodded, allowing herself to get caught up in the younger girl's excitement. "Sure," she said. "Let's go."

"Is it always this dark here?" Lucky asked, as they ascended the stairs, the automatically conjured torches lighting their way.

Alicia shook her head. "It depends on the phase of the moon. When the moon's full, the light is very bright, almost magical. But when it's waxing or waning, the light is dimmer. When the moon is in its dark phase, there's no light at all."

"That sounds like our moon," Lucky said.

Alicia nodded. "It is like your moon, I believe. When Lilith was banished, she was sent to this place. They say she was told, 'You have chosen Darkness. In Darkness you shall dwell.' We only receive the sunlight the moon reflects, making our day akin to your night."

"Do you know why Lilith was banished?" Lucky asked.

Alicia shook her head.

Lucky didn't pursue that line of questioning any further, but she found herself wondering if Zeke had somehow been involved, if Lilith's banishment was part of the history between the two of them he had once mentioned.

They had reached the second floor, and Alicia turned down the hall to the right. "First, I'll show you where Mother and I live."

Lucky followed as Alicia turned down another corridor and stopped before a large, heavy wood door. Slipping a key from the pocket of her dress, she inserted it in the lock and ushered Lucky inside.

They entered a large sitting room, furnished with a couch and several armchairs, all upholstered in heavy, dark fabrics. Velvet curtains, much like the ones in the bedroom Lucky now occupied, adorned the windows. They were pulled back to allow what light the moon provided to seep through.

A door at one end of the sitting room opened into a combined kitchen and dining room. A door at the other end opened into a hallway that led to two bedrooms and a bathroom.

"That's my mother's room," Alicia said, indicating the closed door of one of the bedrooms. "And this one is mine," she added, opening the door to the other.

Alicia's room, like all the rooms Lucky had seen so far, contained heavy, dark furniture and velvet drapes. But in the dim light filtering through the windows and the flickering glow from the torch Alicia called into being, Lucky could see the girl had added her own touches to the room. Pale pillows with delicate embroidery adorned the bed and window seat. Jars and vases filled with herbs and flowers could be found on almost every other surface: desk, side tables, shelf tops, and windowsills.

"How do the plants get enough light?" Lucky asked.

Alicia appeared puzzled by the question. "They are native to Nadach. They do not need more light. Like me, and the others born Bound, they know nothing else."

"Can you tell me more about the Bound?" Lucky asked. "I still don't understand what it means."

"Well," Alicia said, boosting herself up on the high bed, where she perched on the edge, swinging her legs, "for the most part, the Bound are humans, who have Bound themselves to Lilith for life."

"But what does that mean—they Bound themselves to her?"

"Come and sit."

Alicia waited until Lucky had sat down on the edge of the bed, one leg tucked beneath the other, before she answered the question. "It means they agreed to leave their homes, to come here, to Bind themselves to Lilith and this place forever, until their lives end. They can leave, but only for short periods of time. Then they have to come back."

"What happens if they don't?"

"They die."

"Why would anyone agree to that?" Lucky asked, feeling somewhat nauseated at the thought of her grandmother requiring such a thing of anyone.

"Because they want to learn magic, and the magic extends their lives. That's why my mother did it."

"To learn magic?"

Alicia looked at Lucky as if she had asked the stupidest question in the world. "Of course, magic," she said. "Lilith is one of the greatest sorceresses ever, perhaps *the* greatest. She's your grandmother, and you didn't know?"

Lucky picked up one of the pillows and ran her finger over its embroidered design as she spoke. "I didn't even know she existed, let alone that she's my grandmother, until a couple of months ago."

"Oh," Alicia said, sounding apologetic. "Was that when you were Made Naphil?"

Lucky nodded. "Sort of. I first met Lilith at the Striking. Until then I had no idea I was anything but human."

"And now you're Naphil," Alicia said. "I wish I was something other than human."

"Why?" Lucky asked.

Alicia looked down. "I can't do the magic. I can't seem to learn it. I was born here, and my mother is a very strong sorceress, but I have no power. If I were something other than human, I would. I'd have some sort of Gift."

"Even if you're Naphil, it doesn't mean you have an instant Gift. Mine hasn't revealed itself yet."

"But you will have one."

"So they say," Lucky said. "But I don't know what it will be. I don't even know if it will be something good. Sometimes I miss being human, being the girl I used to be."

When Alicia didn't respond, Lucky continued, "I'm sure there's something you love, something you're good at, even if you can't do the magic."

She glanced down at the pillow in her hands, for the first time noticing the embroidery depicted herbs and flowers. Looking from the pillow to the jars and vases of herbs that covered the desktop, she said, "You're good at growing herbs, and you clearly love them. Maybe that's your gift."

Alicia bit her lip. "Maybe," she said. "Mother says only a weakling would want to work with herbs and roots."

Lucky frowned. How could Alicia's mother so belittle her own daughter's interests? She felt a rush of gratitude for G-Ma, who had always supported her in whatever she wanted to do.

Giving in to impulse, she reached over and squeezed Alicia's hand. "I think your mother's wrong."

Alicia responded with a grateful smile. "That's what Bryn says too." Then she sucked in a breath. "Bryn! We'd better hurry if we're going to meet her in time."

She hopped off the bed. "Come on. We'll do a quick run through the rest. Most of the quarters are like this one. But at least you'll get an idea of who lives where."

After she had closed and locked the apartment door, Alicia turned to Lucky with a smile. "I'm glad you're here," she said, looping her arm through Lucky's. "You and Bryn and I are going to be best friends."

Lucky smiled back, but didn't say anything. Somehow she didn't think Branwen would agree with that statement.

# CHAPTER 4

When the Dominion guards ushered Kev into the Metatron's council chamber after their customary pat down, he found only Margash, the newest member of the Heavens' ruling body, awaiting him.

His surprise must have shown on his face.

"What is it, *Ha-Satan?*" Margash said. "Did you think we are required to appear as a foursome?"

Kev's lips twitched. "Of course not, Most High. Your solitary presence is simply—unexpected."

"Yes, I am sure. We have been on our Most High and Mighty behavior with you, have we not?"

Margash nodded to the guards, and one of the Dominions strode toward a door on the far side of the council chamber. Margash followed the guard, gesturing for Kev to accompany him. The second Dominion fell in behind them.

"The mourning ceremonies are complete," Margash said. "After some persuasion, I convinced the others that you should be allowed to see the body before the Assumption."

"Thank you, Most High."

Kev's gut tightened in anticipation. Months had passed since Jahoel, the former First of the Metatron and an angel far older and more experienced than any of its current members, had been murdered, with all signs pointing to Lucifer, the leader of the Dark and Kev's father, as the killer. Kev knew Lucifer hadn't killed the angel, but he and the other members of the investigation team had made little progress in determining who had. Not least because none of them had been permitted to examine the body. Almost as soon as it had been discovered, the body had been whisked from Elsewhere back to the Heavens for extended mourning rituals. Thanks to Margash, it appeared he would finally get a look at the deceased.

He wanted to see what lay outside this room almost as much as he wanted to see the body. So far, he had experienced nothing of the Heavens besides the chilly council chamber and the even colder ante-room he entered when he stepped through the Gates.

From the council chamber, they entered a long, narrow corridor, with several closed doors to their left and a wall with high, narrow windows to the right. Through those windows leaked the same silvery light that infiltrated the identical windows in the council chamber. At the end of the corridor, they stepped through another door into a shower of light—and warmth.

If he had stood in the doorway, straddling the threshold, a thermometer in each hand, Kev thought, the instruments would have recorded several degrees difference. His bare feet registered with pleasure the shift from icy tile to the unfamiliar, smooth, near body-temperature surface on which he now stood. A faint breeze caressed his skin, erasing the chill he'd come to associate with the Heavens. He couldn't hold back a sigh of pleasure.

Margash smiled at the sound. "Perfect, is it not?"

Kev had to agree.

They stood at one end of an immense plaza. On all sides crystalline structures glittered in the silvery light that shattered into color as it passed through their prisms. In a fountain at plaza's center, water rose and fell, rainbows whispering in its spray. A few angels wandered here and there, strolling around the plaza or moving purposefully toward one of the crystalline buildings. Somehow even their motion seemed to be aligned with the falls of colored light and the splashing of the fountain.

"I've never seen such—harmony," he said.

"Indeed," said Margash, "but at what price?"

Kev looked a question at the Metatron's youngest member, but Margash did not elaborate.

"This way."

Kev accompanied Margash around the fountain to the other side of the plaza, one Dominion guard preceding them and the other a discreet distance behind. Some of the angels on the plaza cast suspicious glances in Kev's direction. Some even stared, with expressions of open hostility, at the son of the being they believed had killed their beloved leader. For the first time, Kev realized the guards might be protecting him as well as Margash.

They moved toward a building that looked to Kev like a Gothic cathedral carved out of the world's largest diamond. Its faceted surfaces sparked colored fire.

Kev followed Margash and the first guard inside, while the remaining guard took up a post at the door.

Once inside, Kev registered a drop in temperature, and his eyes had to adjust to the dimness. He wondered how a structure that appeared so transparent could block so much light. Well, he supposed, it did reflect off the surface in a pretty spectacular light show.

Much like those in the Gothic cathedrals it resembled, the ceiling of the structure arched high overhead, light trickling in through more narrow windows. At the center of the great room, more of those windows, in elongated wedges, formed a circle, which rained light onto the raised platform directly beneath it and on what rested on the platform. The guard remained a respectful distance away, allowing Margash and Kev to approach with privacy.

The casket holding Jahoel's remains was transparent—made of glass or some Heavenly crystal. Whatever its medium, it appeared to be all of a piece, as if formed around its contents. Shadows played across its surface, the light from the windows above fragmented by the frames outlining the wedges of window.

Without speaking, Margash pressed his hand against the casket end nearest the body's head. The top of the container rippled, appeared to liquefy, then faded altogether, like vapor. Margash gestured toward what lay inside.

As much as he had wanted a chance to examine Jahoel's body, to see the evidence for himself, now that the body lay before him, Kev could only think about the life that no longer animated the form. He had never spoken to the angel, but he had seen him a time or two in Elsewhere, at a distance. Unlike the current Metatron, Jahoel had refused to confine himself to the Heavens. He had insisted on personally attending meetings, rather than sending an emissary. Perhaps, in the end, that insistence had cost his life.

Kev bowed his head. The angel and his remains deserved respect.

After several minutes, Kev leaned over the body and moved aside the cloth that covered its shoulders. If he hadn't learned from the reports he'd studied that the killer had incinerated the angel's internal organs, he would never have known from looking at the body. Nothing marred its surface but the incriminating sigil seared into the flesh beneath the left collar bone.

That sigil belonged to Lucifer.

And if Lucifer hadn't put it there, who had? A sigil was like an angelic fingerprint. Who could have faked the intricate symbol with such accuracy?

Kev studied the mark for a long time. Then he closed his eyes and traced it with his fingertips, adding texture to the visual image. Something caught at his memory, something that seemed wrong somehow, but he couldn't say what that something was.

He slipped a tiny holographic recorder from the pocket of his black silk trousers and held it out for Margash's inspection.

"May I?" he asked. "I mean no disrespect."

Margash inclined his head, granting permission. "I understand, *Ha-Satan*. Do what you must."

Kev recorded an image of the deceased angel's head and shoulders and a couple of close-ups of the sigil mark. When he had finished, he moved the cloth, soft as a whisper against his fingers, back into place.

He nodded to Margash, who again pressed his hand against the end of the casket. Kev watched the top of the casket reform, mist to liquid to solid. He cast one last glance at Jahoel's still face and then followed Margash back toward the door, the guard trailing behind.

As they crossed the plaza, Kev noticed one female Power and two male Dominions, one very tall, the other sporting a blond ponytail, striding toward them. They came from different directions, but their paths would converge right in front of Margash's entourage. And from the way they looked at Kev, he guessed a friendly conversation with the newest member of the Metatron wasn't what they had in mind.

Margash came to a stop a few feet from the group. Kev followed suit. The guards flanked them, weapons at the ready.

The female took one step forward, her eyes boring into Kev's. "You dare to come here," she hissed, "after what your father did? You dare to look on our departed, his victim? You and your kind, you sicken me."

She spat at his feet. Kev felt a few drops make contact.

"We do not know Lucifer committed this crime," Margash said. "The investigation is not yet complete. In the meantime, *Ha-Satan* is our guest and, as such, should be treated with respect."

The angel's words surprised Kev. Perhaps the views of the Metatron's members differed more than he had believed.

"The mongrel does not deserve our respect," said the taller of the males, stepping forward to stand beside the female. "But, of course, we will respect *your* wishes, Most High."

They stepped aside, allowing Kev, Margash, and the guards to proceed.

"Watch your back, *Ha-Satan*," said the tall Dominion as they walked away. "He will not always be there to protect you."

Lucky and Alicia arrived at the A wing gate a few minutes late, and they found Branwen looking less than patient. She made no secret of who she blamed for their lateness. She greeted Alicia's breathless apology with a warm smile, but when she turned to Lucky the smile turned into a frown, and her dark gray eyes narrowed with suspicion and dislike.

"You have fencing practice today, don't you, Bryn?" Alicia asked, as they passed through the gateway and into an arched tunnel that stretched the width of the wing.

"Yes, you know I do," Branwen answered.

Alicia's cheeks colored. "I thought so, but I wasn't sure."

"Oh, yes, you were." Branwen laughed. "You know my training schedule better than I do. You just want to talk about it so you can mention *him.*"

"I don't know who or what you mean," Alicia said, but the color in her cheeks heightened.

"Mmm-hmm. You didn't watch all my fencing lessons before, but you haven't missed a single one since *he* started training with me. Have you?"

"Well, no," Alicia admitted.

"So you do know who I'm talking about, after all?" Branwen teased.

"Oh, but Bryn, he's so lovely to watch. He moves like a dancer, and—"

"I know," Branwen interrupted, laughing. "His hair and his eyes and his strong but graceful arms." She clasped her hands at her heart and blinked wide-eyed in mock adoration.

"Oh, stop." Alicia giggled and gave Branwen a good-natured shove.

Lucky observed the exchange with interest. The laughing, light-hearted Bryn, who clearly viewed Alicia as a friend, was light-years away from the surly, distant Branwen, who had made a point of telling Lucky she was not. Watching the two of them together reminded Lucky of herself and Josh, and she felt a pang of longing for home. But she couldn't go back—she didn't think she could go anywhere near Zeke without feeling sickened by his betrayal.

The outdoor training area was so large that even the light from the magicked torches surrounding it approximated only a twilight glow. Markers divided the area into fields, each for a specific physical challenge. Trainees and masters occupied most of the fields. Some of the trainees—mostly young men—wrestled while masters coached them on moves and technique. Others raced through obstacle courses, demonstrating both speed and agility. Still others trained with weights or weapons.

Lucky and Alicia followed Branwen to the weapons training field. When she broke away from them to head toward a marked off part of the field, where a middle-aged man waited with fencing gear, Lucky and Alicia moved to the cluster of benches that faced the field.

While Branwen donned her gear, Alicia looked about impatiently.

Before Lucky could ask what or who she looked for, a movement on the far side of the field caught Alicia's attention. "There he is," she breathed.

Lucky turned to look at the object of Alicia's infatuation. The boy was of medium height, slender, and, like Branwen, dressed in black leather. His wavy, chin-length hair looked dark, not as dark as Branwen's, but Lucky couldn't distinguish the exact color in the subdued light. He greeted Branwen and the fencing master as he drew closer and, glancing up, smiled and waved at Alicia. Catching sight of Lucky, his eyes lingered and his brows drew together in a slight frown. Lucky wondered if he, like Branwen, viewed her with suspicion.

Branwen and the boy donned their gear and, after listening to their master's direction, began their practice. The two were well matched—much the same height, both were leanly muscled and, it seemed to Lucky, equally skilled. As she watched, she understood what Alicia had meant when she said the boy moved like a dancer. Branwen's movements were not awkward by any means, but her intense athleticism contrasted with his grace and fluidity. His arm positioned the foil with what appeared to be effortless ease, and his feet seemed hardly to touch the ground.

"I see what you mean about him," Lucky said. "He looks almost weightless."

"Yes," Alicia breathed. "He's beautiful."

Lucky turned to look at her new friend, a smile tugging at the corners of her mouth. Catching her eye, Alicia flushed again.

"Does he know how you feel about him?" Lucky asked.

Alicia shook her head. "He thinks of me as a child."

Lucky glanced at the boy and then back at her friend. "He can't be that much older than you."

Again Alicia shook her head, her eyes following the boy's every move. "He's two years older, but he says"—her voice dropped an octave—"'There are light years between eighteen and sixteen.'"

"So you've discussed it?"

"Not really. I think he mostly meant that *he* is different now than he was at sixteen, but I could tell he intended to point out the difference between us too." She paused for a moment. "I've known Jaime all my life. We played together as children. As we grew older, I didn't see him as much, and then, when he turned sixteen, he left. He is not Bound to this place as I am. He returned a few weeks ago."

Alicia's words drew all of Lucky's attention back to her. "Explain to me again why you are Bound and Jaime isn't?"

Alicia cast a quick glance at Lucky and then looked down at the ground for a moment, before lifting her eyes once again to Jaime. "Sometimes people Bind their children as well as themselves. The stronger the magic they wish to learn, the higher the price."

Lucky gasped. She remembered Alicia saying her mother had Bound both of them to Lilith, but she hadn't grasped what that meant. "Your mother Bound *you* to Lilith so *she* could learn magic?"

Alicia nodded. "Many of my friends are Bound. But Jaime's father Bound only himself. Once Jaime turned sixteen, he was free to leave."

"He can come and go as he pleases?"

"Yes," Alicia said. "He could choose to leave tomorrow."

"And you can't leave at all?" Lucky studied her young friend's face as she waited for her answer.

"Now that I'm sixteen, I can leave, but for no more than twelve hours in any moon cycle." Turning, she caught Lucky's eyes with her own. "And where would I go anyway? My whole life has been here."

"You could visit him," Lucky said, "if he leaves again."

"I suppose," Alicia conceded, her eyes once again following Jaime's dancing feet and elegant swordplay. "If he wanted me to."

Lucky studied Alicia's profile for a moment before turning her own gaze back towards Branwen and Jaime. They took turns practicing some intricate move under their master's instruction. And while she couldn't help but be impressed by Branwen's economical athleticism and Jaime's elegant grace, her thoughts kept circling around Alicia's words and what they revealed about this world and her new grandmother. How could anyone sacrifice her own child's freedom like that? And how could Lilith ask them to?

The Halls of Hell looked nothing like the traditional religious depictions humans had created throughout the centuries. No demons with pitchforks, no torture, no lake of fire. Yes, the Hell Realms were naturally dark, but, true to his name, Lucifer had brought to them an abundance of light. The Halls, the massive palace from which he ruled and which had the property of existing simultaneously within all the Dark Realms but Nadach, beamed in each realm like a small, white sun. The Light had given the palace to Lucifer when he had first been sent to rule the Dark, and it shone with the same silvery light that lit the Heavens. Having finally seen some of what existed outside the Metatron's council chamber, Kev could see the resemblance.

He covered the length of the throne room with purposeful strides, his boot-strikes resounding like gunfire in the vaulted space.

He looked at his father where he all but lounged in the seat of honor.

"The throne room? Really?"

Lucifer sat up. "Sometimes I like to remind myself that I hold a position of power."

"Like you could forget."

Lucifer's eyes flashed. "You may be my son, but you are also in my employ. Do not be insubordinate, *Ha-Satan.*"

A few short months ago, Kev would have let the remark go without comment. Now he decided to push a little further. "Dare I say you prove my point?"

Lucifer's eyes flashed again, but the corners of his mouth turned up in a reluctant smile. "Come," he said. "We will continue this in my study. You are here on a matter of business?"

"Margash allowed me to examine Jahoel's body. I made a recording of the sigil mark."

"And you wish to compare it to the real thing? Others have already confirmed it is mine." A combination of bitterness and impatience edged Lucifer's voice.

"Yes, but those others had a vested interest in finding you guilty. It's my job to prove otherwise. Humor me."

Lucifer raised an eyebrow. "Are we being insubordinate again?"

Kev met his gaze unfazed. "I *am* your son."

Lucifer chuckled as he opened the door into the study and gestured for Kev to enter. "So you are."

Kev took a seat at the conference table that filled one end of the large room. Lucifer sat across from him, both hands up, palms facing Kev. Kev turned on the recorder and positioned it so the image of the sigil mark on Jahoel's chest displayed between Lucifer's upraised hands. Lucifer activated his palm sigils. Kev's gaze moved back and forth between the recorded image and the glowing symbols on his father's palms.

He frowned. "They're the same, but it's like the mark on Jahoel is blurred or something. The edges of the lines aren't sharp like they are on your palms. That's what I felt when I touched the mark. Can you think of any way of faking the sigil that might cause such a thing?"

"I cannot even think of any way anyone could copy my full sigil. The general design is public knowledge, my signature. But whoever did this captured all the details left out of the public copies."

"Except for those softened edges. That must mean something."

Kev killed the hologram as Lucifer deactivated his sigils.

"Yes," Lucifer agreed, "it must. But for now that meaning escapes me."

Kev nodded. "Me too, for now. But at least this gives us something to go on."


"Where is she?" Aidan burst through the door of Zeke's office, not bothering to knock.

Zeke looked up from the scroll he had been studying. "I assume you mean Lucky?"

"I got a text from Ben asking where she had to go in such a hurry. Since I had no idea she had to go anywhere, I called him to get more information. He said she'd left a note for Josh saying she'd be gone for 'a while' and not to worry. Of course—Josh being Josh—that just made him worry more."

Zeke gave him a pointed look.

Aidan sighed. "Yeah, I know. Pot, kettle—got it. So, where is she?"

Zeke shook his head—or heads. The Cherub's morphing features and the transparent shadows of his flurry of blue wings dazzled Aidan, until the angel settled once more into his customary human form.

"I don't know where she is," Zeke said, his usually resonant voice flat. "But I suspect she is with Lilith."

"Lilith? But why…?"

"When Lucky did not show up at my office this morning, I was concerned. She has never been even the slightest bit late without notifying me. I asked Malachi to look into it. He could not locate her, said it was as if she had completely disappeared. He would not sense her if she is in one of the Dark Realms."

"And she would only have gone willingly with Lilith."

Zeke nodded. He reached into the small cabinet beside his desk and withdrew a bottle of cognac. He held the bottle up for Aidan's inspection and looked at him with a raised eyebrow. Aidan shook his head. He might not be training with Lucky, but he had every intention of doing some serious sweating anyway. He'd take a pass.

Zeke poured some of the cognac into a snifter and leaned back in his chair, the drink cradled in his hand. He stared into the glass as if he could find the answers he sought in its swirling contents.

After a few moments, the angel heaved a sigh and looked back up at him. "I should have told her about Sambethe. I knew Lilith was asking questions, and I knew she would find out about the toxin. I had thought to get to Lucky before Lilith did, but I did not want to say anything until I was sure. I did not want to upset Lucky without cause."

Aidan propped himself against the back of the leather armchair behind him. "You think Lilith told her?"

"Why else would she disappear without saying a word to any of us? I'm sure she feels...betrayed."

"There's no way you can contact her?"

"Not directly," Zeke said. "I am forbidden entry into the Dark Realms mentally as well as physically. We could ask your father—"

"Or Kev," Aidan interrupted.

"Yes, as *Ha-Satan*, Kevin could contact her as well. I would suggest we wait a bit though, give her some time to cool down. Perhaps she will come to us, allow me to explain."

"How long do we wait?" Aidan asked.

When Zeke didn't answer, Aidan changed direction. "What is being done about Sambethe?" he asked.

"She can mix potions and practice healing only under strictest supervision. She cannot even enter her own laboratory unless her supervisor grants permission and accompanies her. She risked much by her actions, but she remains convinced she acted with just cause. Since, ultimately, no one came to serious harm, her punishment will not be worse. Perhaps knowing she has lost our trust is punishment enough."

"Who's her supervisor?"

Zeke's lips curled into the hint of a smile. "Raphael himself."

"Raphael? She has to ask him permission for everything?" Aidan whistled. "Better him than Uriel, but still…"

"With good behavior, she may be allowed to work independently again, but that could take centuries. Raphael has all the time in the world."

"Have you spoken to Sambethe—since the sentencing?"

"No. The sentence was just handed down this morning. I confess I do not quite know what to say to her. The last time we talked she still insisted she had done the right thing—the only thing she could have done to ensure the outcome she believed necessary. I, on the other hand, cannot believe she risked both their lives. We can all be thankful Lucky survived the Making." Zeke paused to drink from the snifter in his hand, before continuing, "Perhaps Sambethe will be proven right in the end, but I cannot believe even that would justify her means."

"Lucky must know we weren't part of it." Aidan levered himself off his prop and paced in front of Zeke's desk. "She can't think you or I would have harmed Josh."

"We must give her time, Aidan. I'm sure we will hear something from her soon."

"I hope so." Aidan made for the door. "I've got to move. See you later, Zeke."

Zeke didn't respond. As Aidan pulled the door closed behind him, he could see the angel once again staring at the cognac swirling in his glass.

"What's up with you?"

At the sound of Kev's voice, Aidan gave the punching bag he was beating to smithereens one last slam with his fist. Then, raking his arm across his forehead to wipe off the sweat, he turned toward his brother. "What's up with me, what?"

Kev raised one eyebrow. "Well, you've hit that thing often enough and hard enough the seams are starting to split, and you've been doing it long enough your clothes are drenched with sweat. You don't go at it that hard unless something's bothering you."

Aidan stopped the swinging bag. "It's Lucky."

"Lucky? Did she see the error of her ways and throw you over for someone else?"

"Piss off, Kev." Imagining it was his brother's face, Aidan walloped the punching bag again.

Kev caught the bag as it swung back toward them, stopping its motion. "Sorry," he said.

Aidan directed his eyes toward the floor. "I said 'Piss off.'"

"Come on, Aidan. Tell me what's going on. No more smart ass remarks, I promise."

"I've heard that one before," Aidan muttered.

Turning away from the punching bag, he moved over to the weight machines, grabbed a towel from the nearby stack, and sat down on the bench press. "She's gone. Zeke thinks she's with Lilith, that she found out about Sambethe and believes we all betrayed her."

"Found out what about Sambethe?" Kev asked.

"You don't know?"

"Know what? I've been zipping back and forth between Lucifer, the Metatron, and the murder investigation team for the last day and a half. What did I miss?"

Aidan rubbed the towel over his sweat-drenched hair and then draped the cloth around his shoulders. "Sambethe was the one who poisoned Josh. The so-called 'antidote' she gave him was really the toxin."

"*What?*"

"Yeah, that was pretty much my reaction when Zeke told me. He said he'd suspected for a while, but he didn't know for sure until a couple of days ago. He told me yesterday, after he'd already talked with the Archangels and set a time for the hearing. We were going to tell Lucky today. But it looks like Lilith told her first. At least, that's what Zeke thinks happened."

"Wow." Kev's voice was subdued. "She didn't leave you a message or anything?"

Aidan shook his head. "Not a word."

"If Zeke is right, and she's gone off with Lilith, she probably acted before she had time to think. She'll be back. She has to know you would never have done anything to harm Josh."

"I can only hope." Aidan rose to his feet. He took a few steps toward the shower room door and then turned back to his brother. "Kev, if she doesn't come back soon, would you go find her?"

After a momentary pause, Kev nodded. "Yeah," he said. "If she doesn't come back on her own."

As Aidan exited to the showers, Kev dropped down onto the bench his brother had vacated.

Sambethe? Holy hell. Yes, she'd insisted Lucky undergo the Making, but to force her hand like that...? And, yes, if he were Lucky and thought any of the rest of them had known, he would feel betrayed too. But the thought that she would believe Zeke or Aidan—or him—capable of intentionally hurting her or her cousin was like a wound. He knew how Aidan felt—more than Aidan could ever know.

He hoped Lucky was all right, hoped she would come to her senses, hoped she would come back. But he also wanted to go find her—and he didn't want to wait, didn't want to give her time to come back on her own. He wanted to find her now, make sure she knew he'd known nothing about any of this, that he'd always been—would always be—there for her. But he had to be Aidan's messenger first—had to reassure her Aidan had always been there for her too. Cursing, he stood and strode over to the punching bag to give it a few wallops of his own. Yeah, he knew exactly how Aidan felt.

# CHAPTER 5

Questions about the Bound and Lilith and her own place in Lilith's world still swirled through Lucky's thoughts as she dressed for the evening feast. She had Alicia to thank for the clothes. Her new friend had borrowed a dress and slippers from another girl who was Lucky's size.

The gown was a deep teal velvet with gold brocade trim around the v-neck, sleeves, and hem. Lucky slipped it over her head and studied her reflection in the long oval-shaped mirror that stood in the corner of her room. The flames of the torch she had conjured cast flickering shadows across her image, but they provided enough light for her to see the color of the dress and to admire the way the soft fabric skimmed her body to her hips and then fell into a full, floor-length skirt with a short, pointed train. The sleeves fit snug to the elbow where they flared slightly. Long and asymmetrical, they reached to her wrist in the front, while the backs of the sleeves mimicked the dress's train, their gold-brocade-trimmed points touching the tips of her fingers.

*I look like I stepped out of a Medieval tapestry,* Lucky thought. She decided she'd braid her hair instead of letting it hang loose over her shoulders. That would leave her neck bare, but it would make her feel less like she should be wearing a pointed hat with a scarf flowing from its tip and cradling the head of a unicorn in her lap.

As she began to twist her hair into a French braid, she slipped her feet into the matching velvet slippers. They were soft and almost weightless, but they protected her feet from the chill of the stone floor.

When she had finished the braid and secured the end with an elastic band, she looked in the mirror again. Yes, that was better.

The dress's v-neck framed her locket and the Light-Bringer's Medallion where they rested on her breastbone. She caught the medallion between her thumb and forefinger, rubbing it like a worry stone. Despite her feelings of betrayal, she had never once thought about removing the chain from her neck. The medallion, like the locket, seemed a part of her now.

She let her hand fall to her side, her stomach twisting with anxiety at the thought of being paraded before all the inhabitants of this Dark realm by the grandmother who had forced many of them to Bind themselves to her. To give herself courage, she summoned her wings. Her Gift still hadn't manifested, and her palm sigils had yet to appear, but she did have the wings—and her stronger, more resilient body—to prove she was Naphil.

As the weight of the wings settled against her back, she saw the appendages reflected in the mirror. Folded as they were, the tops reached above her head and the tips almost touched the floor. Their gold-dusted variegated green didn't quite match her borrowed velvet gown, but it didn't clash either. The combination of the gown and the wings made her look magical, unearthly. She looked nothing like her image of herself. Who was that being in the mirror anyway?

Taking refuge in the hope that she was more than she thought herself to be, she dismissed her wings, got rid of the torch, and prepared to face the festivities.

From her place next to Lilith at the center of the head table, Lucky scanned the great room. Conjured flames glittered in the many chandeliers that hung from the high ceilings and blazed on either side of the many doors.

Everyone seemed to be enjoying themselves. Guests filled the benches at the long tables arranged in several rows throughout the room. Talking and laughing, they indulged in the copious amounts of food and drink provided by the servants who weaved among the tables carrying bowls and pitchers and trays. Although the trays appeared to Lucky to be precariously balanced, she hadn't seen anyone drop or spill a thing.

Alicia sat on Lucky's other side, with Branwen in the seat next to her. Alicia's eyes sparkled with excitement, and every time a new dish was placed before her she identified it as either a seldom-served favorite or something she'd never had before but which looked wonderful. Between exclamations, her eyes would shift to Jaime, who sat on the opposite side of one of the tables in the row nearest the head table.

Lucky had to admit that he did look handsome in his black velvet doublet. His hair glowed deep chestnut, the chin-length waves a bit disheveled, as if combed through with his fingers. As the meal progressed, Lucky decided he wasn't as indifferent to Alicia as she believed. More than a few times, Lucky caught him casting his own furtive glances at the blonde girl, though Alicia seemed unaware of his attention.

Lucky couldn't blame him. Even if Jaime had convinced himself Alicia was too young for him, he could hardly help but notice her tonight. She wore a gown cut similarly to Lucky's, but hers was a pale cornflower blue with silver trim. With her straight blonde hair streaming over her shoulders and her sparkling blue eyes, she looked nothing short of lovely.

Branwen, unlike the other girls, had not submitted to the dictates of conventional fashion. She wore the black leather trousers and boots that seemed to be standard issue for her, but she had topped them with a black velvet tunic that hung to mid-thigh and which she had cinched around her slim waist with a wide leather belt. Somehow, the ensemble made her look both feminine and formidable. She had barely said hello to Lucky when she had sat down.

Alicia seemed happy to talk to each of them in turn. And Lilith offered her new granddaughter occasional comments about the food and the décor, as well as questions about how Lucky had spent her first day here. The heavy wooden table was too wide for conversation with the people seated opposite them.

Lucky soon gave up trying to consume more than a few bites of anything. Even so, she felt uncomfortable by the time the last course was served.

When the last servant had left the room, empty tray in hand, Lilith rose to her feet, and the cacophony of voices which had filled the room throughout the feast stilled.

"As you all know," Lilith said, "this party is in honor of my newly discovered granddaughter, Lucky." She paused to give Lucky a smile, which Lucky did her best to return.

"I hope you all have enjoyed the feast. Once you have finished the last course, please feel free to make your way into the ballroom next door for dancing." Lilith gestured toward the doors on the right side of the room. "And if you haven't yet met my granddaughter, there is still time. The evening is quite young." Bestowing a warm smile on the crowd, she gave an airy wave of her hand and added, "Carry on."

When Lilith sat back down, the conversation resumed as if there had been no interruption. Some of the tension that had gripped Lucky at Lilith's announcement dispersed as she realized no one was staring at her. She felt like a fraud, the reluctant guest of honor. Between the real reason for her visit to Nadach and what Alicia had told her about the Bound, she saw little cause to celebrate. She hoped she could keep up appearances for the duration of the party.

The laugh that escaped her caught Lucky by surprise. She hadn't expected to enjoy the dancing. But as the young man—whose name she couldn't remember—swirled her through the complicated steps, altering his own steps to cover her missteps, she found she did. When the dance ended, he promised to claim her for another before the evening was out, and she agreed that he could.

Before she could make her way back to the edge of the room, another man, this one old enough to be her father, asked for a dance. He wasn't as graceful as her previous partner, and their conversation was stilted. Still, he seemed nice enough and patiently showed her the proper steps. He even bowed over her hand when he left her at the edge of the dance floor after the dance ended.

"So, you're Lilith's newly discovered granddaughter?"

Lucky looked over her right shoulder to find the source of the soft, melodic voice. Holding her eyes with his own, Jaime stepped nearer, took her right hand in his, and like the older man who had just left her, bowed over it. The man had meant the gesture as a courtesy, but Jaime did it with such a flourish as to make the act an insult.

Lucky flushed. Why did Jaime and Branwen dislike her so much? She hadn't been here long enough to do anything to either one of them.

"Would you care to dance?" Jaime asked, his lips curling upward in a mockery of a smile.

Lucky pulled her hand out of his. "You don't really want to dance with me."

"Oh, but I do." Jaime took her hand again. "Please do me the honor."

Lucky gritted her teeth and followed him onto the dance floor.

"I suppose I should introduce myself," he said, as he positioned her in his arms. "I'm Jaime."

"I know who you are—and you know I do. I watched you and Branwen fencing this afternoon."

"Yes, you were with Alicia. She told you my name?"

Lucky nodded. "She said she'd known you all her life—except for the years you were gone. Where did you go?"

Jaime spun her around. When she faced him once again, he answered, "I traveled the earth. Why do you ask?"

Lucky shrugged. "Curious—and trying to make conversation."

"What brings *you* to Nadach?"

"Visiting my new grandmother. Escaping my life. Why do *you* ask?"

Again he spun her away from him. When she spun back toward him, his arms tightened around her. "Because I don't trust you. Newly Made Naphil visiting her grandmother in the Dark Realm of the Banished." His eyes lit on the dragon medallion, and he sniffed. "Smells like a spy to me."

Lucky gasped and stopped moving so suddenly he almost tripped over her. *"Spy? Me?"* She laughed in disbelief and disgust. "I came here to get away from things like that."

Dropping into a curtsey which she hoped conveyed as much mockery as his earlier bow, she added, "Thank you for the dance. Sorry I can't bring myself to finish it."

Then, with as much dignity as she could muster, she wound through the dancing couples to the edge of the dance floor.

Lucky scanned the room until she located Alicia, who sipped a glass of lemonade while she too caught her breath. From the way her eyes moved between Lucky and Jaime, Lucky could tell the girl had witnessed their uncomfortable exchange.

Alicia's brows drew together in an inquiring frown as Lucky approached her. "What did Jaime say to you?"

Lucky shook her head. "He thinks I'm a spy."

Alicia giggled. "A spy? That's just silly."

Catching the girl's humor, Lucky chuckled too. "That's sort of what I said."

"He'll come around." Alicia said, taking another sip from her glass. "Do you want some lemonade? I'll go get you a glass, if you'd like."

"Thanks. I'd love some."

"Stay here. I'll be right back."

By the time Alicia returned with the lemonade, Lucky had decided not to worry about what Jaime or Branwen thought of her. Sure, she might be here for a while, but at some point she'd have to go back to her own life—once she could face Zeke—and when she did, it wouldn't matter whether anyone here believed she was a spy or not.

"Are you enjoying the dance?" she asked Alicia, after she had sampled the lemonade, which tasted of herbs—basil and mint?—as well as lemons.

The blonde girl nodded. "Yes. I've danced most of the dances so far, and the dancing is fun. Of course, I keep hoping Jaime will ask me to dance." She hesitated then smiled at Lucky as she continued, "I was almost jealous when I saw him ask you. But neither of you seemed to enjoy it, and then you walked away and left him there."

"Oh, you have no need to be jealous of me. I can see why you like Jaime, but I don't feel the same way about him. Besides, I have a boyfriend." Lucky's voice trailed off as the thought of Aidan brought with it uncomfortable questions about what he might have known about Sambethe. Maybe she had a boyfriend, maybe she didn't.

"You do?" asked Alicia. "What's he like?"

Before Lucky could answer, a smirking boy stepped between them. He appeared to be about Alicia's age.

"Will you dance this set with me, Alicia?" he asked.

Alicia shook her head and backed away from him, almost colliding with Lucky. "No, William, I won't dance with you— this set or any other."

William closed the distance Alicia had put between them. "Oh, come on," he said, the smirk still on his face, his eyes cold, "this once—for old time's sake?"

Alicia backed up farther and shook her head again. "No."

William gripped her upper arm. "You used to want to dance with me. Until *he* came back."

Lucky followed the direction of his glance to the other side of the ballroom, where Jaime stood talking to a group of young men. Her hands fisted at her sides as Alicia struggled to pull her arm from William's grasp.

"I stopped wanting to dance with you long before Jaime came back," Alicia said. "Let me go."

William jerked her toward him. "Just one dance, Alicia."

"She said 'No.' Twice." Lucky's voice trembled with the sudden anger that filled her, and her palms began to tingle. "Do as she said and leave her alone."

Before she could think better of it, she had nudged Alicia from between them and shoved a hand against William's chest to push him away from her.

William released Alicia's arm and knocked Lucky's hand off his chest. "This is none of your business. Why don't you stay out of it?"

Lucky's rage had intensified along with the tingle in her palms, and William became the focus of all her pent up emotions: her confusion and anger at Sambethe's deception and Zeke's betrayal, her bewilderment over Branwen's dislike and Jaime's belief that she was a spy, her misgivings about her grandmother and the Bound, her frustration and anxiety about the changes in her own body and mind.

"Alicia's my friend," she said. "I will not stand by and let you treat her like that."

She shot her right fist into William's nose with enough force to send him reeling. When he recovered his balance and lunged for her, blood streaming down his face, she hit him again, an uppercut to the chin, like Aidan had taught her. She heard William's teeth slam together and watched in satisfaction as he fell back onto the floor.

By that time a crowd had gathered. Two of William's friends lifted him to his feet. He glared at Lucky through narrowed eyes as they led him away.

Her anger subsiding, Lucky unclenched her hands as she glanced around at the staring faces. They showed a range of emotions, from fear to curiosity to satisfaction. She took a deep breath and turned her back on them to find her friend.

Branwen and Jaime now stood with Alicia, and when Lucky approached them, they both greeted her with grins.

"Who would have guessed you'd have it in you?" Branwen said.

"I'm just sorry I didn't get to punch him in the nose," Jaime added.

Alicia smiled at Lucky and pulled her into a hug. "Thank you," she said.

Lucky returned the squeeze. "You're very welcome. What a jerk!"

"Should we ask her?" Jaime said to Branwen, as Lucky stepped away from Alicia.

Lucky looked from one to the other. "Ask me what?"

Branwen grinned again. "Well, since you seem to have an aptitude for fighting and even look like you know something about it, Jaime and I wondered if you'd like to start training with us."

Lucky looked from Branwen to Jaime and back again. "I thought you didn't like me."

Jaime chuckled. "After the way you went after William, we may have changed our minds."

"Since I hit him, I'm no longer a spy?"

Jaime's grin turned rueful. "Our dance had already convinced me of that."

Again Lucky's glance slid back and forth between him and Branwen. "You really want me to train with you?"

They both nodded. "We really do," Branwen said.

"Then I'd like to," Lucky said. "Very much."

"Good," Branwen said. "We start tomorrow. I'll go over the schedule with you at breakfast."

"And I'll fix you up with gear," Jaime added, moving toward the door. "But, right now, I'm going to go make sure William and his pals don't come back here bent on revenge."

Branwen fell in beside him. "Not without me, you're not," she said, adding to Alicia and Lucky. "Catch you two later."

Lucky chuckled and shook her head as her eyes followed Branwen and Jaime until they exited the room.

"See," Alicia said, reaching out to clasp one of Lucky's hands. "I told you we'd all be best friends."

Lucky stood on the balcony, where she had escaped from the crowd, looking down at Lilith's garden. So many people strolled its torch-lit paths, it seemed almost as populated as the ballroom. It all looked magical in the flickering torchlight.

"Mother said I could find you here."

The gravelly voice took Lucky by surprise. She spun to face the speaker. She recognized the voice and the glowing yellow eyes. Otherwise, he bore no resemblance to the man she'd seen at the Medici and who had later tried to kidnap her. That man had appeared middle-aged. This one looked much younger. Wavy dark hair framed a tanned face with high cheekbones and a sharp nose. Still, she knew who he was. Luil. Her father.

Lucky held on to the balcony railing, expecting pain to pierce her head at any moment.

"Do not be afraid," Luil said. "I mean you no harm. I simply wished to see you, to talk to you."

"Why isn't my head hurting?"

A smile curved Luil's lips. "Because I am not trying to hide my eyes from you. There is no glamour for you to penetrate. When I take human form, my eyes always give me away, so I hide them behind a very strong glamour. Your untrained Sensitive mind tried to break it, without your conscious awareness. It even succeeded for a moment."

Lucky didn't reply, but she couldn't keep herself from scanning him from head to foot. Except for the eyes, he looked so different.

"This is not a familiar form to you," Luil said, "but it is how I looked when your mother knew me. Except for the eyes, of course. I hid them from her."

"Did that cause her pain too?"

Luil shook his head. "Her powers had not yet manifested when I met her. She did not resist the glamour."

He pointed at her locket. "May I?"

Lucky hesitated. She didn't want to stand that near him. But she did want to hear what he had to say about her mother, and hard as it might be for her to believe, he was her father. She nodded.

He stepped close, lifted the locket, opened it. He studied the picture inside for several seconds. Then he looked at Lucky, glanced back at the picture, and closed the locket.

"You look like her," he said as he backed away from her. "With something," he waved toward his own form, "of this as well."

It was true. She had her mother's fair skin and freckles, but her face was shaped like Luil's.

"You left her," she said.

He looked puzzled. "We were never meant to last. I loved her—as much as it is in my nature to love—but I knew our time together would be short. I am Shedim." He spoke as if that explained everything. "I did not know about you. I had not thought it possible we could create a child."

"Would it have made a difference if you had known?"

Luil lifted his shoulders. "At the time? I do not know. I suppose I would have at least looked in on you on occasion."

Lucky stared at him. "You suppose? Did you even care when she killed herself?"

"I did not know. I learned of her death only after I learned of your existence. I would have thought Ezekiel would have prevented it."

"Zeke?"

"He has a kind of radar for Sensitives. I assumed you knew. Is that not how he found you?"

Lucky shook her head. "He never knew about me, until Aidan told him he'd met me."

Luil frowned.

"When I was with Marie, I masked the growing seeds of her Sensitive abilities, so she would not see through my glamour, and so Ezekiel could not find her. When I ended the relationship, there was no need to continue the masking. I assumed Ezekiel would find her soon enough."

"And you never checked back in with her? You never thought to follow up and see what happened to her?"

"She would not have wanted to see me again."

"Couldn't you have watched her from the shadows or something?"

"Our time was over. What purpose would such a thing have served?"

"You could have saved her life."

"I did not know she needed saving. As I said, I thought Ezekiel would find her."

"He never found her. She killed herself not long after I was born." Lucky moved to the other side of the balcony, as far away from him as she could get. "It's your fault. If you hadn't masked her powers, Zeke would have found her and helped her. She would still be alive."

Luil shook his head. "It is perhaps my fault, but not because I masked her powers. I believe it may well have been because I gave her you."

# CHAPTER 6

A smile lit Alicia's face when Lucky entered the dining room for breakfast. Lucky sat down beside the younger girl, pasting on a smile of her own to cover her exhaustion.

Alicia had dragged her back into the ballroom right after Luil's revelation the night before, so she hadn't had a chance to ask him for more details. His words had somersaulted through her head most of the night, allowing for little sleep. Like she hadn't had enough to worry about already. She didn't need the additional fear that she had somehow inadvertently been responsible for her mother's death.

She picked up the mug of tea the serving girl had set before her and took a drink. Heat seared her tongue. She swallowed, fully awake now, and thankful for her Naphil body's accelerated healing.

She listened to Alicia's chatter, doing her best to shake off her thoughts about her mother. She'd find Luil and get more information when she could.

Branwen joined them soon after, almost animated in her eagerness to go over Lucky's training schedule. Lucky had feared her cousin's suspicion and dislike might have regrouped overnight, but whatever shift had taken place in the ballroom the night before remained.

The same held true for Jaime. When Lucky and Branwen reached the training area, he had compiled the promised assortment of gear. Branwen helped Lucky find a storage locker for her borrowed things and even gave her a faded black tank top and leggings to change into.

"We'll have to find you some leathers," she said as she handed Lucky the clothes. "I would loan you those too, but mine would be way too long for you."

"Thanks. It means a lot to me, that you asked me to train with you."

Branwen grinned. "Well, go change then, so we can get to work."

By the end of the day, Lucky's emotions had lifted, despite the fatigue that weighted her limbs. After putting her through a series of tests to determine her physical abilities, Branwen and Jaime's trainers—her trainers now too—had worked them all through individualized strength and endurance drills similar to those she had done with Aidan and Malachi. Then they had alternately paired her with Branwen or Jaime for martial arts combat. Lucky knew Branwen and Jaime had more experience than she had, but neither seemed to mind being paired with her, and they both pushed her to extend her limits.

As she and Branwen walked back to the castle to get cleaned up for dinner, she realized that through this whole disruption of her world, she had lost only one day of training.

At least, she could still learn how to deal with the enemies she knew she'd have to face one of these days.

Her next thought stopped her in her tracks. If there was a battle between Light and Dark, one in which she was to play a pivotal role, on which side would Branwen and Jaime fight? Would they all fight for a common cause, or would they be enemies?

"What is it?" Branwen asked, stopping a few steps ahead of Lucky.

"Nothing," Lucky replied, pulling herself back to the present. "I just—thought of something I don't want to think about."

"Want to talk about it?"

Lucky shook her head. She didn't want to risk destroying the beginnings of their friendship by suggesting they might someday be enemies. Maybe that idea had even inspired Branwen and Jaime's initial suspicions. If they might fight on opposite sides, then her presence here did appear questionable—and their offer to train with her surprised her even more. Then again, training together would allow them to learn her strengths and weaknesses even as it exposed theirs to her.

"You sure?" Branwen asked.

Lucky sighed. "Yeah, I'm sure."

"Suit yourself."

Halfway up the stairs leading to their rooms, they met Lilith on her way down.

"Ah, Lucky," she said. "Just the person I wanted to see." Glancing from one of her granddaughters to the other, she added, "It seems my Bryn has coerced you into undergoing physical training with her."

Lucky chuckled. "Branwen didn't coerce me. She offered. And I accepted."

"Oh, well, to each her own," Lilith replied.

Branwen laughed. "I know better than to ask *you*, Grandmother. Why fight with hands and weapons when you can do it with magic, right?"

Lilith nodded. "That's always been my position."

"To each her own," Branwen said, as she started back up the stairs. "I'll leave you two to talk. I've got to get out of these nasty clothes. You did great today, Lucky."

"Thanks, Branwen. I enjoyed it, and I learned a lot. I appreciate you and Jaime including me."

Branwen looked at Lucky, her head tilted to the side as if she were weighing her options. Then she said, "You don't have to use my full name anymore. You can call me Bryn."

As Bryn turned the corner at the next landing, Lilith looked at Lucky with a raised eyebrow. "Well, that's quick work. What did you do to bring Bryn around?"

Unsure of Lilith's opinion of her previous evening's adventure, Lucky felt a blush stain her cheeks. "You've probably heard I hit William last night. I think that's what did it."

"Mm-hm. I figured as much. There's no love lost between them, and I gather you hit him to protect Alicia?"

Lucky nodded.

"Well, I can't say I condone my granddaughter brawling at a party intended to introduce her to my people, but I can understand why you did it—and I can see why it would raise you in Bryn's estimation." She slid an arm around Lucky's shoulders. "But don't make a habit of it, please."

Lucky shook her head. "I won't."

"Good. We can talk on the way to your room, since you too need to get out of your training clothes. I believe your training schedule allows you two free mornings a week. Is that correct?"

"Yes."

"Excellent. I suggest you put that time to use learning some magic. You are my granddaughter, after all. You should know something of the family trade."

"I—all right," Lucky stammered. She had never thought about learning magic. Well, unless zapping herself from one place to another could be considered magic. She certainly hadn't thought about incantations or spells. But it would be handy to know how to make her own wards. And if Lilith used magic to fight, then others would too.

"*All right?*" Lilith sounded offended. "I offer to teach you magic, and you say '*All right?*' Do you have any idea what most people would give to learn magic from me?"

"I didn't mean to sound ungrateful. I was just surprised. And, yes, I do know. Alicia told me about the Bound." Staring into her grandmother's emerald eyes, she added, "If you want me to Bind myself to you and your world to learn your magic, I won't do it."

"I know you wouldn't. And I wouldn't ask it of you. I'm not planning on teaching you all that many of my secrets anyway. But you should know something of the magic you bear. Otherwise, you will be too vulnerable to your enemies."

"Then I'd like to learn what you're willing to teach me."

"Good. We'll start tomorrow. I'm afraid I haven't left you much time to change. You'll have to hurry, or you'll be late for dinner."

"Wait," Lucky said, as her grandmother turned to go. "How would I contact—Luil—if I wanted to talk to him?"

Lilith's features softened. "I will let him know you wish to speak to him. He will come to you."

"Thank you."

Lilith smiled and turned away. Lucky slipped inside her room to get ready for dinner.

The next morning after breakfast, Lucky accompanied Lilith to her chamber to begin her lessons in magic. When Lilith invited her to sit and make herself comfortable while she made tea, Lucky felt a pang of homesickness. She couldn't seem to help missing Zeke, even though he had betrayed her. She resolutely pushed those thoughts away as Lilith handed her a steaming cup and sat down in the chair across from her.

"First, let me tell you what magic is and what it is not. Magic is an awareness of the interconnectedness of all things, a deep knowledge of *how* all things are connected, and the ability, based on that knowledge, to influence or change those connections. Magic is not illusion. It is not a game. And it is not to be taken lightly. Everything in existence is connected in an infinite web, and to influence or change certain strands without causing unwanted changes throughout the entire web takes considerable talent and care. Do you understand?"

"I think so. I mean, not down to the details or anything. But I can see the web when I have my senses wide open—gold and dark threads running everywhere."

Lilith raised her eyebrows. "Very good. That puts you well ahead of most of my students. Then again, I've never worked with a Sensitive Made Naphil before. Perhaps you could tell me a bit about how your powers work when you have your 'senses wide open' as you say. That will help me determine the best way to guide you in the practice of magic. There are different types of magic, different techniques, and each of us is more or less suited to practice each of them. We are strongest when using the type of magic to which we are most well-matched."

Lucky described how she experienced the world in a synesthetic way with her senses at full volume. She explained her "control room" and how she could turn her extra senses on or off, up or down. Lilith seemed pleased and impressed that Lucky had mastered her Sensitive powers so quickly.

"And what about your Gift, dear?" Lilith asked when Lucky had stopped speaking. "As a Naphil, you must have one."

Lucky shook her head. "It hasn't shown up yet."

"I see. Well, it will manifest in its own time. I am quite interested to see what it turns out to be."

*You're not the only one,* Lucky thought.

"In any case, you've given me plenty to work with. Let's start with an overview of the different types of magic. Then in our next session, we'll begin work on those most suited to you and your talents."

Lucky spent the rest of the morning trying to absorb everything Lilith told her. When they broke for lunch, she was more than ready to shift gears and concentrate on training her body during the afternoon.

Kev's boots clattered on the marble stairs as he raced to the second floor of the Allied Council Hall. He never overslept, but he had this morning. By the time he'd awakened and realized he'd somehow slept through the alarm, a shower was out of the question. He'd yanked on clothes, run his fingers through his hair, and called it good. Zapping himself to Elsewhere took a matter of seconds, but he was still late.

And the foggy tendrils of the dream still clouded his mind. He couldn't remember any of the details—but the dream had been about Lucky, and she'd been in some sort of trouble. He shook his head to clear away the residual anxiety.

He slowed his steps as he neared the closed door. He might be late, but he could enter with some decorum. He opened the door as quietly as he could and made his way to the empty seat at the table.

Only after he sat down did he realize someone occupied the place that had belonged to Sambethe. And that someone was no stranger.

"Hello, Mother," he said.

Katrin tilted her head toward him, a cool smile on her lips. "Hello, Kevin. So glad you could join us."

One corner of Kev's mouth twisted in a resigned half-smile. "Yeah, apologies for the lateness. I guess I threw back a few too many on that bender last night."

Several sets of eyebrows raised, and he added, "Kidding. Please proceed."

Several minutes had passed before he tuned in to the conversation. He still felt as if he'd left a good chunk of his mind behind in the dream world, and thoughts of Katrin now filled the part he hadn't. What had it been? Five years? Who or what, he wondered, had convinced her to come out of seclusion?

She looked good—even with the scar that marred her left cheek and caused that side of her mouth to turn slightly downwards. Her dark hair was scraped back into the severe twist he remembered, and her dark green eyes, much like his own, were as penetrating as ever.

It was her name, spoken in Zeke's resonating voice, that caught Kev's attention.

"...Katrin Drake, who has graciously agreed to serve as Sambethe's replacement on the Council."

"Thank you, Zeke," Katrin said. "As you know, I left my position as General of the Forces five years ago, after incurring serious injuries fighting the Zahhak. While I may never fully recover my physical mobility, Zeke has convinced me to stop letting my Gift go to waste. I am pleased to rejoin you as the Fallen's new Healer."

That meant Kev would see her a lot more often. Somehow he doubted it would make them grow any closer. Katrin had never made any pretense of wanting to be a mother to the son she'd borne for the sake of politics. And Kev had long since given up his childish dream of earning his mother's affection.

After everyone had welcomed Katrin to the circle, Zeke turned to Kev. *"Ha-Satan,* do you have anything new to report concerning the investigation?"

"I finally got a look at Jahoel's body—and the sigil mark. It's definitely Lucifer's sigil, but something's off—like it's out of focus. If he'd actually made the mark, it wouldn't be blurred like that. It doesn't give us much to work with, but it was enough to convince the Metatron to grant us more time for the investigation. We just have to figure out how someone could have faked it with such accuracy."

"The mark is the key," Zeke said. "I will keep looking through our records for any leads."

*Do not make the mistake of eliminating what may seem impossible.* Uriel spoke for the first time since Kev had arrived. Even as distracted as he was, he couldn't have tuned out the Archangel's searing voice.

"Do you know something, Uriel?" Zeke asked.

The Archangel shook his head, his flame-filled eye sockets shifting toward Zeke. *I know no more than you do about who did this. But it seems your efforts might be improved if you seek more broadly.*

Great, Kev thought, as if exploring the improbable didn't leave them a huge enough field. Still, maybe Uriel had a point. Maybe the culprit was someone or something they had eliminated out of hand. "Thank you, Archangel. We'll keep that in mind."

Zeke closed the meeting a few minutes later. Uriel exploded into brilliance and disappeared while the others abandoned their chairs.

The sight of Katrin pushing herself up with the help of a cane and limping a few steps away from the table shook Kev. He'd heard what she said about her injuries not healing completely, but he hadn't considered what that might mean. She wore a long dark skirt—a marked change from the black leather trousers she used to wear—so he couldn't see her legs. But from the way she moved, he guessed her left leg was now shorter than her right. A scar similar to the one that crossed her cheek, marked the hand holding the cane.

Kev had taken part in the battle in which she'd been wounded, but his battalion had engaged the lesser demons, while Katrin and her troops had fought the nearly invincible Zahhak. By the time he had learned of her injuries, she had retreated to an undisclosed location to heal, and he hadn't seen her since. He had spared some thoughts for her, had occasionally wondered about her recovery, but for the most part she had been as absent from his mind as she had been from his life.

Watching her now, he realized how difficult it must have been for her to come back, to let everyone see her like this. She had always been vain—more so about her strength than her looks, though she had taken pride in her appearance as well. To return to the public eye in less than perfect physical form had no doubt exacted a huge toll on that vanity, a toll she would have paid with even more inner strength than he had known she possessed.

Kev felt an unwilling swell of pride.

He took a few steps closer to her. He had no idea what to say, but he couldn't leave without saying something. She turned toward him as he approached, her eyes daring him to offer her pity.

"Welcome back, Mother," he said.

Her eyes softened the slightest bit. "Thank you," she said crisply.

It wasn't much, but perhaps it was a start.


Luil was waiting at the A wing gate when Lucky and Bryn returned from their afternoon training session.

He exchanged greetings with Bryn, before turning to Lucky. "You wished to see me?"

Lucky nodded. "Go on ahead," she said to Bryn. "I'll catch up with you at dinner."

Bryn looked at Lucky. "Does this have anything to do with whatever's been preoccupying you all day?" Before Lucky could respond, she shifted her gaze to Luil. "I guess you two could use some father-daughter time."

"That's not..." Lucky let the sentence drop. She stared after Bryn's departing form, resisting the impulse to insist she wanted information and nothing else. She had no interest in establishing a relationship with the man—demon—who had fathered her.

"Not what you had in mind?" Luil asked. "Do not worry. I am under no illusions about your feelings for me."

"It's not as if you're standing there harboring a deep well of fatherly love for me either."

Luil raised his eyebrows. "How do you know what I feel for you? I have admitted it is not in my nature to love as humans do, but I have also told you I loved your mother as much as I am capable of loving anyone. You are my child, her child. Why would you doubt that I would care for you?"

Lucky snorted. "Maybe because you abandoned her. From where I'm standing whatever love you're capable of doesn't seem like much."

"Perhaps that is true. But even a little is something, no?"

"I guess."

"Walk with me?" Luil gestured toward the path that led toward the wing's living quarters.

They had taken several steps before Lucky could shape her question. "I wanted to know more about what you said the other night. What did you mean when you said you might have caused my mother's death by giving her me?"

"You told me yourself Ezekiel did not know about you until Aidan told him. How do you think you escaped his detection? You are part Shedim. You have the same masking ability I have. I believe that ability activated in you the moment you were conceived, probably because I was using the power at the time. As you grew inside your mother, your power masked both you and her."

What he said sounded plausible, but Lucky didn't want to believe it. "You're saying I have this masking power I never knew I had?"

"You have other powers you did not know you had."

She couldn't argue with him there. But she still didn't quite get this whole masking thing. "I'm not masking my powers anymore, right? If I didn't know I had masked them in the first place, how did I know to stop?"

"Once your powers were no longer a secret—to you or to Ezekiel—you unconsciously dropped the mask." Luil looked at her. "I am guessing, you understand?"

"It makes sense." How Lucky wished it didn't. She had had no control over what had happened, but she still felt responsible for her mother's death. Even though she knew the real culprit walked beside her.

Luil frowned. "You blame yourself?" he asked, as if sensing her thoughts.

Lucky shrugged.

"Do not. As you pointed out last time we talked, the fault is mine." After a few steps, he continued. "If I had known Marie would die because of our involvement, would I have walked away from her at the beginning? I do not know. I wanted what I wanted. If faced with the same situation now, would I act differently? I would like to think so, but I am not even sure of that." Luil shook his head. "I am Shedim."

Lucky frowned. "You say that like it's an excuse."

"I am what I am."

"But you can change, can't you? If you want to do better, to be better?"

"Perhaps." He stopped, studied her face. "Do you want me to change? To be better, as you say?"

Lucky looked away. "I don't want anything from you."

"No?"

Lucky didn't reply.

He pointed to a third floor window. "My quarters are there, should you change your mind and wish to find me."

"I have to go, or I'll be late for dinner," Lucky said.

Then, not wanting to seem ungrateful—after all, he had sought her out as she'd asked—she added, "Thank you for the information."

"I am happy to talk to you any time you like—daughter."

Lucky jogged back down the path toward Lilith's part of the castle, Luil's final word echoing in her head in time with her rhythmic footfalls.

# CHAPTER 7

If the looks cast toward him and Zeke were any indication, Kev thought, more than a few of the Heavenly residents held the same opinion of the Dark and the Fallen as the two Dominion males and the female Power who had confronted him on his last visit. Many of the Light had greeted them civilly, and some bestowed on Zeke the warm smiles and hugs reserved for a long-time friend. But at least an equal number stared with open hostility.

It wasn't as if they could hide in the crowd. On his own, Zeke in his ivory robes might have managed to blend with the sea of unadulterated white, but Kev's red and black, as well as their accompanying Dominion guards, shouted their outsider status. Their position to the side of the gathering also marked them as observers instead of participants in the Assumption.

The crowd had gathered in a huge circular plaza behind which soared the main façade of the Metatron's palatial headquarters. Kev had never seen the building from the front, and he had to admit he found it even more impressive than the one in which Jahoel had lain in state. Light and color flashed fire from the facets of its lofty towers. On an elevated platform in the center of the plaza, Jahoel's crystal casket winked like a chip cut from the palace's gargantuan diamond.

The Metatron stood on a kind of balcony supported by flying buttresses that extended from the building's front past the edge of the crowd. There they could be both a part of the ceremony and still separate from the throng.

Silence descended at a sudden charge in the atmosphere, as if before an electrical storm. Kev shielded his eyes from the blinding bursts of light that heralded the Archangels' appearance at evenly spaced positions on the circle's perimeter. At full stature, they towered above the crowd, taller even than the Metatron's balcony.

No one spoke as Adrigon disappeared from the balcony and then reappeared on the raised platform that held Jahoel's casket. He pressed his hand into the casket's end, and as Kev remembered, the crystalline cover wavered like water before seeming to evaporate. His task complete, Adrigon too faded away, reappearing once again on the balcony with Tatriel, Galiel, and Margash.

In unison, the Archangels extended their wings, the spans so great their wing tips touched, enclosing the gathered crowd within their collective embrace. The iridescence of their wings reflected the colors glancing from the faceted buildings around them.

The atmosphere super-charged again, and a thrum filled Kev's ears. The air hung heavy and still, but the ends of his hair lifted, floating as if on a breeze.

The Archangels raised their arms, and all the light from their explosive appearance coalesced into a column that shot down from the sky into Jahoel's casket. Kev's hair whipped about his face. He squinted through it at the shining column.

Then the light, the thrum, the heaviness and charge in the air departed, taking Jahoel's body with them. The casket sat upon the platform, open and empty.

The Archangels lowered their arms and their wings and shrank until they were only a head or so taller than the tallest in the crowd. It seemed the ceremony was over. The Metatron disappeared into their diamond palace, and the crowd began to disperse, gathering in smaller groups to talk, as the Archangels moved among them.

The Dominion guards stepped forward, Kev and Zeke's cue to head back toward the Gates. Since the Alliance, though frayed, was still intact, they had both been invited, even obligated, to attend this brief affair of state, but lingering would mean overstaying their welcome.

They followed the guards across the plaza, winding through the crowds, pausing for Zeke to exchange greetings with old acquaintances or friends. They had nearly reached the entrance to the palace, when two Dominion males Kev recognized blocked their way.

The taller male speared Kev with his gaze. "One would have hoped you would have had the decency to stay away from this ceremony, *Ha-Satan*." He spat the title like venom. "Since it would not have been necessary but for your father."

"My father did not kill Jahoel. Despite their differences, he held him in high esteem. I would have been remiss if I had not come to pay my father's and my respects on this day."

"If Lucifer were innocent, you would have found Jahoel's killer by now. I do not know what you have said to stay the Metatron from nullifying the Alliance, but time grows short." He rested a hand on the hilt of the sword that hung at his side. "Many of us find these delaying tactics tedious."

"What my friend means to say," said his ponytailed companion, "is that under different circumstances, we would draw our swords and cut you down where you stand."

At these words, the guards the Metatron had assigned Kev and Zeke readied their weapons.

"Ah, but circumstances being as they are, we are the Metatron's invited guests." Zeke's words underscored the warning of the guards' raised swords.

"Pardon, Ambassador," offered the taller Dominion. "We did not notice you, intent as we were on your companion."

"Mmm. I suppose I can be easy to overlook."

The corners of Kev's mouth curved in response to Zeke's desert dry words.

"If you would step aside, we will depart your world without further disturbance," Zeke said.

The two Dominions nodded to Zeke and stepped back. The ponytailed male leaned forward as Kev brushed past him. "You would do well to heed my friend's earlier warning," he said in Kev's ear. "Watch your back, *Ha-Satan.*"

Between her training with Bryn and Jaime and her magic lessons with Lilith, Lucky's days fell into a routine. Almost before she knew it, she had spent two weeks in Lilith's Dark world.

Her days were too filled to allow much opportunity to think about or miss her home and her friends. And if thoughts of home, of Josh and G-Ma or Mo or Aidan or Zeke, crossed her mind before she fell asleep at night, she did her best to push them away. She figured she could give herself at least another week before she forced herself to confront Zeke and demand an explanation—after which she'd have to decide if she accepted it.

And if she didn't? What would she do then? Come back to Lilith and take up permanent residence with the Banished and Bound?

She couldn't bear to think about it too much, so she pushed herself harder and harder in her training. If she went to sleep as soon as she lay down each night, she would have no time to think.

She let herself collapse to the ground as she rounded the track after completing one more set of sprints than her body needed. Her breath came in gasps, and she felt exhausted enough to fall into bed right now.

"What's with you, girl?" Bryn asked, dropping down beside her. "You've been pushing harder every day. I know you're all Naphil and everything, but don't you think you're overdoing it a bit?"

"Maybe. I don't know. It keeps me from having to think."

"About what?"

Lucky hesitated. She still hadn't told Bryn what had brought her to Nadach. She wanted to confide in her, but putting it into words would make it even more real.

"Did Lilith ever tell you why I was Made Naphil?"

Bryn shook her head.

"I have another cousin, back home. He's more like my brother. Anyway, after I found out I was a Sensitive and got dragged into this world, someone attacked Josh. This oracle and healer, a woman named Sambethe, she gave him something she said would save him. But it was really a poison. If I hadn't been Made Naphil, so my blood could cure him, he'd have died and become a Wraith. I didn't know it was Sambethe who poisoned Josh until a couple of weeks ago, when Lilith told me. But I think all my so-called friends among the Fallen knew. I know Zeke knew, and he never said anything to me. When I found out, I couldn't stay there. So Lilith invited me to come here. I know I have to go back and face them, but I still don't know how I'm going to do that."

"You aren't a spy, after all," said Bryn, grinning.

"Nope, still not a spy."

"You know I was kidding, right?" When Lucky nodded, Bryn added, "And you know your friends probably have an explanation, if you give them a chance to share it?"

"I know." Lucky pulled a blade of grass and twisted it in her fingers. "But I haven't been ready to listen."

"Well, at least you have the opportunity to cut and run for an extended period of time," Bryn said. She leaned back on her hands and looked up at the gray sky.

Lucky turned to look at her. "Alicia told me she's stuck here because her mother Bound her. Are you Bound too?"

"I'm Lilith's grandchild—the only daughter of her only daughter. I inherit the same limitations that were placed on her, and which she then placed on her Bound." Bryn made no attempt to hide the bitterness in her voice.

Lucky fingered the dark moon birthmark on the inside of her left elbow, her eyes noting its twin on Bryn's left arm. "But I'm Lilith's grandchild, and I'm not Bound."

"Don't think I haven't noticed that. That's partly why I didn't want to like you. Your mother was human and your father—well, my uncles can take on various forms. They are Lilith's children, born of her blood, but they weren't born of her body. My mother was the only child she ever bore. I think the Banishment, Binding, whatever, passes from daughter to daughter."

"Oh," Lucky said. Then, "Where is your mother?"

"She's dead."

"What happened?"

"That's something *I* don't want to talk about," Bryn said, rising to her feet. "Come on. I'm starving."

They walked toward the edge of the field, and Lucky noticed someone leaning on the fence watching them. William. He raised two fingers in a mocking salute, and his eyes followed them all the way off the field. Lucky hadn't seen him since the night of the dance when she had bloodied his nose, but her anger rose up anew as she looked at him, and her palms tingled in response. He may not have done anything yet, but from the looks of things, he didn't intend to remain passive for long.

Aidan couldn't slow down—or, at least, he didn't want to. Racing to a quickly scheduled rehearsal session provided just the kind of distraction he needed. He cranked his Ducati motorcycle to the maximum speed he could manage while weaving through city traffic. The sounds of car horns and squealing breaks accompanied him all the way to Ben's Lincoln Park loft.

"Jesus, Aidan," Eric greeted him as Ben let him in to the apartment. "You booked us for a birthday party? Seriously?"

"She's the mayor's daughter, Eric. She loves us. How could I tell him no?"

"Easy. It's just a two-letter word, man. It's not that hard."

"He's paying us. It's not like we're doing it for free."

"Yeah, but we've already got another gig later that night, and another the next day, and two the following day. You're killing us." With that, Eric moved to the other end of the room to make some adjustments to his drum set.

"Let it go, Eric," Ben said. "We're already booked for all those gigs. We have to do them. But, Aidan, he's right. You've got to stop adding shows to our line-up. We've got a full schedule as it is."

"Yeah, I know." Aidan took off his leather jacket. "I'm sorry. I just have to keep busy, or…" His voice trailed off, as his shoulders drooped.

"You miss Lucky, and you're worried about her," Ben said. "I get it. But you can't keep using the band as a pressure release valve." He lowered his voice. "The humans can't take much more."

Aidan raised his hands. "I'll stop. I promise. No more impromptu gigs. I'll find another way to work off my excess adrenaline."

Ben chuckled. "Let Malachi beat you up a few more times a week. That ought to do it."

Aidan grinned. "Where do you think I am when I'm not with the band?"

"Well, start teaching that ferret of yours to do tricks or something then," Ben said, as he went to open the door for the remaining band members. "But give us a break, okay?"

"You got it," Aidan said. He hung his jacket on the coat rack near the door and went to help Eric with setup.

"Gang's all here," Ben called. "Let's get this party started."

"Tomorrow is the full moon," Lilith said, handing Lucky a cup of tea. "Today's lesson will be about the powers of the moon and blood magic."

"Blood magic?" Lucky asked.

"Yes. But first, the moon." Lilith settled into the chair across from Lucky. "I have explained to you how everything is connected and how magic is the art of influencing those connections. The moon in its phases is a natural influence, so adding the power of the moon to one's magic multiplies the force of any spell. The moon's power is at its height when it is full, as it will be tomorrow."

"That makes sense," Lucky said when Lilith paused for a sip of tea. "But what does it have to do with blood magic?"

Lilith smiled. "Be patient. I will get to that."

She took another sip from her cup and then set the cup on the occasional table at her side. She lifted a small curved blade from the table top and, turning the tip downward, pressed it into the end of her index finger. A red drop welled. She tilted her finger to examine the drop.

"Blood is a very potent substance," she said. "It carries within it a being's life force, essence, signature. A single drop can magnify a spell's effect several times over. With as many as three drops, a spell is next to impossible to break." She raised her finger to her lips and licked away the spot of blood. "My blood is especially powerful when linked with the moon. As you might have guessed from the form of your birthmark, my powers are strongest when the moon is dark."

Lucky glanced at the dark moon shape on the inside of her left elbow and then pressed her fingers over the mark.

"When I combine my blood and its affinity for the dark moon with the force of the moon in full light, the powers of the dark and light moons unite, and I can share that power with all of my Bound."

Lilith replaced the curved knife on the side table and retrieved her cup of tea. Lucky waited, her fingers pressing into her arm, while Lilith drank from the cup.

"When performing blood magic," Lilith said, "it is of the utmost importance to use only your own blood and only a few drops. Too much and you can lose control of the magic. Tomorrow, my blood will call the moon to enhance the individual spells of the Bound." She tilted her head. "Too bad you are not yet ready to practice spells."

"Why is that?"

"Because you are of my blood, of course. The enhancement would be even stronger for you. You may feel some effect anyway, simply by virtue of being my blood kin."

Lucky suppressed a shiver. She didn't know that she wanted to be influenced by Lilith's blood magic. "I guess I'll have to try a spell another time," she said.

Lilith smiled. "Yes. Another time."

# CHAPTER 8

"Isn't it beautiful?" Alicia said. "This is my absolute favorite day of the month."

They stood on the balcony overlooking Lilith's extensive gardens. The full moon shone down out of a clear, dark sky, painting the world with strokes of silver and casting dramatic elongated shadows. People gathered around the large reflecting pool from which an image of the orb winked up at its source in the sky.

"It won't be long before the ceremony starts. We should go down." Alicia turned from the railing and took Lucky's arm, drawing her back inside and toward the stairs.

They had promised to meet Bryn at the pool, and they wound through the gathering crowd to their designated meeting point. They found Bryn waiting for them, and Jaime joined them before long.

Like the feast for Lucky's arrival, the Full Moon ceremony was a formal celebration, and everyone had dressed in their finest. Lucky wore the same teal velvet gown she had worn to the feast. Alicia wore a similar gown of the palest pink. In honor of the Full Moon, Bryn had traded her black velvet tunic for one of pale silver-gray that shimmered like the moonlight itself, and Jaime's black doublet boasted a silver collar.

A hush settled over the crowd, and the four moved closer to the edge of the pool so they could see Lilith where she stood at the pool's end, robed in silver and black. She raised her arms above her head and began to speak. Thanks to Lilith's magic lessons, Lucky understood a few of the words.

When Lilith had completed her invocation, she turned ninety degrees and spoke the words again. She repeated the invocation twice more, turning ninety degrees after each repetition, until she once more faced the pool.

Chanting, Lilith knelt in front of a large shallow bowl, which Lucky knew was filled with salt. She took a small curved knife from the folds of her robe and made a cut on each of her palms. Holding her hands over the bowl, she let a few drops of her blood fall onto the salt. Without breaking her chant, she stood, lifted the bowl of salt over her head toward the light of the moon, and then poured the blood-marked salt into the reflecting pool.

As the salt dissolved in the pool, the moon's reflection took on a reddish glow. Lucky glanced up at the moon where it floated in the sky, its surface as silver as before. Then, even as she watched, red tinted the moon's silvery surface, as if the moon in the sky reflected the one in the pool.

"The sacrifice has been accepted," Lilith declared. "The moon is yours."

The crowd dispersed. Lucky knew some returned to their normal duties, while others hurried to cast the spells that had waited for the fullness of the moon. She had no such spells.

She only wanted to stroll through the moon-drenched garden with her new friends. The full moon provided the closest thing to daylight she'd seen since she'd arrived. She wanted to soak it in for as long as it lasted.

For a while the four of them walked together, but gradually Jaime and Alicia fell behind.

When she and Bryn had moved far enough ahead that she knew she couldn't be overheard, Lucky asked, "Should we sneak into the forest and leave them alone?"

"You want to go into the forest?" Bryn asked in amazement.

"Why not? I've been wanting to walk through the trees, and I bet it's beautiful in the moonlight."

"Yes, it is," Bryn said, "but right now people are casting spells in there, and they won't want to be disturbed."

"Oh, come on. You must know some places where no one is likely to go for spell-casting."

Bryn thought for a minute or two, then she said, "Okay, I can think of a couple of spots. You have to stay with me, though. No wandering off on your own. You have no idea what you might run into."

"No wandering off on my own. I promise."

Lucky took one last look back at Alicia and Jaime before she followed Bryn into the woods. They had circled back to the pool and sat on its edge, deep in conversation. She and Bryn would not be missed.

Lucky tried to make as little noise as possible as she wove through the trees after Bryn. The silvery moonlight filtering through the branches created a fairy-tale world. She caught glimpses of fires, and she smelled wood smoke and the fragrant scents of burning herbs. The tree bark felt rough beneath her fingers, and sometimes leaves touched her face and hair like small hands.

They wound deeper and deeper into the forest, Lucky careful to keep Bryn's silvery tunic in view.

Then Bryn was gone. One minute the flash of silver was before Lucky's eyes, the next it was nowhere to be seen.

"Bryn," Lucky called quietly, so as not to disturb any magic-makers. No answer.

She raised her voice. "Bryn!"

A rough arm closed around her, pinning her arms to her side, while a hand clamped over her mouth.

"Your friend is up ahead," a male voice said in her ear. "You'll see her when we get to the clearing."

Lucky fought, but she couldn't pull free of her captor's arms.

"All your training counts for nothing when we've got the moon on our side," sneered the voice in her ear. William. He had decided to take his revenge tonight. Well played. She wondered how strong his magic was. There had to be a weakness somewhere.

He dragged her into the clearing, and she saw Bryn. The girl knelt several yards to Lucky's left, two of William's friends standing guard, one on either side. She struggled as if she were bound, but Lucky could see no rope. Magic.

Across the clearing, a tall man in a dark cloak stood near a fire, his hands drawing symbols in the air, while he muttered incantations.

Lucky still couldn't move her arms, even though William had released his hold on her. The magic confined her like it did Bryn.

William smirked at her. "Don't even bother trying to scream. With Father's spell, no one will be able to hear you."

"A bit of overkill, don't you think?" Lucky said. "All this as payback for a bloody nose?"

"Oh, this is about way more than that. Little spy, coming here to search out our secrets so you can share them with the Light."

"You've got to be kidding me. Do you think Lilith would have brought me here if I was a spy for the Light?"

"Lilith is blinded by her affection for her new grand-daughter. She can't see what you are."

Lucky smirked. "Not only are you a bully, but you're also an idiot."

William's hand flashed out to hit her cheek, spinning her head to the right and causing her to stagger. "That was payback for pushing me," he snarled. "And this is for punching me in the face." He drew back his fist and slammed it into her stomach.

Lucky groaned. "Well, aren't you the brave one?" she said. "It takes a lot of courage to hit a girl when she can't begin to fight back."

At that, William laid into her with both fists.

Lucky gasped and fell to her knees, then onto her side as he continued to rain blows on her. She couldn't fight back. She could do nothing but endure the pain as he hit her again and again. Her cheek burned from where he'd struck her earlier, and her head throbbed from a blow to her temple. Her ribs and sides ached when she drew breath. When he kicked the side of her back below her ribs, she feared she might lose consciousness.

But underneath that fear, the spark of anger flared into leaping, flaming life. The emotion she had felt the night she stood up for Alicia was like a half-snuffed candle in comparison. This was an inferno. It filled her core and ran through her limbs and burned like coals in her palms.

Looking up, she could see the full moon through the trees, the moon with its reddish glow, from Lilith's blood. Lilith's blood. *She* was Lilith's blood. The sacrifice had been accepted. The moon was *hers*.

With a cry of rage, she ripped her arms free of the magic that had bound her and whipped out a hand to grab William's arm as his fist came at her again. She felt the heat in her palm at the same moment she heard William scream. He yanked his arm away from her and stumbled backward as she lunged to her feet.

"She burned me!" he cried.

"Lawbreaker!" shouted William's father, who had left his fire to run to his son's side. He glanced from his son's arm to Lucky's outstretched hand. "The use of the palm sigils in combat is forbidden. You will pay!"

Stretching out his hand, he began to chant, but before any spell could take effect, Lucky had stretched out her own hand. The white-hot flame of her anger flashed down her arm, and power shot out of her palm, capturing and holding both William and his father motionless.

"Lucky?" She heard Bryn's voice as if from afar. "Lucky, what are you doing?"

She held them in her power, William and his father. And they had begun to realize how the tables had turned. She could sense their self-righteous anger and confident despotism shifting to fear. She could see the strands of thought and emotion, and she knew precisely what it would take to turn up the volume. A twist here, a little knot there, and they would feel a terror so extreme as to be just this side of madness. And if she pushed a little more, tangled the strands a bit, she could tip them over the edge. She could. She could do it. They would pay for their actions with their sanity.

"Lucky! Lucky, stop!"

Lucky barely heard Bryn's voice. It would be so easy. And so satisfying. Her lips curved into a smile of anticipation.

"Lucky." Lilith's voice joined Bryn's. "You must stop. You don't want to do this."

Oh, but she did. She wanted this more than she had ever wanted anything in her life. Nothing could ever give her the satisfaction she would feel as she watched William and his father tumble into madness from a mere flick of her wrist. That's all it would take. One little twist. She tilted her hand. William and his father both screamed.

Lucky laughed, then cried out as the dragon medallion on her chest heated to near unbearable intensity.

The pain lasted but a moment, and it didn't distract her enough to cause her to lose her hold on her playthings.

She tilted her hand the other way, and they screamed again. She supposed she could toy with them for a while. But she wanted to watch them come apart at the seams, destroyed by the fear and madness in their own minds. And she could do it with one tiny motion. A twist to a strand, a shift of the wrist.

"Lucky!"

That was a new voice, but one she recognized.

Keeping her hand unmoving, she turned her head toward the sound. Kev stood a few yards away from her, on the opposite side of the clearing from Bryn and Lilith.

"Lucky, you need to stop this. Now!"

She couldn't stop. Not when her task was so close to completion. She tore her gaze away from Kev and directed all her attention back toward her captives. She smiled and flicked her wrist.

"NO!"

Bryn's cry was muffled by the unearthly roar that came from where Kev had stood, a spot now occupied by a dragon even bigger than the one that had appeared to Lucky when she called her Makers.

Lucky felt something impact the shaft of power shooting from her palm in the same instant flames engulfed her arm. She screamed and dropped her arm in time to see Bryn fall.

Then she too crumpled to the ground.

Shifting back to his human form, Kev raced toward Lucky, while Lilith ran to the pixie-haired girl who had flung herself between Lucky and her victims just as Kev had played the dragon card. He snuffed out the remaining flames on Lucky's arm before the rest of her gown could catch fire and then pulled the remnants of sleeve away from her burned flesh.

The wounds had already begun to heal. He released the breath he hadn't been aware of holding. He hadn't wanted to flame her, but he hadn't seen any alternative. She had been beyond listening to reason. And he had known he could control the fire well enough to hit nothing but her arm. She would be fine when she came to—well, physically at least. He couldn't vouch for her emotional state.

Laying her gently on the ground, he joined Lilith where she knelt beside the dark-haired girl.

"How is she?" he asked, crouching down near her.

"She's unconscious. She has a pulse, but it's thin." Lilith's voice was unsteady, and Kev could see tears on her cheeks.

"She got hit by both Lucky's power and my flame. I didn't see her coming until I'd already released it. She just got a partial dose of both. Still…"

"She's my granddaughter," Lilith said. "My only daughter's only daughter. And I can do nothing to save her. My magic cannot heal this. It is useless to her."

"I could take her back to my world—with your permission, of course. My mother is a powerful Healer, and my brother has a Gift that, well, could help your granddaughter."

"What happened to Bryn? Did I do this to her?"

Kev looked up in surprise. He hadn't heard Lucky approach. Her voice was faint, and she swayed on her feet, looking like she might topple over onto her unconscious friend. Kev stood and wrapped an arm around her, pulling her against his side.

"We both did this to her," he said. "But we'll take her back to Zeke's with us. We can tend to both of you there."

"No! I can't go back there, and Bryn—she'll die if she's gone too long."

Kev's attention shot back to Lilith. "Is that true? Is she Bound, Lilith?"

Lilith let out a sob as she clutched her granddaughter's hand.

"Lilith, answer me," Kev demanded. "Is she Bound?"

Lilith shook her head. "No," she said. "I told her she was, because I couldn't bear to have her leave me. But, no, she's not Bound. Take her. If you can save her, take her."

"Right, then." Kev looked down at Lucky, where she leaned against his side. "You wait here. I'll take Bryn first. Then I'll come back for you."

"Kev, I can't go back. I can't face Zeke—and, after what I just did, I'm a danger to everyone."

"Well, you certainly can't stay here." The voice came from the tall, dark-cloaked man Lucky had held in her power when Kev had arrived after answering the medallion's summons. "In fact, you should be prosecuted. Lilith, did you know she burned my son with her palm sigil? Show her, William."

William held out his right arm. Kev could barely see the small red mark on his skin.

"It wasn't intentional, Mather," Lilith said. "Her palm sigils and Gift manifested for the first time tonight. I doubt she even knew the sigil was on her palm when she touched him."

"But you saw what she did to us, what she tried to do."

Kev could almost feel Lilith collecting her scattered composure before she spoke. "Yes, I did. Fortunately, we stopped her. My granddaughter is very strong. I can hardly wait to see what she'll do when she is in full control of her powers."

"I would see her punished."

Fire lit Lilith's eyes, and Kev almost felt sorry for the loose-tongued man. Lilith rose to her full height, her regal bearing draping her like a cloak.

"*You* would do well to keep your mouth shut. From what I have observed, you and your son instigated the situation. Neither of my granddaughters would have been injured but for you. And you provoked what Lucky did to you. Perhaps you'll think twice before attacking the possessor of such raw, untamed power again. I will absolve *you* of all punishment for your crimes, and you, in turn, will make no claims against my granddaughter."

The man blew out a breath, but took two steps back in the face of Lilith's reply. "Very well, but she must leave."

"That is not *your* choice!"

"He's right, Lilith," Lucky said. "I can't stay here. Not after this, not after what I did to Bryn." Looking up at Kev, she continued, "But I can't go back to Zeke's either. It wouldn't be safe. I'm too angry with him, and I don't know what I might do."

"All right," he said, squeezing her shoulder. "I know a place where you can go. Wait here, while I take Bryn to Zeke's. I'll be back for you soon."

Lucky nodded.

Kev started to slide his arm from around her shoulder, but her voice stopped him. "Kev?"

"Yeah?"

"Did you know? About Sambethe? Did you know?"

He shook his head. "I found out about Sambethe when I heard you'd disappeared." His hand closed on her shoulder in a quick squeeze. "Hang tight, okay? I won't be gone long."

Lucky swayed as he moved away from her. Then she lowered herself to the ground beside the unconscious Bryn.

"You get better, Bryn," she said. "You're too strong for this."

When she looked up at Kev, he could see the tears shining in her eyes. "Take good care of her."

He nodded. "We will."

Then he scooped the girl up in his arms and dematerialized.

# CHAPTER 9

"Where is he? He should have been back by now—and Lucky with him." Aidan clenched and unclenched his hands as he paced in front of Zeke's desk.

Zeke picked up the two glasses of scotch he'd poured and came around the desk to face Aidan.

"We have no idea what situation Kevin might have found when he arrived in Lilith's world. We can make no guess as to when he should return." Handing one of the drinks to Aidan, he added, "Sit—before you wear a hole in my rug."

"I can't sit still, Zeke. If I don't move, I'll jump right out of my skin."

Zeke reached for Aidan's glass. "Then give that back to me. Twenty-year-old scotch should not be consumed mindlessly."

Aidan stopped pacing. "Twenty years old? You brought out the good stuff."

"Everything in the cabinet is good stuff," Zeke said. "Please, sit, have your drink, try to calm down. We can do nothing until Kevin returns."

Aidan dropped into one of the large leather chairs. Zeke sat down across from him. Raising his glass to his lips, Aidan took a sip of the scotch. Zeke was right. It should be savored. He allowed the smoky taste on his tongue and the warmth in his throat to slow his racing thoughts and calm his emotions.

He wished he knew what had happened. He and Kev and Zeke had been sitting right here in the study, discussing Katrin's return and the possibility that she could help Aidan develop the power of creation that accompanied his Gift. He had felt a sudden mental tug, the familiar pull of the Light-Bringer's Medallion, but before he could process what the feeling might mean, Kev had leapt to his feet, calling Lucky's name—and then he had disappeared.

Aidan's awareness of the medallion had remained until several minutes after Kev had gone. Then that awareness had faded too. He assumed that meant the danger had passed. So where was Kev? Why hadn't he returned? Why hadn't he brought Lucky back? And why had *he* gotten the whole message when Aidan hadn't?

Aidan took another sip of his scotch and almost choked as Kev appeared across the room, an unconscious figure in his arms. Aidan plunked his unfinished drink onto the table and shot across the room to his brother.

"Is she—?" he began, and then realized the girl in Kev's arms wasn't Lucky. "Who—?"

Kev paid no attention to Aidan's questions. "Call Katrin," he said to Zeke. "We'll be upstairs. You," he added, looking at Aidan, "come with me."

They both took the stairs two at a time. When they reached the second floor, Aidan turned the knob for the only guest room that wasn't occupied—besides Lucky's.

As Kev placed the girl on the bed, Aidan heard Katrin's voice in the hallway. Then she and Zeke stood beside him, looking down at the unconscious girl.

"Her name is Bryn," Kev said, tugging off the girl's boots. "She's Lilith's granddaughter—the only daughter of her only daughter, Lilith said. She got caught in the crossfire of Lucky's power and my flame. Lilith said her magic couldn't help Bryn, so I brought her here."

"How much time do we have?" Zeke asked. "Is the girl Bound?"

"Lilith says no."

Katrin had already started examining the girl.

Kev moved to Aidan and took his arm. "Help her," he said. "I think this one might need your Gift too."

Aidan nodded. "Yeah, sure. And Lucky?"

"She's all right—or she will be. Her Gift manifested, and it's not a fun one. She needs some time to adjust to it, to deal with her powers."

"You're bringing her back, right?"

Kev shook his head. "She refuses to come back. She's still upset about Sambethe, and now with her Gift—she's afraid she'll be dangerous. And, from what I saw, she's got a point."

"She's staying with Lilith then?" Zeke asked, his usually resonant voice almost flat.

Again Kev shook his head. "After what just happened— and, no, I don't have time to go into that right now, even if I had all the details—she can't stay there either." He paused for a moment. "I have a place I can take her. She'll be safe there. I'll stay with her for a few days. See if I can convince her to come back." He turned toward the door. "I have to go. I promised her I wouldn't be gone long."

"But where—?" Aidan began. "How—?"

"If you need me, you can call me on my cell. Or if that doesn't work, Zeke has his ways," Kev said. Then he disappeared—again.

Aidan cursed, raking both hands through his hair, and went to help Katrin with her patient.


After Kev disappeared with Bryn in his arms, Lucky remained kneeling, staring at the ground where her new cousin and friend had lain moments before. It was all she could do to stay upright. She wanted to curl up in a ball on the ground and sob herself to sleep. What had she done? What had she *wanted* to do? She pushed the memories to the back of her mind. She couldn't begin to face them yet.

Placing her hands palm up on her knees, she stared at them, willing the sigils she guessed she now had to activate. She felt a slight burn as they flared to life, miniature versions of the black and gold design that marked her back between her shoulder blades. She let them fade away, like dying coals, as tendrils of memories forced themselves to consciousness, filling her mouth with the taste of ashes. She pressed a trembling hand against her lips to keep herself from screaming and pushed the memories away once more.

A gentle arm slid around her shoulders as Lilith knelt beside her. Lucky looked up to find that she and her grandmother were alone in the clearing. Lilith must have persuaded William and his father to leave. Lucky let her head drop to

Lilith's shoulder, and Lilith took one of Lucky's hands in her free one.

"I didn't mean to hurt Bryn," Lucky whispered.

Lilith's hand tightened on her shoulder. "I know that, dear girl. She did what she did to protect *you*, you know, more than William and Mather."

Lucky nodded, the fabric of Lilith's robe soft against her cheek. "I know," she said with a sniff.

"Come on." Lilith urged Lucky to her feet. "Let's go back to the castle, so you can get out of this smelly, burnt dress and pack up your things."

"Kev said to wait for him here."

"Yes, well, I'll leave him a guide to bring him to us when he returns." Lilith waved her hand, and a glowing figure took shape in the middle of the clearing. "Come, lean on me. You're about to fall off your feet."

Lucky accepted Lilith's assistance as they made their way back to the castle. When they left the forest to re-enter the garden, she kept her eyes on the path in front of her, avoiding the stares of those milling about. She could hear whispers as she and Lilith passed through the crowd, but she couldn't make out what was said. She guessed William and his father had already started spreading the tale—and with embellishments, no doubt.

Her legs felt leaden as she climbed the stairs to her room, and she leaned more heavily on Lilith. They reached the landing and turned down the hallway that led to her room. Alicia sat on the floor outside the door, and she scrambled to her feet as Lucky and Lilith approached.

"What happened?" she cried. "William and his father are saying Lucky tried to kill them and that she almost killed Bryn. I can't believe they're telling the truth, but what *did* happen?"

Lucky stared at her friend in anguish. "It *is* true," she whispered.

"What?" Alicia's eyes widened, and even in the dimness of the hallway, Lucky could see the color drain from her face.

"She was provoked," Lilith said impatiently. "From what I could gather, Mather and his son attacked Bryn and Lucky, using the power of the Full Moon to their advantage. Unfortunately for them, Lucky's Gift came to her rescue. Bryn's injuries were an accident."

"Where is Bryn?"

Lilith remained silent for a moment, as if the question brought her back to the reality of her other granddaughter's condition, causing her to regroup. *"Ha-Satan* has taken her to the human realm—where she can be healed."

Alicia's face grew even paler. "But she's Bound..."

"No." Lilith shook her head. "No, she isn't."

Lucky tightened her hold on Lilith as her legs came close to buckling.

Lilith took her weight and gestured to the bedroom door. "Lucky needs to lie down. Alicia, will you please help me gather her things?"

"Gather her things?"

Lucky half-heard Lilith's response as she let her grand-mother guide her to her bed and then collapsed into the softness of the covers. She sensed Lilith and Alicia moving about the room and caught the murmur of their voices, but she was grateful she couldn't tell what they said. She didn't want to hear the story again. She didn't want to think about it at all. She managed to stay awake long enough to allow Lilith and Alicia to help her out of the ruined dress and into a pair of jeans and a t-shirt. Then she sank back down onto the bed and gave herself up to sleep.

When Kev zapped himself back to the clearing in Lilith's forest, Lucky and her grandmother were nowhere to be found. He looked around, puzzled, and then chuckled as a glowing, transparent gold shape curled in the center of the clearing unfolded itself into a dragon about the size of a large dog. It moved its head and neck in a gesture Kev took to mean "follow me" and trundled toward the edge of the clearing.

Kev chuckled again, falling in behind Lilith's guide. The woman was a bundle of contradictions, but he appreciated her sense of humor.

He also appreciated having a few minutes to think as he followed the dragon guide through the forest. The rapid fire of events had allowed him no time to reflect on what had happened.

One minute, he had been talking to Aidan and Zeke. The next, the fact that Lucky needed help and the knowledge of exactly where to find her had hijacked his mind.

But he didn't know why the Light-Bringer's Medallion had spoken so forcefully to him. Aidan was the one Lucifer had given it to, the one who'd worn it for so long. But Kev had seen both Lucky and the medallion in the vision he'd had when Lucky called her Makers. Maybe that had established the connection. Whatever the case, the medallion now seemed to be a link between him and Lucky. He wondered what *she* had seen when she'd called him as a Maker. He would have to ask her. It looked like they'd have plenty of time for conversation in the next few days.

His heart picked up speed at the thought. Yeah, taking her to the cabin seemed like both the best possible solution and the worst idea he'd ever had. She'd be safe there, and he hoped she'd find the place as much of a sanctuary as he did. But the near-giddiness he felt at the thought of spending a few days alone with her warned him that doing so was not the wisest of calls.

He took a deep breath. He would help Lucky deal with her Dark Gift, nothing more.

The dragon led Kev out of the forest and into an elaborate formal garden with winding paths and a large fountain and reflecting pool. Several people strolled the garden paths or clustered in groups, talking and laughing.

Conversations hushed as the garden's occupants caught sight of Kev and his dog-sized guide. Kev could sense their suspicion. Whether that feeling stemmed from a knowledge of who he was or the fact that he was a stranger, he didn't know, nor did he care. Being *Ha-Satan* allowed him free entry into Nadach, which had enabled him to be there when Lucky needed him. Nothing else mattered.

The dragon delivered Kev to what looked like a servants' entrance and sat beside him until the door opened.

"There you are," said Lilith, and the dragon guide faded away, having turned its charge over to its creator.

"Come with me," Lilith commanded.

Kev fell into step beside her, thankful for the free-floating torches that flamed to life to light their path. The moon, full though it was, didn't cast much light through the castle windows.

"How is my granddaughter?"

"She's still unconscious, but I left her in good hands. My mother and my brother will take good care of her."

They mounted a set of heavy stone stairs.

"Your mother is Katrin Drake, if I remember correctly," Lilith said.

"Yes," Kev replied. "She has returned to the Council to act as Healer."

"Ahhh. In Sambethe's stead?"

"Yes," Kev said again. "Sambethe has been removed from the Council and disciplined for her actions."

"I am sure Lucky will be glad to hear that. You know why she came to me, do you not?"

"What Sambethe did shocked us all—Zeke as much as anyone. He never meant to betray Lucky in any way. His only fault was keeping his suspicions quiet for too long. If you hadn't talked to Lucky when you did, she would have heard the news from Zeke the following day." Kev directed a sharp glance at Lilith. "I can't help but wonder if your timing was coincidental."

She looked at him, one eyebrow raised. "You may wonder all you like."

At the fourth floor landing, she turned to the right. "Lucky's room is this way. She was sleeping when I left her. She barely made it back to the castle."

"How does she seem otherwise?" Kev asked.

"She's upset, of course—worried for Bryn, scared of her power, devastated by what she almost did to Mather and his son."

"What *did* she try to do to them? We could all tell she intended them harm, but do you have any sense of what her Gift would have enabled her to do?"

Lilith paused with her hand on the door to Lucky's room. "Not having asked her what she experienced, I can't be certain. But if I had to hazard a guess, I would say my granddaughter has the Gift of Madness."

"I'll hold the field for you, while you reconnect the damaged neurons and receptors in her brain."

Aidan could hardly hear Katrin's voice over the pounding of his heart. When Kev had told him to assist Katrin, he hadn't hesitated. But now? He couldn't do this. He hadn't used his Gift on a living being since he'd had such disastrous results with his mother. Katrin sounded so matter-of-fact. Couldn't she see involving him was asking for trouble?

"Aidan? Are you all right? Aidan?"

Katrin's words reached through the fog of thoughts. "I— I don't know," he answered. "I don't think I can do this."

"You have to," Katrin asserted. "This girl needs you. I've done everything I can. I can't heal the damage to her brain, but *you* can. I'll guide you, but you have to do the work."

Aidan willed himself to focus, even as the flush of panic enveloped his entire body. He took deep, even breaths in an effort to slow his heart. After several minutes, he pushed the images of his mother to the back of his mind. This time would be different. Katrin would help. They would do this together.

"Okay?" Katrin asked.

"Yeah," he breathed.

With one hand on the girl's head and the other on Aidan's arm, Katrin closed her eyes. Aidan felt a slight electrical shock throughout his body as she opened the connection. Then the sight of the girl on the bed, Katrin's hand on her head, was overlaid with another image, that of the girl's brain, neurons and receptors shining like colored lights in a pinball game. He closed his eyes, letting the image Katrin projected fall on the dark screen of the inside of his eyelids.

Katrin's mind guided his to the damaged neurons, their colors faint and muddied. Aidan let himself drop into his Gift and the felt sense of the girl's brain, discerning the difference between the healthy, glowing neurons and the damaged ones. When he had located the broken connections, he placed his fingertips on the girl's head and opened his mouth.

The combination of notes he heard himself singing surprised even him. A chorus of mixed voices issued from his throat, melody, harmony, point, and counterpoint overlapping and entwining in an intricate pattern. As he sang, the muddied colors of the damaged circuits in the girl's brain began to clear and brighten. He held the song until the colors matched those of the healthy receptors.

"Stop."

Katrin's voice jarred him, and Aidan wavered for an instant, his song continuing for a heartbeat as the image of the girl's brain in his mind shifted to that of a twisting strand of DNA.

His voice faded to silence as Katrin ordered, "Stop! Now!"

When he opened his eyes, the girl lay before him on the bed as she had earlier, but a streak of white now swept through the pixie-short hair that had been black as a raven's wing.

"Did I do that?" Aidan asked.

"Yes, you held on a bit too long. No real damage done, though I don't know what she's going to think of her unplanned makeover." Katrin's hand tightened on his arm. "Otherwise, you did well. She should recover fully, thanks to you."

"And you," Aidan said, his hand moving to cover hers where it rested on his arm. "I couldn't have done it without you. I wouldn't have even been brave enough to try."

Katrin lifted her eyes to his, and they were so like his brother's that Aidan caught his breath. He had almost forgotten this woman was Kev's mother.

"We'll work on that," Katrin said, her lips curving into an abbreviated smile. "Go get some rest. I'll sit with our patient for a while."

As Katrin's hand dropped away from his arm, Aidan drooped. The healing had exhausted him.

"Thanks," he said. "I'll spell you after I've had a nap."

He collapsed onto his bed as soon as he reached his room, but he fell asleep feeling as if he'd at last lived up to some of his potential.

# CHAPTER 10

She was toasty warm, snuggled in something soft. Lucky wasn't sure she wanted to wake up. And as she swam upward into consciousness, and the memories came flooding back, she knew with certainty that she didn't.

She pushed the memories aside as best she could and concentrated on the softness of the fleece blanket wrapped around her. Light and shadow flickered across it, and she caught the scent of wood smoke just as her eyes turned toward its source, a fireplace with a crackling fire—one that had been going long enough to generate substantial heat.

She lay on a couch in front of a fireplace—where? And how did she get there?

Lucky raised herself to a semi-reclining position, and saw a figure seated on the floor leaning against the arm of the sofa nearest her feet, an open book on his outstretched legs. Kev. His head turned toward her as she moved.

"You're awake," he said.

"Where am I?" She spoke in little more than a whisper.

She was about to repeat the question, fearing he hadn't heard her over the crackle of flames, when he answered. "Somewhere safe."

"But where?" she asked, a little more loudly.

"My cabin. It's where I come to get away from the rest of the world."

She pushed herself up to sitting and tucked her legs beneath her so she could look around the room. The space was lit only by the glow of the firelight and a small lamp at the far end of the couch, so the edges of the room were cast into shadows, but she liked what she saw. The room was of medium size and seemed to serve as both living and dining room. Bookshelves rose on either side of the fireplace, and a comfortable-looking chair sat at an angle to the fireplace and the couch. Three of the room's four windows had inner shutters closed over them. A small table with a couple of chairs stood in front of the fourth, which was bare. Outside it, she could see moonlit trees through a veil of falling snow.

She rose and walked slowly to the window, noting the change of textures beneath her feet as she stepped off the wool rug onto the smooth boards of the floor. Though not quite as warm as the rug, the wood did not feel cold to her socked feet. But she felt a chill radiating from the window as she drew closer. Ahead, she saw nothing but trees, their branches covered with snow. Off to the right, a few yards away, stood another building, a large shed or perhaps a small barn. Snow blanketed the structure's roof.

She turned away from the window to find Kev's gaze on her, as if he'd been taking in her reaction with as much interest as she took in her surroundings. For an instant, she couldn't speak, couldn't even remember what she'd meant to say. Then he glanced away, and she found her voice.

"It's lovely here."

When Kev nodded in silent agreement, she added, "And where is here?"

"Colorado. In the mountains. The middle of nowhere." Kev's voice caressed the words. Lucky's breath hitched in her throat.

She padded back to the couch and sat down, drawing her feet up beside her and tucking the discarded blanket around them. She stared into the flames. A log cracked and fell, spilling sparks.

Kev moved to the fireplace, readjusted the burning logs with one of the cast iron tools placed to one side of the hearth on its stone surround, and added another log from the ready supply on the hearth's other side. When he repositioned himself on the floor, he moved a little closer to the center of the couch and turned toward her, one arm resting on the sofa cushion. If she straightened her leg, Lucky thought, she could touch his hand with her foot.

"How are you?" he asked. "Are you okay?"

At his words, the memories she'd shoved to the back of her mind rushed forward once more, and her mouth filled with the acrid taste of ash. She shook her head.

"No. I didn't think so." Kev's voice was gentle. "Can I get you something? Tea? Hot chocolate?"

Tears threatened to spill from her eyes, and she blinked them away. She had to clear her throat before she could speak. "Hot chocolate sounds nice."

"Hot chocolate it is then." Kev gave her blanket-covered foot a quick squeeze as he uncurled from his position on the floor. "And not just any hot chocolate either. You're going to get my Nana's special recipe. I promise it will be the best cocoa you've ever tasted." He held out a hand to her. "Come with me."

She hesitated, but when he didn't drop his hand, she placed hers in it and let him draw her to her feet.

The kitchen was larger than she had expected and well-appointed. But then, she supposed, if you lived in the middle of nowhere, you'd have to be able to cook for yourself. Takeout and delivery weren't exactly options.

She leaned against the granite countertop while Kev opened cabinets and drawers, spreading ingredients and cooking implements across the counter's surface. After pouring milk into a small saucepan and putting it on the stove to heat, he stirred cocoa and sugar together in a measuring cup with a little salt, a little cinnamon, and a dash of cayenne pepper. When the milk had heated, he whisked the dry ingredients into the pan.

"Mmm, it smells wonderful," Lucky said, as he poured the steaming cocoa into two large mugs and handed her one.

Kev grinned. "And it tastes every bit as good as it smells."

Back in the living room, Kev abandoned his place on the floor for the couch. He sat at the opposite end from Lucky, angled toward her.

She blew on the surface of her hot chocolate to cool it and took a first small sip. "Yummy," she said. "You were right. It is the best I've ever had."

"And guaranteed to make you feel better, no matter what ails you. My Nana used to make this for me when I was small, and it never failed. I was always smiling by the time I reached the bottom of the mug. Later, when I got older—when I couldn't even tell her what my problems were—she still made me cocoa. And while it didn't solve anything, it still made it all seem easier to bear."

Lucky stared into her chocolate, her fingers tight on the mug. She took another sip, savoring the mix of flavors and the slight tingle of the pepper, before she spoke.

"I wanted to kill them," she said bleakly. "I've never felt anything like that in my entire life. I wanted to hurt them, wanted to feel their minds come undone." She turned to Kev, her eyes desperately seeking and holding his. "I *wanted* it, Kev. How could I have *wanted* that?"

Kev studied her in silence, his eyes searching hers. He didn't turn away in horrified disgust, but gazed at her with a compassion that was a balm to her bleeding soul.

"Dark Gifts are the hardest to bear," he finally said. "Even the Light ones have a Dark side—ask Aidan." Lucky nodded. She knew what he meant. "But the Dark ones, sometimes it's harder to find their Light side."

"I'm not sure my Gift has a Light side."

"It does. You'll see. You just have to wrestle through a lot of dark and murky to get there."

Lucky looked at him out of the corners of her eyes. "Is that what you had to do?"

Kev chuckled. "You've seen my Gift and the form it takes. What do you think?"

Lucky remembered the huge dragon bearing down on her, breathing fire, and her lips curled upward.

Then she lost the smile. "Did it make you—want to do terrible things?"

"Sometimes," Kev said. "And sometimes it did them, whether I wanted to or not."

Lucky turned fully toward him then. "You talk as if it has a life of its own, apart from you."

He nodded. "It does. I've learned to manage it, to work with it, but it's still—other. It—he—doesn't think like me, doesn't feel like me. When I'm him—or he's me—or we are—it's like two minds sharing the same space, overlapping, with one of us in the lead. These days that's usually me. In the early days, it was mostly him."

Lucky digested his words, washing them down with sips of chocolate. "Mine—didn't feel separate. It didn't feel like—struggling with someone else for control. It was more like I became someone I didn't recognize, someone who want-ed..." Her voice faded away.

When she continued, fear and self-loathing shadowed her words. "It was horrible, and at the same time, I felt like I was more me than I'd ever been." She shuddered. "Kev, what if that's really who I am?"

"But it is," he said, and she gasped in hurt surprise, searching his face for some clue as to why he would be so cruel to her. And he said it again, calmly, gently, matter-of-factly. "It is."

Lucky's eyes flooded with tears. When she spoke, she had to force the words past the lump that filled her throat. "But I'm not like that. I don't want those things. I don't want to hurt people, to destroy them. That's not me."

"Yes, sweetheart, it is you. Just as my dragon, separate though he is, is somehow me. You have to accept that, learn to work with it. Pushing it away will get you nowhere."

Lucky wiped away the tears that streaked her cheeks. She blinked back the rest, while she sipped her cocoa in silence. She knew Kev had the experience to back up what he said, but she didn't want to accept the destructiveness she had felt toward William and his father as integral to her being. Yes, she had been angry at them. William had beaten her, and his father had bound both her and Bryn so he could do it. She had every right to be angry and to defend herself. But to want to destroy them? That made her as bad as them. And saying "That's who I am" sounded too much like the "I am Shedim" Luil used as an excuse for whatever he did. She didn't want to be like him.

Kev's quiet voice intruded on her thoughts. "Can you tell me more about how it felt? What you saw? What you wanted to do? *Knew* you could do?"

Lucky shook her head. She couldn't talk about it anymore. She might never feel like talking about it again. She changed the subject. "How is Bryn? Do you know?"

"I called Zeke about an hour ago for a report. She's still unconscious, but her vital signs are stable. Katrin and Aidan have done what they can to heal her. She should be fine."

Lucky looked at Kev. "Katrin?"

"She's our new Healer." Kev caught her eyes. "Sambethe has been relieved of her responsibilities and can act only under Raphael's supervision. She's under a kind of house arrest. She was sentenced the day after you left."

Lucky didn't reply.

"Zeke never meant to hurt you, Lucky. He didn't want to tell you until he was sure his suspicions were correct. Then, once he was sure, he directed all his efforts toward the hearing. If you'd stuck around, he would have told you."

"You said you didn't know either?"

"No. Zeke didn't involve me. He knew I had other things to deal with. Aidan told me what Sambethe had done—and about her sentencing—when he told me you'd gone."

"Aidan knew?" Lucky asked flatly.

"He hadn't known for long. I don't believe Zeke told him more than a day before."

"He still should have told me."

"Zeke asked him not to."

"*Zeke* should have told me. She gambled with my cousin's life and my own. I deserved to know."

As the words left her lips, she felt the now familiar tingle in her palms. Holding the mug of cocoa in one hand, she turned the other palm up. A faint sigil showed there, partially activated. She willed it to activate fully, and the tingle changed to a burn as the sigil flared to life. She held her hand up, her palm facing Kev.

"They show up when I get angry," she said. "I burned William."

"Not very badly." Kev slid closer and curved his fingers around the back of her hand, holding it in place as he studied her palm. "There was barely a mark on his arm."

"I—I don't think they were fully activated when I touched him," Lucky said. She found it hard to concentrate with Kev's warm fingers spanning the back of her hand. She wondered if he realized he was stroking her wrist with his thumb. "William's father said I should be—prosecuted."

Kev released her hand and moved back to the other end of the couch. He took a sip of cocoa before he responded. "It's forbidden to use the palm sigils in combat. But it's not as if you did it on purpose. You didn't even know your sigils were there."

"Why is it forbidden?"

Kev looked at her, a small frown between his brows. "I don't remember the whole story, but at some point pre-Alliance, some of the Dark used their sigils as a kind of brand. Angels and Nephilim can heal from most injuries, but a burn from a fully activated sigil leaves a permanent scar. Anyway, when they codified the Alliance, they included the restriction among the rules of agreement."

"If you—burned an enemy with one of them, would they get some of your power, the way I did in the Making?"

"No." Kev shook his head. "The activation is different, and so is the mark. The marks on your back are more like tattoos than scars, right? The Making isn't about wounding but about a conscious bestowing of Power."

He set his mug of cocoa on the coffee table and turned his right hand up to look at the palm.

"I felt my Power go out of me—and into you—here," he said, his voice almost inaudible. He stroked his palm with his left thumb the way he had stroked her wrist. "And when it stopped, when it came back into my hand, it—brought something of you with it."

Lucky's heart kicked in her chest as she slid close to him, her gaze on his thumb as it moved against his palm.

He turned his head to look at her, his eyes catching and holding hers. "What did you see?" he asked. "When you called me as a Maker, what did you see?"

"Your dragon," she said. "He roared and breathed fire, and then lay down with his head on his front feet. I—I patted his head."

Without thought, she brushed her fingers through the hair that fell across Kev's forehead, pushing the silky strands away from his face. When his breath caught, she lowered her hand and turned it palm up. "Then he—he shrank so small he fit in my hand, and he ran up my arm and disappeared into the medallion."

She reached for the medallion at the same time Kev did, and his hand closed around hers, guiding both their forefingers to touch the amulet.

Time hung suspended as Lucky stared into Kev's eyes, his hand warm around hers, his finger brushing the amulet where it rested on her chest.

Then he cleared his throat and leaned away from her, releasing her hand. "That explains it then," he said.

"What explains what?" Lucky asked, sliding back to her end of the couch, feeling both as if she had had a narrow escape and as if she had lost a treasure that had never been hers to lose.

Kev retrieved his cocoa and stared into the mug as he answered. "I'd wondered how I knew where you were, how to find you, why the medallion chose me."

"Oh," Lucky breathed.

She hadn't even thought to ask how Kev had found her, come to her rescue. She remembered the medallion burning against her skin, but she hadn't connected it to Kev's presence. She had been so caught up in her Gift and its consequences, she hadn't even wondered at his sudden appearance. Once she had come to herself, she had just been grateful he was there.

"Thank you," she said, "for coming for me."

When Kev spoke it was as if the whispered words forced themselves from his lips without his volition. "I'll always be there for you."

Then he jerked to his feet and strode toward the kitchen.

Her heartbeat accelerating, Lucky swallowed the rest of her cocoa in two large gulps. "There's not a smile at the bottom of my cup, Kev," she said, hoping to break the tension.

It worked. Kev gave a startled bark of laughter. "But you still feel better, don't you?" he asked.

Lucky found herself beginning to smile after all. She nodded, a slight frown knitting her brow. "Yeah," she said. "Strangely, I do."

"Nothing strange about it," he replied, coming back to take her empty cup. "Nana's cocoa does it every time."

Kev escaped into the kitchen. He needed to put some distance between himself and Lucky. *"I'll always be there for you"*? What the hell had he been thinking? He couldn't say that to her. He couldn't even think it. Even if it was true. She belonged with Aidan, not with him—and that was as it should be.

*The medallion thinks she belongs with you,* insisted a treacherous thought. He did his best to ignore it. This sense of closeness, of rightness, he felt when he was with her—it was just a result of the Making. The ceremony had linked them—nothing more. The intensity of his feelings would fade.

He took his time rinsing the mugs, pan, and utensils and placing them in the dishwasher. Then he took his time wiping down the counter and the stovetop. He knew he had to stop his delaying tactics when he'd straightened the dishtowels on the rack for the third time. He took a deep breath and went back into the living room.

Lucky sat snuggled under the blanket, staring at the dying fire, her eyelids drooping.

"You should go to bed," he said. "I'll show you where I put your things."

Lucky stood up and stretched, clapping a hand over her mouth to cover a yawn. "Sorry," she said.

Kev smiled. "It's late—and you've had a rough day."

He led the way toward the open wood staircase that mounted to the loft-like second level where the bedroom and bath were located. Lucky trailed behind him, and he waited on the landing that overlooked the living area, leaning against the wooden railing and watching her climb the stairs.

"The bedroom's here," he said, when she reached the landing. He gestured toward the open door. "Your things are on the chair beside the bed. The bathroom is the other door off the landing." He pointed at it as he spoke.

"Where will you sleep?" Lucky asked, noting only the two doors.

"I'll crash on the couch or something."

"I don't want to kick you out of your room," Lucky said around a yawn.

Kev chuckled. "You need the bed more than I do. I'm not even sleepy. Get some rest. I'll see you in the morning."

"Okay," she said. "Thanks again. And goodnight."

"Goodnight, Lucky," Kev said, as she entered the bedroom and shut the door behind her.

As soon as he was certain Lucky had fallen asleep, Kev zapped himself to his father's palace. An idea about the possible source of the mark on Jahoel's chest had sparked to life while he had talked with Lucky about sigils and scars. Since Lucifer, like Zeke, never slept, Kev figured he might as well go looking for information now.

This time he found the throne room empty, so Kev headed for his father's study. The door was open, and voices spilled into the hallway. Lucifer had company.

Kev tapped on the doorframe.

Lucifer and Ba'al-zebul, his second in command, turned at the interruption.

"Kevin, what brings you here?" Lucifer asked. "Isn't it late in your world?"

"I have some questions for you, and I'd rather get answers than sleep. Do you have a few minutes?"

"Come in." Lucifer gestured toward one of the empty chairs at the table he and Ba'al-zebul occupied. "Have a seat."

Kev sat.

"What are your questions?"

Kev glanced at his father's second.

"Do not mind Ba'al. You may speak freely."

A grin split Ba'al's dark beard. "You should know by now your father does not keep secrets from me, *Ha-Satan*. Have I not proven myself trustworthy?"

"You have, Ba'al." Kev grinned in return. "Though I understand from my history lessons that you caused my father much pain in the beginning."

"That is true. But he earned my respect."

"You said you have questions, Kevin?" Lucifer asked.

"Yes. You know how the sigil mark on Jahoel seemed blurred? Could that be because whatever was used to mark him was somehow copied from a scar? Is there someone you once marked who might have done this to get back at you?"

"Good question," Ba'al said. "You must have marked someone in the days before the Alliance."

Lucifer shook his head. "No, not then. I fought on the side of the Light in those days, and we did not mark those we defeated in battle as the Dark did."

"But you have marked someone?" Kev asked.

"Yes, but they are all dead."

Kev frowned. "Dead?"

"The Watchers," Lucifer said. "They were the original members of the Light who, thousands of years ago, were tasked with watching over humans, observing them, learning their ways. But they did not stop at watching. Against the Light's orders, they interacted with humans, married and mated with them, creating the first Nephilim. As punishment for their disobedience, they were imprisoned in a cave deep in the earth."

"And you marked them?"

"Later. After we formed the Alliance, I requested their release. After all, they had done nothing more than other members of the Dark and Fallen had done. Why should they continue to be punished once interaction and intermarriage with humans was acceptable?"

Lucifer looked at Kev as if seeking an answer to the rhetorical question. Kev nodded his understanding.

"The Metatron doubted the wisdom of their release. They consented, but they insisted I mark the Watchers, to indicate my responsibility for them. They were mine to watch over— and police, if need be. The Metatron washed their hands of them."

Lucifer stared at the glossy surface of the table as if it were a window into the past. "The Metatron was right, as it turned out. Hundreds of years in the bowels of the earth, coupled with the loss of their human and half-human families, had unfitted most of the Watchers for reintegration into any form of society. Some created such havoc that eternal imprisonment or Disintegration were our only options. They chose death rather than be imprisoned again. Others requested Disintegration because they could not bear the pain of living with all they had lost."

Lucifer turned his gaze from the table to Kev. "One survived. Your grandfather."

"Semyaza." Kev knew some of the story of his grandfather, and what he knew wasn't pleasant. "He too requested death, after his punishment for what he did to my grandmother."

Lucifer nodded. "He was the last of those I marked. There are none left to seek revenge on me."

"Had my mother been born when he was Disintegrated?"

"No. It happened a month or so before her birth."

Over fifty years. A long time for a human, but not long at all in angelic terms. "Where was he kept before the Disintegration?" Kev asked.

"In one of the palace's holding cells."

"Was he allowed visitors?"

"Yes, though I do not believe he had many."

"Would you have a record of visitors?"

Lucifer looked at Ba'al, who shook his head. "We do not log visitors in and out."

"Then the only record would be in the Book," Lucifer said.

"The Book?" Kev asked. "*Uriel's* Book?"

"The Book does not belong to Uriel. He is merely its Keeper."

"Figure of speech," Kev said. "Can we see that record?"

"*We* cannot. But perhaps you can. Generally, each being's records can be accessed only by that being—unless said being grants permission. But since you are Semyaza's grandson, you could argue that his history concerns you. Uriel might grant you a dispensation."

Kev pushed back his chair and stood. "That's good enough for now. I'll let you two get back to whatever you were talking about when I barged in. It was good to see you, Ba'al." He inclined his head first to his father's second and then to Lucifer. "Father."

"Goodnight, my son."

Kev exited the study before he dematerialized.

Back at the cabin, Kev made sure Lucky still slept and then slipped out the kitchen door into the mudroom. He located his lined barn coat on one of the wooden pegs along the wall, shrugged into it, and pulled on the gloves he found tucked in its pockets. He should call Zeke and ask him to request an audience with Uriel, but that could wait until tomorrow. He'd stayed out of the studio as long as he could.

The snow came down harder now, and the wind had picked up. It swirled the snow around him and drove the flakes against his face as he crunched through the white blanket to his studio. He turned the key in the lock—no sigil-activated doors here—stepped inside, and closed the door behind him, shutting out the blowing snow.

Even inside, the cold had a bite. Before he did anything else, he needed to start a fire.

A ready stack of dry wood waited next to the stove. Kev pulled off his gloves and squatted in front of the stove. He gathered a small pile of kindling, struck a match, and as the flames licked upward, he placed a couple of the smaller, thinner logs on the pile. Once they caught, he arranged some larger ones over them, making sure to leave spaces for the air and flames to move. Then he closed the stove door, stood, and surveyed the studio.

Except for the bathroom tucked into the back corner, the space was all one large room, filled with work tables, shelves, equipment, and the metal sculptures that were the reason for the studio's existence. Kev worked with found objects, salvaging old tools, mechanical parts, and discarded industrial steel, and turning them into art.

The craft was perhaps a natural one for someone with his Gift, since he often had to heat the metals he worked with, either to bend them, shaping them to his artistic will, or to weld them together, uniting many disparate discarded objects into a single coherent whole. But he never used his Gift to create his art. He considered the cabin and the studio places apart from his normal life among the Dark and the Fallen, separate from his role as *Ha-Satan*, and off-limits to the dragon.

Not that he didn't make an appearance every now and then inside Kev's head. Kev had learned it was impossible to shut the dragon out completely, and unwise even to try. But he never called the Fire to work the metals. He used human tools: blow torches, arc welders, and on occasion—when he felt the need to hammer something into submission—an old-fashioned forge.

As the room began to warm, Kev discarded his coat and made his way over to an empty work table, where he opened the drawer and pulled out a sketch pad. Positioning the work stool, he perched upon it, turned to a blank page, and started to sketch. After a few quick strokes, the image began to take form, and he relaxed a bit. The picture had burned in his brain ever since he'd materialized in the clearing in Lilith's forest to see Lucky more than successfully fending off her attackers, and he knew from experience that it would continue to burn there until he captured it on paper before recreating it in metal.

Once he'd completed the sketch, he sat and studied it for a while, picturing the sizes and shapes he would need to create the piece. Then he moved past the tables and shelves of tools and sculptures, finished and in process, to the far wall, which held bins and racks laden with salvaged metal waiting to be repurposed. Searching through the hodgepodge of materials, he found what he looked for. After carting the pieces to the work table, he reviewed his sketch, returned to the stash of supplies, and selected a few more items.

Before he began to work, he checked the fire and added more logs. Once he'd started creating a piece, he had a tendency to forget about other things, like keeping the fire stoked. He remembered at least one occasion when he'd been so involved in the process he hadn't come back to awareness of his surroundings until his fingers, even inside the welding gloves, had gotten too cold to unwind from the welder. He had a feeling this piece would have the same effect on him.

Fire tended, he returned to his project table and positioned the two pieces that would form the sculpture's base. Then he pulled on his welding mask and gloves and began the process of joining the two into one.

# CHAPTER 11

The first tendrils of morning light were creeping through the windows when Lucky awoke, feeling surprisingly refreshed. Although it had taken her a long time to fall asleep, once she did, she had slept deeply. She sat up, puzzled for a few seconds, before she remembered where she was. Kev's cabin. Kev's bedroom.

She pushed her long hair back from her face and scanned the room. Like those of the living room, the furnishings were simple but warm. An American Indian blanket woven in a pattern of muted red, brown, and green covered the bed. The bedside table held a lamp that appeared to be fashioned from reclaimed metal, a paperback mystery novel, and a clock that confirmed her impression it was early morning.

Lucky glanced from the clock back to the lamp. Something about its lines reminded her of the metal sculpture in the courtyard of the training center's meditation space. She studied the lamp for a moment and then turned her attention to the rest of the room.

A bookshelf spanned the wall across from the bed, its shelves adorned with a mixture of books, rocks, and gnarled pieces of wood. Lucky walked over to the shelf and picked up one of the rocks to examine it more closely. It was about the size of a baseball, and it wasn't a simple rock. It was a geode, rough and gray-brown on the outside, its hollow interior, visible where a part of the stone had broken away, lined with sparkling crystal formations.

Lucky held the geode, tilting it in different directions so the morning sunlight danced on the crystals. Then, feeling as if she'd been given a gift, she set it back on the shelf and turned toward the wooden straight-back chair beside the bed, where her travel bag sat.

After pulling on jeans and her heaviest sweater, Lucky stepped out of the bedroom onto the landing overlooking the living area. She didn't see Kev in the living room, and she didn't hear any sounds coming from the kitchen. She called his name as she descended the stairs, but received no answer.

When she reached the main floor, she crossed over to the unshuttered window and looked out upon a white world. The snow had stopped falling, but not before several more inches had been added to the quantity that had blanketed the ground the night before. After her weeks in Lilith's dark world, the sight of the sunlight reflecting off the pure white snow seemed like a miracle. And it felt so peaceful. She understood why Kev came here to escape from the rest of the world.

Stepping into the kitchen, she filled the tea kettle and put it on the stove to heat. While she waited, she wandered back into the living room and made the rounds of the shuttered windows, opening the shutters so she could see outside. All the windows showed much the same scene: snow-covered trees stretched in every direction. At the front of the cabin, the trees sloped downward and away, giving Lucky some sense of how high up the mountain the cabin was located. A drive wound through the trees on one side, leading to a cleared area in front of the cabin. An unbroken layer of white adorned it all.

Lucky had never seen so much pristine snow in one place before. In the city, white soon became gray—gray slush in the streets and gray-tinted piles of snow pushed to the side by the snow plows. Here, nothing marred the whiteness. Not even footprints broke its smooth, frosting-like surface.

That thought made her frown. She wondered where Kev had gone.

The tea kettle whistled, drawing her to the kitchen.

As she passed by the larger window overlooking the back, she saw the object of her thoughts coming toward the cabin. The sun highlighted the lighter streaks in his shoulder-length hair. His footprints in the snow led back to the other building she'd noticed the night before. About halfway to the cabin, Kev stopped and turned to survey his surroundings. After making a full circle, he raised his face to the sky, and a brilliant smile lit his features. The smile stayed in place as he moved toward the cabin again.

Lucky's breath caught in her throat. He looked so at home here—so happy. She felt as she had when she had held the geode, watching the sunlight sparkle on its crystalline interior.

Kev moved around the corner of the cabin and out of her line of sight, and Lucky again became aware of the screeching of the teakettle and hurried into the kitchen. She had just lifted the kettle from the stove when she heard Kev in the small mud room that served as entryway into the cabin. By the time he opened the kitchen door, she had two cups of tea steeping.

When he stepped into the room, that smile still lighting his face, she forgot to breathe again. Their eyes met, and neither said a word. They looked at each other in silence, Kev smiling that smile. Before she broke eye contact, Lucky felt a similar smile stretching her lips.

"Good morning," Kev said.

"Morning," Lucky replied, knowing her cheeks had flushed and feeling self-conscious. She picked up one of the cups of tea and handed it to him. "I made tea."

"Perfect. Thank you." Kev's eyes moved back to her face. "You slept well?"

Lucky's thoughts scattered when she looked into those clear, deep green eyes with their flecks of gold like little pieces of sunlight. Pulling her thoughts together, she nodded. "Very well, thanks. Did you?"

Kev shook his head. "I didn't sleep at all."

"I'm sorry. I took your bed." Lucky felt the flush on her cheeks deepen.

"No need to apologize. I could have slept on the cot in the studio. I didn't feel like sleeping. I worked all night instead."

"Worked?"

"In the studio."

"Studio?" The word finally penetrated Lucky's consciousness. "Does that mean you're an artist?"

"I suppose," Kev said, leaning back against the counter and crossing one wool-socked ankle over the other. "Though I've never tried to sell any of my pieces. Instead of saying I'm an artist, it's probably more accurate to say I make art."

"What kind of art?" Lucky settled in against the counter across from him and took a sip of her tea.

"Metal sculpture. Out of salvaged parts, found objects."

"Like the lamp in your room?" Lucky asked.

"Yes," Kev said, looking surprised. "I made that lamp."

"And the sculptures in the meditation space at the training center?"

Kev nodded, his surprised look taking on a hint of admiration. "Those too. You have a good eye."

"So do you. I like those pieces."

Kev smiled. "Thanks."

Lucky tilted her head in the direction of the studio. "And that's what's out there? More sculptures?"

Kev nodded. "Sculptures, tools, lots of scrap metal."

"Can I see?"

"Sure, later." Kev pushed off from the counter and moved toward the refrigerator. "Right now, I'm hungry. What do you say to breakfast?"

"Mmm. Sounds good to me."

A loaf of bread, still in its bakery bag sat on the counter, and Kev pulled items from the refrigerator to place beside it.

As eggs, veggies, bacon, butter, and a jar of preserves joined the bread, Lucky asked, "You don't live here all the time, right? Where did all this food come from? It doesn't look like there's a store anywhere near here."

"There's a couple who take care of the place for me, look in on it when I'm not around, turn the water on and off, stuff like that. I call them to let them know when I'll be here, and they bring in supplies. I was planning on coming this weekend anyway. I didn't know I'd have company." Kev looked up from the bowl and whisk he'd placed next to the carton of eggs to give her a smile. "Fortunately, they had everything arranged a day early."

"Don't they wonder how you get here? No car in the driveway and all?"

"I seldom see them. Most of our contact is by phone or email. They know I want to be alone when I'm here, and they respect that. And I do have a car here—another Jeep, as beat up as the one you've seen. There's a garage on the other side of this wall, accessed through the mud room."

Snagging a knife from the rack, Kev pulled a retractable cutting board out from under the counter's edge. "Do you want to start on the veggies or deal with the bacon?" he asked.

"Veggies, please." Lucky took the knife from his outstretched hand and drew the bags of vegetables closer to the cutting board. "I suck at cooking bacon. I try to get it crisp, but I always burn it."

Kev's eyes lit with laughter. "And you're going to trust *me* to do it? You've seen me play with fire."

Lucky chuckled. "You do fine as long as you're in human form. Just don't turn into the dragon and breathe all over it." Even as she laughed, she couldn't quite believe she was teasing him about his dragon. That thing was seriously huge and terrifying, and she knew he could easily have killed her the day before.

"Yeah, not the best plan, since I don't want a kitchen re-model." Kev grinned.

"There's the stove," Lucky said, pointing the knife she held toward the appliance. "Use it."

Chuckling, Kev placed a skillet onto a burner and lined it with bacon.

Lucky smiled down at the red pepper she was chopping. She could get used to this.

And the feeling didn't go away. She and Kev chatted and joked and teased each other all through the preparations for breakfast, and as they carried their plates of garden omelets, bacon, and toast out to the living area and sat down at the small dining table by the window, Lucky couldn't imagine any place she'd rather be.

After they finished breakfast, Lucky asked if she could visit the studio. Kev suggested a walk first. After spending the whole night in the studio, he said, he wanted to get out into the fresh air and sunlight. Looking out the windows at the sun sparkling on the snow, Lucky readily agreed.

She had brought boots and a coat and gloves, since she'd worn those when she had left her apartment to spend time with Lilith. However, the warmest sweater she had packed, and which she wore now, wasn't all that heavy.

In one of the closets, Kev found a sweater that would do, since it had shrunk until it was too small for him. Too small for Kev still meant baggy for Lucky. The bottom of the sweater reached mid-thigh and the sleeves covered her hands. Kev chuckled as she began cuffing the sleeves. She stuck her tongue out at him, which made him laugh out loud.

His laughter was deep and rich, like chocolate. He still laughed as he went to get her coat, and Lucky stared after him, stunned, silently declaring his laugh one of her favorite sounds in the world. At that moment, she wanted to make him so happy he'd laugh often and with ease.

"Get a grip, girl," she whispered to herself as she began cuffing the second sweater sleeve.

She couldn't afford to be indulging in such thoughts. Kev wasn't hers to make happy or not. But, she thought, as he came back across the room toward her, her coat in his hands and a warm smile on his face, she could enjoy this interlude with him while it lasted.

She smiled back at him as she reached for the coat, but he held it for her so she could shove her arms in the thick baggy sweater into the coat's sleeves. They both laughed at her struggles. Kev stood close enough that Lucky not only absorbed the richness of the sound of his laughter but could feel the rumble of it as it moved through his chest. He adjusted the fit of the coat, tugging it into place around the bulk of her borrowed sweater, and his hands came to rest on her shoulders for a few seconds, before sliding down over her upper arms. Then he stepped away from her, and despite her layers of clothing, Lucky missed the warmth of his body close to hers.

Bundled into coats, hats, and gloves, they stepped out into the cold and snow and light. So much light. Lucky laughed at the joy of it. She now knew where the light missing from Lilith's dark abode had gone.

Kev broke a path towards the woods, and Lucky followed. They walked without talking for several minutes, the silence broken by the sound of their breathing and the crunching of their boots in the snow.

Then Kev pulled back an evergreen branch and let it go, sending the snow that covered it into her face. Lucky's gasp of surprise turned into laughter, and as Kev started to run, she took off after him with the promise of payback. Scooping up a handful of snow she packed it into a loose ball and sent it sailing toward him. It struck the back of his neck.

"Yes!" she said.

She couldn't gloat for long though, because Kev had launched a missile of his own toward her. She jumped aside and scooped some snow off a nearby branch.

When she looked up, Kev had disappeared. She had to find him before she could beat up on him.

Laughing, she ducked around the tree, scoping out the other side. No Kev. She followed his footprints and had almost realized they made a large circle, when she felt something cold slide down the collar of her coat at the same time as she heard Kev's laugh.

She turned toward him, handful of snow at the ready.

"That was evil," she said, shivering as the snow melted down her neck and back. "But so is this."

She shoved the snow into his laughing face.

He tried to dodge as his hands came up to push her away, but his foot slipped out from under him. He fell into Lucky, tumbling them both to the ground. Lucky sank into the snow, half-trapped under Kev's body.

"See what you started?" She laughed into his face. "Now we're covered in it."

Kev laughed too. But when his eyes met hers, the laughter in them shifted to something warmer and far more dangerous. His gaze dropped to her mouth, and Lucky's heart began to hammer against her ribs.

Then with a shake of his head that sent snow flying from his hat into her face, he rolled away from her. Rising to his feet, he stuck out a hand to help her up. She placed her gloved hand in his and let him pull her upright. He dropped her hand as soon as she had her balance.

They walked several feet without speaking, their boots crunching in the snow.

"How old are you, Kev?" Lucky asked.

He turned to look at her, eyebrows raised. "Twenty-two. Why do you ask?"

"Just curious," Lucky said. "I would have guessed older."

Kev chuckled. "Compared to you I'm practically ancient."

"You are not." Lucky smacked his arm. "You're younger than Josh."

"In years maybe."

"Wait." Lucky stopped in her tracks. "You're not that much older than Aidan. It didn't take Lucifer long to move on from your mother to his, did it?"

This time Kev's chuckle lacked humor. He didn't look at Lucky when he spoke. "My parents weren't exactly an item. They felt nothing for each other besides a mutual respect."

Lucky frowned but said nothing, waiting for him to continue.

"Lucifer wanted a child. He had learned of a prophecy that said his son would restore the balance between Light and Dark, reunite them. Katrin was a strong half-Seraph Naphil with a high-ranking position in the Forces of the Fallen. He chose her to bear that son. After some consideration, Katrin agreed. Neither of them could have predicted that Lucifer would fall for Aidan's mother soon after."

"Katrin? The new Healer? She's…?"

"My mother. Yes."

After a few crunching steps, Kev added, "I hadn't seen her in almost five years. It was something of a shock to walk into the Council meeting and find her there."

"How could you have gone for five years without seeing your own mother?"

"Katrin and I have never been close. She didn't really want to be a mother. When she had me, she was only doing what she saw as her duty. Nana was more a mother to me than Katrin."

Lucky frowned. "She was your—grandmother?"

"Not by blood, but in all other ways. Nana and Papa were Katrin's adoptive parents."

"Did they know—what you are?"

Kev nodded. "They didn't at first—when they adopted Katrin, I mean. Later, Zeke helped them—and Katrin— understand what she was. And by the time I came along, they knew I wouldn't be the most normal of grandchildren."

"What about your real grandparents?"

"My biological grandmother was some poor girl who was unlucky enough to be raped by a Seraph and then have her memories erased." Lucky had never heard Kev's voice sound so hard. It softened as he continued, "Zeke learned of what happened to her and kept his eye on her until she gave birth to my mother. Then he kept an eye on Katrin—and Nana and Papa—until she was old enough to learn the truth."

"Were you lonely—as a child?" Lucky asked.

"What is this, twenty questions?"

Kev took her arm, tugging her off the path to a steep incline. "Come this way. I want to show you something."

They alternated walking and sliding down the incline for about ten minutes, and then the ground leveled out, before falling away into a small gorge.

"There," Kev said, pointing.

Across the gorge, a narrow waterfall tumbled to a creek below. Ice had built up on the rocks, but water still trickled over the frozen mass.

"It's spring-fed," Kev said. "It never completely freezes."

Lucky looked from the icy waterfall to the creek to the snow-covered mountain and the bright blue sky stretching above it all. "It's gorgeous," she breathed.

"You should see it in the fall," Kev said. Then he laughed. "Or spring. Or summer."

They stood without talking for several minutes. Lucky could hear the trickling of the water flowing over the ice and the soft sound of Kev's breathing. Without thinking, she reached for his hand. She caught herself before she touched him and shoved her hand into her pocket.

The water making its icy way to the creek below reminded Lucky of Lake Michigan and the peace she found in its presence. And that reminded her of the family and friends she had left in Chicago. She missed Josh and Ben and G-Ma. She missed Mo. She missed Aidan and Malachi. And, yes, she missed Zeke. Maybe she had been unreasonable. Sambethe had been punished. Maybe she should consider going back.

Except now she had the not-so-small problem of her Gift to contend with. Maybe Kev could give her pointers and Gift-taming lessons or something here in the middle of nowhere, where no one could get hurt. She trusted his dragon could hold his own against her Gift if it got out of hand.

"Hey." Kev's quiet voice interrupted her thoughts. "Where'd you go?"

Lucky gave him a rueful smile as she shook her head. "Thinking about home."

He slid an arm around her shoulders and gave her a quick squeeze. Then he turned and looked up at the incline they'd descended.

"Race you to the top," he said, grinning.

Lucky didn't wait long enough to reply. She took off running, with Kev's dark chocolate laughter following after her.

# CHAPTER 12

"Where am I?"

Aidan's eyes popped open at the sound of the husky, no-nonsense voice. He'd almost fallen asleep as he sat watch over his and Katrin's patient. He straightened in his chair to see the girl in the bed pushing herself to a seated position.

"And who are you?" Her dark gray eyes locked on his, a frown gathering like a storm cloud on her brow.

The question threw him for a moment. Between his position with the band and his role among the Fallen, he had become accustomed to being recognized.

"I—my name is Aidan," he stumbled. "I've been helping to take care of you."

"Well, then, *Aidan*," the girl said, "where am I?" She didn't sound any friendlier.

"You—you're—we're in Zeke's house, in Chicago."

"Zeke? Chicago?" The girl's eyebrows rose. "I'm in the human realm? With the Fallen?"

"Um, yeah."

Aidan could see the momentary wave of panic cross her face, before she controlled her features. "How long have I been here?" she asked.

"Almost twenty-four hours."

"Twenty-four hours? But—that's not possible." The volume of the girl's voice dropped as the color faded from her face, leaving her skin starkly pale next to her mostly black hair. "I should be dead now," she whispered.

"Oh." Aidan grasped the source of her panic. "You thought you were Bound? Kev made sure you weren't before he brought you here."

"Kev?"

"Sorry. You would know him as *Ha-Satan*. He's my half-brother."

"Oh, yeah. He turns into a dragon, right? The last thing I remember is running at Lucky. He was there, your brother. I think he might have flamed me."

Aidan nodded. "He did. And Lucky's Power hit you too."

"Is she okay—Lucky? Did we stop her?"

Aidan scooted forward on the chair, resting his elbows on his knees. "I think she's okay. I haven't seen her. She's—with Kev somewhere. He said she thought she'd—be a danger to us, if she was here."

"She might be," the girl said. Then, her subdued voice veined with steel, she added, "You said your brother made sure I wasn't Bound. How did he do that?"

"He asked Lilith. She would know, right?"

"Yeah," the girl said, the vein of steel in her voice changing to a mother lode, "she would know. Which means she's lied to me my entire life."

"Lilith told you you were Bound? But you're her grand-daughter."

The girl looked at him like he was stupid. "Familial relationship does not preclude dishonesty," she said, as if tutoring a child.

"I know that," Aidan snapped. "I meant why would she lie to you?"

"Funny, I came up with that question all on my own."

Aidan opened his mouth to respond, then decided to cut his losses and changed the subject. "Kev said your name is Bryn. Is it okay if I call you that?"

The look she shot him made him question his choice of safer topics.

"I'm Bryn to my friends only, thank you very much. To everyone else, including you, I'm Branwen."

"I've been helping take care of you. Don't you think that makes me a friend?"

"No, that makes you a caregiver. You're pretty, but you're not long on logic, are you?"

"Oh, for f—." Aidan stopped before the obscenity left his lips. "Branwen it is then. Are you hungry, thirsty? Can I get you something to eat or drink?"

Branwen smirked at him. "Both actually. I'm starving."

Aidan had already reached the door. "I'll bring up a tray," he called over his shoulder. "You won't want to try tackling the stairs yet."

*Annoying much?* he thought as he jogged down the stairs. Perhaps Branwen had inherited that trait from Lilith. He supposed she must have some friends, since she allowed them to call her "Bryn," but he guessed the group didn't have many members. He wondered if Lucky counted among them.

Branwen had seemed genuinely concerned for Lucky, and he knew the girl had been injured trying to help her. That was a point in her favor. And, as Lilith's granddaughter, she was Lucky's cousin. Another reason to be nice to her. He'd do his best, but it wouldn't be easy. Salving his guilty conscience with the thought that, in a way, he wished her well, he hoped her recovery time would be short.

After Aidan left, Branwen swung her legs over the side of the bed. She wanted to find a bathroom, and she was none too sure how steady she would be on her feet. Her head pounded, and her limbs felt heavy. At least the head of the bed sat against the wall. She could make it to the door using the wall for support.

Once in the hall, she stopped for a moment to check the other doors. The closed ones likely led to additional bed-rooms. An open door on the other side of the hall and a few yards to her right looked like the best candidate for a bath-room.

Holding on to the wall, she took the several slow steps necessary to position herself across from the open door. She'd guessed correctly. She just had to make it across the hall. Three steps should do it, but she wouldn't have anything to hold onto. She supposed she could crawl across the hall if she had to, but she'd rather die than have Aidan come back up the stairs and find her on her hands and knees.

She gritted her teeth and let her hand fall from the wall. Although she wobbled with every step, she reached the open door without falling. She allowed herself to rest against the doorframe for a few seconds before hauling herself the rest of the way into the bathroom and shutting the door behind her.

She had made it back across the hall when she heard Aidan climbing the stairs. A couple more minutes and she could have been back in bed, with him none the wiser. Instead, he would see her leaning against the wall like a complete weakling. She tried to increase her pace, but she had to stop and rest at the bedroom door.

Aidan saw her as he reached the top of the stairs. "Let me help you," he said, setting the tray he carried on the floor.

Bryn pushed herself away from the doorframe. "I don't need your help," she asserted.

"Right, *Branwen*," Aidan said. He retrieved the abandoned tray. "Excuse me for even offering."

Bryn wished she could think of something biting to say in reply, but she had to focus all her energy on getting back to the bed. To his credit, Aidan didn't comment on her slow progress. He held the tray and waited until she'd climbed into the bed and leaned back against the pillows. Once she was settled he handed her the tray, holding on to it until it was steady on her lap.

"Do you want some company, or would you prefer to eat alone?" he asked.

He didn't sound too excited at the prospect of keeping her company, and Bryn almost let him off the hook. But she didn't want to eat alone. Her weakness coupled with the knowledge that Lilith had lied to her all these years had left her feeling more vulnerable than she wanted to admit. She needed the distraction of someone else's presence—even someone who annoyed her.

"You can stay if you want," she said.

Aidan lowered himself onto the chair he'd occupied earlier.

Bryn studied the items on the tray. He'd brought her a bowl of brothy soup, a thick slice of bread with butter, a banana, a glass of water, and a cup of tea.

"Sorry if it doesn't look like much," Aidan said. "Since you haven't eaten in a while, a light meal seemed best."

Bryn glanced at him. He hovered on the edge of the chair, like he thought she might throw the bowl of soup in his direction.

"It looks great. Thanks," she said.

Aidan relaxed into the chair as she began to eat. And he didn't offer to help her—even when her trembling hand threatened to spill the soup from the spoon before it reached her lips. She picked up the bowl and held it close to her mouth while she sipped the soup from the spoon.

"Would you mind telling me what happened—when you were hurt?" Aidan asked after she'd set the soup bowl back on the tray. "What were you trying to stop Lucky from doing? Why did her Power hit you, and why did Kev flame you?"

Bryn drank the entire glass of water while she collected her thoughts. She didn't know what Lucky had tried to do to William and his father, but it hadn't looked good. And she didn't know if Lucky had finished what she started or not. Aidan hadn't answered that question, so perhaps he didn't know either. She set the empty glass back on the tray. She guessed she should start at the beginning.

She told Aidan how Lucky had stood up for Alicia and how William had enlisted his father's help in seeking his revenge.

"William's friends grabbed me first. As soon as we crossed into the clearing, the magic took hold of me. It felt like my arms and legs were tied. I saw William drag Lucky into the clearing, and the same thing happened to her. He gloated, and Lucky started taunting him. Then he hit her."

Bryn watched Aidan while she spoke, and at those words, his eyes flared and the muscles of his jaw flexed as he clenched his teeth. She wondered how close he and Lucky were.

"And he kept hitting her," she continued. "She couldn't fight back. The magic bound her like it did me. When she fell, he started kicking her. Then—I don't know what happened—but she broke free from the magic and grabbed his arm. He screamed something about her burning him. And then she held out her hand, and both William and his father were caught in her Power. The magic released me then too."

Bryn paused to take a sip of her tea. Aidan was on the edge of his seat again.

"I don't know what she did to them, but it hurt them. And it looked like she wanted to do more than that. I yelled at her, but I don't think she even heard me. Then my grandmother showed up. She must have sensed Lucky breaking Mather's spell. Anyway, she yelled at Lucky too, but Lucky didn't hear her either—or she was too far gone to listen, if she did. Not long after that your brother materialized on the other side of the clearing. He called to her, and I guess she heard him, because she looked at him. She didn't release William and Mather though. And your brother didn't hold her attention for long. He yelled at her to stop, but she didn't. And I could tell she was going to do it—going to kill them. And I knew she would never be okay if she did. So I started running. I thought if I could knock her off balance, I could make her lose her hold on them. At the same time, your brother went green and scaly. I must have hit Lucky's arm at the same time he flamed her."

When she finished speaking, Bryn realized how much her body had tensed while she related the tale. She leaned back against the pillows and took a deep breath. "Do you know if we managed to stop her?" she asked.

"Kev didn't say," Aidan answered, "but I'm sure you did. He would have told us if Lucky had—killed someone." A frown creased his forehead, and he spoke the final words as if they left a bad taste in his mouth. Bryn knew the feeling.

Aidan scrubbed a hand over his face. "Kev said Lucky's Gift wasn't a fun one. Sounds like that was an understatement. I can only imagine what she's going through now."

"Yeah," Bryn agreed.

She picked up the banana, but then placed it back on the tray. She seemed to have lost her appetite. She also seemed to have depleted her little store of energy. She wanted nothing more than to curl up under the covers and go to sleep.

Aidan must have noticed her drooping. He collected the tray, leaving the banana on the bedside table—in case she wanted it later, he said. Bryn snuggled down in the bed, her eyes already closing as he left the room.

# CHAPTER 13

"That'll keep going for a while, and there are plenty more logs here if you need them," Kev said, standing from where he'd crouched in front of the fireplace. "Are you sure you don't want to come with me?"

"I'm sure," Lucky said. She had curled up under a blanket on the couch again, a cup of tea in her hands and a book within reach. "I'd rather stay here and rest. For some reason, I'm really tired. And I don't want to be around other people yet."

"You're still recovering from yesterday," Kev said.

Lucky's mouth twisted into a grimace.

Kev wanted to thread his fingers through the curtain of dark curls that fell forward when she looked down at the mug she held. Instead, he shoved his hands into his pockets. "You rest then. I'll be back in a few hours. You should have everything you need."

"Thanks, Kev," she said.

His fingers flexed when she tucked the fallen hair behind her ear. Yeah, it was time to go.

He strode through the living area into the kitchen and out into the mud room, where he pulled on his boots and coat, before entering the attached garage. He could zap himself to the little gem store instead of driving down the mountain, but like everything connected to the creation of his art, he wanted to do this the human way—even if the drive would take him well over an hour each way. Besides, he needed the occupation of driving on the steep, windy road in the snow. He figured it would give him the same kind of focus he found in practicing *tai chi*—albeit with the added zing of physical risk.

The old Jeep started on the first try. With its dents and black paint giving way to rusty patches in places, it looked like hell, but it ran like a charm. He turned the heater up and backed out of the garage.

As he waited for the garage door to lower, his eyes shifted to the living room windows. He both hated leaving Lucky behind and looked forward to a few hours alone. Not that he didn't like her company. On the contrary, he liked it too much. He couldn't afford to get used it.

He turned the Jeep around and started down the narrow road that wound through the trees. He hoped Lucky could rest while he was gone. He knew yesterday's adventure had taken a lot out of her. The onset of a Gift expended a huge burst of energy, kind of like a growth spurt. That coupled with what Lucky had then done with her Gift, not to mention the emotional after-effects, had to have left her exhausted. Their morning's hike seemed to have used up what energy she had managed to recoup.

A large branch had fallen part way across the road in front of him. Kev maneuvered around it and, leaving the Jeep running, hopped out to toss the branch to the side of the road, so he wouldn't have to worry about it on the way back. He put the Jeep back in gear, grateful the trees grew so close to the road. No other vehicle had broken a path through the snow, and without the trees to mark its edges, he wouldn't have been able to find the road.

After about thirty minutes of navigating the steep, snowy curves, Kev had become accustomed enough to the drive that a part of his mind returned to the problem of the forged sigil. He had meant to call Zeke, but Lucky had so preoccupied him, it had slipped his mind. He would give the angel a call when he reached the little town. Too bad they couldn't ask Uriel to access the record of the murder itself, but that record would be sealed to all but the murderer, now that the victim was no longer in the picture.

Snow had started to fall when Kev pulled into one of the three parking spots in front of the tiny gem store. He dialed Zeke's number but got no answer. He left a message saying he needed to talk to Uriel and asking Zeke to call him for details and an update. Then he jogged through the falling snow to the shop door.

Lucky sat curled on the sofa, staring into the fire. She had awakened from a fitful nap about a half hour earlier to find that dark had fallen, and she'd shuttered all the windows except the large one overlooking the back yard and studio. She liked having that one uncovered, but somehow with the others unshuttered, she'd felt the darkness closing in on her. She had picked up the book she had been reading before she fell asleep, and when it no longer held her attention, she had spent several minutes searching Kev's bookshelves for something distracting. But after reading the same paragraph over and over and still not remembering what she'd read, she'd given up on the distraction of books. So she stared into the fire and worried.

Kev had left hours ago, and snow had been coming down hard for a while now. She hoped he would return soon. He'd probably driven on that road in the snow countless times, plus he was a near-invulnerable Naphil—but she couldn't help worrying about him.

Nor could she keep from worrying about herself and her newly manifested Gift.

Throughout the morning and early afternoon with Kev, sharing breakfast, playing in the snow, hiking to the waterfall and back, and then lingering over lunch, she had let herself forget the events of the day before, forget who she had become in those moments when she'd held the minds of her attackers in her power, forget what she'd wanted then, what her desire had told her to do.

Alone and staring at the flickering flames and the shadows they cast, the memories pressed in on her like the night outside the windows. She forced herself to face them instead of pushing them away. Kev had said she had to accept that part of herself. She couldn't do that yet, but she could at least acknowledge the memories.

Sorting through the images and the crush of emotions they brought with them, she found the worst one: that instant when the realization of her own power had rushed over her, filling her with the horrible, gleeful knowledge that with one small shift of her thoughts, she could twist the minds of her attackers enough to break them, enough even to end their lives. The desire to do it, to shift her thoughts that little bit, had been irresistible. She would have given in if Kev's dragon hadn't flamed her arm.

Lucky let herself remember, let herself be pulled back into that moment, that feeling, let herself touch the desire to harm, to destroy. In retrospect, the memory sickened her. But in the moment, in the instant between desire and action, she had felt a burning need to make the desire a reality. The only thing better than knowing she had the power to crush the minds of William and his father would have been using that power to crush them.

Thank God Kev had intervened in time. She knew that if she had used her power to destroy her attackers—whatever deep satisfaction the Dark part of her might have felt—when she came back to herself, the knowledge of what she had done would have destroyed her. The promise of satisfaction had been a lie. The reality would have been utter devastation.

Kev had told her to acknowledge the dark, destructive thing she wanted to disown as a part of herself, so she could learn to work with it, channel it, collaborate with it, as he did his dragon. But how could she? How could she find anything worthy of her cooperation in the part of her that wanted to kill, to destroy? She couldn't get rid of it either though—even if she wanted to.

She remembered Uriel's words: *Exactly what this means remains to be seen. May your Making be of benefit to us all.* The Archangel hadn't known what the results of her Making would be, because she was descended from Lilith. What if the powers given her at her Making mixed with the extra bits she'd received from Luil made a deadly combination? What if they had created a monster? Maybe she couldn't help save anyone. Maybe instead she would bring about the very destruction they all hoped to avoid.

Grabbing her head with her hands, Lucky groaned in frustration. Her thoughts were terrible company. She should call Josh.

She had plugged in her cell phone earlier, before she'd fallen asleep. It had been dead when she had dug it out of her backpack, whatever charge it may have had when she had packed it having disappeared during her time in Nadach. By now it should have enough of a charge for her to let her best fam know she was okay and back in the human realm.

*The human realm.* She sounded like Bryn. She smiled as she remembered her first meeting with her new cousin. Then she remembered how Bryn had looked the last time she'd seen her, and the smile faded. She'd have to ask Kev for an update on Bryn's condition when he finally returned.

She stopped by one of the front windows to open the shutter and peek outside, to look for Kev's headlights through the trees. No luck. Sighing, she reclosed the shutters and bounded up the stairs to find her phone.

Josh picked up after the first ring. "Lucky! Are you all right? Where have you been?"

Lucky's eyes filled with tears when she heard his voice. "Yeah, I'm okay, Josh," she replied, sniffling a little. "I've missed you."

"I've missed you too, and I've been crazy worried about you."

"I left you a note, told you not to worry." Lucky automatically defended herself against the accusation underlying her cousin's words.

"Right. Like that's going to stop me."

Lucky relented. "I know. I'm sorry. I'd have been crazy worried too, if you had disappeared, leaving me nothing more than a note."

"So, where are you? When are you coming home?"

"I don't know," Lucky said. "I mean, I know where I am, sort of—Colorado somewhere. But I don't know when I'm coming home."

"You ran away to Colorado?"

"No. I was with Lilith—in her world, Nadach—until yesterday. Now I'm in Colorado."

"What are you doing there? And why don't you know when you're coming home?"

"I'm here—with Kev." Lucky hesitated. She didn't want to go into the whole awful story, but she couldn't leave it there. "It's complicated. The short version is that he—well, he rescued me from an ugly situation in Nadach. I'll explain it all when I see you. And I don't know when that will be, because there are some things I have to figure out. But I wanted you to know I'm okay—and I miss you."

"Come on, Lucky. You've got to give me more than that. What's going on? Are you sure you're okay?"

Lucky sighed. "I'm mostly okay. It's just—my Gift showed up—and I'm having a hard time with it. Kev seems to have experience with this sort of thing though, so I'm hoping he can provide some guidance."

"All right," Josh said. "I guess that'll satisfy me for now. I'm glad you called. It's good to hear your voice."

Lucky's eyes filled again, and her words thickened with tears. "Yours too. I love you, Josh."

"Yeah, I love you too." From the sound of his voice, Josh had choked back some tears of his own.

After Lucky ended the call, she started scrolling through her contacts to find Mo.

The phone fell from her hand when the dragon medallion resting on her chest began to burn, and a vision, clear as a movie scene, filled her head. A Jeep half off a narrow, snow-covered road, a large branch splayed across the dented hood and cracked windshield, Kev slumped behind the wheel, and a ponytailed angel with a sword bearing down on the vehicle.

Leaving her phone where it had fallen, Lucky focused all her thoughts on the scene that filled her mind. Then she added herself to the picture.

For a moment, she was nowhere and everywhere all at the same time. Then she stood in the snow four or five feet behind the sword-bearer.

Panic swelled when she felt the tingling in her palms, but she forced it down and allowed the power to fill her. She couldn't fight the angel single-handed. Her Dark Gift was the only weapon at her disposal.

Activating all her senses, she directed her power toward the angel. His fingers had closed on the door handle, but he jerked toward her when she entered his mind.

Lucky fell to her knees. His thoughts and emotions, much more powerful than those of William and Mather, threatened to overwhelm her. But even as she faltered, she felt the cold, dark, gleeful desire to destroy worming through her. The panic retreated before it, and with nothing to stop her, and every reason to use whatever power she had, she gave in.

The angel screamed as she twisted and knotted the strands of thoughts and emotions. When she snapped a thread, he grabbed his head in his hands and toppled over, his screams growing louder.

Lucky smiled. A little more…

"Lucky, stop."

Kev's voice penetrated the dark fog of destruction, even as she felt his hand close on her arm.

"Let him go. You don't want to do this."

Lucky stopped tormenting the angel, but she didn't release him. "He was going to kill you."

"I know. But you've done enough already. Trust me. You don't want to go any further."

Reluctantly, she tore herself from the angel's mind, and he sagged, weeping, whimpering. She sat back on her heels, energy flagging as the rush of power departed. She shivered in the cold, only now noticing she had no coat or shoes.

She saw Kev kneel beside the bent angel. He pulled the obsidian pendant he wore as *Ha-Satan* from beneath his shirt and enclosed it in one hand, speaking words she couldn't hear.

Within seconds, a blinding light filled her vision. She closed her eyes. When she opened them again, Uriel stood next to Kev. They exchanged a few words, and the Archangel glanced in her direction. Then he picked the blond angel up in his arms. Light began to gather around him, and Lucky waited for the flash of his departure. Kev stayed him with a raised hand. The Archangel listened to whatever Kev said and offered a brief response. Then light exploded, taking him and the angel he carried away.

The afterimage of the flash still burned on her retinas when Lucky felt Kev lifting her up out of the snow. He took off his coat and wrapped it around her, then picked her up and carried her to the car. The engine was still running, and even with the driver's side door open, all the heat hadn't escaped. He placed her in the passenger seat and buckled her seatbelt. She shivered and collapsed against the seat back.

She watched, detached, while Kev pulled the tree limb off the hood of the car and tossed it to the side, before climbing in the car, buckling himself in, and maneuvering the car back onto the road.

"How're you doing?" he asked.

Lucky rolled her head toward him without lifting it from the headrest. "I'm tired, but I'm not quite as cold as I was. I didn't even think about shoes and a coat when…" Her voice trailed off. When what? How could she explain the clearness of the vision and her certainty of Kev's location?

"Let me guess," Kev said. "When you got the vision of what was happening to me—Hi-Def and detailed and complete with its own 100% accurate GPS?"

"Yes. That's it exactly."

"Did you notice anything else?"

"The medallion—it got hot all of a sudden. Like it did when I called you as a Maker, and like it did in Lilith's world, when I…" Again, her voice trailed away into silence.

"Needed my help," Kev finished the sentence for her. "Like I needed yours tonight."

Neither of them said anything more for the rest of the short ride home.

Back at the cabin, Kev sent a partially revived Lucky to change into dry clothes, promising her hot chocolate would be waiting when she came back downstairs. While the milk heated, he tried Zeke again. Still no answer. He left a message letting Zeke know he'd already made contact with Uriel, but asking him to call anyway for a general update.

He was whisking the cocoa, sugar, and spices into the hot milk when Lucky returned. A smile curved his lips when he saw that in addition to leggings and a pair of thick socks, she wore the oversize sweater she had borrowed from him that morning. She had probably chosen it for the warmth factor, but he couldn't help hoping her choice had had something to do with him.

"Nice sweater," he murmured, his smile growing as her cheeks turned pink.

"It's warm," she said.

He poured the cocoa into mugs and handed her one.

Lucky curled into the corner of the couch. After adding another log to the fire, Kev settled in the armchair. He needed to put what distance he could between them. Holding her in his arms to carry her to the Jeep had felt too good.

And knowing she'd raced to his rescue like he had raced to hers made him wish for things he couldn't have.

"Who was he?" Her question broke through his thoughts. "The angel with the sword?"

Kev shook his head. "Some Dominion who's convinced my father murdered Jahoel. He and some friends expressed their displeasure on my last couple of visits to the Heavens."

"How did he find you?"

"We're not that difficult to track, if someone's looking hard enough. Each of our energy signatures is distinct. It takes some time to find the right one and track it, but it can be done."

Kev took a sip of hot chocolate, stared at the fire, took another sip. "Thank you," he said, "for what you did tonight. If you hadn't been there, he might have succeeded in his mission."

Lucky shivered. "I'm glad I could help." She caught his eyes, held them. "I would have killed him—if you hadn't stopped me."

Kev nodded. "I know. And I appreciate that—even though I'm glad you didn't."

"I'm glad too. Thank you for stopping me."

"He's not getting off easy, you know. You may have done permanent damage. And he has Uriel to deal with."

Lucky gripped her mug so tightly Kev could see her knuckles whiten. "I still can't believe I can do that—hurt someone so badly without even touching them."

"Gifts can be hard to get used to. You did well tonight. You had more control. You stopped it when I asked."

"I wouldn't have though, if you hadn't told me to."

"It's still progress. Every little bit counts."

Lucky nodded, but she didn't look as if she believed him.

*One minute William was kicking her, and the next he screamed as her hand closed on his arm. Then she held him and his father in a wave of power that streaked down her arm and out of her hand, a wave of power that enabled her to see all the intricate threads that made up their thoughts, their dreams, their desires, their fears. She tilted her head and shifted the position of her hand ever so slightly. A wave of satisfaction washed through her as they writhed in agony. She shifted her hand again, increasing their suffering, and a pair of dark, cold arms closed around her. She knew those arms. They had held her when she had succumbed to the poison from the Power's sword. They had threatened to pull her deeper into the darkness, so deep she would never be able to escape. They closed around her now as if welcoming her home. Cold hands slid up and down her arms in a gesture of approval. Yes, if she shifted her hand a bit more...*

*No, she thought. She didn't want this. No, no, no. One dark arm tightened its grip, while the other hand slid down her arm to her outstretched hand, wrapping around it, shifting that extra tiny bit.*

*"No!" she screamed. "No, no, no, no, no!"*

Lucky struggled against the hands that closed around her arms. She yanked one arm free and struck her captor as hard as she could. Then her eyes flew open as she heard a crash and Kev's loud curse. By the time she'd scrambled to her knees, he'd regained his balance and righted the chair he'd knocked over when she'd hit him.

"That's some backhand you've got there," he said, rubbing his cheek and jaw.

"Kev, I'm so sorry." Lucky spoke through the hands she had clasped over her mouth. "I'm so, so sorry. I didn't mean—I wouldn't—I—"

"It's all right." Kev sat down on the bed beside her. "It was my fault. You were having a nightmare. I shouldn't have touched you. But you were screaming, and I didn't stop to think. I just wanted—to get you out of it."

Lucky lifted her hand to touch the red mark on his cheek. "Does it still hurt?" she asked.

He shook his head. "Not so much."

Giving in to impulse, Lucky leaned forward and pressed a kiss on his cheekbone, where the fading red mark was darkest.

"Lucky, don't," Kev whispered.

She ignored him. Moving her lips lower to the next darkest spot, she kissed him again. When her lips touched his cheek a third time, Kev's hand slid into her hair to cup the back of her head.

"Lucky," he said, the word half-whisper, half-groan, as he turned his head, so her next kiss fell on his parted lips.

Both hands in her hair, he held her head in place while he deepened the kiss. His touch licked through her veins like flames, burning away her inhibitions, igniting her senses, and leaving her with a strange empty feeling it seemed only he could fill. Her hands went to either side of his face, sliding down over his stubbled jaw, his neck, to close over the hard muscles of his shoulders. She moved so she straddled his hips, one knee on either side of him. His hands left her hair and slid down her back, drawing her closer. His mouth left hers to trail kisses over her jaw and down her throat.

Lucky breathed Kev's name. Her hands glided down his chest and stomach to the hem of his t-shirt. She tugged it upward, and he released her long enough to remove the shirt and toss it aside. Then she was back in his arms, held close against his chest, his mouth hard on hers. Sliding her hands over the muscles of his back, she could feel the warmer, slightly raised pattern of his sigil. She traced bits of the pattern with her fingertips and felt Kev shiver. His hands slid beneath her t-shirt.

She leaned away from him so he could pull the shirt over her head. But instead he moved his hands from under the shirt to press her arms back down to her sides. Holding her shoulders, he leaned his forehead against hers, his breathing ragged.

"We have to stop this," he whispered.

"No, we don't," she whispered back, her hands moving to caress the sides of his waist.

He groaned and pressed a small kiss to her mouth.

"Yes, we do," he said, resting his forehead against hers once more.

They remained like that until their breaths quieted.

Then Kev shifted Lucky's body so she sat on his lap. He pulled her close. She lay her head on his shoulder, one arm around him, the other hand resting on his chest. When she turned her head to plant a tiny kiss on his shoulder, he chuckled.

"Don't start that again."

She smiled against his skin. "I wasn't starting anything."

"Mm-hm. So you say." Lucky could hear the smile in his voice.

"I wasn't. I just wanted to kiss you."

Kev's hand slid up and down her arm. "I want that too. But if I kissed you again, I would definitely be starting something."

"Would that be such a bad thing?"

"I'm pretty sure it would be a very good thing. But you're vulnerable right now. And I'm not going to take advantage of that."

Lucky lifted her head from his shoulder. "You think I don't know what I want? That I don't know how I feel about you?"

It took Kev some time to answer. "I think you might be confused—and you have every reason to be. You're still angry with Aidan, your Gift has ripped you apart, and here we are, thrown together, with the medallion sending us messages about each other. Hell, I'm confused."

"You don't know what you want?" Lucky asked.

Kev grasped her shoulders. "Yes, I know what I want. But I'm not sure I should want it. Look me in the eye and tell me honestly that you don't still have feelings for my brother."

Lucky stared into his eyes—those gold-flecked green eyes that made her want to fall inside them—and she couldn't do it. She remembered all the things Aidan had done for her, all the times he'd held her in his arms, comforted her, kissed her. She thought about how he'd feel if she arrived back home to tell him she was with his brother now. And she couldn't do it. She didn't want to hurt him. Whatever she felt for Kev, she still loved Aidan too.

She stared into Kev's eyes until she saw them through a veil of tears, and she felt her face crumple. "I can't," she whispered. "I'm sorry, but I can't."

Kev pulled her head to his shoulder once more. "It's okay. You don't have to be sorry. I never thought you could."

For some reason, his words triggered more tears. Lucky clung to him and sobbed, while his hand stroked her hair.

As he held Lucky, her curls soft beneath his hand, her tears wet against his skin, Kev wondered what was wrong with him, that he could comfort her after she'd admitted she still loved his brother and be grateful to have her in his arms. Was he a masochist or what?

But it wasn't like he'd been disillusioned. What he'd told her was true. He hadn't ever believed she could tell him she no longer loved Aidan. Kev knew she had feelings for him as well—which may be why he was able to hold her now and be grateful—but he knew she hadn't let Aidan go. Their relationship hadn't ended—it had only been interrupted. And he didn't want to interfere with it any more than he already had. *Yeah, right. Then why are you still holding her?* he thought.

All right, so he wanted her to want him. How could he be blamed for that? But he didn't want to make the choice for her, didn't want to force her hand. She had to choose him because she wanted *him*, not because she was hurt, or scared, or lonely—and he happened to be there at the time.

And if she didn't choose him? If she chose Aidan? Kev sighed. Then so be it. It would hurt like hell, but he would live through it. Better that than all three of them suffering. Maybe he was a masochist, after all.

Lucky's sobs had quieted, and he stopped stroking her hair, resting the tips of his fingers instead on her tear-damp cheek.

"Do you think you can go back to sleep now?" he asked.

"I don't know. Maybe." Lucky sniffed, raising her head and sitting up.

Without her warmth snuggled against him, the tears she'd left on his skin made his chest feel cold.

"Sorry—about all this." Lucky's fingers brushed the patch of wet skin.

Kev shivered, as much from her touch as the cold. "It'll dry."

He stood up, his hands moving away from Lucky as soon as she was steady on her feet.

She stared at him for a moment, and it took all his strength not to fold her in his arms again.

"Stay with me?" she whispered.

Kev felt as if his heart would split open. Every cell in his body screamed "Yes," but he shook his head. "I can't," he said, repeating her words to him. "I'm sorry—but I can't."

# CHAPTER 14

Lucky awoke the next morning feeling like she imagined it would feel to have a hangover. Her head hurt, her eyelids scratched like sandpaper, and she felt empty inside. She didn't know how she would face Kev. She couldn't believe she'd asked him to stay with her—after she'd told him she still cared about Aidan. What must he think of her?

She'd cried herself to sleep after Kev had left. He had been right. She was confused. She didn't know how to tell right from wrong anymore. She didn't even know what she wanted. Mostly because she didn't know if she could trust her feelings.

When she had held William and his father in her power, the desire to destroy them had seemed strong and real. But once the power of her Dark Gift no longer overwhelmed her, she knew that desire was false, its promises were lies, and acting on it would have brought nothing but devastation.

Was her desire for Kev equally false? Was the sense of belonging she felt with him a lie, the completeness she imagined he could bring her a fantasy? If she acted on her feelings for him, would she end up similarly devastated—knowing she had broken faith with Aidan and perhaps destroyed the relationship between the brothers? And, worse, what if the need to destroy was somehow at the root of her desire for Kev? What if she was turning into an instrument of destruction? What if, like Luil, she wanted what she wanted, whatever the cost?

She pulled the covers over her head, wanting to hide in bed and refuse to meet the day. But the idea of staying there with nothing but her thoughts for company terrified her even more than that of facing Kev.

A shower helped Lucky regroup, but her heart thudded against her ribcage as she descended the stairs to the living area. She smelled coffee, and she could hear the sounds of a drawer opening and the crumple of a bread bag, so she knew Kev was in the kitchen. She pressed a hand to her stomach to quell the icy fear that sliced through it.

Her shoeless feet made no sound as she approached the kitchen door and stopped just inside it. Kev's back was to the door, but he must have sensed her presence, because he turned his head almost as soon as she entered.

"Good morning," he said.

The warmth of his smile almost bowled her over. She rocked back in surprise and caught the doorframe with one hand to steady herself. She had been sure he must be thinking awful things about her.

"Good morning."

Kev poured a cup of coffee and handed it to her. "You look like you could use this," he said. "Did you manage to get any sleep at all?"

"Not much," Lucky admitted.

"Yeah, me either."

Kev picked up his own coffee and took a swig. "Drink up. We've got work to do today."

"Work?"

"Yep. Not being at Zeke's doesn't mean you get to slack off on the training." Kev started slicing bread for toast.

"Hey, I trained while I was at Lilith's," Lucky said.

Falling into the rhythm of breakfast making, she opened the fridge and rummaged around. "How about a mushroom and cheese omelet?" she asked.

"Sounds good to me," Kev said, handing her a bowl for the eggs. "What kind of training did you do?"

"Strength and endurance drills. Martial arts. Fencing."

"Who did you train with?"

Lucky spilled an egg from its shell into the bowl. "Bryn— and a guy named Jaime. How is Bryn, by the way? Have you heard anything more?"

Kev shook his head. "I left Zeke a message yesterday, but he hasn't called back. I'll try him again while you fix the omelets. If I can't reach him, I'll call—Aidan."

Kev's hesitation before saying his brother's name brought the memory of the previous night crashing back in vivid detail. He left to make the call, and the tension broke.

He came back in a couple of minutes, wearing a frown.

"What is it?" Lucky asked.

"Neither one of them answered. And it's not like Zeke to wait this long to return a call. I'm worried."

"But if there was a major problem, someone would have contacted you, right?"

Kev raked a hand through his hair. "Yeah, probably."

"You could call someone else—like Malachi."

"If Zeke and Aidan are tied up, Malachi probably is too."

Lucky hesitated a moment before offering her next suggestion. "What about your mother?"

Kev's head snapped back as if she'd slapped him.

"Wow. She's the obvious choice for an update on Bryn, isn't she? And it didn't even occur to me to call her. What does that tell you about our relationship?"

Even as he spoke, he headed toward the door, phone in hand.

*Well, that was as awkward as I'd imagined it would be,* Kev thought as he ended the call with Katrin. At least he knew Bryn had awakened and seemed to be on the way to recovery. He also knew Malachi had summoned Zeke and Aidan the previous afternoon regarding an incident with some of the Dark, and neither had yet returned. Katrin didn't have any more details—just that she had agreed to stay with Bryn in the meantime. She promised to let Kev know if the situation worsened or if he could help in any way.

The call had lasted less than five minutes, and Kev had learned what he needed to know. But the conversation had been stilted—from the moment Katrin had answered the phone, clearly surprised to find her son on the other end of the line, until he'd ended the call with a gruff "Thanks."

Gods, the woman was his *mother.*

And therein lay the problem. He'd have been more comfortable calling a stranger—someone from whom he didn't want or need anything but information. As much as he wanted to feel nothing for Katrin, to be as cool toward her as she was toward him, he still kept hoping for some acknowledgement that he was more to her than the son of the leader of the Dark, current *Ha-Satan*, and asset in the service of the Fallen. Well, give it another twenty-two years. Maybe by then he wouldn't care anymore.

He sighed as he headed back toward the kitchen to give Lucky the news.


Lucky dripped with sweat, despite being outside in the Colorado winter and having stripped down to one layer of workout gear. Kev hadn't been kidding when he'd said work. He'd pushed her harder than any of her other trainers ever had, Malachi included.

First, they'd hiked deep into the woods to a large clearing, one side of which ended in a near-vertical drop of at least 100 feet to a rocky outcrop. Then, after manifesting the dragon long enough to vaporize the snow from the clearing, the steep cliff, and the rocky ledge below, Kev had led her through a punishing routine that included running, weight training with rocks, tree climbing, and multiple descents and ascents of the rocky cliff—first with, and then without, the aid of a rope.

Her body more than ached. She could feel the muscles in her legs and arms shaking as she forced them to pull her body back up the last few feet of rocky cliff. She dragged herself up over the cliff edge and collapsed on her back on the ledge, her lower legs dangling over the drop.

"No sleeping," Kev said, dropping down beside her and plunking a bottle of water on her stomach. "Grab a drink. Then it's on to the next round."

Lucky sat up and twisted the cap off the water bottle. She downed half its contents before she spoke. "You're killing me, Kev."

"No whining either," he said. "Get up. Break's over."

Lucky almost smacked him. She would have been angry with him for the unrelenting pace he'd demanded, except he'd worked himself even harder than he had her.

"Okay," he said. "Let's see those wings of yours."

The heavy weight of the wings had settled against Lucky's back almost before she was aware of having summoned them. Even though she hadn't logged much actual flight time, she had practiced summoning and dismissing the wings so often the actions had become second nature.

Kev nodded toward the cliff edge. "Show me what you've got."

Lucky raised her eyebrows at the command, but she did as he requested. Spreading her wings, she jumped off the cliff edge. She did a few easy loops and turns before circling back and landing beside him.

"That's it?" he asked. "That's the best you can do?"

Lucky threw him a look, then gritted her teeth and launched herself into the air again. She hovered long enough to remind herself of what Aidan had taught her, then she shot upward in a vertical climb. She didn't reach the height she wanted, so she did it again. Better that time, but she needed more practice and more power. She shifted to barrel rolls.

Definitely not her strong suit. She tried several, but she still couldn't quite manage the minute muscle shifts required to move the wings just so, and all the rolls fell flat.

She abandoned the effort. She had gone flying with Aidan several times, but, except for the one lesson he had given her at the training center, those flights had been purely for fun. Relaxing flights over Lake Michigan at night, giddy loops through the obstacle course of the downtown skyscrapers, and heart-pounding races high above the city to blow off steam. She'd already tried the relaxed option. The tree cover was too dense to fly through, so the obstacle course option was out. That left speed.

Before she could put thought into action, Kev appeared beside her, gold-dusted dark green wings beating the air.

"That was pathetic," he said.

She frowned at him. "Why are you being such a jerk all of a sudden? I'm exhausted, and I haven't had very many flight lessons. Maybe instead of criticizing me, you could give me some tips."

"Lessons? Tips? Flying is supposed to come naturally. Maybe this is one of those places where being a demonic descendent of Lilith's puts you at a disadvantage."

Lucky couldn't believe her ears. That mocking tone didn't sound like Kev at all—and the look of scorn on his face made him almost unrecognizable.

"Fine," she said. "If that's the way you're going to be, I'm done with this training exercise. I'll see you back at the cabin. Maybe by dinner time your evil twin will have gone back into hiding."

Of course, the dignified turn she'd intended came out wobbly and uneven in execution. Great, give him something else to snark about. Once she'd retrieved her things, she'd fly back to the cabin and get some practice that way.

Before she'd gone far, Kev's arms closed around her, pinning her wings to her side. "You're not getting off that easily," he said in her ear. "Get away from me. Show me what you've got."

"I was trying to get away from you, you jerk. Let go of me."

"Make me."

Lucky gritted her teeth and twisted in his arms, trying to make contact with an elbow or her heels.

Kev laughed at her. "You don't have it in you, do you?"

"What is wrong with you?" she yelled. "Stop being such an ass and let me go."

"You heard what I said. Make me." As Kev spoke, he tightened his hold on her until his grip on her arms became cruel and punishing.

Lucky struggled against him, but her strength was no match for his. The fruitlessness of her efforts made her feel almost as if she deserved to be called pathetic and reminded her of her futile struggles against the shadow creature Luil had sent after her at Mo's stepfather's country club all those months ago. She had been human then, but she wasn't anymore. She was stronger now. She had the body of a Naphil. She was not helpless. *She would not be helpless.*

Her frustration and anger increased, her palms began to tingle, and she felt the power of her Gift begin to build inside her. She forced the sigils not to activate—she knew now not to use them as weapons—and pushed down the wave of panic that threatened to swamp her as the power rose higher.

Then she bit back a cry of pain as Kev's hold on her tightened even further.

"Show me what you've got, Lucky," he growled in her ear.

Her panic disappeared as her Gift swept through her, and she reached out with her power for the tendrils of Kev's thoughts. Oh, she'd make him let her go, all right.

She felt his start of surprise as he felt her in his mind, and taking advantage of his loosened hold, she dismissed her wings. Without their bulk, she slipped through his arms and dropped toward the ground far below. As soon as she fell free of him, she summoned the wings again. The adrenaline rush of her Gift gave her added strength, and she shot back upwards, turning to face Kev from a few yards away.

She held out her hand, and drawing the power up from her core, she directed it down her arm and out her palm. She didn't want to destroy as she had with William and his father, but she did want to show Kev she was no one to mess with.

Before her power could touch him though, he transformed. Where Kev had hung supported by his dark green wings, the dragon who had breathed fire on her arm now hovered.

So it was the dragon's mind she saw and felt, not Kev's. And that mind was both similar to the human minds she'd touched and utterly alien. The tendrils of thought formed different, oddly beautiful patterns. Seeing and touching them, she found she didn't want to control, didn't want to change the beast's thoughts or twist his emotions. She only wanted to know them. Just as she had felt an irresistible urge to pat the dragon's head when she'd called him as a Maker, so she now let her power stroke over the dragon's mind like a palm.

Then she gasped as she felt him reach through her power to touch her mind. The shock of the touch of the dragon inside her head made Lucky lower her hand and break their connection. She hovered in the air, staring at the beast that was both Kev and not Kev, while he stared at her. She wondered if he felt as altered by the exchange as she did.

Then the dragon shifted, and Kev flew to her side.

"Sorry about those," he said, his fingers brushing the bruises he'd left on her forearms.

Lucky looked at the dark marks. "They'll fade soon."

He gestured toward the clearing. "Ready to call it a day?"

She nodded and, with a few beats of her wings, landed in the clearing. She dismissed the wings as soon as her feet touched the ground.

"You did all that on purpose?" she asked, as Kev touched down beside her, disappearing his wings. "You weren't really running for king jerk of the universe? You just wanted to make me mad enough to let my Gift out?"

Kev nodded. "That was the general idea. What did you do to my dragon anyway?"

Lucky looked at him in surprise. "Nothing. I don't know. I touched his mind. And he—returned the favor."

"Hmmm," Kev said. "Interesting."

"What did you think I did?"

"I didn't know. I felt you—in my mind—for a moment. Then when you reached out again, the dragon manifested. I didn't call him. He just showed up. And then, after, he felt—I don't know—more familiar—than he ever has."

"Yeah," Lucky said thoughtfully. "I got that too. My Gift feels more—manageable. Not that I know what I would do in a situation with real danger. You made me mad, but I never imagined you would actually hurt me."

Kev grimaced. "Except for the bruises."

Lucky held out her arms. "They're already gone."

She shivered and pulled her sleeves down. Now that she wasn't working so hard, she could feel the cold.

"You couldn't feel me when I touched the dragon's mind?" she asked as she pulled on her coat.

"Not really." Kev put on his own coat and wrapped his scarf around his neck. "I could tell you were there, but that's about it. The dragon's mind is separate from mine. It's hard to explain, but we don't merge. It's more like we communicate with each other. That communication is pretty much instantaneous, but it's not like I know all his thoughts and emotions or he knows mine. The physiology of our brains is different. I don't know if it's even possible for us to share exactly the same thoughts."

Lucky thought about Kev's reply as they gathered the rest of their things and started back toward the cabin. When her Gift manifested, she didn't feel a foreign presence in her head. It was more like she didn't know herself, that the Gift brought out thoughts and feelings she wouldn't have thought she possessed. The experience hadn't been as marked today.

She had even found the clarity to free herself from her emotions enough to figure out how to get away from Kev. Still, her experience was less like being invaded by an alien presence and more like becoming alien to herself.

"Would you tell me more about what it's like for you?" she asked. "How did your Gift first manifest?"

Kev took a deep breath. After a long exhale, he answered.

"I was eleven," he said. "Fortunately, Zeke—and Katrin—made sure I knew what I was from an early age. They'd told me my Gift would show up someday, and they'd given me some ideas of what that Gift might be. Certain Gifts are more likely to manifest for certain types of angels— and, by extension, Nephilim. You know Zeke has the Gift of Knowledge, right? Well, that Gift will most often manifest for someone from the order of Cherubim. They'd explained to me the Gifts most likely to manifest in someone who was three-quarters Seraph."

Kev paused in his story long enough to help Lucky navigate across the icy rocks of a small stream.

"I knew I might receive the Gift of Fire," he said, once they had crossed the stream. Grinning, he added, "I thought that would be pretty awesome—to be able to create fire with no more than a thought, to manipulate it. I hoped it would be my Gift." The grin faded from his face as he continued, "I did not know that Gift could come in the form of a dragon who took over my body and my mind."

"You were only eleven when it happened?" Lucky asked.

He nodded. "I had gone to a park a few blocks from Nana and Papa's house. One of the neighborhood boys had told me he and his friends met there to play basketball on Saturday mornings, and I had hoped I could make some friends. About twenty minutes into the game, I got dizzy and achy, and then I wasn't me anymore. I was this huge thing breathing fire and melting the ball, warping the hoop—and giving second degree burns to a few of the boys unlucky enough to be anywhere near the path of the flames."

"Oh, no! What did you do?"

"Zeke has his ways of watching out for those in his care. He and Katrin showed up almost immediately. He got into my head and helped me change back to—me. Then Katrin healed the boys' burns while Zeke altered their memories. Then they got me out of there. I'm not sure how the boys explained the melted ball and the warped hoop. I never saw them again. Except for Nana and Papa, I did my best to stay away from normal humans after that."

"How were you able to do that?" Lucky's heart went out to the eleven-year-old Kev, so young and, after such an experience, afraid to even try to make friends.

"I never went to school anyway. Zeke, Katrin, Lucifer, and the other members of the Fallen gave me all my classes and training. Before the melted basketball incident, I'd tried to make human friends a few times, without much success. I was small for my age as a kid, and I was different. I didn't know the TV shows they talked about, didn't know much about their games. And since I couldn't tell them what I learned in my school, I was pretty quiet. After the dragon showed up, I stopped trying, figured it was safer not to be around humans. Then Aidan started training with me a few months later. I found out I had a brother and got my first real friend, all at the same time."

Lucky stumbled and caught herself on a nearby tree. Aidan had been Kev's *first* friend? No wonder Kev was so glad to have his brother back in his life. And no wonder he had walked away from her last night. Every word he'd uttered made her want to hold him more—and made it even less possible for her to do so.

# CHAPTER 15

Aidan rematerialized back in his room at Zeke's to find Harley hopping out of a half-opened dresser drawer with a sock in his mouth. He shook his head as he pushed the drawer closed. He knew better than to leave any drawer unclosed or any door ajar, but he'd left in a hurry. The fact that he'd relocated his pet to his temporary digs had slipped his mind.

The ferret chittered and skipped sideways in a war dance.

"Not now, Harley," Aidan said. "Sorry, but I'm too tired."

He pulled off his boots and dirty clothes and let them lay where they fell. He'd deal with them later when he didn't feel like he might fall over. Snagging the towel he'd hung on the back of the door, he wrapped it around his waist before grabbing a change of clothes and heading for the shower down the hall. Tired as he was he didn't want to hit the sheets without cleaning up first.

He and Zeke had responded to Malachi's summons expecting to deal with a routine—if surprising—instance of containment after a demon had gotten carried away and used his powers in front of a group of humans. What they'd found had been much worse and not so easily taken care of. A pair of Wraiths had appeared at a suburban mall in broad daylight and decided to treat the patrons as items on a smorgasbord.

Confining the Wraiths in a glamoured and warded holding area until they could be transported back to their domain, where they were free of the frenzy brought on by the scent of human blood and the hunger for human souls, hadn't taken long. But healing the wounded and tracking down all the witnesses so their memories could be altered had taken hours.

Then, when they'd returned their two captives to the Dark world the Wraiths called home, they discovered that the wards that kept the soul-suckers locked away from the human realm had deteriorated so much as to be ineffective. Several more of the creatures had escaped while they dealt with the mess created by the two they'd captured. They'd alerted Lucifer and left him and his colleagues to repair the damage, while they rounded up some more of the Forces to scout out the rest of the escapees and help with damage control.

By the time all the creatures had been captured and re-stored to their particular Hell realm, more than twenty-four hours had passed, and Aidan, Zeke, Malachi, and their companions were blood-stained and bone-weary—not to mention reeking of Wraith. But somehow they had managed to locate all the witnesses and adjust their memories of the event, and to heal most of the wounded. Most. Aidan wished they'd been able to save them all, but a couple of the victims had been beyond healing when the Fallen had reached them. Both times he'd made an anonymous 911 call to bring an ambulance to the scene. The deaths would be attributed to some medical condition, and no human would realize the victims had died as a result of a Wraith attack.

*And to think Josh could have become one of those things,* Aidan thought now, as he let the hot shower wash the blood from his skin and the smell of demon from his hair.

The thought of Josh reminded Aidan of Lucky's other cousin, who lay recovering in a room down the hall. He supposed he should check on her before he climbed between the sheets. He didn't have the energy for an argument, but he also didn't want to shirk his responsibilities.

He toweled dry, pulled on the clean clothes, and prepared to beard the lioness in her den.

"There's something I need to discuss with you," Branwen said as soon as he walked through her door.

*Perfect,* he thought, falling into the chair beside her bed. Why hadn't he crashed when he finished showering? He craved the softness of a pillow beneath his head. He didn't think even Harley yanking on the covers could keep him awake. But, no, he'd decided to check on his ill-tempered patient before falling into bed. The more fool he.

"And what would that be?" he asked.

Branwen pointed at the white streak in her hair. "I finally looked at myself in a mirror today. Katrin says I have you to thank for this."

"Yeah," Aidan said. He probably should apologize, but he wasn't in the mood. "You also have me to thank for the fact that your neurons are working properly and your mind isn't messed up. The hair was—an unexpected casualty."

"You don't have to get all huffy about it," Branwen said.

Aidan snorted as he stood up. Time for bed. There was no way he could win this.

Her voice stopped him before he reached the door. "I actually kind of like it."

He didn't reply, but he felt his lips curve into a reluctant smile as he left the room.

Kev had just stretched out on the couch when his phone rang. He snatched the cell off the coffee table, hoping the ring hadn't wakened Lucky. After she had gone to bed a few hours before, he had headed out to the studio to work on the sculpture. The stones he had gotten at the gem shop were perfect, but it had taken him a while to get them positioned right. Once he'd managed it, he'd decided to hit the couch. A few more touches and he'd finish the piece, but he couldn't do it tonight. At three-quarters Seraph, he required less sleep than a human or even most Naphil, but two sleepless nights in a row had left him wiped.

"Yeah?" he said.

"Kevin," Zeke's voice resonated in his ear. "My apologies for taking so long to get back to you. I was—otherwise engaged."

"I heard. I ended up calling Katrin when I couldn't reach either you or Aidan."

"What did she tell you?" Zeke asked.

"That Malachi had summoned you and Aidan to deal with something demon-related. And she let me know that Bryn seems to be recovering well. She also said she couldn't have cured her without Aidan's help. She seemed very—

proud of him." The words caught in his throat, and Kev hated himself for it.

"Have you heard from your father?"

Kev sat up. Something in Zeke's tone made him sure he needed to be fully awake for this. "No. Should I have?"

"Not necessarily. I just wondered if he had told you."

"Told me what?"

"The warded barrier to the Wraith's realm was breached. Over a dozen of them ported into the earthly realm. That's what Aidan, Malachi, and I, along with several other members of the Forces, have been dealing with."

"Human casualties?"

"Two. We healed the rest, but those two were too far gone when we reached them. They died soon after."

"My condolences," Kev said. He knew every loss was personal to Zeke. "I assume the breach has been repaired."

"Yes. Lucifer, Ba'al-zebul, and a couple of others took care of it."

"Any idea what caused it?"

"None. Lucifer said everything seemed normal when they checked the barrier yesterday morning. Yet the first two escaped yesterday afternoon."

"At least the barrier is working again."

"Yes. For now. I would like to believe this event was an anomaly, but something tells me it is not. I can hardly wait to see what happens next."

Kev had never heard the angel sound so tired and cynical.

"You need to get some rest, Zeke. I know you don't sleep, but do something to recharge, okay?"

"I will, Kevin, thank you. But, first, tell me what you need with Uriel."

Kev shared his theory about the forged sigil mark. Then, without going into too many details about his and Lucky's encounter with the pony-tailed Dominion, he explained that he'd already spoken to Uriel and that the Archangel had agreed to grant him access to the Book.

"When?" Zeke asked.

"I don't know. But he said he'd make it happen."

"Keep me informed."

"Will do. And you'll do the same?"

"Of course."

Kev put the phone back on the coffee table and rested his head in his hands. He hoped nothing would happen that Zeke would need to inform him about, but the way things were going, he feared the odds weren't in his favor.

Lucky jerked awake, unsure of what had awakened her. Then she heard Kev cry out—again. She couldn't understand what he said, but it sounded like he was having a nightmare. She lay unmoving for several seconds, debating the wisdom of trying to wake him. Maybe she should let the nightmare run its course. She didn't want to risk a repeat of last night— or make him think she hoped for one. Even if her pulse did pick up at the thought.

Then she heard a crash—and she was out of bed, out the door, and down the stairs, all thoughts scattered.

She'd flipped on the light at the top of stairs, and when she reached the bottom, she could see Kev crouching beside the overturned coffee table. Its contents, including the fragments of a couple of broken mugs, littered the floor.

Kev's head was lowered, and he emitted a noise somewhere between a growl and a hiss. Lucky could see his back rise and fall with his breath.

"Kev?"

He lifted his head by degrees, and the eyes that met hers were the vertical-pupiled eyes of the dragon. She had seen those eyes in Kev's face before, when he'd stepped forward to Mark her at her Making. But then, even though the dragon had been present, Kev had been in the lead. She had recognized him behind those dragon eyes.

This was different. The presence looking at her through those eyes wasn't Kev. It was the dragon whose mind she had touched that afternoon—and it had slipped Kev's rein.

A shudder shook Kev's body, and Lucky realized he was on the verge of shifting. Her heart beat faster and her stomach knotted. If he shifted to dragon form with the dragon in charge, who knew what damage he'd do. His size alone could destroy the cabin.

Holding the dragon's eyes with her own, she lowered to her knees and inched toward him.

"Hey," she crooned. "You remember me. We said hello this afternoon."

He cocked his head to study her, and a shiver ran up Lucky's spine. He looked like Kev—except for those eyes—but he moved like a beast.

She reached a hand toward him, stopping the motion in midair when he hissed and drew back.

"It's okay," she breathed, holding out her hand for his inspection. "I won't hurt you."

His eyes never leaving hers, he leaned closer to her hand and sniffed, nostrils flaring.

Lucky swallowed.

He sniffed her hand again, and a spark of recognition lit those uncanny eyes. This time when Lucky moved her hand toward him, he didn't pull away.

"See? You know me," she whispered.

She placed her hand on his head—as she had when she had called her Makers—and he pushed his head into her palm, like Shu or Tef when they wanted to be petted. She swallowed again. Okay, this was a little weird.

She ran her hand over Kev's hair, noting once again its silky texture beneath her fingers. He no longer growled or hissed, and his eyelids were half lowered.

"That's good," Lucky said, continuing to stroke his hair, "I need you to let Kev come back, okay? Can you do that? It's all right. Everything's okay."

Gradually the beast's eyes changed, vertical pupils becoming round, irises shifting from yellow-gold to gold-flecked dark green. Then Kev looked out at her from his own eyes.

As recognition dawned, he pulled away from her hand. Blowing out a breath, he dropped from his crouch to a seat.

Lucky too relaxed, settling onto the floor beside him.

"You okay?" she asked.

Kev shook his head. "I'm not sure."

Lucky leaned back against the couch and regarded him in silence.

Kev scrubbed a hand over his face and then turned to look at her. "That hasn't happened in a very long time."

"Want to tell me about it?"

"It was a nightmare. One I used to have a lot. The fear and anger pushed me over the edge, and the dragon took over. It was like I was watching from the sidelines. I couldn't control anything."

"How was this different from this afternoon? You said you didn't summon the dragon then, that he just appeared."

"This afternoon, he didn't shove me aside. I know it's hard to understand. Most of the time, I'm me, but I always know the dragon's there. He's a constant presence in the back of my mind, seeing what I see, experiencing what I experience. I feel him there, and parts of our minds overlap, so we each enhance the other's senses. But I'm in the driver's seat—meaning I summon him. This afternoon, he came without a summons, but he didn't take control. When I—we—shift into the dragon's body, his mind is the primary perceiver, but I still make the decisions. We work as a team. When—we—are in this body"—he gestured toward his torso—"I'm both the primary perceiver and the driver. Tonight, he pushed me out of the driver's seat."

"Why didn't that cause you to shift forms?"

Kev shook his head. "I don't know why we—he—didn't shift right away. But he would have if you hadn't calmed him down. *I* couldn't have stopped him."

"Do you think what happened tonight is related to what happened this afternoon?"

"Maybe. I don't know."

"Was it because of me?" Lucky asked. Her hand gripped Kev's arm. "Did I cause this?"

Kev's hand moved to cover hers. "I don't know. It's possible. But it may have been due to something else entirely. Don't blame yourself. I certainly don't. Besides," he added with a smile, "you talked him down. If you hadn't been here, we'd have probably burned the house down."

Lucky's lips curled upward at his words, but they didn't set her mind at ease. She feared her afternoon's encounter with the dragon had somehow altered the balance between him and Kev.

# CHAPTER 16

The leggings were too short and the t-shirt was too big, but Bryn didn't care. She was grateful to be out of bed and wearing something that wasn't a hospital-style gown or pajamas. Her leather pants, velvet shirt, and boots had been cleaned and placed in the closet of her room. But they were hardly appropriate for a workout—and Bryn had every intention of getting some exercise. She hadn't even had to argue with her healer about it. When Katrin had come to check on her, Bryn had said she wanted to get up and moving. To her surprise, Katrin had agreed and recruited Aidan to find Bryn some workout clothes and escort her to the gym. Aidan had even found her a pair of athletic shoes.

She was tightening the laces of the shoes when she heard a knock on the door. She opened it to find Aidan waiting in the hall, wearing sweat shorts and a t-shirt.

"I thought I'd get a workout in too, while we're at it," he said. "If you don't mind."

Bryn shook her head. "Not at all." She gestured at the clothes she wore. "Thanks for these."

"No problem. The t-shirt's an old one of mine. I found the leggings in Lucky's room."

At the mention of Lucky's name, Bryn wondered again what kind of relationship Lucky had with the blue-eyed Naphil—and his brother, with whom it seemed she was staying.

"Have you heard any more from her?" she asked.

"Not directly. Zeke's talked to Kev though, and he says she's okay. The gym's this way."

As she followed Aidan through the main floor, Bryn registered impressions of an unused-looking formal living room and a large, comfortable dining area. Then Aidan directed her down another set of stairs to the house's lower level.

When they reached the bottom of the stairs, Aidan led her to the end of the hallway, where he pushed aside a tapestry and pressed his palm against a security panel. At his touch, a door swung open, and they walked into an expansive and well-equipped gym.

"You're welcome to use whatever you like," Aidan said, tossing her a towel from a stack near the door. "But take it easy at first. Let me know if you need help with any of the equipment."

"I will. Thanks."

"Do you mind if I turn on some music?"

"Not as long as it's good music."

The grin Aidan tossed her held more than a hint of mischief.

As the music filled the room, Bryn looked around wondering where to start. She opted for the treadmill for a warm-up. A light run would get her blood moving. Then she'd hit the weights and, before she finished, she would have a go at the punching bag. She'd had plenty of time to reflect on Lilith's years-long deception about her being Bound, and the idea of hitting something as hard as she could held enormous appeal.

Even the treadmill wasn't loud enough to drown out the music Aidan had started. As she warmed up, her movements fell into pace with the beat. Given the way he'd grinned, she assumed he'd thought she wouldn't like his musical choice, but she did. She couldn't make out the words, but the rhythm made her want to make her body move and her heart pump.

After twenty minutes on the treadmill, she moved to the free weights. Aidan worked the bench press nearby, but he didn't speak as she chose her weights. He seemed focused on his own workout—or absorbed in his own thoughts.

Upper and lower body weight training complete, Bryn headed toward the punching bag. She had hit it twice, sending the bag flying away to rebound back, when Aidan appeared beside her. He grabbed the swaying bag and positioned himself on the far side from her.

"I got this. Beat it up as much as you want."

Bryn did. By the time she finished punching and kicking the bag, she was breathing hard and covered with sweat. Aidan held it steady for her the whole time.

"Return the favor?" he asked, when she stopped to catch her breath and grab a drink.

She nodded and latched on to the bag.

Aidan evidently had some aggression of his own to release. Bryn got an additional workout holding the bag still against the onslaught of his punches.

When he kicked the bag, he lifted her off the floor.

"Whoa!" she laughed as she found her feet. "Take it easy, angel-boy."

In response, Aidan gave the bag another kick that took her airborne.

Bryn rode the bag for a couple of swings before she dropped to the floor.

"Feel better now?" she asked.

"Yeah. You?"

"Yeah."

"Were you swinging at anyone in particular?"

"My grandmother. I can't believe she's lied to me for as long as I can remember. I thought I could only leave that place for a few hours at a time. I thought I was stuck there for life."

"Now that you know you can come and go as you please, will you go back?"

Bryn sighed. "I'll have to sometime. It's home. And I have friends there. I'd like to get to know this world better though. See what it's like when I'm not an invalid."

"You don't seem to be an invalid anymore. At least you don't punch like one." Aidan grinned.

"Yeah, well, you'd know about punching, wouldn't you? Who were *you* beating up on?"

"The Wraiths. Sambethe." Aidan hesitated before adding more quietly. "My brother."

Bryn's gaze lasered in on his. "Your brother?"

"Yeah." Aidan looked away. "He's off who-knows-where with Lucky, and the only information I get is through Zeke."

"You love her."

Aidan stilled. This time his eyes caught hers. "I guess. Maybe. I don't know. I miss her. We were—dating."

Bryn had suspected as much. Alicia had told her Lucky had mentioned a boyfriend, and Aidan had seemed the obvious choice. But Lucky wasn't talking to him, and she'd disappeared with his brother. Yeah, that had to hurt.

Zeke burst into the gym, saving Bryn from a response.

"Aidan, get geared up. Wraiths have appeared at the River East multiplex. Ben is there now, but he could use some help. Malachi and Gareth are on their way as well."

"Ben's there?" Aidan asked, as he followed Zeke to a large closet at the back of the gym, where they both began donning protective gear and weapon sheaths.

"He and Josh had gone to a movie. He is doing what he can, but he is somewhat outnumbered."

By the time Zeke finished speaking, both he and Aidan were fully outfitted.

Then Zeke stepped inside the closet, and a section of the back wall slid away to reveal an extensive cache of weapons. Bryn gasped.

"I can help," she offered. "Let me come with you."

Aidan and Zeke had already made their selections, and Zeke re-entered the closet to activate the mechanism that slid the wall back into place.

"That is out of the question," he said, closing the closet door. "This is your first day out of bed after your injury, and you are"—his gaze raked over the mark on her throat—"an unknown quantity. I will not endanger you, the members of the Forces, or the humans we strive to protect by putting you into battle when I have no way of knowing how you will react. If you will excuse us."

He grasped Aidan's left shoulder with his right hand as Aidan did the same to him, and then they were gone.

After materializing into the chaos of the concessions area of the River East, Aidan scanned the room. Popcorn, soda, and their respective containers littered the floor where prospective moviegoers had dropped and then trampled them as they ran from the red-eyed, gaunt-featured Wraiths that poured out of a tear in space near the side wall and roughly halfway between the escalators and the concession stand.

He spotted Ben, who was fighting three of the creatures, at the same time as Malachi, Gareth, and two other members of the Forces materialized nearby.

A couple of feet from Aidan, a Wraith grabbed hold of the long hair of a young girl and dragged her, screaming, toward his gaping, sharp-toothed mouth. Pulling a dagger from one of the sheaths strapped to his thigh, Aidan drove it into the creature's arm. The Wraith let go of the girl and turned to confront him, red eyes blazing. Aidan yanked the dagger free, and blood spurted from the Wraith's arm. The creature growled and grabbed the front of Aidan's jacket. Pulling him close, he licked the side of Aidan's neck. Aidan drove the dagger into the Wraith's chest. The hand loosened from his jacket, and the creature dropped to the floor.

As he watched the life fade from the Wraith's red eyes, behind him Aidan could hear Zeke's resonant voice speaking the spells to create the necessary containment wards. Their goal was not to kill the Wraiths, but to capture them and return them to their own world. Well, add one to the list of those for whom capture was no longer an option.

Banishing the twinge of regret, Aidan dived into the tangle of Wraiths and screaming humans. He inserted himself between two Wraiths and the family they pursued. Grabbing one Wraith by the shirtfront, he spun him into the other. Then, before they could recover their equilibrium, he used a series of blows and kicks to maneuver them the short distance to the translucent silver lines that marked Zeke's containment zone. Once even a part of their bodies crossed into the area, they would be unable to escape.

No sooner had both Wraiths stumbled over the silvery threshold, than a strong, bony arm wrapped around Aidan's throat, dragging him backward. Locking one hand onto the arm, he yanked it away from his neck while twisting his body in the opposite direction. As he turned to face the Wraith, a female this time, she sank her teeth into his left shoulder. Though the thick leather of his jacket blunted the impact, her sharp teeth still broke the skin. He grabbed her by the throat and pushed her away. His shoulder had already begun to sting and burn. He hadn't experienced a Wraith bite in a while—and he hadn't missed the sensation one bit. The venom would cause him no lasting ill effects, but for the next few hours his shoulder would feel like it had been attacked by a whole nest of wasps.

The female's eyes took on a neon glow. That meant she'd gotten enough of his blood to enable her to latch on to his soul if he was careless enough to let her lock those glowing eyes on his. He might be only half human, but even a quarter was enough to make him potential Wraith food.

Biting back a curse, he spun them around and pushed her backward toward the containment area. Zeke saw her coming and pulled her the last few inches into the zone, before picking up another Wraith and flinging him in behind her.

Aidan spun back around, surveying the situation. Several containment areas now held a number of Wraiths, but far more of the creatures remained out than in. At least it looked like someone had managed to close the portal. The hole from which the Wraiths had been pouring when he and Zeke had arrived was gone.

Now they had to deal with the hundred or so creatures that still filled the room.

They had fought the Wraiths for what seemed like hours, and Aidan's shoulder felt like hundreds of bees had used it to park their stingers. But less than a dozen of the Wraiths remained—and from the looks of things, human casualties had been minimal.

Aidan's eyes landed on a Wraith kneeling over a screaming teenage girl he had pinned to the floor with his knees. The creature held the girl's bleeding arm to his mouth with one hand, while the other held her head in place. That neon glow began to emanate from the Wraith's eyes even as Aidan ran toward the pair.

Before he could reach them, a figure detached itself from a group of humans clustered beside the concession counter and dragged the Wraith off the screaming girl. The man flung the creature back and dropped into a crouch.

Aidan felt a shock of recognition. Josh.

Josh stared at the Wraith through blazing red eyes, his lips curled back as he let out a hiss.

"What the—?" Aidan muttered.

The Wraith leapt at Josh, and before Aidan could offer to help, Josh had caught the creature in one arm and twisted its neck with the other.

"Josh?"

Aidan moved into a defensive posture. Lucky's cousin seemed to be on their side, but with his glowing red eyes and Wraithy hiss, he wasn't quite himself. Best to be on guard.

Josh turned toward him with a snarl, but recognition dawned in those uncanny red eyes.

"I couldn't let him hurt her," Josh said, his voice deeper and gruffer than normal.

"Are you okay?" Aidan asked.

"I don't know. I was helping get people to safety, and one of the Wraiths bit me. It hurt—a lot—and things were a blur for awhile. But when I saw that thing kneeling over that poor girl, my vision went red and hazy. I knew I had to get him away from her." Josh looked down at his now trembling hands. "I think I—killed him."

When he looked back up at Aidan, the red had faded from his eyes, leaving them their normal warm brown.

"Yeah, you did."

Aidan scanned the room. While he'd been preoccupied with Josh, it looked like the rest of his team had rounded up the remaining Wraiths. "Hold on for a minute, and I'll get you back to Zeke's so Katrin can take a look at you, okay?"

"Yeah. Okay."

In moments, Aidan had alerted Zeke and Ben and returned to Josh's side.

Josh's body was shaking. He had curled in upon himself, as if trying to contain the energy moving through him.

Aidan crouched beside him and wrapped an arm around Josh's shoulders. With his other hand, he covered the hands Josh had clasped at his knees. "I'm going to get you out of here, okay? I need you to do your best to concentrate on where I'm touching you, to stay connected to me. Can you do that?"

Josh nodded, his head jerking against Aidan's shoulder.

"Okay. You hang on. I've got you."

Aidan tightened his grip on the trembling young man, and then dematerialized them both.

# CHAPTER 17

Kev's heart pounded as he unlocked the door to his studio. When he and Lucky had finished their afternoon training session, Lucky had asked to see it again, and he could find no reasonable excuse to keep her out of it. At least his latest piece was hidden under a sheet. It was almost complete, except for the patina. Still, he wasn't ready to show it to her. He didn't know if he ever would be.

"Wow," Lucky breathed as she surveyed the room and its contents. "You made all of these?"

"Yeah." Kev did his best to suppress the thrill that shot through him at the admiration in her face and voice.

She stepped up to one of the closest finished pieces, a large sculpture with simple sweeping lines enclosing a finial pendulum. She reached a hand toward the piece, then stopped and turned to look at him. "May I?"

Kev nodded. "Go ahead. They're all touchable."

Lucky wandered through the room, pausing in front of some of the sculptures to study them or run her fingers over a piece. Kev followed her, inserting the occasional comment about his inspiration for a design or where he'd found the objects to create it.

"You found all these metal pieces and parts and turned them into art? That must have taken years."

"It did. Papa taught me to weld when I was young, about the time the dragon showed up. He knew I was having a hard time, and he thought learning the skill—and the art—would give me a focal point. My world outside Nana's and Papa's home was all about being Lucifer's son and training to take on a leadership role with the Fallen. But when I was with my grandfather, I was just a boy, learning at his hands. He taught me how to look at a piece of scrap metal and see its potential, how to combine shapes, textures, and lines to create beauty or convey emotion. What he taught me, this work, it helped me survive until I could control the dragon."

"Do you still have some of your early pieces?"

"Yeah. They're over here."

Kev led Lucky to the back of the room and a grouping of his first sculptures. Most of the pieces were anywhere from one to two feet in height, with one that stood roughly four feet tall. He picked up the oldest piece, the first one he'd ever done. It was simple, a rusty double-bladed axe head welded to three curving, pointed pieces of steel that had made him think of flames. The welds were clunky and uneven, the work that of a novice, but he could still remember the desperation that had fired him when he had begun the piece—as well as the flare of satisfaction he'd felt when he held the finished product and the pride he'd seen in his grandfather's eyes when he'd flipped up his welder's mask.

"Good work, son," Papa had said, "good work."

Kev handed the sculpture to Lucky. "This was my first."

She took the piece from him, holding it in one hand and running the forefinger of the other over the curves of the flames. She studied it in silence, before setting it back in its place and picking up the piece sitting next to it. Kev's anxiety had faded away. He liked watching Lucky examine the sculptures, liked the way she held and touched them as if, instead of rusted metal, they were something precious. He had never shared these pieces with anyone but his grandfather. But somehow it seemed right to share them with her.

Kev refused to examine that feeling of rightness too closely.

As she studied the sculpture in her hand, Lucky felt her heart swell for the young man standing next to her—and the boy he had been when he created it. The sculpture was formed of two crescent-moon-shaped pieces of metal mounted on a round base. The points of the moons came together to create a rough circle with a lens shaped opening in the middle. Suspended in the opening by wires attached to the inner curves of the crescent moons was a small flame-like shape colored red and gold.

"It's your Gift. The dragon's eye and the Fire."

Kev nodded.

Lucky examined the remaining pieces one by one. Images of flames and vertical-pupiled eyes repeated. All of the pieces witnessed the young Kev's struggle with his dragon.

When she reached the tallest sculpture, she almost stopped breathing. The piece was black and gray, charred-looking, and shaped like a warped basketball hoop. Glued to its base was a boy's action figure, its limbs twisted, blackened, and melted.

"Oh, Kev," she whispered.

She stared at the sculpture with tears in her eyes and an ache in her chest. The pain that had fueled the piece was palpable—and all too familiar. The solitary action figure tore at her heart. It represented more than the boys Kev's dragon had burned. It stood for Kev himself—broken by his own Dark Gift. And alone. So alone.

She knew that feeling too, as she knew the grown Kev carried it as deeply as had the eleven-year-old boy.

She couldn't bear for him to feel so alone.

She turned and flung her arms around him. Pressing herself against him, she held him as tightly as she could.

Kev remained motionless for several seconds, but Lucky refused to let him go. She wouldn't allow him to push her away. Finally, his arms closed around her, and he whispered her name into her hair.

He didn't resist when she pulled his head down to press her lips to his. He tightened his embrace and kissed her back.

Her heartbeat accelerating, Lucky threaded her fingers through his hair. She shivered as the silky strands brushed her neck when Kev moved his mouth from hers to nuzzle under her ear.

Then she gasped as an undeniable need to see Zeke filled her mind, eclipsing all else.

"Zeke's." Kev's urgent whisper indicated he'd gotten the same signal.

"Now," she said.

He gave a quick nod. Worried eyes locked on one another, they dematerialized.

Lucky and Kev still held each other when they rematerialized in Zeke's basement study. Kev's hands rested low on her back, and Lucky's fingers tangled in his hair.

Blushing furiously, she stepped away from him, aware of the shocked stares of the room's other occupants.

"I hope my summons didn't come at an inopportune time," Zeke said.

Lucky couldn't meet Aidan's eyes, though she could feel the intensity of his gaze boring into her.

"While you were—otherwise occupied," he bit out, "we've been risking our lives fighting Wraiths—and trying to keep your cousin from turning into one again."

"Aidan," Zeke barked in warning, as Lucky gasped.

"Josh?" she said, her eyes homing in on Aidan's, her embarrassment a paltry consideration beside her concern for her cousin. "What happened? Why is he turning into a Wraith again? Does he need more of my blood? Where is he?"

"We are not sure what is happening to him, Lucky," Zeke said. "The Wraiths attacked at a downtown multiplex—where Josh and Ben had gone to see a movie. Josh—changed—during the attack. A Wraith bit him, and the bite seems to have triggered some residual toxin in his blood, but we cannot say for sure. He is upstairs in your room, with Katrin. She will be able to give you a more up-to-date report."

Lucky barely registered Kev's fingers closing around hers before she ran for the door.

"The Wraiths attacked a multiplex?"

Kev's question drew Aidan's attention from the empty door through which Lucky had departed. His jaw clenched as he glanced at his brother.

"I have been in touch with the other Fallen leaders. This was one of several attacks around the world," Zeke said.

"How many Wraiths?" Kev asked.

"Swarms," Aidan said, dropping into one of the leather chairs. "I'll try not to get your chair too dirty, Zeke, but I don't think I can stand anymore."

In fact, he felt as if the ground had dropped out from under him. When Lucky and Kev had materialized all wrapped around each other, the pain in his chest had nearly knocked him over. He almost preferred fighting the Wraiths. At least then he knew to be on his guard against getting hurt.

"The Wraiths couldn't have done this on their own," Kev said. "Someone else must have orchestrated it."

"That's pretty obvious," Aidan muttered.

Kev shot him a look, but Aidan turned away.

"Whoever did it had a direct portal into Wraithland," Ben said. "They just kept coming."

"Lucifer said thirty percent of the Wraiths escaped their realm," Zeke added. "We dealt with a few hundred of them."

"A few hundred?" Kev asked.

"Yeah," Aidan said, "some of us have had work to do."

Zeke sighed. "And we could all do with showers, clean clothes, and some food. Why don't we table this conversation until later, when Malachi can join us? Food and drink will be available in the dining room in an hour. We will take this up again then."

Aidan rose to follow Ben and Zeke out of the room, but Kev stopped him before he had taken more than a few steps.

"Look, Aidan, I know you're pissed at me, and I understand. You have every right to be."

"I have every right?" Aidan chuckled bitterly. "Thanks. That makes it all so much better."

"I didn't intend this to happen—"

"Really? It looked pretty intentional from my angle. I doubt anyone forced you to put your hands where they were, and I'd bet Lucky didn't get hers tangled in your hair all accidental-like."

"Aidan—"

"I can't listen to you right now." Aidan moved toward the door. His back to Kev, he added, "I can't even look at you."

Lucky stopped outside the open door to her room and tried to compose herself. She went to wipe her eyes with her sleeve and realized she still had on the coat she had worn to Kev's studio. She stripped it off, dropped it on the floor, and wiped her eyes on her sweater sleeve. Then she took a deep, shaky breath and stepped into the room.

Josh was sitting up in the bed, propped against a stack of pillows. Despite the various instruments strapped to him, he looked fine.

"Josh?" Lucky said.

He turned his head toward her, and Lucky sucked in a breath. His normally brown eyes were the Wraith-red they had been after Sambethe had given him the toxin. She glanced from his eyes to the straps looped around his arms and chest and legs, binding him to the bed.

"Lucky," he said, "you're back. Zeke said he was going to summon you, but I didn't expect you'd be here so soon."

"Josh?" Lucky asked again. He stared at her with those frightening red eyes, but he sounded like himself. "You— sound normal..." Her voice trailed off.

"His vital signs are good at the moment, if odd."

The remark drew Lucky's attention to the woman who monitored the various instruments attached to Josh. She wore a long skirt and a long, belted cardigan. Her dark hair was drawn back into a severe bun. One hand gripped a cane.

"Odd?" Lucky asked.

When the woman turned toward her, Lucky had the disconcerting experience of seeing Kev's eyes in the woman's face. They lacked the gold flecks that made Kev's look like they contained little pockets of sunlight. Otherwise, they were the same: the same shape, the same dark green, fringed by the same dark lashes.

"You're Katrin?" Lucky asked.

The woman nodded. "And you are Lucky," she stated.

"Yes. You said his vital signs are odd?" Lucky prompted.

"His heartbeat is faster than normal for a human, and his blood pressure is high. But he has stabilized again—for now."

She swabbed the inside of Josh's arm where it bent at the elbow before inserting a needle into his vein. She pulled back the plunger, and Lucky watched the syringe fill with the deep red of her cousin's blood.

"For now?" she asked.

"He has been experiencing bouts of intense muscle spasms when all his vitals spike off the charts. The spasms are followed by chills and trembling, during which his heart rate and blood pressure plummet. Then he stabilizes for a time."

Lucky swallowed. "What's happening to him?"

"I'm changing," Josh said. As he spoke, Lucky watched the red fade from his eyes. "We don't know what I'm turning into, but I'm changing."

Lucky looked to Katrin for confirmation.

She replied without glancing up from the bandage she pressed against Josh's arm. "The spasms are caused by changes at a deep cellular level. The chills and trembling are a reaction to the body's assimilation of those changes." She held up the blood-filled syringe. "Once I analyze this, I'll have a better idea of what those changes mean."

Leaning on her cane, Katrin moved to the far corner of the room, where a makeshift lab had been erected. Lucky watched the healer place a drop of blood from the syringe on a slide, then she turned her attention back to her cousin.

Sitting on the edge of the bed, she rested tentative fingers on the back of his hand. "How do you feel?"

Josh shrugged. "Right now, I feel okay. When the spasms hit—well, they feel sort of like a full-body charley horse, so…"

For the first time, Lucky could see the fear in his brown eyes. She squeezed his hand, and his fingers closed on hers.

"At least, they don't last long," he said, offering her a lop-sided smile.

"Does he need more of my blood?" she asked, twisting her head toward Katrin and her makeshift lab. "Will that stop the changes?"

"It's too late to stop the changes," Katrin said, her voice both preoccupied and matter-of-fact, as if the statement wouldn't shake the foundations of Lucky's world.

Lucky leapt up from the bed. "But we can't let him turn into a Wraith. I became Naphil to save him. I won't let that happen!"

"Lucky, it's okay." Josh's hand tightened on hers, at the same moment Katrin looked up from her work to give Lucky her full attention.

"Your cousin will not turn into a Wraith," she said. "I thought we had established that. But he is no longer human either. The venom from the Wraith bite seems to have triggered some mutation caused by the combined effects of the residual Wraith toxin and your—hybrid—blood. When the spasms first hit, I feared the worst, but, based on what I've seen here"—she gestured at the instruments attached to Josh and the temporary lab area—"I no longer believe he is in any real danger. But I want to monitor him throughout the transformation process to be sure."

As she finished speaking, Katrin turned back to her blood work, as if her attention had already been diverted for too long.

Lucky turned wide eyes to Josh. "My blood is part of what caused this to happen to you?" she whispered.

"Hey." He squeezed her hand. "You saved me. You kept me from dying and turning into a Wraith. *This*—is something else." His lips twisted into a semblance of a smile. "I guess we can think of it as a sort of impromptu Making."

Lucky choked back a sob. "How can you be taking this all so well?"

Josh gave a humorless chuckle. "I killed a Wraith tonight. Then I thought I would die myself. And then I thought, instead of dying, I would become the thing I killed. Trust me, not being human anymore, but being otherwise okay, seems a much better alternative."

Lucky reached to hug him, but Josh shoved her away. His back arched, and the feral red invaded his eyes.

"Get back," he growled. "You don't want to be near me for this."

"In fact, you should leave now," Katrin said, moving toward the bed as quickly as her limp would allow. "You won't want to see him in pain, and you will be in my way." She waved toward the door. "Please, let yourself out."

With one last look at Josh's body arching and straining against the bonds that held him to the bed, Lucky complied.

# CHAPTER 18

The meal was strained to say the least. Everyone ate—or pretended to eat—in silence. Zeke and Malachi's attempts to renew the discussion of the Wraith attack had met with as much success as Kev's own efforts to get Aidan to glance in his direction.

Kev's gaze shifted to his brother again. He could almost see the waves of tension radiating out from Aidan's body as he lifted his fork, chewed, swallowed, and then washed the food down with a long drink from the glass of beer near his plate.

Kev knew Aidan sensed his stare, but his brother's eyes never wavered from the food and drink in front of him. Either he refused to acknowledge Kev's attention in order to hurt or anger him, or—and Kev swallowed back a curse at the thought—Aidan really couldn't bear to look at him, just as he'd said.

This was exactly what he'd hoped to avoid. Exactly why he had tried to push Lucky away. Exactly why he hated himself for giving in to his feelings and pulling her close instead.

Kev picked up his own beer and drained the glass.

Bryn, who sat across from Aidan, kept casting furtive glances at both Aidan and Kev. Even though she hadn't been in the study when he and Lucky had arrived, she must have heard something. Or perhaps she simply wondered what had caused the friction between them.

Ben, the final member of their awkward little party, sat across from Kev. He went through the motions of eating, like a man who knew his body needed fuel and would do his duty by it, but who found no pleasure in the act.

Kev knew the feeling.

He was about to excuse himself from the tension-laden table when Lucky entered the room. She sat down in the empty chair beside him, and he noticed the muscles in Aidan's jaw clench.

"How is he?" Ben asked, the prospect of information about Josh's condition transforming him from robot to flesh-and-blood in an instant.

"He's having another spasm now." Lucky swallowed a sob. "Katrin seems to think he'll be all right once the transformation is complete. We just don't know—*what* he'll be."

Ben shoved back his chair and tossed his napkin on the table. "I'm going up there. I should be with him."

"Katrin might not let you stay," Lucky said. "She asked me to leave."

"Let her kick me out then," Ben said as he strode from the room, his tone leaving no doubt as to his belief about the odds of her being able to do so.

Ben's departure left the atmosphere even more electric with tension than before. The light clinks of serving utensils against dishes as Lucky put food on her plate seemed as loud as gunshots in the awkward silence.

When she asked Kev, in little more than a whisper, to pass the rolls, Aidan exploded from his chair and stormed out of the room, as if, Kev thought, the sound of his name on her lips was more than Aidan could bear.

Lucky closed her eyes, forcing back the tears that threatened with stinging intensity. This was all her fault. She should never have come back—and certainly not in Kev's arms. She should never have kissed him. She should never have left in the first place. Dear God, how would she ever make things right? She didn't know how to begin. She didn't even know what *right* would be.

When she felt sure tears wouldn't stream down her face, she opened her eyes and blinked down at the food on her plate. She had no desire to eat any of it now.

Zeke cleared his throat. "Katrin believes your cousin is out of danger then?" he asked.

"Yes," Lucky said. She lifted the offending roll from her plate and broke it in two pieces. She tried to keep her hand from trembling as she spread butter on both halves of the roll. "She said his vital signs are good, but they're not— human anymore."

"And how did he seem to you?"

The cloud-like softness of Zeke's voice prompted more prickling behind her eyes.

"He seemed okay, considering. He joked about this being his own version of a Making."

"If Katrin says he'll be okay, he will be," Kev said. "She doesn't sugar-coat anything."

He was close enough to touch, but Lucky couldn't bring herself to look at him. She had known that hurting his brother was the last thing he'd wanted to do, but she had refused to take no for an answer. Now Aidan acted like he couldn't bear the sight of either one of them.

And somehow Kev could still be kind to her.

"Yeah, I got that impression," she said into her plate.

Kev swore under his breath and shoved back his chair. Then, like his brother, he left the room.

Lucky lost all pretense of even trying to eat. "I'm going home," she said, her voice thick with tears. "I'll be back later to check on Josh."

Bryn remained in the dining room for only a few moments after Lucky left. She had eaten all she wanted, and she had no desire to interfere with Zeke and Malachi's conversation. Besides, she had a feeling Aidan might need a friend, and she had a pretty good idea of where he might be.

In her room, she changed into workout clothes. Then she made her way back down the stairs to the gym. Finding the door ajar, she stepped inside.

Aidan was running on one of the treadmills, the track spinning so fast she was surprised it wasn't smoking.

Bryn grabbed a towel and, after a quick warm-up, started a circuit on the weight machines. When she had repeated the circuit, she stepped on the treadmill next to Aidan's. Adjusting the track to a speed several times slower than his flat-out sprint, she jogged for a few minutes before speeding up to a run. Even then, she still moved at about half Aidan's pace.

She cast a few sidelong glances at him, but she said nothing. Then she settled into the rhythm of her run.

After several minutes, she noticed that Aidan had slowed until his pace now matched hers. She offered no comment, but a small smile curved her lips as she continued to run.

When she slowed to a walk and then switched off the treadmill, Aidan did the same. He went to grab a towel, and Bryn noticed his soaked-through t-shirt and sweat-darkened hair. She had worked up a bit of a sweat herself, but he looked almost as wet as if he'd showered.

Bryn snagged a towel for herself while Aidan stripped off his wet shirt and dropped the soggy cloth on the floor. With efficient movements, he dried his chest and hair and then draped the towel around his neck.

When he finally raised his eyes to hers, the mix of emotions on his face floored her. Pain, anger, pride, despair. All shot through with a weariness that stemmed from more than the battle with the Wraiths.

She reached to touch his cheek, his shoulder, something, in order to offer some comfort. But before her fingers made contact, he gripped her upper arm and yanked her to him.

His kiss was angry, more desperate than passionate. And it had nothing to do with her—and everything to do with Lucky and his brother.

Bryn felt her own anger flare. She pulled away from him as her hand shot out. Her palm struck his cheek with enough force to turn his head.

"I came down here to try to comfort you," she snapped, as Aidan's hand rose to his reddening cheek. "But I will *not* be used to punish Lucky or Kev. You got that, angel-boy?"

Throwing her towel on the floor in disgust, she turned and stalked out of the gym.

It felt strange to be back in her own apartment after such a long absence, especially with Josh still at Zeke's. But with him in her room, and Bryn in the remaining available guest room, it had made sense for her to come home.

Besides, someone had to feed Shu and Tef.

Feeding done, Lucky sat on the couch trying to pet the two squirming cats who alternately walked on her or head-butted her for attention.

Her thoughts were equally insistent. Worry for Josh and anxiety about what to say to Zeke when she saw him next warred for her attention with images of Aidan's face when she'd appeared in Kev's arms and the memory of each of them, separately, stalking out of the dining room.

If she hadn't run away in the first place, she would never have grown so close to Kev, and she wouldn't have hurt Aidan. And neither of them would hate her.

Now that she was back—and Zeke had been nothing but kind—her motivation for running away seemed foolish, the intensity of her belief in his betrayal, a pale and distant thing. Whatever Sambethe had done, Zeke would never have been a part of it. And Aidan—well, before she and Kev had shown up in Zeke's basement the way they had, he would have found any such act of disloyalty to her all but impossible. Of course, he had kept silent because Zeke had sworn him to secrecy until they could be certain of Sambethe's actions. Running away from them had been selfish and stupid.

And the consequences of it couldn't be undone.

A buzzing sound interrupted her thoughts. Someone was at the door.

Booting the cats off her lap, she went to activate the intercom. "Yes?"

"I hope you're decent, girlfriend," Mo's voice said through the speaker.

Lucky laughed and pressed the button to let her friend into the building.

"It's good to see you, Mo," she said, as her friend mounted the last flight of stairs to the landing. "But how did you know I was here."

Mo waggled the cell phone she held in her left hand. "Zeke said you could use some company."

Lucky's eyes filled with tears yet again, and she threw her arms around the blonde girl. When she stepped back from the embrace, she sniffed, blinking away the tears.

"I'd intended to give you crap about running away without saying good-bye—and without so much as a phone call for the weeks you were gone—but I guess I can save it for another day," Mo said as she followed Lucky into the apartment. "You being all sad and weepy takes the fun right out of it."

Lucky chuckled. "It's okay, Mo. Go ahead and give me crap. I deserve whatever you can dish out."

"Really? You want to hear my spiel? I rehearsed it a lot."

Lucky nodded, the corners of her lips twitching.

Mo stood up straight, put her hands on her hips, and glared at Lucky. "Now that you're, like, half-angel and everything, you think you can just walk out on your family and friends—and your boss—with no more than a note scribbled on a whiteboard? How irresponsible can you get? 'Don't worry,' she writes. Yeah, like that's supposed to keep big brother Josh from biting his nails. And 'Let Mo know'? What kind of crap is that? I don't even rate my own individual whiteboard scribble. I'm, like, a P.S. to Josh's. Please. What kind of BFF are you, anyway?" She interrupted herself, adding as an aside, "I gotta say, this whole Naphil thing has totally wacked your BFF skills."

She took a breath. "Okay, where was I? Oh, right. What kind of BFF are you, anyway? I mean, I get that a vacation in Somewhere, Colorado, with Kev could have its attractions, but—"

"I didn't go on vacation with Kev. I was with Lilith most of the time. I only spent a few days with Kev. Because I couldn't face coming back, and because my Gift—well, it scares me—and he was helping me with it."

"Um-hm. Tell me you didn't kiss him at least once."

Lucky felt herself blushing. Would she ever grow out of that?

"Ah-ha!" Mo pounced. "You did! You did kiss him." Her eyes widened. "And Aidan found out, didn't he? No wonder Zeke said Aidan's shorts are in a knot."

Lucky giggled at the thought of those words in Zeke's voice. "Zeke did *not* say that," she said.

Mo tossed her head. "His sentiment, my words."

Lucky giggled again, then sobered. "It isn't funny. Aidan's really hurt. He's only said a few words to me. He won't even look at me—or Kev." She sighed. "I never wanted to come between them."

"Well, then, you shouldn't have been kissing both of them, should you?" Mo scolded.

"I know. I know. But—I don't know. I care about both of them. Aidan has been so good to me. He taught me so much and protected me when I couldn't do anything to protect myself. And he's so beautiful—and his voice—"

"But?" Mo prompted.

"But even when I was dating Aidan, I kept thinking about Kev. It's like he crept inside my mind, almost the moment I met him, and the feeling got even more intense after the Striking, and then after the Making, after he burned his sigil into my back..." Her voice trailed off as she shivered.

"He wasn't the only one, though. I mean, other angels or Nephilim were involved in the Making, right?"

Lucky nodded.

"You don't feel that way about any of them, do you?"

"No! Geez, Mo. Zeke and Malachi are like—I don't know—uncles or something. And the *Archangels?* Seriously? And Sambethe—well, I'm kind of sickened by the thought of being Marked by her, after what she did."

Mo gave her a knowing look. "Yeah, that's what I figured. So, how's your Kev reacting to all this?"

"He's not *mine*—and we haven't talked about it, so I don't know what he's thinking. But I know he's not happy. He never wanted to hurt Aidan. He told me we couldn't… But then I kind of forced myself on him, and… We were—kissing—when Zeke summoned us, and—"

"Oh my god," Mo exclaimed. "You didn't show up with your tongues down each other's throats, did you?"

Lucky felt herself blushing again. "It wasn't that bad. But we were—holding each other, and my hands were in his hair. It was pretty obvious what we'd been doing."

Mo whistled. "You do lead an interesting life."

"Yeah, *too* interesting sometimes."

"Seriously, are you okay? I know things have to be hard—with what's going on with Josh, and Aidan and Kev and everything. Can I do anything to help? 'Cuz I guess I forgive you—even for the whiteboard scribble P.S. business." She resumed her lecturing pose. "But don't do it again."

"I won't. And you've already done something. Seeing you was exactly what I needed." She wrapped Mo in a hug. "Thanks for still being my friend."

"Still?" Mo asked. "You haven't done anything all that awful. Even if you sometimes tick me off, I'm not going anywhere. Face it, girlfriend, you're stuck with me."

# CHAPTER 19

"You look like you could use a cup of tea."

Zeke's warm, resonant voice enfolded Lucky like a blanket, counteracting the cold of the early winter morning and calming the anxiety she had felt about ringing his doorbell. She kept expecting him to berate her for her disappearing act, make her feel guilty for not trusting him, or, at the very least, inform her she no longer had a job. Instead, he had treated her more kindly than she felt she deserved.

"That sounds wonderful," she said, following him into the brownstone. "I came to see Josh, but tea would be great."

"I just finished steeping a pot. You can take a cup with you to visit your cousin."

Lucky slipped off her coat, and Zeke hung it and her scarf in the closet, before leading the way to the kitchen.

A tea tray bearing a selection of antique china cups, milk, and sugar sat on the granite counter. Zeke poured tea into two of the cups and handed one to Lucky.

"Thanks, Zeke." She inhaled the aroma of the steaming cup. "I know we need to talk. I owe you an apology, but—"

Zeke stopped her words with a raised hand, and when he spoke, his words brought tears to her eyes. "It can wait,

Lucky. You came to see your cousin. I understand. Come and find me whenever you are ready."

She nodded, blinking away tears, and turned to leave.

She stopped when she reached the door. "Thanks again—for everything—including the tea."

"You are very welcome, my dear." A catch reverberated through the angel's resonant voice. Then he cleared his throat. "When this pot is empty, I will steep a fresh one. Help yourself to more if you like."

"Come in."

Josh's response to Lucky's knock sounded strong.

When she entered the room, teacup cradled in one hand, she found him sitting on the side of the bed, fully dressed. Katrin stood beside him, her fingers at his wrist.

"Your heart rate, like your blood pressure, is now higher than normal for a human, and so is your body temperature," she said, as she released his wrist. "But all those signs have stabilized. The readings have been consistent since the spasms stopped. How do you feel?"

Josh stood and stretched. "Okay, I think. Tired, a little sore, but otherwise okay. And I'm hungry."

"Do you want me to bring you some breakfast?" Lucky asked.

"If it's okay with Katrin, I'd rather get out of this room," Josh said.

"You may go downstairs," Katrin said. "I'd like you to remain in the house for a few more hours. Everything indicates the transformation is complete, but I want to be sure. Check in with me once every hour and if you start to feel anything out of the ordinary. If there are no additional changes by midday, you are free to go. Please keep me updated on any changes in behavior—eating and sleeping patterns, things like that."

At the healer's words, Lucky's hand tightened on her teacup. And she saw Josh tense as his gaze homed in on Katrin's. He asked the question that spun in Lucky's mind. "Eating patterns? I'm not going to start craving human souls or blood or anything, am I?"

"No, Josh. You are not a Wraith. There's no reason you should start behaving like one. But your body is different now. And it may have different needs than your human one."

Some of the tension drained from Josh's body. "Well, right now it could use some eggs and bacon, or pancakes, or waffles, or all of the above."

Lucky chuckled. "Come on. I'll make sure you get some breakfast. I hope Zeke's cupboards are full enough."

"Have fun," Lucky said to Josh a few hours later as he descended the steps in front of Zeke's brownstone. "And call me if you need anything at all."

Josh grinned at her over his shoulder. "Katrin said I'm fine, Lucky. And Ben will get me back here if anything happens. You go have that talk with Zeke."

Lucky nodded and waved. She took a deep breath as she closed the brownstone's door. No more excuses.

She crossed the formal living room and headed toward the stairs to Zeke's study. She had taken only a few steps when Bryn popped through the stairway door, her sweat-damp hair and clothes and the towel draped around her neck indicating a return from the gym.

"Lucky!" Bryn exclaimed, her eyes lighting with pleasure.

To Lucky's surprise, Bryn followed the exclamation by pulling her close for a hug.

Lucky hugged Bryn back, realizing she hadn't talked to her cousin since they had left Nadach. She had barely registered Bryn's presence at dinner the night before, so preoccupied had she been with Josh's transformation and her own drama with Aidan and Kev.

Bryn seemed to have recovered from the effects of the dual blast of powers. Gratitude tightened Lucky's arms for a moment.

As she stepped back from the embrace, Lucky's eyes fell on the white streak running through Bryn's raven-black hair.

"That's new," she said.

"Yeah, you can blame that on Aidan."

"Aidan?"

"He used his Gift to help heal me, and while he was at it, he did this—unintentionally. I have to say, I kind of like it."

"It looks good on you." Lucky gestured toward the black tattoo that swooped across the front of Bryn's throat. "It goes with your tattoo."

"It's not a tattoo," Bryn said.

"Oh. Then it's sort of like a sigil?"

"Something like that."

Bryn gestured to the seldom-used living room chairs. "Let's sit. And catch up."

"I wanted to talk to Zeke. Not that I don't want to see you too, but—"

"He's not here," Bryn said, curling up in one of the chairs. "And neither are Aidan and Kev. Or Katrin. They're all at some meeting of the Fallen Council or something. No doubt talking about the Wraiths and how in bloody hell they've been getting out of their realm and showing up here so often."

Lucky pulled off her boots and curled into the chair facing Bryn. "Well, then, tell me everything."

Before Bryn could comply, she added, "It's good to see you, by the way. I'm glad you're recovered. And I'm sorry— for what I did to you. I never intended—"

"Stop." Bryn held up her hand. "You didn't zap me on purpose. I'm the one who made myself your target."

"Which you should never have had to do." Lucky's gaze dropped to her upturned palm. "If I—"

"It wasn't your fault. If anyone's to blame, it's William— and maybe Mather. If they hadn't attacked us, your Gift wouldn't have manifested in such an overwhelming way. Then there would have been no reason for me or Kev to do what we did. He apologized to me too, by the way."

Lucky looked up at the mention of Kev's name. She shouldn't ask, but she couldn't help herself. "How is he?"

"Aidan won't speak to him unless he has to—like with today's meeting. I don't think Kev's too happy about that."

"I *know* he's not." Lucky hesitated. "Have you talked to Aidan?"

Bryn nodded.

"And?"

"And he's angry—and hurt. You already know that." Bryn's eyes searched Lucky's. "What are you doing, Lucky? You don't seem like the type to get her kicks by playing one brother off against another."

Lucky felt the color draining out of her face. Was that what they thought she was doing? She felt sick.

"That's not what I intended, not what I—want."

"Then what *do* you want?" Bryn asked, as if she really wanted to know. The question held no judgment, no condemnation.

"I don't know," Lucky answered. "I wish I did, but I don't."

Bryn stood up. "Well, you better figure it out, or you're going to lose them both."

# CHAPTER 20

*Council meeting or family reunion?* Kev thought as he and the other members of the Council took their seats. Zeke and Malachi were the only people at the table to whom he wasn't related by blood. Katrin sat at one end, opposite Zeke, with Aidan to her right. And Lucifer sat across from Kev, to Zeke's left.

Kev couldn't remember the last time he had been in the same room with his mother, father, and half-brother. Nothing like persistent, repeated Wraith attacks to bring a family closer together.

Not that they were a family in the true sense of the word. Especially now that Aidan refused to speak to him.

Because Kev had let down his guard and done what he wanted to do, ignoring the consequences. Against his better judgment, he had allowed himself, for a second time, to return Lucky's kisses.

And, for a few moments, he'd felt whole.

Then they'd shown up at Zeke's, and the world had shattered.

Kev forced the thoughts to the back of his mind and tuned in to Lucifer's report.

"All the captured Wraiths were contained within holding cells inside their realm until the frenzy passed. The wards on the portals have been repaired and reinforced, and guards have been posted at the portals and throughout the realm."

"And you still have no idea what caused the wards to fail again?" Zeke asked.

Lucifer shook his head. "No. Like last time, they were working as they should, then, without warning, Wraiths started pouring out into the human realm. It shouldn't happen again. But it shouldn't have happened the last two times." Turning to Malachi, he added, "Be on your guard, and have the Forces at the ready. At this point, we can't take any safety measures for granted."

"Already prepared," Malachi replied, his deep voice grim. "We are doing everything we can to monitor the portals from our side. And teams have moved to the barracks at the training center, so they can deploy at a moment's notice. Aidan, you will join us there later today?"

"Yeah. I'll have to sneak away for a few hours tonight. The band has a gig. Otherwise, I'll be there."

Kev wondered if his father was aware of the emotions that crossed his face as he listened to his younger son. Love, sorrow, bitterness, regret. Gods, they looked so much alike. Aidan's features were softer, the gold of his hair less intense and the blue of his eyes unadulterated by the bits of gold that flecked Lucifer's, but their kinship was apparent.

Kev looked more like his mother, the lighter streaks in his hair and the gold flecks in his eyes all that betrayed his paternal parentage.

"And you'll run interference with the Metatron." Lucifer said to Kev, the words less request than order—or simple statement of fact.

Kev nodded. "As soon as we're done here."

As the meeting continued, his thoughts turned to the upcoming conversation with the Metatron. He would have to do some fast talking to mitigate the damage done to Lucifer's already shredded reputation by two Wraith attacks in a matter of days. Combined with the investigation team's lack of progress in determining Jahoel's killer, the attacks put him at even more of a disadvantage than usual.

The sound of chair legs sliding over the floor told Kev the meeting had ended.

Navigating around Zeke, he stopped Lucifer before he had taken more than a few steps away from the table.

"Did Zeke tell you I spoke with Uriel?"

Lucifer raised an eyebrow. "With the Wraiths to preoccupy us? What do you think?"

"Yeah, that's what I figured. Anyway, I don't know when or how, but Uriel said he'll get me access to the Book."

"You might not want to share that information with too many others."

"I've told no one but you and Zeke."

"Good," Lucifer said. "Keep it that way."

Kev zapped himself back to his room at Zeke's to change before going to see the Metatron. Given the level of damage control he had to deal with, he figured he should observe every possible formality. He shivered as he slipped out of his seasonally appropriate clothing and into the loose-fitting black trousers and open-fronted, blood-red robe. Whoever designed this garb had never lived through a Chicago winter—or sat through a meeting in the Metatron's council chamber.

He jogged down the stairs to the main floor, heading toward the basement and the Gates of Heaven that would take him to the council chamber's even less welcoming ante-room. Only as he stepped off the bottom stair and into the formal living room did he realize the usually empty room was occupied.

Lucky sat in one of the armchairs, and Bryn stood nearby.

Kev froze. His feet refused to move another step, and his voice didn't seem to work either.

"Nice outfit," Bryn said.

When Kev didn't move or respond, she added, "I'll just—go to my room." Then she brushed by him to run up the stairs he'd descended.

Leaving him alone with Lucky.

His eyes locked on hers, but he still couldn't find his voice. She looked so sad. He wanted to put his arms around her, hold her close, bury his face in her hair. But he knew better than to give in to that desire again. He'd already done enough damage.

"Hey." Lucky broke the silence.

"Hey," he said. Once he'd spoken, he found he could move his limbs too. He took a few steps closer to her, but stopped with several feet still between them. "How are you doing?"

She shrugged. "What about you?"

"Pretty much the same."

"Yeah." She stood and closed some of the distance between them. "We need to talk. We can't—you and Aidan and I—we can't—"

She didn't finish the sentence. An expletive interrupted her as Aidan came bounding down the stairs, stopping dead when he saw them.

Kev cleared his throat. "I have to go. Meeting with the Metatron. We'll talk later, though, okay?"

"Sure. Later."

The misery in her eyes made it very hard for him to leave. But he didn't have time for the kind of discussion they needed to have. And he definitely didn't have time to talk things through with her *and* Aidan. The meeting with the Metatron couldn't wait. This would have to.

He felt his brother's eyes drilling holes in his back as he walked away.

"Sorry to break up your little party," Aidan said, once Kev had disappeared. "Next time you might want to pick someplace more private."

"Aidan, please. Don't be that way."

"What way?"

"All cold and snarky. You know what I mean."

"How do you want me to be, then, Lucky? Am I supposed to yell at you for cheating on me? Beg you to come back to me? Congratulate you on moving on to my brother? What do you want me to say?"

"I don't know what I want you to say, Aidan!" Lucky shouted. "But I don't want you to hate me." Then she added more quietly, "And I don't want you to hate Kev."

Aidan scrubbed his hands over his face, before raking them back through his hair. "I don't hate you," he muttered.

"And Kev?"

"I don't hate him either, all right?" Aidan's blue eyes blazed into hers. "But I *am* mad as hell at both of you, okay? Gods! You were my girl—well, you were supposed to be my girl—and you ran away without even contacting me. I found out you were gone when Ben called me after Josh found your note. And, then, when you get into trouble in Lilith-land, you turn to Kev instead of me. No, I couldn't have rushed to your rescue in the realm of the Banished. Only Kev could do that. But you could have let him bring you home. If you'd cared about me, you would have."

"You didn't see what I did there, Aidan. I was afraid I would hurt you."

Lucky could almost taste the bitterness in Aidan's chuckle. "Good thing you were looking out for me. I would hate to have been hurt."

"I'm sorry." Lucky collapsed onto the sofa, feeling small enough to crawl under it. "I was afraid I would hurt you *physically*. You—and Zeke."

"But you didn't have any such qualms about Kev?"

"I wasn't mad at Kev."

After a moment, Aidan sat down in the chair closest to her. Leaning forward, he rested his elbows on his knees. He didn't look at her as he spoke but stared down at his linked hands. "You shouldn't have been mad at me—or Zeke either."

"I know that now."

"Lilith's timing, like before, was—"

"—impeccable," they said together.

Their gazes caught, held.

"I'm sorry," Lucky said again. "I never intended to hurt you. You've been so good to me, and I—I do—love you."

Aidan's lips curled in a pale imitation of a smile. "But you don't want to be my girlfriend anymore, right?"

Lucky shook her head. "No. Would you really still want me to be?"

"I don't know." Aidan rubbed his eyes. "I can't get the image of you in my brother's arms out of my head. I'm assuming that's not the only time you kissed him."

Lucky winced. "No. I'm sorry."

"Sorry you kissed him? Or sorry I found out?"

"I'm sorry I hurt you."

"But if you had it to do over, you'd kiss him again?"

"Aidan—"

"Who made the first move? Did you succumb to my brother's charm, or did he succumb to yours?"

Lucky sighed. "Does it matter?"

"No, I guess not. The end result is the same."

"I'm sorry." Lucky didn't know what else to say.

"Stop saying that, okay?"

"But I am."

Aidan looked back down at his hands. "I know. I am too." Then he raised his eyes to hers. "Do you love him?"

Lucky squirmed. She *so* did not want to have this conversation.

"Right. I guess I don't need you to answer that."

Aidan stood up. He looked down at Lucky for a few seconds and then held out his hand. After a moment's hesitation, she took it and let him draw her to her feet.

When he pulled her into his arms, she went willingly. Her arms wrapped around him, drawing him close, her heart aching as she relived all their past embraces. She knew breaking up with him was the right thing to do, but that didn't mean it didn't feel like losing a part of herself.

Aidan's arms tightened as he dropped a kiss on the top of her head. Then he let her go and turned and walked away.

# CHAPTER 21

After Aidan left, Lucky curled up in the chair again, her eyes filling with tears. The conversation had gone as well as she could have hoped. Still, she felt as if one of her vital organs had been pulled out of her.

She had known better than to try to patch things up with Aidan. She was past pretending she could ignore her feelings for Kev. She loved Aidan, and she probably always would. But what she felt for Kev went beyond that. She and Kev were alike—in ways she and Aidan never could be. The Making had woven Kev into her very being. He seemed as necessary to her as the air she breathed.

But did he feel the same way about her? How would he react when she told him about her conversation with Aidan? Would he be pleased? Disappointed? Breaking things off with Aidan didn't mean she could dive into a relationship with Kev. She didn't know if either of them was ready for that.

Aidan and Kev being brothers made it all so complicated. Despite Aidan's admission that he didn't hate Kev, she knew his relationship with his brother wouldn't be the same, especially if she and Kev were together. Did Kev feel enough for her to weather that? Or would he choose his brother—his first real *friend*—over her? And what would she do if he chose Aidan? What would she do if he chose *her?* Things would be awkward and uncomfortable for them whatever happened. She almost wanted to run away again, despite her promise to Mo.

She should go talk to Zeke. Since Kev and Aidan had both returned from the Council meeting, he probably had as well. But she couldn't face him yet. Not after the encounter with Aidan.

She retrieved her coat and scarf from the closet and stepped out into the cold winter day. At least the sun was shining. Maybe a walk in the cold would help clear her head.


"And how, we must ask, does Lucifer explain the escape of countless numbers of Wraiths into the human realm? Have he and his helpers lost the ability to create effective wards? Or has his existence become so boring he purposely released the creatures in order to manufacture some excitement?"

Kev gritted his teeth at Tatriel's taunting words. The detached smugness exhibited by all the members of the Metatron except for Margash, who had so far kept silent, made Kev want to hit something—or someone. He suspected Margash might be more sympathetic than his fellows, but he knew the other three didn't care about the humans the Wraiths had attacked. They just wanted another complaint to lodge against Lucifer. He wondered how such cold beings had risen to such power.

He schooled his response into calm, measured tones. "I assure you, Most High, the release was not intentional. We have yet to determine how the wards were breached. But they have been repaired and strengthened."

"And the Wraiths?" asked Galiel.

"The frenzy has passed now that they are back in their own world. They have been released from the holding cells."

"Then let us hope, *Ha-Satan,*" said Margash, "that they remain in their world."

Kev inclined his head. "Indeed, Most High."

"Another such incident, and we may be forced to take action," inserted Adrigon. "In keeping with the Alliance, we must ensure the peaceful relations between the Dark, the Fallen, and the people of earth."

Kev kept his expression neutral, but he felt a cold hand clench around his heart. Why would Adrigon cite the importance of the Alliance? He feared it could mean nothing good.

Lucky touched down in the alley across the street from the assisted living facility, dismissed her wings, and, after making sure she was alone, released the glamour that had hidden her from human eyes.

Pushing her gloved hands deep into her pockets, she crossed the street to the facility's entrance. As always, the need to see G-Ma, a need that had presented itself before she had walked more than a couple of blocks from Zeke's, warred with the desire to run away from the truth of G-Ma's condition. She wanted to ground herself in her grandmother's presence, but she feared the Alzheimer's-induced absence she might find instead.

After checking in, she made her way to G-Ma's room, where she found her grandmother standing at her art table, paintbrush in hand, contemplating the painting before her. A furry, gargoyle-like Still One crouched in the corner.

Lucky nodded to the creature.

"Hi, G-Ma," she said.

G-Ma looked her way, eyes empty of recognition, before putting the brush to the canvas.

Lucky swallowed the ache inspired by that vacant glance and crossed the room to stand beside her grandmother. She looked down at the painting and frowned.

She had seen it before—twice, in varying stages of completion—and both times it had disturbed her. Now, almost finished, it unsettled her more than ever.

When Lucky had last seen the unfinished piece, she had suspected many of the shapes on the right had wings. Now she recognized several of the figures because of the color of those wings. Her own variegated green pair appeared near the front of the group, flanked on the right by a figure with Kev's dark green wings and on the left by a figure with white wings and Aidan's unmistakable golden hair. Another shape had wings of bronze—Ben—and still another bore Zeke's multiple blue wings. She recognized one of the two black-winged figures as Malachi. The rest of the group she didn't know, but she knew they faced a common enemy.

The vaguely anthropomorphic dark cloud filling the right third of the canvas loomed over the much smaller winged figures and the outline of the city beneath them. It seemed to pulse on the page, breathing, and gathering power with every breath. When G-Ma touched the dark mass with her paintbrush, deepening some of the shadows, Lucky fancied the darkness would rise off the painting to consume its creator. She wanted to snatch her grandmother's hand away from the thing.

"What are you painting, G-Ma?" she asked.

"What is to come," said G-Ma, in a voice as distant as the eyes that had glanced at Lucky. "I paint what comes."

"How do you know?"

G-Ma turned from the painting, and her gaze speared Lucky's. For an instant, instead of her grandmother's eyes, Lucky saw those of the Archangel Gabriel as he had appeared when he stood in G-Ma's place at the Making—pupilless, like blue skies chased with white clouds. Then the illusion was gone.

"Lucky!" G-Ma smiled. "How do I know what, dear?"

"I—I asked about the painting."

"Painting?" G-Ma looked from the brush in her hand to the canvas. "Oh." She shook her head. "I don't know what this is. But I think it's done now." Shaking her head again, she added, "I don't like it though. Do you?"

"No, G-Ma," Lucky said. "I don't think I do."

After a day spent dealing with the aftermath of the Wraith attack and running drills with the Forces, about the last thing Aidan wanted was to get on stage for an Icarus performance. At least he had a couple of hours to chill before the show.

Instead of going to Zeke's, he'd decided to stop off at his condo for some alone time, "alone" being the operative word. With Harley hanging out at the Hyde Park brownstone, the condo felt even emptier than usual.

After hanging up his jacket, he made his way to the liquor cabinet. The sound of his boots striking the marble tiles seemed to echo off the walls. Whenever he got around to getting more furniture, he maybe ought to think about adding some rugs to the order.

He sloshed some scotch into a glass and then stepped over to the wall of windows and stared out at Lake Shore Drive and Lake Michigan beyond.

How had everything gotten so screwed up? Between the Wraith attack with Josh's subsequent transformation and Lucky and Kev's unintended reveal, his life had taken a sudden, sharp turn southward.

And he'd gone and made it even worse by kissing Branwen—when she'd come to him as a friend.

He tossed back half the scotch and felt its slow burn down his throat.

He owed the girl an apology.

He would cut his visit to the condo short. Once he'd showered and changed, he'd go talk to her. She'd said she wanted to see more of the human realm. Maybe she'd accept an invitation to the Icarus show as a peace offering.

Aidan was in a *band?* That fact alone surprised Bryn more than his apology. She had intended to make him work for her forgiveness, but his invitation threw her so much she accepted it before she had time to think. Aidan was in a band. This she had to see.

"Great," Aidan responded. "Meet me in the living room in about an hour."

"I'll be there."

"And—Branwen, I am sorry. About what I did." His blue eyes never wavered from hers as he spoke.

"I know you are," Bryn said. "Consider yourself forgiven."

Aidan smiled. "Thanks. See you downstairs."

"In an hour."

Bryn closed her bedroom door, yanked off her workout clothes, and pulled on the voluminous robe she'd borrowed from Zeke. If she was going out, she needed a shower.

At least she didn't have to worry about what to wear. Other than her borrowed workout gear, she had only the one outfit. And although she had limited knowledge of this world, she thought her leather pants, velvet shirt, and boots wouldn't be at all out of place where Aidan was taking her.

She smiled in anticipation. An evening's entertainment in the human realm. She could hardly wait.


"Mo, Branwen. Branwen, Mo," Aidan said by way of introduction. "Mo is Lucky's best friend. Branwen is Lucky's cousin—on Lilith's side of the family."

The eyes of the girl with the messy blonde hair widened. Bryn was a little surprised herself. She hadn't expected Aidan to mention her grandmother. Since he had, she gathered the human girl knew about her best friend's non-human connections.

"Hi," she offered.

"Have a seat," Mo said, gesturing to the chair beside her. She studied Bryn, her curiosity evident. "From Lilith's side of the family, huh? So what does that make you?"

"Excuse me?" Bryn raised her eyebrows, making no effort to hide her annoyance or to sit.

"Sorry. That came out rude, didn't it? But I didn't mean it that way, I promise. I'd love it if you'd sit down and talk." Mo lowered her voice. "This angel, half-angel, demon, whatever thing is all kind of new to me. Since you're from Lilith's side of the family, I know you're not human, right? But you're also not Naphil. I wondered what you are, what you can do. Just curious, you know? I didn't mean to be offensive. Great outfit, by the way."

"Oh, um, thanks." Bryn sat. The girl's sincerity disarmed her. "And I am half-human. My mother was Lilith's daughter, but my father was a human male."

"A human male. Right. Well, does being the daughter of Lilith's daughter grant you any special powers?"

Bryn supposed she had what the girl would call "powers," but she had never once thought of describing them as "special." They had always felt more like a burden to her.

"If you're asking if I'm capable of doing things humans can't, then, yes," she said.

When she didn't continue with any details, Mo's eyebrows popped up. "And those things would be...?"

"I'm—what we call a Raven," Bryn hedged.

"A Raven? Like the bird?"

Bryn nodded. "Yeah, sort of." She didn't like talking about that side of herself.

"Okay, so you're a Raven. What can Ravens do?"

"You don't want to know."

"Yes, I do."

"Well, then, I don't want to talk about it." Bryn's eyes locked on Mo's as she spoke. She didn't care what the girl wanted to know. She was not about to go there. She had already said more than she should.

"Fine. I won't ask again."

Mo took a sip of her Coke. "It's weird not having Lucky here. I mean, she missed a lot of shows while she was gone, but now that she's back…" She sighed. "I know why she didn't come, but it still feels like she should be here."

Bryn had no idea how to respond. She would have liked for Lucky to be there too, but given the tension between her cousin and Aidan, Bryn knew Lucky's presence would have caused some discomfort for everyone. Remembering Aidan's angry kiss the night before, she wondered if he would have felt compelled to flirt with her if Lucky had been there. He had apologized for his behavior, and she knew the apology was sincere, but she guessed he might still be tempted to use her to get back at Lucky if the opportunity presented itself. Not that she didn't sympathize, but if he treated her like an object again, she'd do more than slap him.

"Josh!"

Bryn looked up at Mo's exclamation to see a young man with curly dark hair pulling out a chair on the other side of the table.

"Hey, Mo. Who's your new friend?" he asked.

"You haven't met?" Mo asked.

Bryn and Josh shook their heads.

"Huh," Mo said. "Since you've both been at Zeke's, I just assumed... Branwen, this is Josh, Lucky's cousin from the non-Lilith side of the family."

Josh smiled. "You're Branwen. It's nice to meet you. Aidan mentioned you were staying at Zeke's for a while."

"You knew about her even though you hadn't met her?" Mo exclaimed. "Aidan told you about her? And neither of you bothered to pass the information on to me? Does everyone in your family need friend lessons?"

"Sorry, Mo. I've been a little busy."

The blonde girl looked contrite. "No, I'm sorry. How are you anyway? Did you get permission to be here?"

Josh chuckled. "Katrin cleared me this morning. Whatever transformation I went through seems to be complete. No more painful spasms, no more erratic vital signs." He took a deep breath. "Now we wait and see what I turn out to be."

"Have you seen Lucky today?"

"Yeah, she came to visit me this morning, before Katrin had okayed my release. Then I saw her at home before I came here. I think she planned on hanging out with Zeke while we're here."

"That makes sense. Girlfriend's got a lot of patching up to do."

"Yeah, I guess she does."

"Not that she doesn't deserve a certain amount of grief," Mo remarked, "for leaving us with no more than a whiteboard note."

"You got that right," Josh agreed.

Bryn listened as Mo and Josh laughingly outlined the payback Lucky deserved for running off and leaving them in the first place, and she couldn't help wondering if her friends had thought or said similar things about her. Jaime would probably kick her butt whenever she went back to training with him, and Alicia…

Guilt constricted Bryn's heart. Alicia was like a little sister to her, and Bryn wasn't there to take her part anymore. At least Alicia and Jaime had each other. The last time Bryn had seen them, they had seemed almost oblivious to Lucky's and her presence. She took comfort in knowing that, in her absence, Alicia had Jaime to care about her and to counterbalance her mother's criticisms.

Drumbeats interrupted Bryn's thoughts, and the music swept her up as the other instruments joined in. When Aidan strode toward the microphone and began to sing, she laughed out loud. She recognized the song as one he'd played during their workout.

It still surprised her that the Naphil who had helped to heal her also sang in a human band. How had he managed to integrate so easily into the human world? When he'd invited her to come to the performance, she hadn't known what to expect in terms of quality—getting out of Zeke's house was excitement enough. But Aidan was good. Better than good. He had an incredible voice. And the musical skills of the other band members matched his vocal talents. Before long she found herself clapping and whistling with the rest of the crowd.

She liked life in the human realm.

# CHAPTER 22

Standing on Zeke's doorstep, snow falling around her, Lucky felt even more alone than she had that morning. Most of her friends had gone to the Icarus show. But, given the state of her relationship with Aidan, she had decided not to join them. It wouldn't have been fair to him, and she couldn't have relaxed enough to have had a good time anyway.

The thought of spending the evening alone held no appeal. And she didn't have the courage to call Kev. She hadn't seen him since their brief encounter before he'd left to meet with the Metatron, and she still didn't know what she had done to prompt him to stalk away from the dinner table the evening before. She had no idea if he would want to see her.

It seemed like the perfect time to have that talk with Zeke. If he was available.

She rang the bell a second time, wondering if perhaps the angel wasn't home after all. She had hardly lifted her finger from the button when the door opened.

"Come in, come in." Zeke ushered her inside. "Sorry to keep you waiting in the snow. Kevin was leaving, and I wanted to see him off."

"Leaving?" Lucky asked.

Zeke helped her out of her coat.

"Yes, he said he had some things to take care of at the cabin."

"Oh." The thought of Kev at the cabin made her long to be back there with him.

"He will return soon. I believe he wanted to get everything stowed and locked away, after your unplanned departure. He said he'd bring your things back when he returns."

"I'd forgotten about them."

Zeke squeezed her shoulder. "You have had plenty of other things on your mind."

He gestured toward the hallway. "Let's go downstairs where we can be more comfortable."

Inside the angel's study, Lucky curled up in the embrace of one of the big leather armchairs. Zeke sat across from her, his elbows on his knees, his long wheat-blond hair spilling over his shoulders.

"How are you, my dear?" he asked.

That was all it took for the floodgates to fall.

Zeke found a box of tissues somewhere and pushed them across the oak table toward Lucky. He didn't say anything as she plucked a few from the box and pressed them to her eyes.

When the tears had run their course, Lucky rested her head against the chair back, spent. "Zeke," she whispered, "I've made such a mess of things. I'm sorry I ran away."

"I am sorry too. Sorry I did not tell you about Sambethe. Sorry you had to hear it from Lilith instead of me." His kind gray eyes searched hers. "You must know I did not intend to deceive you. I wanted to be sure before I spoke to you."

Lucky nodded. "I know that now. At the time, I thought—I thought maybe you wanted to protect Sambethe." Her eyes filled with tears again. "And I couldn't bear the thought that you—any of you—had betrayed me—and Josh."

"Forgive me for asking, but did Lilith suggest that I betrayed you?"

"No." Lucky shook her head. "In fact, she said I should give you a chance to explain."

"Did she?"

"Yes. But I couldn't face you—or Aidan. I had to get away." Lucky sighed. "Now it seems so stupid. If I'd stayed and talked to you and continued my training, everything would have been okay."

For a moment Lucky saw all four of Zeke's faces, and they all looked surprised. When his form merged back into Zeke the man again, his eyebrows were raised. "Everything would have been okay?" he asked. "How so? Do you think your staying here would have prevented the Wraith attack?"

"No, but—"

"And would your staying here have prevented your Gift from manifesting?"

"No, but—"

"And would your staying here have prevented you from having feelings for Kevin?"

"No, but—" This time Lucky stopped herself without Zeke's interruption, when she realized what she'd said.

"You have cared about him for some time, have you not? But you believed you could ignore those feelings. Because you did not want to hurt Aidan."

"I didn't want to hurt Aidan or Kev. They'd finally gotten to be friends again. Now they're hardly speaking, and it's all my fault."

Zeke shook his head, the ghost of a smile curving his lips. "It is not *all* your fault. Aidan and Kevin are responsible for their own feelings and actions and reactions. You must all find a path through this. And you would all have had to find that path whether or not you had run away."

"I didn't want to hurt them."

"And I did not want to hurt you." Zeke leaned back in his chair. "If I have learned anything in all my very many years, it is that pain is an inevitable part of life. If you live, you will hurt others—and others will hurt you. Sometimes the hurt is intentional, but most often it is not. Our lives rub against each other, and sometimes the friction of that rubbing causes pain. To ourselves, to others. We should never cease to care if we hurt others, but we have to understand that we will, whether we want to or not. We cannot eliminate the possibility of pain. We have to figure out how to live with the hurt. Sometimes our wounds can become our greatest strengths."

Tears washed Lucky's eyes once more. "I've missed you, Zeke," she whispered.

"I have missed you too," the angel responded. Leaning forward in his chair, he opened his arms.

Lucky flew into them. As his arms enclosed her, she saw the shadows of his great blue wings enfolding her as well.

Then she tumbled out of his arms as he stood to face the battle-garbed Naphil who had materialized beside the heavy oak table.

Malachi's deep voice boomed into the peace of the study. "The Wraiths are attacking again. We need every hand we can get. They're spread out in various parts of the city. The latest attacks are along the Magnificent Mile and—" he glanced at Lucky "—at Lucky's grandmother's assisted living facility. We need help in both locations. Split the others into two teams and send them as soon as you can."

Malachi's form faded even as he finished speaking.

"I want to help," Lucky said, but Zeke didn't respond. The angel had closed his eyes, and his form wavered before her, man, eagle, lion, and bull sliding over and merging into one another amid a cloud of blue wings.

"Follow me," he said as he opened his eyes. Lucky jogged to keep up with his long strides.

When they reached the gym, Kev was already there, pulling gear from a large closet at the back of the room.

"What's up, Zeke?" he asked. "I got the message to get here and get geared up, but what am I getting ready for?"

"We need your help to quell another Wraith attack. They have appeared on the Magnificent Mile and at the assisted living facility where Lucky's grandmother stays. I want you to go to the assisted living facility. When Aidan and the others get here, I will divide them into teams."

After exchanging the Chuck Taylors he'd been wearing for a pair of heavy boots, Zeke strapped on leather guards.

"I want to help," Lucky repeated.

Zeke looked from Lucky to Kev and back to Lucky. "Do you think that is wise? Can you handle your Gift in this situation, given your unquestionable emotional involvement?"

"Don't make me stay here while everyone else is out there doing something, Zeke. Let me at least do what I can to save my grandmother."

"Let her help, Zeke. She needs to do this." Kev's eyes found Lucky's as he spoke. His head tipped forward in a small nod of encouragement before he looked away. "I'm good to go. Give me the coordinates."

Zeke blinked.

"Got 'em," Kev said. And then he faded away.

"These should work for you," Zeke said, handing Lucky a pair of leather trousers, which she tugged on over her jeans.

"We will try to contain as many of the Wraiths as we can in holding areas," he explained as he found a leather jacket for her as well. "If possible, get them into those. Kill only if you must. And if one manages to taste your blood, do not look into his eyes. That is how they take your soul."

He shook his head as he studied the weapon sheath he held. "You have not even begun weapons training yet. How can I send you in there?"

"I've had a lot of practice with hand-to-hand. I kept training these last few weeks. And I have my Gift. I haven't mastered it, but it's powerful. Please. I need to do this, Zeke."

"Right," he said. "Put these on." He handed her a pair of boots. "I will fill you in on how this works while we wait for Aidan and the others."

They had almost finished the second set when Aidan felt Zeke in his head. Who else could be responsible for his sudden compulsion to get to the gym at the brownstone

ASAP? He rescued the lyric he'd almost fumbled and signaled the band to wrap up the song. When he glanced toward Ben, the other Naphil gave a small nod, which told Aidan Ben had gotten the same message. Good thing they had only a couple more songs left in the set. The rest of the band could manage to pull something off without him and Ben.

As the last notes of the song faded, he thanked the crowd and made his and Ben's excuses. Then he hopped off the stage and headed toward the table occupied by Branwen and his other friends.

His *other* friends? When had he started to think of the often surly girl as his friend? He couldn't pinpoint when it had happened, but he found he did—even if she hadn't given him permission to use her nickname.

He leaned down so he could speak near her ear. "We need to take off. Something's up."

Branwen stood up at once, no questions asked.

Across the table, he saw, Ben had communicated similar information to Josh. They made their good-byes to Mo and then hurried out the door.

Aidan had brought Branwen here on his Ducati. He'd thought she'd enjoy the ride—and he knew for sure he would. He didn't like the idea of leaving the motorcycle parked on the street, but he also knew they didn't have the time for human transport at the moment. Zeke's compulsion wormed its way deeper into his brain by the second.

He ducked into the closest alley and held his hands out to Branwen.

"Give me your hands," he said.

"What for?" she asked.

"Because we have to dematerialize. Don't argue. Just take them."

"Do what he says," Ben said, grabbing both of Josh's hands. "We gotta go now."

Aidan could almost see the questions on Branwen's face, but she took his hands without voicing them.

"Ready?" he asked.

At her nod, he closed his eyes and zapped them back to Zeke's.

"It's about time," Zeke said, as soon as the quartet re-formed in his study. His resonant voice crashed like a wave.

Lucky's "What took you so long?" rang through the din.

Only their worried looks and the fact that both were fully geared up kept Aidan from commenting that no more than ten minutes could have passed since he'd first received Zeke's summons.

"More Wraiths?" he asked instead, as he and Ben yanked their own gear from the closet.

"What else?"

"Bloody hell," Aidan swore. "Where?"

"Everywhere. Members of the Forces are fighting them off all over the city. Aidan and Ben, I need you to get to the Magnificent Mile. Lucky and I will go to Lincoln Park, to the facility where Lucky's grandmother lives."

"Hand me some gear too," Branwen demanded, stripping off her velvet tunic to reveal a black tank. "If Lucky's going, I'm going."

"And you might as well include me, because there's no way I'm getting left out of this," said Josh.

Ben passed leathers to Josh while Aidan found some for Branwen.

He was about to hand her the clothes when he noticed Zeke studying the dark mark that swooped across her neck.

"Are you sure you can handle this?" Zeke asked, his gaze lifting to meet hers.

Branwen's lips tightened. "It seems to me you need all the help you can get."

For a second, Zeke held her defiant gaze. Then he nodded. "Very well. Branwen, you go with Aidan and Ben. Josh, you are with Lucky and me. I will give you the coordinates, and then we are off."

Aidan felt the location's coordinates slide into his mind as Zeke reached for Lucky's and Josh's hands.

"Hold on, you two," Zeke said, and the trio faded away.

# CHAPTER 23

Malachi had already set up a containment area when Kev materialized in the commons room of the assisted living facility. Leaving Malachi to start containing the Wraiths, Kev did his best to corral the staff. He collected as many of the terrified workers as he could find and ushered them into an office, instructing them to lock the door behind him.

"Wait." A voice stopped him as he started to shut the door. A pretty, young, dark-skinned woman moved to the front of the group. "What about the residents? Someone has to save them from—whatever those things are."

"We'll do our best, DeShawn" he promised, shifting his gaze from her nametag to her frightened yet determined eyes. "You have my word. Stay here and keep the door locked until we let you know it's safe to leave."

He had warded the office door as well as the residents' doors on both sides of two corridors before Malachi's shout sent him racing back to the commons room. Kev hoped he could ward more of the doors later, but for now he would have to trust the Still Ones to protect their charges from any Wraiths who made it beyond the commons and into the other residential areas.

Back in the commons room, he found Malachi up to his leather-clad armpits in Wraiths. A second portal had ripped the space on the far side of the room, and the creatures poured through like ants fleeing a scattered ant hill. Many of them had already entered the residential hallways that opened off that end of the commons.

Kev warded the entrances to the hallways to prevent any more of the creatures from getting through—at least as long as the wards would hold. Warding an open threshold was much more difficult than warding a door, but it was the best he could do. He could do nothing about the Wraiths who had already made it into the residential area. He'd have to trust them to the Still Ones.

A quick glance down the hallways revealed the furry gargoyles on duty at their doorways, fangs bared and claws at the ready. And he could see Zeke, Lucky, and Josh near the end of one of the corridors, as well as the silvery lines that marked the containment zone Zeke had already constructed. Good. He and Malachi could focus on containing the Wraiths in the commons and closing the portal before the entire population spilled out of their world and into this.

Kev took over containment duty from Malachi, freeing the other man to concentrate on closing the portal. Malachi's abilities to navigate the realms of life and death and the dimensions in between made his the better portal-closing skill set. Kev could get scaly and flame the blasted thing, but it wouldn't accomplish anything besides toasting some Wraiths and raising the temperature on the other side of the portal by a few degrees. Better for him to keep the Wraiths out of

Malachi's braids long enough for the amber-eyed Naphil to work his magic.

Summoning his broad sword and shield, Kev stepped between Malachi and the Wraith swarm. With his sword slicing the air and the shield serving less as protection and more as a herding device, he maneuvered the creatures toward the containment zone. He handled the sword with care, trying not to wound any of the Wraiths. They hadn't yet fallen victim to the frenzy he could tell had already gripped their fellows in the warded hallway, and the smell of even their own blood could tip them over the edge. Sooner or later, the scent of the blood spilled in the hallway would reach the commons area. He hoped Malachi would have closed the portal by then.

Kev shoved the Wraith bundle across the perimeter of the containment zone, filling the silver-marked area. He paused only long enough to speak the words that would send the Wraiths back to their world, emptying the warded zone, before he crossed back to the portal.

He was two steps away when the rip in space folded in upon itself. Malachi had found the key.

"You have this now, right?" Malachi yelled, as he ducked and spun the Wraith that had lunged at him in Kev's direction.

Kev answered in the affirmative, catching the Wraith in the shield-extended length of his arm and sending it and a couple others skidding toward the containment zone.

"Then I'm headed to the Magnificent Mile. If you haven't heard otherwise by the time you get things cleaned up here, come join the party. The more the merrier." Malachi's form faded with his last words.

And what perfect timing. The scent of blood had reached the commons, and the room full of Wraiths began to look at Kev like he was lunch.


The hallway outside G-Ma's room looked to Lucky like a macabre version of her initial encounter with the horde of Still Ones. The creatures massed in the doorways, fangs bared and claws extended, as they confronted the gaunt, crimson-eyed invaders entering the hall. Lucky glanced from the Wraiths to the Still Ones and back again, forcing herself to breathe through the terror making her heart race. As danger-ous as the furry creatures seemed, they didn't appear to stand a chance against the rabid-looking Wraiths, who exuded a frenzied ferocity that prevented Lucky from equating their gauntness with weakness.

Even as Zeke began marking off the holding area he'd told her about, one of the Wraiths yanked a struggling Still One from its doorway. Before Lucky could think what to do, the creature had sliced its sharp nails across the Still One's throat and tossed the furred body aside. Lucky swallowed her horror. Dear God, *that* was what Josh could have become?

As a second Still One, this one larger, stronger, and fierc-er than its deceased colleague, leapt at the Wraith with extended claws and bared fangs, Lucky scoped out a plan of attack. Zeke had said to capture as many of the Wraiths as they could, to kill only if necessary. Lucky didn't quite understand the logic of that, since the Wraiths seemed to have no qualms about killing anything that got in their way. But if Zeke said to contain, she'd do her best.

She lunged to her left, grabbed a tall, long-haired Wraith approaching G-Ma's door, and knocked him off balance, shoving him toward Zeke's containment area. Before he could regain his balance, she kicked a booted foot into his back, sending him sprawling over the silvery line demarcating the containment zone's edge. Once across the line, there was no escape. She heard the Wraith's frustrated growl as she spun to confront her next opponent.

Blood splattered the hallway before her, spilling from the body of a Still One, which despite its many wounds, stood its ground against the Wraith trying to enter G-Ma's room. As the Wraith lunged at the bleeding Still One, the furry, gargoyle-like creature ducked and sank its razor-sharp claws high in the Wraith's thigh, near the groin, opening a vein. The Wraith hissed and backhanded the wounded Still One hard enough to knock it to the floor.

Lucky leapt at the Wraith as it moved toward the door. No way would she let that thing get to G-Ma.

At the impact, the Wraith's wounded leg buckled, and Lucky's body followed the Wraith's downward. She bent her knees to move into a crouch, holding on to the Wraith with one hand, the other drawn back into a fist she intended to slam into the creature's face. But her boots skidded on the blood-covered floor, and she fell backward, pulling the Wraith down on top of her. The creature's foul breath hit her face as her head struck the tiles.

Bryn was no stranger to violence, but she'd never seen anything like this before. Human bodies lay crumpled on the sidewalks, while those lucky enough to be separated from the Wraiths by the two first-responding members of the Forces huddled together, screaming, behind the warriors who battled their attackers. Elsewhere more of the crimson-eyed soul-suckers, looking even more rabid than normal, chased after fleeing humans or turned their attention to the store fronts, searching for prey.

For an instant, Bryn wondered if maybe she shouldn't have been quite so adamant about coming along to help.

Then her warrior instincts kicked in. And as Aidan and Ben joined the fray, she was right there with them. The two Nephilim had each summoned weapons—swords, spears. She'd heard they could do that. She couldn't, but then again, she didn't need to. She had built-in weapons. She didn't like to use them much, but if ever a situation called for them, this one did.

She screamed at the pain that bit through her as she shifted her hands into the talons she'd been born with, and the scream sounded in her ears like the hoarse cry of the Raven she was. Calling her wings to her back, she launched herself at the nearest Wraith, and before he knew what had hit him, her beak had separated his head from his shoulders.

Nearby, one of the red-eyed nasties had pinned a human male against the side of a building. He raised his hand, sharp nails ready to open a vein in the man's throat. Yeah, that wasn't happening. Bryn grabbed the Wraith's shoulder with her taloned hand and spun him away from the terrified human. While surprise still marked his ghoulish face, she sliced her beak across his throat.

Two down, dozens to go.

Gods, they were everywhere. Aidan raced after a Wraith and shoved his sword through the thing before it could open the throat of the human it held. The Wraith toppled, and Aidan opened the nearest door, checked to make sure the room was Wraith-free, and shoved the screaming human inside.

"Lock this," he ordered. Then he closed the door and turned back toward the street.

It was chaos. There was no way they could contain all the Wraiths. Too many of them covered too large an area, and he counted far too few of the Fallen. They would contain the Wraiths they could, but with their limited numbers, choosing to spend time creating additional containment areas would mean allowing humans to die. Aidan didn't enjoy killing—even when his victims were Wraiths—but if he had to choose between saving humans and saving Wraiths, he'd choose the humans every time.

Ah, good, they had one more to add to their side. Malachi must have materialized while he had gotten the human behind a locked door.

As Malachi marked off another containment area, Aidan summoned his wings and flew toward a trio of Wraiths that stood between him and the holding zone. Spreading his arms, he scooped up the Wraiths and shoved them across the silvery barrier.

Then he winged upward, scanning the block to see where he was needed most.

Just when Lucky thought she would become Wraith food, the weight of the thing lifted off her. She opened her eyes to see Josh standing over her, teeth bared, eyes Wraith-red, and muscles she didn't know he had stretching the leather of his fighting gear. Holding the Wraith at neck and crotch, he flung the creature straight toward Zeke's containment zone.

"Holy transformation, Batman," Lucky muttered as she got to her feet, careful not to slip again on the blood-slick floor.

"Are you all right?" Josh asked. His voice was deeper than normal and edged with a growl.

"Yeah, thanks. Are you?"

Josh's hands clenched. "I'm good. Let's send the rest of these soul-suckers back where they belong."

As if he'd heard Josh's words, a Wraith leapt toward him, long, sharp nails aimed as his face and throat. Growling, Josh caught the creature by the arms and spun it around over his head. Two more of the creatures lunged toward Lucky, and she ducked. When the body of the Wraith Josh swung slammed into its fellows, they went flying over Lucky toward the containment area. She saw that they didn't quite make it to the silvery barrier, but they landed close enough that Zeke made short work of getting them the rest of the way across.

Zeke must have captured several of the creatures on his own, because the containment area looked filled to capacity. As Lucky watched, he gestured with his right hand and spoke some words she couldn't hear over the noise of combat. The translucent silvery lines demarcating the holding zone flared, and the Wraiths inside disappeared.

Too bad so many of the red-eyed monsters remained uncontained.

Lucky clenched her teeth and dived back into the melee.

Shoulders sagging with relief, Kev spoke the words that would empty the containment zone and sent the last of the living Wraiths in the commons back to their own world. The bodies of the casualties would have to be dealt with later. If the scent of blood hadn't reached them, he might have been able to complete the job without killing, but the aroma had sent their desire to feed into orbit. Too many of them had wanted a piece of him, and he'd had to take out some of them in order to avoid being taken out himself.

With the commons area as cleared as it could get for the moment, he ran to the warded hallway entrances. Most of the action seemed to be happening in the hallway where Zeke, Lucky, and Josh, along with several Still Ones, continued to engage a sizeable number of Wraiths. The Still Ones seemed to have taken care of the few soul-suckers who had entered the other residential corridor.

Kev did a quick pass down the quiet hallway to make sure no Wraiths had managed to enter any of the residents' rooms, then he hurried to the other corridor to help his friends, wondering what had drawn so many of the Wraiths to that particular corridor.

By the time Lucky became aware that Kev had joined their party, the numbers had already shifted in their favor. More of the Wraiths had been contained and shipped back to their Wraithy world—or killed—than remained. The red-eyed creatures still outnumbered the Fallen and the Still Ones, but their numbers seemed manageable now.

Plus she no longer had the distraction of worrying about the creatures getting to G-Ma and the other residents. In addition to his Wraith containment and transport duties, Zeke had somehow managed to ward the residents' doors.

*We can do this,* Lucky allowed herself to think as she determined her next move. The end of the battle was in sight.

It seemed the shift in numbers had energized the Still Ones as well. They appeared to be engaging the remaining Wraiths with new ferocity.

A small Still One whose silky dark fur was smattered with blood caught Lucky's attention mere seconds before it leapt from the floor, slamming its feet into the back of a Wraith and sending the creature careening toward Lucky. Lucky grabbed the soul-sucker's arm, pulled, and released as she spun to the left. The Wraith pinballed in Zeke's direction, and the Cherub made quick work of maneuvering him into the containment zone.

Lucky chuckled. How was that for teamwork?

The sound died in her throat as she turned around. Halfway down the hall, G-Ma stood in her open doorway. What was she doing? Why had she opened the door?

Lucky started running even as the questions flooded her mind, and she could see Josh sprinting from the hallway's opposite end. She had run only a few steps before she realized more doors had opened and other residents had stepped into the hall. No, no, no, no. They were supposed to stay safe in their warded rooms.

"Lucky!" Zeke's voice boomed in the corridor. "On your right!"

She pivoted in time to see two Wraiths descending on a white-haired man whose blank expression and vacant eyes indicated that in his mind he was somewhere other than this hellish hallway. Oh God, she didn't have time for this—she had to get to G-Ma. But she couldn't leave the poor man to the Wraiths. She dived toward the Wraiths just as a Still One grabbed the man, pulled him back toward his room, and placed itself between the Wraiths and their prey.

Lucky caught the nearest Wraith's frustrated growl. Then she crashed into the creature, and the growl turned into a howl of rage. Sharp nails pierced the leather of Lucky's borrowed jacket, scoring her rib cage. The Wraith pivoted and pinned her against the wall. He pushed her head to the side, stretching her neck and exposing her jugular vein.

Lucky tried to kick, but the creature had trapped her legs against the wall with his own. One of her arms was pinned to her side, and the other pressed tight into the wall above her head. The Wraith pushed her head farther to the side, and panic rose inside her as his breath hit her neck. His teeth pierced her skin, and she felt the warm trickle of blood.

The Wraith grabbed her chin and turned her face toward his. His eyes glowed neon red. Those eyes probed hers, and she screamed as something inside her began to unknit.

*Do not look into his eyes.* Zeke's remembered words rumbled beneath her scream like distant thunder. Her eyelids were doors with rusted hinges, and it took all the strength she had to force them closed. But when they dropped, shutting out the Wraith's neon glow, power pulsed through her, and the now familiar tingle-and-burn filled her palms. She gathered the energy in her core and blasted it toward the Wraith.

Time stilled for Lucky. She could see the creature's mind. She held his life in her hands. The sense of power she'd felt over William and his father filled her again. She could do anything. All it would take was a little turn, a little push. The Wraith would never threaten her—or anyone else—ever again. With a mental finger, she strummed a thread of his thought. The Wraith shrieked, demonic, inhuman, agonized.

Something about the cry penetrated Lucky's consciousness, and she remembered Zeke's mandate to contain, not kill. Though the dark side of her Gift beckoned seductively, she could see other ways to use her power. A different twist to a different strand, and the Wraith would be docile as a lamb—at least for as long as it took her to contain him.

She turned the selected strand the tiniest bit, and the Wraith stared at her, puzzled, as if he couldn't quite remember why he held her against the wall. His hold on her relaxed, but before he could release her, there came a crash, a tremendous roar, a blast of heat in front of her, and the Wraith fell to the floor in a pile of ash.

"Kevin, no! Stop!"

Zeke's command reached Lucky's ears as another group of Wraiths crumbled to ash, followed by yet another. She caught the acrid scent of burning hair and realized some Still Ones had been close enough to the flames to get singed.

Her eyes swung to the dragon that more than filled the end of the hallway. Plaster, brick, and splintered wood littered the floor around the beast. Wires, broken ceiling tiles, and mangled metal framing dangled above him. He lashed his tail, and another section of wall fell to pieces. Shaking his head, he roared again as flame leapt from his mouth.

He didn't stop until he had reduced all the remaining Wraiths to piles of ash. Then he directed a geyser of fire at the walls and ceiling he'd mangled. As the flames died out, Lucky saw dark night and city lights and felt the cold winter air sweeping in through the gaping hole.

Stepping through the hole, the dragon spread his huge green wings and lifted into the air.

"Kev!" Lucky yelled.

She had taken two steps toward the rubble, when she remembered G-Ma. She hesitated, torn between the two, then turned and scanned the hallway.

Her eyes found Josh's leather-clad figure cradling G-Ma in his arms. She raced to kneel beside him.

"Is she all right?"

"She'd been bitten by the time I got to her, but the Wraith didn't get her soul. She's still alive."

"I will take her to Katrin," Zeke said.

He crouched next to Josh and took G-Ma from his arms. "When I return, we will clean up loose ends here. At least Kevin's dragon gave us an alternative explanation for what happened."

G-Ma's eyes fluttered open when Zeke rose to his feet. "Lucky?" she said weakly.

"Yes, G-Ma," Lucky said. "I'm here." She caught G-Ma's searching fingers in hers.

G-Ma's fingers fluttered in Lucky's hand as her eyes found Lucky's. "Help him," she said. "Help your dragon."

Lucky blinked back tears. "How?" she whispered.

"One." G-Ma fingers slipped from Lucky's. "Only one."

"I will be back shortly," Zeke said, and he and G-Ma disappeared.

With a couple of hours of fighting behind her and most of the Wraiths quelled, Bryn had lost count of the number she'd killed. Her human side felt sickened by the carnage, while her Raven side rejoiced and searched for its next victim.

It didn't take her long to find him, or rather, them.

Two Wraiths stalked Aidan.

While he ran his sword through another of the creatures, one of those at his back reached to grab him, so the other could sink its teeth into his throat.

"Aidan!" she yelled. At least, she meant to. But what came out was the Raven's cry. Curse it! She'd never get used to losing her voice to the Raven's beak with every shift.

But that beak made a deadly weapon. Diving over Aidan, she pecked out the eyes of one of the Wraiths, while she wrapped her talons around the other's throat.

Holy hell! Wraith blood sprayed Aidan's back. He leapt forward, over the body of the Wraith he had skewered, and turned to see the black-winged, taloned, beaked figure that had dived over him tossing aside two dead Wraiths like so much garbage. The tall, leather-clad body and the white streak in the pixie-short black hair identified the being as Branwen. Otherwise, he would have been hard-pressed to name his rescuer. He had caught glimpses of black wings during the fighting, but he had been too preoccupied to realize they weren't always Malachi's.

His eyes scanned Branwen's figure, noting the blood that marked her beak, talons, clothes, and hair. Given the amount of the stuff, he guessed the two Wraiths she'd saved him from could be added to numerous others she'd dispatched. He would bet she'd racked up a considerable tally. The way she'd rescued him proved she was as lethal as she looked.

"Thanks," he said, when he could stop gaping long enough to find his voice.

Branwen's beak opened and issued a Raven's harsh cry. Shaking her head, she turned away. Over her shoulder, Aidan could see Ben ushering the final remaining Wraiths into a containment zone.

Aidan called Branwen's name as she spread her wings. "Ben's got the last of them. It's over. Don't go."

Bryn lowered her wings as Aidan had requested. But she kept her back to him when she shifted to her human form. She didn't want him watching her face while she transformed. Like always, the shift sent pain ripping through her. Her scream began with the harshness of a Raven's call but ended as a very human cry of pain.

"Branwen?"

Aidan's question reached her ears as the sound of her scream faded. She opened her eyes to find he had come around to face her.

"Are you okay?" he asked.

Bryn opened her mouth to reply and nearly gagged at the taste of Wraith blood. She wiped her mouth with her hand, but it didn't do much good, since her hand was bloody too. Unzipping the leather jacket that had come from Zeke's closet, she lifted the hem of her tank and wiped her face. Then she wiped her hands on the shirt as well.

"I'm okay," she said. "The shift always hurts."

"You're a Raven."

Bryn snorted. "Whatever gave you that idea?"

"Sorry. Sometimes I like to state the obvious. I've never met a Raven before. I didn't realize there were any living."

"There aren't any others like me," Bryn said. "Some of Lilith's more gifted followers eventually master the art of shifting and can take Raven form, but they're not like me."

"What do you mean?" Aidan asked, as he began to walk toward the containment area where the other members of their group gathered.

Bryn fell into step beside him. "I didn't learn the shift through magic. I was born this way." She didn't know why she continued speaking. She usually hated talking about her Raven birth, and she had already revealed more than she had ever told anyone besides Alicia. But for some reason, she added, "Worse luck for my mother."

"She didn't like you being a Raven?"

Bryn suppressed a bitter chuckle at Aidan's innocent question. He couldn't be expected to understand what she'd meant. "I don't know if she even realized I was one. Maybe for a moment she did. I was born with talons on my hands and feet. They ripped her apart, and she bled to death."

Aidan stopped walking and turned to face her, her pain reflected in his expression. "Gods, I'm sorry." His hand closed over her arm, his mouth working to form words. "I know what it's like," he finally said. "Losing a mother—and being responsible for her death."

Bryn stared at him. She hadn't expected that reply. "You do?"

"Yeah, I do." Aidan released her arm and started walking again, more slowly this time. "My mother was badly wounded in a conflict between Light and Dark. I tried to heal her, but I didn't know how to control my Gift, and I couldn't stop the growth of new cells. Instead of healing her, I killed her."

Bryn didn't know what to say. Without speaking, she caught Aidan's hand in her own.

He stopped, looked down at their linked hands, and then glanced up to meet her eyes. He didn't say anything either, but he didn't drop her hand. Instead, his fingers tightened around hers.

# CHAPTER 24

After almost a quarter of an hour of winging it over the city Kev finally wrested control from the dragon. It also took that long for his emotions to settle enough that he didn't feel like breaking things, punching someone, or obliterating anyone or anything that tried to hurt Lucky from the face of the earth.

Gods, this was not good.

Shifting back to human form, he summoned his wings and continued the flight as he cast his thoughts back to his recent activities at the assisted living facility.

He'd heard Lucky's scream, seen the Wraith staring into her eyes, and he'd shifted to the dragon in an instant, incinerating the soul-sucker before he could finish what he'd started.

The next thing he knew, the dragon was ashing every Wraith in sight—and Kev wasn't giving the orders. Not that he didn't share the dragon's satisfaction every time one of the red-eyed monsters dusted to the floor. But he knew better than to indulge his desire to kill them all because one of them had tried to take Lucky's soul.

Didn't he?

Maybe he did, maybe he didn't. He may not have been driving, but the dragon did no more than what he wanted to do at the primitive level beneath all the layers of civilization and training that told him to contain if at all possible and to kill as a last resort.

He hadn't lost control of the dragon in years. Once he'd finally mastered the power, he'd always been in charge. Until his time with Lucky at the cabin. Until he'd dropped his guard and let her in. Until he'd accepted her embraces and kisses and returned them in equal measure. Even while he knew he shouldn't because of her relationship with his brother.

This was so not good.

When he had taken Lucky to his safe haven, he had thought he could help her deal with her Dark Gift. After all, he had one too—and he'd mastered it long ago. Yeah, not so much, as it turned out. At least, not where Lucky was concerned.

He wasn't safe around her. Others weren't safe around him when he was around her. Maybe he should hole up at the cabin alone for a while, until he could get these feelings under control.

But that couldn't happen anytime soon. Once he pulled himself together enough to go back down to ground level, he had to help with clean-up duty, both at the assisted living facility and on Michigan Avenue and wherever else the blasted Wraiths had punched through from their domain.

And after that he'd have to book it to see the Metatron. He didn't know if any amount of fast talking could cover the damage done by a Wraith escape of this magnitude, but his duty as *Ha-Satan* bound him to give it his best shot. Maybe

Lucifer would have some golden words to give him to pass on to the quartet.

Or maybe he should send Aidan and let him sing to them. If his brother used the full force of his Gift, even the Metatron might be swayed.

Kev blew out a breath and banished the distraction of his thoughts. No need to prolong the inevitable. Best go back down there and deal with the mess.

Lucky was helping Josh and Zeke clean up the blood and other signs of battle, when Kev strolled through the gaping hole his dragon had created. They had already removed the Wraith bodies from the commons area, along with the piles of ash from the damaged hallway.

"Go on," Josh said. "I can get the rest of this while Zeke works his memory-switching magic. Go talk to your dragon."

"He's not—," Lucky began.

Josh raised his eyebrows. "He turned a roomful of Wraiths into ash for you. Go."

Lucky went.

She and Kev both stopped when they met in the middle of the ruined hallway. Neither of them spoke. Lucky studied Kev, while he kept his eyes directed to the floor.

"Are you okay?" she asked.

"I should be asking you that." He still didn't look at her.

"You already know I'm all right. You made sure of that. But I'm not so sure about you."

At her words, his eyes lifted to hers, and the bleakness in their green depths clenched a fist around her heart.

"I lost control," he said. "After the first blast, when I got the one that attacked you, the dragon took over. I wasn't driving. If I had been, I wouldn't have… But I wanted to. I wanted to. And he knew it."

"Kev," Lucky breathed.

She reached for him, but he backed away.

"I can't be with you," he said. "I can't feel this way. This has to stop."

"Kev?" she said again.

"I have to find Zeke and finish triaging this mess." Stepping around her, he jogged down the hall and through the exit to the commons.

*Coward,* Kev thought. He was every kind of coward for running away from her, but he couldn't afford to let her touch him. If her fingers had so much as brushed his shoulder, he would have pulled her into his arms and held on so tightly their shapes would have imprinted on each other's bodies. And that couldn't happen. He could no longer afford to cater to his feelings. He had succumbed to the selfishness of taking what he wanted, and he had loosed the monster. No more. He had to get the dragon back under control, and that meant leaving Lucky alone and forgetting he'd ever felt more for her than he should feel for his brother's girlfriend.

Kev found Zeke in one of the residential hallways, exiting one of the resident's rooms.

"You came back," the Cherub said.

Kev rubbed the back of his neck. "Sorry about—back there."

"Are you all right to finish this?"

"Yeah. The danger has been contained, so the beast is under wraps."

After a moment of silence, Zeke said, "I would like to talk to you after all this is settled."

Kev gave a jerky nod. "Of course."

"Right, then," Zeke said. "I will finish scrubbing memories while you make this look more like an electrical fire and notify the authorities."

Twenty minutes later, with fire trucks arriving and the memory-scrubbed staff busy moving residents from the ruined hallway, Lucky, Josh, Zeke, and Kev left the assisted living facility and materialized on Michigan Avenue amid all the post-battle mess.

Lucky couldn't keep her eyes from straying to Kev. He hadn't spoken to her since he'd left her in the hallway. He'd hardly looked at her. Now he surveyed the aftermath of battle, his eyes moving everywhere but in her direction. She shoved the hurt into a mental closet.

She followed Zeke and the others toward the containment field where Malachi was sending the last of the Wraiths back to their world. From the looks of things, the battle here had been even worse than the one at the assisted living facility. She guessed that made sense. More space to move increased the possibility the Wraiths could escape and made containment much more difficult. The team here would have had to kill even more of the creatures. Then again, Kev's dragon had upped their kill quota considerably.

She swallowed as she stepped around the bodies of several fallen Wraiths. Scenes from tonight would haunt her sleep.

Ben jogged to greet them, his body silhouetted against the fading silvery lines that had marked the containment zone. His eyes settled on Josh's transformed body. "Who's the red-eyed hunk, and what have you done with my boyfriend?"

Lucky chuckled. Leave it to Ben to lighten things up.

Josh grinned. "I'm still riding the adrenalin surge from the fight. I'll be back to normal once everything calms down. I hope that doesn't disappoint you."

"Honey, I've got no problems with you either way. Red-eyed muscle-man or brown-eyed scholar, you still have my heart. But I gotta say, I do like the way you fill out those leathers."

"Down, boy," Lucky teased. "We've still got work to do."

Within minutes, Zeke and Malachi started handing out assignments. Lucky took her place with the rest of the crew charged with disposing of the evidence of the night's battle, while Zeke and Malachi went in search of all the humans whose memories had to be altered.

Exhaustion weighting her legs, Lucky climbed the stairs to the room in Zeke's brownstone she'd once thought of as hers. In the last couple of days, it had become less bedroom than makeshift hospital room. She was tired of seeing her loved ones lying in beds with instruments strapped to them while she worried they would never recover.

She couldn't help but blame herself. Neither Josh nor G-Ma would have been drawn into any of this but for her.

She tapped on the door before opening it to step inside. Katrin sat beside the bed, and she looked up at Lucky's entrance, a finger pressed to her lips.

"How is she?" Lucky whispered, her eyes lighting on G-Ma's still, slight figure before shifting back to Katrin.

"She's sleeping. The Wraith took enough blood to weaken her. With the transfusion and rest, she should be fine."

Lucky glanced at the bag of red fluid attached to G-Ma's arm.

"That's all?" she asked. "She's not in any danger of being changed by the bite?"

Katrin shook her head. "No. Wraith bites typically have no side-effects. Your cousin was an exception, because of the toxin he had received and because of—"

"My mixed-up blood."

"Yes."

"Well, I guess I'll come back when—"

A tap on the door interrupted her. Seconds later, the door opened, and Aidan entered the room. Unlike Lucky, he had exchanged his battle-soiled leathers for clean clothes, and his hair was post-shower damp.

His eyes skipped over Lucky to settle on Katrin. "Zeke said you wanted to see me."

"Yes. I thought you might use your Gift to heal the bite wound. You did an excellent job with Branwen. It is time you try again."

Aidan glanced from Katrin to G-Ma before turning to Lucky. "She's your grandmother. Is it all right with you if I try to heal her wound?"

Lucky could hear the hesitation in his voice, and she knew he was remembering what had happened to his mother. Since he'd told her the painful story, she knew he also wondered if she would be afraid for him to use his Gift on G-Ma. "Of course, it's all right, Aidan," she said. "I trust you."

As she heard her words, Lucky cringed inwardly. She might trust him, but she knew, on some level at least, he could no longer trust her.

"Okay, then," Aidan said, turning back to Katrin. Lucky saw the muscles in his jaw clench.

Katrin must have sensed his nervousness as well. "You will do fine, Aidan," she said. "I will be right here with you."

Lucky stepped closer to the bed, so she could better see what happened.

Katrin removed the bandage from G-Ma's shoulder, exposing the jagged wound. Aidan placed his hand over the mark, closed his eyes, and opened his mouth.

Lucky had heard Aidan sing with Icarus, and she had witnessed the inhuman song he sang to alter the wards that protected his home, but what he sang now was something else altogether. It sounded like a single note, but in multiple octaves, some of which she sensed even though they were pitched too low or too high for her ears to hear. She opened her senses, and she could see the sounds twining around each other, like strands of DNA, but parted like the halves of a zipper. As Aidan held the note, the rungs of the double helix ladder took form, zipping the strands together. When the last of the pieces joined, the note died away.

Aidan lifted his hand from G-Ma's shoulder, and Lucky could see the wound had healed. Unmarked skin covered the area where the jagged teeth marks had been.

G-Ma had slept undisturbed through the process.

"Well done, Aidan," Katrin said. "Not so much as a mark to prompt her caregivers to ask unanswerable questions when she is returned to the facility."

Aidan nodded. "Right. I'm out of here then, if it's okay with you. Zeke wants us to gather downstairs in half an hour or so, and I could use a few minutes to rest."

"Of course."

Lucky followed Aidan into the hall, stopping him before he entered the room he'd claimed as his own.

"Thank you," she said. "That was amazing, Aidan. What you can do—it really is a Gift."

He nodded, unsmiling, as his blue eyes met hers. Then he turned, went into his room, and shut the door behind him.

Lucky closed her eyes against the sting of impending tears. For a few moments, she stood, unmoving.

Then, straightening her shoulders, she returned to the room where G-Ma slept. She retrieved some workout clothes from the dresser and a pair of sneakers from the closet, said her good-byes to Katrin, and headed downstairs to the gym showers where she could discard her filthy borrowed leathers and do her best to wash away the memories of the night's battle.

# CHAPTER 25

The ante-room was as cold as ever, and Kev had waited much longer than normal for admission to the Metatron's council chamber. He had begun to feel as if his entire body, from the soles of his bare feet to each hair on his head, was transforming into the same icy crystal as the Metatron's council table and the uncomfortable chair they assigned him during the meetings. His mind filled with a momentary vision of himself, no longer flesh and blood, but a piece of transparent sculpture, tucked into a corner of the council chamber to serve as a warning to whoever might replace him as *Ha-Satan*.

He glanced at the Dominion standing guard over him, but the angel's impassive face revealed nothing—no impatience, no discomfort, and no smug certainty indicating he knew any more than Kev about his companion's extended absence. Whatever the Dominion knew or didn't know remained hidden behind his disciplined blankness.

Kev directed his gaze back to the floor a few feet in front of him. If the Metatron wanted to keep him waiting, then wait he would. When they got around to admitting him, he would assure them the entire Wraith domain was now on lockdown. In the hours since the latest escape, Lucifer and his most trusted lieutenants had worked new wards to seal all known portals and to block any attempts of unauthorized egress or ingress at any point in the realm. No more Wraiths would escape any time soon.

Too bad his father hadn't taken such drastic steps before tonight's attack. But how could Lucifer have known someone would rip new portals into the space between the Wraith's world and the human realm, allowing the creatures to pour through the way they had?

With an inward sigh, Kev allowed his thoughts to return to the more personal problem of his dragon. Once he was done here, he had to have the promised conversation with Zeke. He hadn't decided how much he wanted to share with the Cherub, even though he had mentally rehearsed the encounter in various versions. The idea of telling Zeke everything both filled him with a sense of relief and terrified him. If he told Zeke, he wouldn't have to carry the burden alone, but it would also mean admitting he may never have mastered the dragon at all. If he wasn't in control now, maybe he never had been.

And what did that say about his qualifications for serving as *Ha-Satan?*

Kev's heartbeat picked up as his mind leapt to a possibility he hadn't yet allowed himself to consider. What if he lost it while he was with the Metatron? If that happened, he would put more than himself in danger. The entire cause of the Dark and the Fallen would be at risk.

*That won't happen.* Kev forced his thoughts to move forward, and his heart slowed its pace in response. Granted, his emotions seemed more volatile in general lately, but he'd only ever lost control when Lucky was involved. No matter how infuriating he might find his encounters with the Metatron, he could trust himself to remain in diplomatic mode and keep the dragon safely contained—couldn't he?

He looked up as the door to the council chamber opened, revealing the long-absent Dominion.

"*Ha-Satan,* you may take your leave," the guard said. "The Metatron has asked me to inform you that they have no interest in the excuses Lucifer or you may have concocted regarding this incident. They will contact you as soon as they have determined the appropriate response to Lucifer's blatant negligence."

Anger bubbled in Kev at the high-handed response, but he schooled his features to reveal nothing. Then fear flooded through the anger as his vision shifted. *Holy hell.* He had to get out of here. He lowered his gaze to hide what he knew were now vertical-pupiled irises and tilted his head to the Dominion in silent response. Then he turned and stepped back through the Gates.

When he exited on the other side, the shift was already on him. As his human body morphed into the massive, scaly form of his alter ego, he offered a silent apology to Zeke for whatever damage he would cause.

Only when he found himself back in human form and dangling from the huge hand a very angry-looking Uriel had locked around his throat did he realize he hadn't stepped through to Zeke's basement. He was in a stark white room he'd never seen before.

*Do you have your beast under control again, Dragon?*

Kev didn't know which hurt more, the bruising hand cutting off his air supply or the Archangel's question running flaming laps in his brain. Uriel's words always seared the senses, but he'd never been the recipient of the Archangel's anger before.

He tried to answer, but no sound could escape through the choke-hold. He could hardly even breathe. Still, he assumed the question hadn't been rhetorical—and that Uriel didn't intend to kill him without getting an answer first. Looking into the Archangel's flame-filled eye sockets, Kev gestured toward the hand that enclosed his throat.

Uriel let out a growl.

Then the back of Kev's body slammed against a wall, and the hand pinning him there by the throat loosened.

Kev sucked in a breath, noting the emptiness of the room, blank white walls, white floor, no windows.

"I don't know," he said as soon as he could speak.

Uriel growled again as his hand began to tighten.

"I think so," Kev added. "But the change came on me pretty quickly back there, so I can't be sure."

*When you are sure, let me know, and I will release you.*

Suspension by the throat wasn't the ideal situation for deep breathing, but Kev did the best he could.

"Okay, I'm good now," he said, after several breaths.

Uriel released his hold. Kev's knees hit the floor.

*You wanted to see the Book?*

Kev got to his feet, any dignity he might have possessed in tatters. "Yeah, I did. The Book is here?"

*Not* here *precisely. This is merely an entry point, one that mimics your sense of space.*

The Archangel laid a hand on Kev's shoulder, and for a second the world spun.

*The Book is here.*

The space where they stood seemed to Kev both like a room and unlike any room he'd been in before. It somehow managed to convey the sense of enclosure and unlimited spaciousness all at the same time.

And it hummed. A music more layered and nuanced than any Kev had ever heard flowed around them like water.

Enclosed in a series of giant singing spheres, they stood on a small, clear platform that seemed to float, suspended. Beneath them, above them, all around them, stretching away into infinity were stars and planets, constellations and galaxies.

Closer in, like spheres inside spheres, myriad flickering transparent images played on countless clear screens as if on sheets of water, circling in every direction, like electrons around the nucleus of an atom.

Too many images flickered on too many layers of the circling water-like spheres for Kev to focus on any one of them, and they moved too quickly for him to track even if he could have focused on one. But he could grasp impressions. Skies filled with birds. Oceans full of fish. Deeper oceans populated with bioluminescent creatures. Trees. Flowers. Animals of all sorts. People. Angels. Demons. Nephilim. And creatures he didn't recognize at all. Beings beyond his experience and even his comprehension.

Suspended in the center of the rotating series of spheres, somehow simultaneously an infinite distance from him and close enough to touch, was the Book. He'd only seen it at Strikings, when it looked, well, somewhat more like an actual book than it looked now. But he knew what it was. The Book of Life. The one Uriel had altered, rewritten, when he agreed to allow Lucky to be Made Naphil. There in the center of all those spheres, it glowed, the nucleus to their electrons. One Book, yet uncountable Books, pages open and spilling out the creatures and beings that flickered on the spheres and lived and breathed in their respective worlds.

Kev closed his eyes against the impossible immensity of it all. Taking it in was like trying to look at Zeke's morphing form multiplied several thousand times over.

His breath sped up as his heart rate increased. He stood in the space where the Book of Life—what? Was stored? It wasn't exactly the kind of book you kept in a library. This was where it—lived. Where *everything* lived.

He opened his eyes for another look and then closed them again.

"Uriel, this is too much for me. Is there another way to— look at things?"

Again Uriel's hand closed on his shoulder. Again the world tilted.

*This should better suit your senses, Naphil.*

Kev opened his eyes.

They now stood in what appeared to be a kind of viewing hall. The images that had swirled on the infinitude of watery spheres now flickered on screens that filled the walls to either side. The walls stretched away as far as he could see in either direction.

*You wanted to access information about your grandfather?*

"Yes. I'd like to know who visited him before his Disintegration."

*Has your grandfather given you permission to access these records?*

For a moment, Kev was at a loss for words. "Uh, no. He was Disintegrated before my mother was born."

*Time has no meaning here.*

As Uriel spoke, the screened walls disappeared, and Kev found himself alone in another white room. White walls surrounded him on three sides. The fourth stretched out in a long hallway.

In the distance, he could see something moving toward him. Faint and blurred at first, it seemed to gather form as it approached. That form solidified a few yards from Kev into a dark-haired man, tall but stooped. When he drew nearer, Kev saw his mother's dark green eyes in the man's care-worn face.

"Semyaza?

The angel inclined his head. "Grandson. Your name is Kevin, I believe?"

Kev nodded.

"What do you want of me, Kevin? What makes you summon me to this form that causes me such pain?"

The rush of empathy took Kev by surprise. He knew the history of his mother's birth. The last thing he'd expected was to feel anything but hatred for the angel who sired her. But Semyaza radiated such loss, such self-loathing, such remorse, that much of Kev's animosity faded away.

"I would like permission to access the records of your imprisonment—before your Disintegration. I would like to know who visited you."

"Why? What does it matter?"

"Jahoel has been killed. He was marked with Lucifer's sigil. As were you."

Semyaza raised his right arm, turning it palm up. "As was I," he said.

Kev stared. There on the inside of Semyaza's lower arm was Lucifer's mark. The scarred skin looked leathery and tough.

His hand moved toward the scar before he had time to think. He stopped before he touched the angel's arm. "May I?" he asked.

"If you must."

Kev traced his fingers over the pattern. Yes, the unevenness in the edges felt familiar.

"Thank you," he said. "Can you tell me who visited you?"

"I hardly remember." Semyaza sounded weary. "It will be in the records. You have my permission to view them."

"Thank you," Kev said again.

Semyaza already moved back down the hallway. After a few steps, he stopped and turned around.

"Tell your mother I am sorry," he said. "It is too late to apologize to her mother, but please tell Katrin I regret my actions. I do not ask for forgiveness. I simply want her to know."

Kev nodded. "I'll tell her."

"Thank you," Semyaza said.

Kev watched him walk away, his form disintegrating as he went.

When Semyaza disappeared, Kev found himself again in the viewing room filled with flickering screens, Uriel at his side.

*Permission has been granted?*

Kev nodded, then frowned. "Uriel, if Semyaza could appear to me despite his Disintegration, why can't you ask Jahoel who killed him? Or ask for permission to access the record of the murder?"

*I am the Keeper of the Book. I am not permitted to know its secrets. I can only help others access small parts of records that concern them and serve as a conduit to rewrite records, as I did for your friend Lucky during her Striking.*

"Couldn't Zeke or someone ask to see Jahoel's record? Could I?"

*If Jahoel had granted permission in life for you or Zeke to access his record, it could be done. He did not. A bond of blood could summon him, as your blood tie summoned Semyaza, but Jahoel had no family. There is no blood to call him.*

"That would be a 'no' then. Do we have time for you to show me Semyaza's record now?"

*I told you time has no meaning here.*

Uriel waved his hand, and the long hallways shrank, all the screens disappearing, save one. The flickering images it displayed resolved into an image of Semyaza inside a cell.

*Watch as much as you like. Your thoughts can speed or slow the record. When you have seen what you wished to see, the screen will fade, and I will return.*

Kev lost all sense of time as he stared at the screen. He learned to control the pace of the playback with his thoughts as Uriel had indicated. He sped through the hours when Semyaza sat or paced alone, slowed when anyone appeared to break the angel's solitude.

Guards. Ba'al. Lucifer. Lucifer and Ba'al. Ba'al. Guards. The same visitors repeated over and over.

Kev was almost ready to call it quits, convinced the record was a dead end after all, when a cloaked and hooded figure entered the frame. He slowed the record, a frown gathering his brow. In all the previous visits, Semyaza had interacted with his visitors. This time, he seemed unaware of the cloaked presence. His eyes looked straight ahead, unseeing.

The figure approached the seated Semyaza and lifted his right arm, exposing the mark from Lucifer's sigil. From the appearance of the hand the figure pressed against the mark, Kev guessed the cloaked figure was male. His eyes widened as the man's fingers and thumb disappeared, his hand flattening and melding like warmed wax. After a moment, his fingers and thumb reformed, and the man lifted his hand away from Semyaza's arm. The shape of Lucifer's sigil showed on his upturned palm. His fingers closed around the copied sigil, and he moved out of frame.

Kev never saw his face.

Feeling almost normal again after her shower, Lucky slid into one of the remaining empty chairs at Zeke's big table. She sat across from Josh and Ben, avoiding the seat next to

Aidan. She figured they would both be more comfortable with some distance between them.

She began to question her choice of seating when Kev entered the room. He had arrived last for the post-battle post-mortem, and the only empty seat was next to her. His glance flitted over her as he sat down, his lips tightening and a muscle moving in his jaw as if he'd clenched his teeth. Lucky sighed. She should have tried harder to make sure she sat nowhere near either of the brothers. Right. How exactly could she have done that?

"Looks like everyone is here. Kevin, why don't we start with you?" Zeke said. "How went your meeting with the Metatron?"

Kev shook his head. "It didn't. They refused to see me. According to the Dominion guard, they will be contacting us soon with their response to, and I quote, 'Lucifer's blatant negligence.'"

Zeke's gray eyes sharpened as the tension in the room ratcheted upward. "That is not good news."

"No," Kev agreed. "I did make some unexpected progress in the murder investigation though, which I'd like to share with you privately."

"We will discuss it further when you see me later regarding the other matter of which we spoke."

Lucky watched Kev nod in agreement, wondering what "the other matter" might be. A part of her mind continued to gnaw the question, as Zeke reported on the increased security in the Wraith's world, and the members of each team filled each other in on the major details of their respective battles.

"There is one final matter," Zeke said, once the information exchange was complete. "For various reasons, we had an inordinate number of kills tonight—both on Michigan Avenue, where it was to be expected, and at the assisted living facility, where, one would have hoped, containment was a more viable option. While we are all aware we must sometimes kill in situations such as these, I believe we all also agree that containment is preferred if possible. The Wraiths are not deadly in the confines of their own world. Only when they cross into the human realm do they become dangerous."

He paused, looking around the table. "Did everyone do their best to contain instead of kill?"

Kev spoke up first. "You know I didn't, Zeke, there at the end. But up until then, yes, I contained if possible."

"What happened at the end, Kev?" Aidan asked. "That doesn't sound like you."

It was Josh who answered. "A Wraith attacked Lucky, and Kev's dragon flamed every Wraith in the vicinity."

For a moment stunned silence filled the room. Then Aidan said, "I should have guessed."

Lucky flinched at the bitterness in his words, and she saw Kev do the same. She wanted to reach for his hand, but knew such a gesture would make matters worse.

"I had it under control," she said.

Everyone looked at her.

"What do you mean, Lucky?" Zeke asked.

"The thing with the Wraith," she said. "I was about to contain him when—he turned into ash."

She glanced at Kev. His face had gone white.

"He wasn't a threat anymore?" he asked.

She shook her head.

"You didn't even need my help, and I ashed every Wraith there."

After a moment of silence, Zeke asked, "Anyone else?"

"I didn't," Bryn said. "I didn't even try to contain. I killed every Wraith I encountered."

Lucky looked at her cousin in surprise. Regret stained the girl's hard expression.

"And why is that, Branwen?" Zeke asked.

"I'm a Raven. Once I started, I—couldn't seem to stop."

"You will come to my study tomorrow morning, please, to talk more about this." The gentleness of Zeke's tone made the words more request than order.

"Of course," Bryn whispered. To Lucky, her usually tough cousin sounded close to tears.

"Anyone else?" Zeke asked again.

"All of us on the Magnificent Mile killed more than we normally would have," Ben said. "The space was too open. We couldn't contain them all."

Zeke nodded. "I understand that, Ben. We all did what we believed necessary. Still, we must work to do better in future."

He pushed back his chair and rose to his feet. "Thank you all for your time. You are free to take your well-earned rest." His eyes swung to Kev. "Except for you. I will see you downstairs."

Kev nodded.

Lucky stood along with the rest.

"Kev?" His name had left her mouth before she had time to think better of it. And her hand reached for his arm almost without her volition.

She felt the muscles of his forearm contract at her touch, but at least he didn't yank it from under her hand.

"What is it, Lucky?" he asked.

He sounded so defeated, Lucky couldn't think of a single response. She searched his eyes, willing them to reveal something of his thoughts.

He lifted her hand from his arm and held it for the barest second before releasing her and turning away. Her eyes followed him as he followed Zeke out of the room.

Lucky waited until everyone else had had plenty of time to find their way to bed or wherever else they might be going before she exited the dining room and headed upstairs. Maybe G-Ma would be awake now.

Knocking softly on the bedroom door, Lucky stepped inside. She relaxed when she saw no one but Katrin keeping watch. She had feared Aidan might be there as well.

"She's awake," Katrin said, pushing herself up from her chair with her cane, as Lucky moved into the room and closed the door behind her. "She's been talking about you, something about how you need to help 'your dragon.'" Katrin's rapier gaze probed Lucky's. "I assume she refers to my son. Do you have any idea what she might mean?"

Lucky shook her head. "No. I mean—yes, I think she is talking about Kev. But I don't know how I'm supposed to help him—yet."

"Is my son in danger?" Katrin's eyes narrowed.

"I don't know that he's in danger." Lucky frowned. "But he's having trouble with the dragon."

"Trouble? What kind of trouble?"

"He—he lost control of the dragon tonight." After the words had left her mouth, Lucky wished she could take them back. Kev might not want her sharing that story with his mother.

"Lost control?" Katrin asked. "What happened?"

"I—It's probably best if you ask Kev about that."

Katrin moved toward the door. "Does Ezekiel know?"

"Yes, but—"

"I will give you some privacy while you visit with your grandmother." The door clicked closed on Katrin's words.

Lucky had no doubts about where Katrin was headed. Poor Kev. Then again, perhaps he'd be grateful for his mother's concern. For concerned she was. By Kev's account, Katrin had never been the most demonstrative of parents, but what Lucky had seen flash in the woman's eyes was the kind of protectiveness she used to see in G-Ma's.

"Lucky? Is that you?"

Ignoring the now unoccupied chair, Lucky sat on the bed beside her grandmother, drawing her legs up under her and taking one of G-Ma's hands in both of hers.

"Yes, it's me. I wanted to see how you were doing."

"Oh, I'm fine, dear. But I'm worried about you—and your dragon. You have to help him, Lucky."

"How, G-Ma? How am I supposed to help him?"

G-Ma's finger tapped Lucky's temple. "You will know."

"I will?"

G-Ma nodded. "Not two, Lucky. Only one."

"What?"

"Not two. Only one."

"I don't understand. What's only one?"

"Would you get me some water, dear? I'm thirsty."

"Sure."

A pitcher of water and a glass sat on a tray on the bedside table. Lucky filled the glass and then helped G-Ma sit up so she could drink the water. After she'd set the empty glass back on the tray, she curled up beside G-Ma again.

"G-Ma, what's not two, only one?"

G-Ma looked at her blankly. "I don't know what you mean. What are you talking about?"

"Never mind," Lucky said. "I'm not sure what I meant either."

G-Ma patted her hand. "I'm glad you came to see me."

"Me too," Lucky said around a yawn.

"You should get some sleep, dear."

"Yeah, I should."

The door opened and Katrin re-entered the room.

"I'm heading home to bed now." Lucky leaned down to kiss her grandmother's forehead. "Goodnight, G-Ma."

"Goodnight, my Lucky." G-Ma pressed her hand to Lucky's cheek. "I love you so."

Lucky blinked back tears. "I love you too."

Stepping close to Katrin, Lucky said, "Thank you—and Aidan. She seems to have recovered from the attack."

"Yes. I have recommended that Ezekiel take her back to familiar surroundings in the morning."

Lucky nodded. "Thank you—again."

"You are welcome."

Lucky had opened the door when Katrin's voice stopped her. "Can you help my son?"

"I don't know," Lucky said, looking over her shoulder at the other woman. "But I'll do whatever I can—once I know what that is."

After she'd closed the door behind her, Lucky stood in the hallway, hesitating outside Bryn's room. She didn't want to wake her cousin, but based on the emotional turmoil she'd seen on Bryn's face earlier, she guessed sleep would be a long time coming for the girl. And Bryn had looked like she could use a friend.

Her soft tap on the door was greeted by an alert "Come in." When she entered the room, she found her cousin still dressed except for her boots, reclining against the headboard, a book in her hands.

"I thought you might be awake," Lucky said.

"Yeah. I had hoped reading would make me sleepy, but it hasn't worked so far."

Lucky kicked off her shoes and curled up on the foot of the bed. "Do you want to talk about it?"

"What's there to say? I ripped the throats out of more Wraiths than I can remember. And each time I did it, I wanted to move on to the next."

"Every time?"

Bryn pursed her lips. "Well, I felt a little regret, but my Raven side won out."

"What does that mean—you being a Raven?"

Lucky kept her eyes on Bryn's face while she waited for her response. After a while, Bryn stood beside the bed, her hands out in front of her. As Lucky watched, Bryn's fingers lengthened and twisted into talons. Her face changed shape, her nose and mouth morphing into a large-size version of a raven's beak. The shift looked painful, and the hoarse caw Bryn gave before the transformation completed sounded to Lucky like a muffled scream.

Bryn gave another quiet scream-caw as black raven wings took shape on her back. She turned in a circle, as if modeling a costume or a new dress.

Then she closed her eyes, and a frown knotted her forehead as she re-transformed. Lucky could see the sheen of sweat on her cousin's brow as she returned to the bed and collapsed back against the headboard.

"It hurts when you transform." Lucky's words were half statement, half question.

Bryn nodded. "Always."

"Is the transformation always partial?"

"I can change completely if I want, but my Raven form is Bryn-sized, so lots bigger than a normal bird. And even when I do a partial shift, I get the beak. I can never speak."

"That must be frustrating."

"It is. But feeling like my mind isn't all mine is worse."

"Yeah. I know what you mean."

Bryn's gaze shot to Lucky's. "That's how you felt when your Gift manifested, and you had William and his father in your power. I understand why you thought you couldn't come home."

"Speaking of home," Lucky said, "have you talked to Lilith? Have you thought about going back?"

Bryn shook her head. "She lied to me, Lucky. She told me I was Bound, and I never was. How could she do that to me?"

"Maybe you should ask her, give her a chance to explain." As Lucky heard her own words, she remembered Lilith saying much the same thing to her about Zeke.

"I guess I'll have to. I've always known I would have limited time here, and Zeke won't want to keep me around now. He'll probably give me my marching orders tomorrow."

"I didn't get that impression. I think he wants to help you."

"I'm not so sure about that. I guess I'll find out."

"Do you want me to come with you—to talk to him?"

Bryn searched Lucky's eyes. "You'd do that?"

"Sure. If you want me to."

"Yeah." Bryn nodded. "I do."

Lucky covered her cousin's hand with hers and squeezed. "Then I'll be there."


Kev entered Zeke's study to find the Cherub pouring scotch into one of two glasses nestled among the books, papers, and scrolls that littered his desk. After he'd filled the first glass, Zeke held the bottle over the empty one and looked at Kev with a raised eyebrow.

"Yes, please," Kev said.

Zeke filled the second glass and replaced the bottle of scotch in the cabinet behind his desk. Then he picked up the two glasses and handed one to Kev, tilting his head toward the leather chairs.

Kev dropped into the chair across from Zeke and raised the glass to his lips.

"What happened tonight, Kevin?" Zeke asked.

Kev took a sip of the scotch and let the warmth sliding down his throat clear a path for the words. "I lost control. The dragon ran the show."

He told Zeke everything, including how Lucky had talked the dragon down that night at the cabin and how he'd come close to shifting in the Metatron's ante-room. It felt good to unburden himself, despite his fear of how Zeke might react.

He need not have worried. While Zeke shared Kev's concerns about the dragon's capacity for destruction, he seemed to think the emotional disruption might be what Kev needed.

"You have been too controlled for too long, Kevin," Zeke said. "I was beginning to worry about you.'

"And you're not worried now?" Kev asked.

"I am concerned, yes, but I think the conflict is unavoidable—and, in some ways, overdue. You can't ignore your feelings, Kevin. You have to figure out how to work with them, channel them, use them."

"That sounds like what I told Lucky about her Gift."

Zeke said nothing, only raised his eyebrows.

Before either could say more, the study door flew open, and Katrin barged inside. She faced Kev, ignoring Zeke.

"I hear you lost control of your dragon?"

The concern on his mother's face disarmed Kev, and he spilled the story without thinking.

After he'd finished speaking, Katrin turned to Zeke.

"Is my son in danger?"

Kev's heart almost stopped in his chest. He'd expected her to be worried about the danger he might cause, not any he might face.

"I do not believe he poses a threat to himself, no."

The qualified nature of Zeke's response did not escape Kev, but his answer seemed to satisfy Katrin. Turning back to Kev, she searched his face. "All right, then," she said, and exited the room as abruptly as she'd entered.

Kev broke the silence left in her wake to fill Zeke in on the cloaked figure he'd viewed in Semyaza's records. Zeke's brows drew together as he listened.

"I can think of a few beings who might be capable of such a thing," he said. "But I cannot understand how any of them would have benefited from Jahoel's death. Let me make some inquiries. I will also ask Uriel to let you view the record again. If you look at it from other angles, perhaps you can see the figure's face or something else that might be helpful."

"Other angles?"

"Yes. Uriel did not explain that you can alter the position from which you view a record?"

Kev shook his head. "No, he didn't."

"It may not help anyway. But you might learn something more. I will let you know Uriel's response. You get some rest."

Thoughts spinning and emotions jumbled, Kev left Zeke's office and headed upstairs to the bedroom he'd claimed as his own. He didn't want to contaminate the cabin—his refuge, his escape—with the chaos in his head and heart, and the very idea of the sterile room at the barracks in Elsewhere that had served as his normal residence for years put a gaping hole in his stomach. Over the last few months, Zeke's brownstone had come to feel like home. He needed that tonight. His conversation with Zeke and the unexpected encounter with Katrin had shredded his defenses.

Kev had hoped to reach the privacy of his bedroom without encountering anyone, but his hopes were dashed when the door of the room next to his opened, and Aidan joined him in the hallway.

"I thought I heard you," Aidan said. "All done with your meeting with Zeke?"

"Yeah. All done."

"Did he tell you to get your feelings for Lucky under control before they get you or someone else killed?"

Kev took a deep breath and blew it out. "No, Aidan, he didn't tell me that."

"Well, maybe he should have. From what I could gather, you not only incinerated a whole roomful of Wraiths but destroyed part of the building. Gods, Kev. When you decide to let go, you don't do it by halves, do you?"

"What's that supposed to mean?"

"For one thing, when you finally decide you can drop your precious control for someone, why did it have to be for my girl? But I guess I know the answer to that, don't I?"

"And again I ask, what's that supposed to mean?"

"You always thought I stole the relationship you should have had with our father. I guess my messing that up by accidentally killing my mother wasn't enough. You still had to go and steal something from me to even the score."

"Aidan, are you hearing yourself? You can't believe even half of what you're saying."

"Oh, come off it. Deep down you've always resented me—because Lucifer loved *my* mother, and because, even though you were conceived to be the subject of that blasted prophecy, it turned out to be about me, and because I screwed up and walked away two years ago."

"Fine! Yes, I have resented you. Yes, I dreamed of having parents who loved each other—and who loved me like Lucifer and Sarah loved you. Yes, I wanted the prophecy to be about me. It was why I was conceived. Without it, I had no reason for being. And, yes, when you walked away, I envied you—because you *could*."

"You could walk away if you wanted to, Kev."

"No, I couldn't. This is the only life I'm fit for. I may not be the subject of the prophecy, but I'm still Lucifer's heir. And I could never pass for human long-term as well as you. I turn into a freaking dragon!"

"Which you can no longer control, because you've got a thing for *my* girlfriend! That didn't quite work out as planned, did it?"

"You think I planned this—in order to get back at you for old resentments? Holy hell, Aidan! You're my brother—and my best friend. I may have resented you at times, but I love you. And I never wanted to hurt you. I don't want to feel this way about Lucky. It's tearing me apart, destroying me. She's the last girl I should have fallen in love with, and if I could make myself stop loving her, believe me, I would. It would be better for everyone if I could."

Time slowed for Kev as the words left his lips. He saw Aidan's shocked expression, saw the door down the hall open as Lucky and Bryn ran out, looking as shocked as his brother, and he felt the reins of his control slipping out of his hands. When Lucky ran toward him, he saw her through the dragon's eyes.

# CHAPTER 26

*He's in love with me.* The words spun in Lucky's head as she ran to Kev. *But he doesn't want to be.*

She and Bryn had had no choice but to overhear the last part of Aidan and Kev's conversation. And when the brothers' voices had grown even louder—and the Light-Bringer's Medallion had flared against her skin—Lucky had leapt from the bed and run to the door. She had reached the hallway in time for Kev's declaration.

She wanted to ask him to repeat the words, to say them to her. But the insistent heat of the medallion on her chest and the vertical-pupiled eyes staring at her from Kev's face forced her attention to other matters. When he sank into a crouch and cocked his head in that animalistic way, she dropped to her knees beside him.

"Kev?" she whispered, her fingertips lighting on his tensed forearm. "I know you're in there."

His head swung toward her, the dragon's eyes narrowing.

"We've been here before, haven't we?" Lucky said, the calmness of her voice belying the pounding of her heart. "You know me. It's safe, I promise. There's no threat here. Let Kev come back, okay?"

The dragon's unblinking eyes looked back at her.

Lucky stared into those eyes, her fingers pressing against Kev's arm. Opening her senses—and ignoring the now near-deafening beat of her own heart in her ears—she reached for the dragon's mind.

There. She could see the tendrils of the beast's thoughts, the coiled ribbons of his emotions. Beautiful. Alien.

Holding the image, she reached further, searching for Kev. Finding him was a struggle, but she finally located the human consciousness the dragon had pushed aside. Iridescent threads of thought, sparking lights of emotion.

She studied the two, the mind of the beast and the mind of the man, feeling her way. What could she do? How could she help? How could she get the dragon to cede control to Kev once again? Or should she help Kev take control? No. The dragon was the key. But how?

She took a deep breath, steadying herself. She had touched the dragon's mind once before. She could do it again. Tentatively, she reached out, an observer no more.

Lucky felt the shock as the dragon recoiled at her touch. It broke her concentration, caused her to lose her connection to both the dragon's mind and Kev's. But it also seemed to break the dragon's hold on the reins. Kev blinked, and his gold-flecked dark-green eyes flashed to her face.

"Stay out of my head," he said hoarsely. Then he disappeared.

Kev's whole body shook as he rematerialized in the mud room of the cabin. Yanking his old barn coat off the hook, he shoved his arms in the sleeves, thrust his hands into the pockets, and stepped outside. He walked a few quick laps around the cabin, letting the sound of the snow crunching under his boots and the touch of the cold, crisp air on his face calm the fear that made his heart thud in his chest and his trembling hands fist in his pockets.

When he no longer felt as if his body would shake apart at the seams, he stopped, took a couple of deep breaths, and dropped his head back to look up. Countless stars filled the clear night sky, tiny lights blinking in the soothing blackness. He lowered to the ground and lay back in the snow. Staring at the sky, he sank into the starry blanket and breathed in the cold. He emptied his mind, letting it go black as the night, and then he filled it with stars. Gradually, his heartbeat slowed to normal.

Kev had no idea how long he lay on his snowy bed before the cold penetrated his clothes, causing him to shiver and jarring him back to the present. He ignored the shivers for a few more breaths. Then he stood, and after searching his coat pocket for the keys he always kept there, he crunched through the snow to his studio.

Inside, he lit a fire, wondering how long it would take before the wood stove would produce enough heat to keep his breath from forming white clouds. No matter. He had plenty of time.

After his argument with Aidan and the internal drama with Lucky and the dragon that had followed, any desire to sleep had deserted him. He knew his disappearance had probably worried the others, but all he could think about when he'd snapped back into control was putting as much distance as possible between him and anyone he could harm.

Well, that and keeping Lucky out of his head.

He supposed he should be thankful for her interference, since it had made the dragon drop the reins. But the thought of her messing with the crumbling balance he had with the dragon chilled the blood in his veins. He'd seen what she could do, and he respected her power. But he also knew her control over her Gift was as tenuous as his had become. If either of them cracked during such a proceeding, they could both die.

Lucky. Had he really told Aidan he loved her? And had she really overheard him? He'd intended to keep that to himself—just as he still intended to let the feelings go, get over her, and let her and Aidan take up where they'd left off. While his confession—and Lucky overhearing it—might complicate things a bit, it didn't change anything.

When the room had warmed enough that he could take his hands out of his pockets, Kev crossed to the unfinished sculpture he'd begun the night he'd brought Lucky to the cabin. He removed the sheet from the piece and examined it with his artist's eye. A medium to dark brown patina would work well, with a bit of blue-green.

He selected the necessary chemicals from the storage cabinet and placed them on a work table before making a quick trip back to the cabin to retrieve some distilled water. Once he'd mixed the formulas, he prepared the piece, using a torch to heat the metal to the appropriate temperature to apply the brown patina. He worked on a small area at a time, so he could keep the temperature as even as possible. After he'd finished with the brown, he added a few touches of the blue-green, this time heating both the formula and the metal.

When he had finished, he surveyed the piece with satisfaction. It had turned out even better than he'd hoped. His beautiful, powerful Lucky.

No. He pushed the thought aside, doing his best to ignore the pain that wound its way through his heart. The sculpture might belong to him, but the real girl never could. He'd indulged himself long enough. It was time to let her go.

He put away his tools and cleaned up the work space before giving the piece one last look. The exhaustion he'd been holding at bay crashed over him. After adding several more logs to the fire, he pulled off his boots and slid into the cot tucked away at the rear of the studio. He was asleep almost as soon as the blankets covered him.

Lucky rose to her feet, her gaze moving from the now empty space Kev had occupied to scan the faces of her companions. She had been so focused on Kev, she had forgotten about Aidan and Bryn. She didn't know when Katrin had joined them, but she must have arrived in time to see her son disappear. The healer braced herself on her cane, as her eyes, so like her son's, locked on Lucky.

"Well?" she asked.

"I didn't do anything," Lucky said, "besides startle the dragon enough to give Kev a chance to grab control."

"What did he say before he dematerialized?" The concern in Aidan's question contrasted with his earlier anger.

"He told me to stay out of his head."

With the crisis passed, Lucky's emotions threatened to overcome her. Her legs trembled as she leaned back against the wall and allowed herself to slide to the floor. Dear God, she'd intended to mess with his mind. And, she realized with surprise, she hadn't felt the burn of her palm sigils even once.

The thought of what she'd attempted to do terrified her. After her experience with the Wraith, she knew she could exert some control over her Gift, but she still didn't have any idea of what she needed to do to help Kev, didn't even know what to look for. What if she'd done something wrong? She silently thanked the dragon for kicking her out. If she'd done anything to damage Kev, she couldn't have lived with herself.

She crossed her arms over her ribs and held on as she began to shake.

When Bryn sat down beside her and put an arm around her shoulders, Lucky leaned into the offered support.

She had stopped shaking by the time Aidan crouched across from her. "Hey, are you okay?"

Lucky lifted her head from Bryn's shoulder and sat upright. "Yeah. I'm all right."

"Any idea where he might have gone?"

Lucky nodded. "I think I know where he is. And he's okay. I'd know if he weren't."

Aidan's expression made her regret adding that last bit. It had seemed like a necessary clarification, but she knew it underscored how much their relationships had changed.

"He says he's in love with you."

"Yeah. I heard."

"Are you going after him?"

"Not now. He needs some time to calm down—and so do I."

"But you will try again?" The question came from Katrin.

"Yes. No. I don't know." Lucky met Katrin's eyes, her own filmed with tears. "What if I make it worse?"

Katrin's gaze never faltered. "You won't."

Lucky wished she could share the woman's sense of certainty.

"You will try again," Katrin stated. Then, leaning on her cane, she turned and went back into G-Ma's room.

When Bryn stood and held out her hand, Lucky took it and let the other girl pull her to her feet.

"You need to get some sleep," Bryn said. "You want to crash with me? You don't look like you could make it home."

"Thanks, Bryn. That would be great."

Muttering goodnight to Aidan, Lucky followed Bryn back to her room, where she climbed under the covers and collapsed against the pillow. The sound of Bryn's even breathing soothed her, and after a matter of minutes, she succumbed to sleep.

# CHAPTER 27

"Let's go," Bryn said. "I want to get this over with."

For the second time that morning, Lucky rapped her knuckles on Zeke's office door. She pushed it open and stepped inside. Her eyes moved from her cousin, who had tensed beside her, to the scarlet-haired woman seated across from Zeke in one of the big leather chairs.

"Hello, Lilith," she said.

Lines of strain marked Lilith's face, making her seem older than before, but her smile was warm. "Hello, granddaughters," she said.

Bryn did not return the greeting.

Zeke gestured toward the two unoccupied leather chairs. "Please join us. Lilith cannot stay long."

Lucky took the chair next to Zeke, leaving Bryn the one nearest Lilith. Bryn shot her a look. Lucky lifted a shoulder. The point of this meeting was for the two of them to talk.

Which she hoped they'd do soon.

Lilith finally broke the uncomfortable silence. "Ezekiel said it took some effort to convince you to see me."

Bryn still said nothing, but she looked at Lilith for the first time since she'd sat down.

Lucky wondered how Lilith would explain her long-term deception. She also wondered if Bryn would find any explanation acceptable. Lucky remembered how hurt and angry she'd been when she'd believed Zeke had deceived her. She knew Bryn's sense of betrayal ran even deeper.

"I never should have lied to you, Bryn." Lilith's voice trembled. "My only excuse is that I loved you so much."

Lucky had never fully trusted her new grandmother, but even she couldn't doubt the sincerity she heard in Lilith's voice.

Lilith turned to face Bryn. "Look at you," she said. She reached as if to touch the flash of white that streaked through Bryn's black hair, but she let her hand drop when Bryn drew back. "Even your brief time here has changed you."

"It was a result of what happened in your world." Bryn's quiet words were clipped.

"My world." Lilith looked pained. "It used to be our world."

Bryn shook her head. "No. It was never my world. It was my prison."

The anguish that flashed across Lilith's face made Lucky want to slip away, to allow the two to finish their conversation in private. But she had promised Bryn her support. So she stayed, even though she felt like an eavesdropper.

"No, Bryn. I never meant it to be a prison for you. I made sure you had every opportunity. I provided you with the best teachers I could find. And when you wanted to train for combat, I never discouraged you. I let you choose your trainers, find your own way. I gave you your independence."

"But you told me I could never leave—for more than a few hours at a time. How does that not make it my prison?"

"It was your home."

"You gave me no choice. I should have been allowed to choose."

"It was *my* home. One *I* could never leave." Lilith's voice broke as tears streaked her cheeks. "I had already lost your mother, Bryn. I couldn't bear to lose you too."

"You lost her because of me."

"No. She came back to me because of you. You have no idea how many years had gone by since I had seen her. I had lost all hope of ever seeing her again. And then there she was, beautiful and happy and expecting a child."

"A child who killed her." Lucky winced at the pain and self-loathing contained in her cousin's softly spoken words.

"You did not kill her, Bryn. I did." Lilith's voice hardened as she cast a glance at Zeke. "And those who banished me." When she turned back to Bryn, her voice softened once more. "Your Raven form is a result of *my* curse. And your mother's death was a part of *my* punishment. It was not your fault, Bryn. It was never your fault."

"Then why punish me? Why tell me I could never leave?"

"Oh, Bryn. You are the only daughter of my only daughter, and she was the only child I ever bore. I wanted to keep you safe, to keep you near me. I couldn't bear for you to leave me the way she had. I couldn't bear to lose you too. In my weakness, I lied to you. But I couldn't keep lying when you were hurt. I knew your best chance of survival lay in leaving my world and coming here."

Again her hand moved toward the white streak in Bryn's hair. This time Bryn did not back away.

"Your ordeal has marked you." Lilith's fingers dropped from her granddaughter's hair to brush her cheek. "Ezekiel says he has offered to let you stay here, to train, to serve among the Fallen."

Bryn looked at Zeke. "He said the Forces could use someone like me."

Zeke nodded. "That I did."

"You wish to accept his offer?" Lilith asked.

Bryn's gaze shot back to her grandmother. "I *have* accepted his offer. I'm not asking your permission. I'm telling you." She glanced at Zeke again, her mouth set in a stubborn line. "Because he said I had to."

"That was very—sensible—of him." Lilith took a deep breath. "I am sorry I lied to you, Bryn. I know it was selfish. Can you forgive me?"

Silence stretched as Bryn hesitated. Then she nodded. "I guess so. What you did wasn't right, but I get why you did it."

Lilith smiled. "Thank you. And you will come visit me?"

Bryn nodded.

"Good. You can come as often as you like. And, of course, you can come and go as you please." Lilith went to Bryn and folded the girl in her arms. Bryn returned her grandmother's embrace.

When she released Bryn, Lilith turned toward Lucky.

"Now, what is this I hear," she said, "about you beginning to master your Gift of Madness?"

Lucky stared. "My Gift of—what?"

Lilith glanced from Lucky to Zeke and back again. "Your Gift of Madness, dear. Has no one told you?"

*Madness?* Scenes from memory replayed in Lucky's mind, eclipsing the woman standing before her. William and Mather in her power, their thoughts open to her, her awareness that she could turn those thoughts toward madness. G-Ma confused and anxious, a Still One perched on her shoulder. Her mother's paintings, her letter: *I know I'm losing my mind,* the death certificate saying she'd committed suicide. Kev's eyes locked on hers as he rasped, "Stay out of my head."

Her mother had gone mad when she was pregnant with her. G-Ma had been living with her when she'd lost herself to Alzheimer's. Had she been some kind of madness carrier even then? And Kev. Oh, God. What might she have done to him if the dragon hadn't kicked her out of his mind?

Lucky struggled to pull air into her lungs and then push it out again, that involuntary act almost beyond her. She recalled Uriel's words: *Exactly what this means remains to be seen. May your Making be of benefit to us all.* Benefit? Hardly. Madness wasn't a Gift. It was a curse.

Kev awoke with Lucky filling his senses. He could smell her hair, taste her lips, feel her in his arms. He'd dreamed of her again, and in his dream no Aidan had come between them.

He swung his legs out of bed and sat up. He rubbed his fingers over his closed eyes as if he could wipe away the remains of the dream. This had to stop. No more thoughts, no more dreams, no more longing.

He pushed the memories and dream images away, re-solved to bury them so deep they couldn't resurface. His was a life of battle and diplomacy, of dragon fire and the icy chill of the Metatron's council chamber. There was no room in it for her smell, her taste, her softness. She threatened the control he'd spent half his lifetime cultivating. She was an indulgence he couldn't afford.

He had started to close the lid on the box into which he'd packed away his memories and his dreams, when the dragon flared to life inside him. The instant Kev felt the beast stir, he raced out of the studio. He'd barely cleared the door before the shift hit. With one lash of his tail, the dragon took out a section of the studio's front wall. The part of Kev that was still human looked on helplessly as the dragon let out a roar and blasted the snow-frosted evergreens with a wall of flame.

"Lucky. Lucky, look at me."

Zeke's voice rang through the noise of her thoughts like the chiming of cathedral bells. The angel knelt in front of her, one hand on each arm of the chair, as he leaned forward, his gray eyes searching her face. When her eyes focused on his, he gave a small nod.

"Good. Now breathe. In, and out. In, and out."

Blocking out everything else, Lucky followed his words, inhaled and exhaled in time to his commands. She calmed.

*Madness.* All calm disappeared, taking Lucky's ability to breathe along for company.

"Lucky."

Zeke's hands framed her face. His eyes anchored hers.

"Stay with me," he said. "Stay right here with me."

"I can't. I can't, Zeke. I can't."

"Yes, you can. Remember that place deep inside you that you found on your birthday?"

"My control room."

Zeke nodded. "What can you do there?"

"I—I can turn my senses on and off."

"Right. You can do that now. You can turn these thoughts off too."

Lucky shook her head. "But they—"

"They are not real, Lucky. They are thoughts. *You* are real. You are here, now, with me. Okay?" Zeke's hands steadied her, not allowing her to break contact with his eyes.

Lucky swallowed, nodded.

"Say it with me," Zeke said. "Here."

"Here."

"Now."

"Now."

"With me."

"With you."

"Again."

This time she and Zeke said the words in unison.

When Lucky had whispered them one more time, her breathing had almost returned to normal.

"You are going to be okay," Zeke said. His hands moved from her face to close around her cold fingers.

Lucky shook her head, moisture welling in her eyes.

"Of course you are, darling," Lilith said. "You have an incredible power."

Zeke sighed. "Lilith, please."

"I must leave anyway. My time here is almost up. Be well, my darlings." Lilith blew kisses to both Lucky and Bryn before she faded away.

Lucky felt Zeke's fingers tighten on hers. Then all awareness faded into the vision that filled her head as the medallion seared her skin.

Snow, golden eyes in a green-scaled face, green wings, charred trees. The dragon was loose.

"Kev," she breathed.

She let the vision take her. The world tilted and swirled. Whatever part of her could sense anything had the uncomfortable, though increasingly familiar, sensation of being both everywhere and nowhere. Then she stood in the snow behind Kev's cabin, the dragon from her vision a massive, fire-breathing reality before her.

# CHAPTER 28

Bryn stared at Zeke, who stood in front of the empty chair where Lucky had sat.

"Where did she go?" she asked.

"She said Kevin's name. I assume she went to him. He did much the same thing when he went to her in Nadach." Zeke sat down in the chair and looked across at her. "And then he brought us you."

"Thank you for letting me stay. When you said you wanted to talk to me, I thought you planned to ship me back to Lilith, that you didn't want a Raven hanging around."

"I have no problem with Ravens—and especially not with you—but I do know how dangerous and unpredictable an untrained Raven can be. That is why I hesitated to allow you to fight with us."

"And you were right. I killed all those Wraiths."

"But you killed only Wraiths. I have known Ravens who would not have stopped there. I have seen some so maddened by bloodlust that they moved on to friends after they defeated their enemies. Your training has served you well."

Bryn looked down at her hands. "I asked for permission to train because it helped to quiet the Raven urges."

"Training, like any form of practice, offers discipline. You were wise to seek it out."

Bryn looked up at him. She didn't think anyone had ever called her "wise" before. "I was?"

Zeke smiled. "You were. You are. I meant what I said, you know. With your abilities and your discipline, you will be an asset to the Forces."

Bryn grinned. "Yeah, I will."

Zeke laughed.

Bryn stood and held out her hand. "Thank you, Zeke."

"Thank you," he said, his fingers closing around hers. "I will let Aidan and Malachi know you will be joining them for training."

Bryn took a couple of steps toward the door, then turned back, hesitating.

Zeke must have known what worried her. Maybe because it worried him too. "Lucky will be all right. If I do not hear from her or Kevin soon, we will go find them. I promise."

Lucky dived headfirst into the snow as a swathe of flame shot toward her head. She caught the whoosh and crackle of the trees behind her igniting, before the sound drowned in the dragon's roar.

She pushed to her knees, barely noticing the bite of the snow on her gloveless fingers. She knelt in the snow, staring at the beast, wondering what had possessed her to answer the medallion's summons without so much as a word to Zeke. What could she do for Kev? Now that she knew her Gift was Madness, she didn't dare venture inside his head.

She'd managed to talk the dragon down twice before, but the shift hadn't been complete either time. It had seemed much easier to deal with the dragon when he was in Kev's body than it did now, with him all huge and scaly, lashing his tail and snorting flame.

The beast swung his head in Lucky's direction and let loose another fireball. She leapt sideways and rolled to her feet. When the next blast came toward her, she dodged and rolled again.

She didn't want to risk taking her eyes off the dragon to see how many trees he'd ignited, but from the crackles that filled her ears and the heat that warmed her back, she guessed a sizable portion of the woods bordering the cabin was aflame. She hoped the heavy snow would keep the fire from spreading too far. She had to figure out a way to stop the dragon soon before he lit up the whole mountainside.

And from the look of it, he'd done some additional damage. During her last leap she had caught a glimpse of Kev's studio. A good chunk of the front wall was missing. Maybe she should take this fight off the ground, before the dragon destroyed anything else.

She felt the weight of her wings even as the thought took shape. When the dragon opened his mouth to blast her again, she shot upward, far out of reach.

He roared through the smoke and flames.

In the beat necessary for him to lift and spread his wings to come after her, Lucky directed her power toward him and opened her senses. Madness or not, she didn't see any other way of calming the beast. She would do nothing more than she had done to the Wraith. She would temporarily lessen the dragon's aggression, make him more docile. With any luck, that would give Kev a chance to reclaim the reins.

When the dragon took to the air, she saw the movement as if through a film. The dual image of the dragon's mind overlaying Kev's filled the foreground of her vision. She willed herself to focus on the image and not the dragon winging toward her.

She scanned the landscape of the dragon's thoughts and emotions, searching for the thread or ribbon she could use to calm him. She found what she sought just as the dragon sent a fireball in her direction.

She dodged, but not far enough. The smell of burning feathers told her one wing had caught fire. Ignoring the pain as the flames burned through feathers to the skin and bone beneath, she reached out with her power and stroked the tendril she'd located in the dragon's mind.

The dragon stopped in midair. His wings lifted and fell, holding him in place, the head that had snaked toward her now cocked to one side.

When he opened his mouth, Lucky wondered if she'd been mistaken and prepared to dodge another blast. But instead of a fireball, the dragon emitted a loud, low-pitched vibration. With her senses wide open, Lucky could see the sound waves radiating toward her burning wing. When they washed over it, the flames died out.

The dragon veered away from her toward the trees he'd set alight earlier. Flying laps, he swept the burning trees with that low-pitched tone until all the flames were extinguished.

Then, in mid-air, the dragon transformed into Kev, dark green wings holding him aloft.

Lucky drooped with relief.

Kev waved to her, gesturing toward the clearing, and when he lowered to the ground, she touched down beside him.

"Are you okay?" he asked. His hand moved toward her wounded wing. "I keep hurting you."

"It wasn't you. It was the dragon."

"But I couldn't stop him. I was stuck in there watching him spit flames at you. When I saw your wing catch fire—"

"It's already feeling better. It will heal soon." As she spoke, Lucky dismissed her wings. Or at least she tried to. She thought them gone, but the appendages didn't go anywhere.

She tried again with the same results.

She frowned. "Why can't I—?"

"Trying to dismiss them?" Kev asked, his own wings disappearing. "You can't, until that one heals. The energy is in flux because of the healing, so it can't disperse."

"Oh. You think I can squeeze these things through the cabin door? I'm getting cold."

Kev chuckled. "I think we can manage that."

He led the way toward the cabin, and he stumbled a couple of times. She frowned. "Kev, are *you* all right?"

He grimaced. "Fighting the dragon—or at least trying to fight him—took a lot out of me. It gets harder each time."

He held the mudroom door while Lucky ducked and turned, maneuvering her wings inside. They repeated the procedure with the door to the kitchen, and then Kev went to the fireplace and began arranging logs for a fire.

"How about some of the beverage that makes everything better?" Lucky asked.

"Sounds good to me."

In the kitchen, Lucky gathered the makings for Nana's hot chocolate, taking care not to knock anything over with her wings. By the time she had mixed the ingredients and put them on the stove to heat, the pain in her wing had faded. She felt the weight disappear from her back when she lifted the pan from the stove to pour the heated cocoa into two waiting mugs.

"Looks like you've healed," Kev said from the doorway.

"Yeah." She handed him one of the filled mugs. "What about you?"

"I'm getting my strength back."

She followed him into the living room. They each took a seat at either end of the couch and stared at the flames licking the logs in the fireplace.

"The fire is mesmerizing," Lucky said.

"Yeah." Kev paused for so long Lucky thought he might not continue. "I've often wondered how something could be so beautiful, so necessary for our survival—and at the same time hold such potential for destruction."

"And for creation. You of all people should know that." Lucky gestured toward the window and the studio beyond. "You couldn't do what you do out there without it." She paused to take another sip of hot chocolate. "And we couldn't make Nana's cocoa."

Kev chuckled, but the sound held an undercurrent of sadness. "Yeah. It's just that I seem to be playing mostly on the destructive side these days." He turned to look at her. "I don't know how long I can keep fighting the dragon."

"Then maybe you should stop."

"What?"

"Maybe you should stop fighting him."

"Are you crazy?" He stood, paced to the fireplace and back. "We can't go on like this. I have to get him back under control. Like he was. Before you."

Kev wanted to take the words back as soon as they left his lips. The stricken look on Lucky's face cut him to the core.

"So this thing with your dragon is *my* fault?" she asked.

"I didn't say that."

"Yes, you did. You had it under control, you said, until me. God, Kev, you're such a hypocrite." Lucky pointed at the couch. "You sat right there and told me I had to accept this—this—thing inside me, that I had to learn to work with it. And you can't accept your own big bad dragon. 'He is me, but he's not me. Sometimes he's in control, sometimes I am. We don't think alike. It's like there are two of us.' There aren't two of you, Kev. There's only one. He's you."

Lucky's eyes widened, and her jaw dropped. "Not two, only one," she whispered. "That's what she meant."

"What who meant?" The truth of Lucky's accusations had hit Kev like a punch in the gut, but her whispered comment got through to him even as he reeled.

"G-Ma. She told me I had to help you. And then she said, 'Not two, only one.' I didn't know what she meant. But now I know she was talking about you and your dragon."

"But we are different. We don't share the same thoughts, the same mind."

"I know. I've seen that. But I think it's changing—*you're* changing. When I got into your head last night—and today— it seemed different than before. I hardly noticed it at the time. I mean, I noticed it, but I didn't know what I noticed." She frowned. "It was like your minds were—more alike some-how. Still separate, but not so—alien to each other."

Kev set his mug on the coffee table. He couldn't drink any more, not with the churning in his stomach. He dropped down onto the sofa, sitting sideways so he could lean back against the arm, his own arms crossed over his chest. "Am I changing him, or is he changing me?"

"I don't think it's one or the other," Lucky said. "I think you're both changing, becoming like each other."

"And that's why I'm having trouble controlling him? Not because I've gotten weaker or he's gotten stronger, but because we're—integrating somehow?" Some of the tension left Kev's shoulders.

"I think so," Lucky said. "But why would you trust me? You said yourself that my getting into your head caused this."

"I did *not* say that."

"Yes, you did. You were okay, you said, before me."

"That's not what I meant." Kev took a deep breath. "I said I was in control before you, but I didn't mean you did this to me. At least not like that."

"Then what did you mean?"

Kev said nothing for the space of two heartbeats. Then, he answered, "You overheard my argument with Aidan last night. This didn't happen because of anything you did. It happened because of how I feel about you."

Lucky stared at Kev, her stomach tightening. Funny, she felt almost as frightened as she had when she had been dodging the dragon's fireballs.

"You said you were in love with me," she whispered, "but you didn't want to be."

Kev pinched the bridge of his nose. "Yeah."

"And this thing with the dragon is why you don't want to be?"

"It's a big part of it." Kev gazed into the fire as he spoke. "There's also Aidan."

Lucky watched Kev watching the fire. She wished he would look at her.

"I broke up with him," she said.

Kev's gaze swung from the fire to her face. "Yeah?"

She nodded. "Yeah."

"Because of—me?"

She repeated his own words back to him. "Because of how I feel about you."

Something like hope flared in Kev's eyes. Then he trained his gaze on the fire once more. "There's still the dragon."

Lucky's next thought had her *more* terrified than when she'd faced the dragon. She set her empty mug on the coffee table and locked her fingers together, while she searched for the courage to say the words. "I—might be able to help with that."

Kev didn't speak, but he turned to look at her again.

"G-Ma thinks I can. But I—" She stopped speaking as tears blurred her vision and choked her throat. "I'm afraid of what I might do to you. It seems my Gift is—Madness."

"You just found out?" Kev didn't seem at all surprised by the nature of her Gift, only by the fact she hadn't known about it sooner.

Lucky stared. "You knew?" She closed her eyes against the new flow of tears. "No wonder you told me to stay out of your head. How long have you known?"

"Since the night your Gift manifested. Lilith told me."

"And you didn't think you ought to share that little piece of information with me?"

"I thought telling you would do more harm than good. I figured you needed time to get used to how your Gift worked, so you wouldn't get caught up in the name. Then— what with everything else—I forgot you didn't know."

"How could I *not* get caught up in the name? How could Madness be any kind of gift."

"Weren't we just talking about how fire can be both creative and destructive? Your Gift is the same."

"Destructive I get, but I'm having a little trouble with the creative part."

Kev studied her in silence, a frown between his brows. Then he got to his feet. "Come with me," he said. "There's something I want to show you."

Kev led Lucky through the snow to the studio, his heart tripping in his chest. On the one hand, he wanted her to see his latest sculpture—to see herself and her power through his eyes. On the other, laying all that out in front of her put more than a few knots in his stomach. For some reason, sharing the piece with her made him feel even more naked than telling her how he felt about her.

Snow fell from the sky again, and the flakes swirled through the gaping hole his dragon had left in the front wall. After he'd shown Lucky what he'd brought her here to see, he'd have to do some makeshift repairs—at least enough to keep the elements and the wildlife out until the wall and door could be replaced.

Surveying the damage his dragon had done, Kev knew he was showing Lucky the sculpture as much for himself as for her. She was right. He had to stop fighting the dragon. And his best chance of doing so was walking beside him. He had started this whole adventure because he thought he could help her learn to use her Dark Gift. But somewhere along the line their roles had gotten all muddled. He needed her help as much as she needed his.

He stopped outside the opening, his hand on Lucky's arm drawing her to a stop as well.

"Close your eyes," he said.

Lucky looked a question at him and then lowered her eyelids.

"Keep them closed."

He guided her through the opening and around the work tables, tools, and supplies until they reached the stand on which the new piece rested. He stood behind her, hands on her shoulders, and positioned her in front of it.

He took a deep breath and stepped away from her, letting his hands slide from her shoulders.

"You can open your eyes now."

Lucky didn't know what she had expected. But what she saw stopped the breath in her throat. The piece mixed realism and abstraction, but its subject matter was clear.

The figure was female, right hand raised before her, long hair flying about her shoulders. Even though the metal rods that represented the hair were still, their interlocking curves gave the illusion of movement. The lines of the body were abstract, making no attempt at realism, but flowing and sensual, conveying both grace and power. The face, in contrast, was painstakingly detailed: the expression focused, powerful, passionate. The eyes were inlaid with sparkling stones that flashed jade green. The face was utterly foreign and completely familiar.

It was *her*—in the moment that haunted her, that instant when she knew she had the power to destroy and was on the brink of using it. And she was beautiful—strong, powerful, terrifying, and beautiful. *That* was how Kev saw her? He had looked on her at her very worst, and *that* was what he'd seen?

She sank to her knees as tears filled her eyes. Her hand flew to cover her mouth, in a vain effort to hold back the wrenching sobs that overcame her.

If anyone had asked her, Lucky couldn't have explained why she cried. Her emotions tangled together, so she couldn't tell where one ended and another began. But something fell away, as if from a hand she had unclenched, and something else bloomed within her. Kev had given form to the promise of what she could be. He could see it, and now she could see it too.

Kev knelt beside Lucky and folded her in his arms. He offered no words of comfort. He didn't try to stop her tears. He just held her while they fell.

When she had cried herself out, he sat on the floor and drew her onto his lap, where she could relax against him, her head on his chest.

After a while, she asked, "Was that really how you saw me that night?"

"It was. It still is. I see that power every time I look at you."

Lucky sniffled again and cuddled closer against him.

"You said you could see only how your Gift could be destructive, not creative. But you've already used it creatively—today with my dragon and yesterday with the Wraith. In both cases, you chose to change something instead of to destroy. That's a lot more than I can say for me and my dragon."

"You and your dragon destroyed the Wraiths to protect me."

Kev's arms tightened around her. "The dragon didn't protect you today."

"No." Lucky raised her head to look at him. "I think he meant to protect *you*—both of you."

Kev frowned. "What do you mean?"

"Well, you said you were okay before me. I'm guessing the dragon thought getting rid of me would solve that problem."

Once more, her words left Kev feeling gut-punched. "That—sounds right," he said, when he could breathe again. The beast had reacted to his thoughts and emotions, but on a more primitive, more literal level. "To think any part of me might want to destroy you…"

He buried his face in her hair, breathed in her scent.

"I don't think he tried very hard. Yeah, he made me work to stay away from his fireballs, and he did burn my wing. But I think he just wanted me to go away. If he'd wanted to kill me, I'd guess he could have."

Again, what she said sounded right, but Kev still shuddered at the thought of what his dragon could have done. His resolve to lock away his feelings for Lucky had been wavering ever since she'd told him she'd broken up with Aidan. Now it came crashing to the ground.

He lifted his face from her hair, framed her face with his hands, and kissed her. Not gently, but with all the hunger he'd tried to deny since that night in his bedroom. She turned her body toward him, twined her arms around his neck, and kissed him back.

His fingers speared through her hair, his hands holding her in place so he could search her mouth. Her fingers stroked the nape of his neck, and he shivered.

Somehow he managed to get to his feet, Lucky cradled in his arms, without ending the kiss. He lifted his mouth from hers, but kept her held close, as he wound through the worktables and stepped out into the snow. Arms locked around his neck, Lucky tilted her head back and laughed. Kev reveled in the sound of her laughter, the brightness of her eyes, the flush in her cheeks.

"I love you," he said.

"I love you back," she whispered against his lips.

What could he do but kiss her again?

They parted in the mudroom long enough to dispose of coats and snow-covered boots. Then Kev picked Lucky up and carried her into the living room. He set her on her feet on the rug in front of the fireplace and dropped a kiss on her smiling lips. He checked the fire, added a couple more logs, and turned back to her.

She sat on the floor, her arms around her bent knees, watching him, not the fire. When his eyes caught hers, she smiled.

He lowered himself to the floor beside her, stretched out on his side. In an instant, she had snuggled against him. He leaned over her, pressing her back into the rug, and kissed her again.

Craving the touch of her skin, he slipped his hands under her sweater. They both gasped when his fingers and palms skimmed over her ribs.

She tugged his shirt from his jeans, slid her hands up over his back, her fingertips brushing his sigil. He shuddered and then stilled, as his vision wavered.

"No," he said, pushing away from her, squeezing his eyes shut, and willing the dragon away. "No. No. No."

"Kev?"

He felt Lucky's hand on his shoulder, forced himself to breathe calmly.

"Is it the dragon?"

He nodded. "I need a minute." He forced the words through his tightened throat.

It took longer than a minute for the dragon to subside, but Kev wasn't about to complain. At least, the beast had obeyed him this time.

He took a deep breath, opened his eyes. He looked at Lucky, kneeling beside him, ready to act if he needed her.

"This has gone far enough," he said. "Will you use your Gift to help me?"

# CHAPTER 29

"Are you sure you are ready for this?"

Katrin looked at Kev, so Lucky assumed she meant the question for him, but it could as easily have been directed at her. If it had been, she would have answered the same way Kev did.

"I'm as ready as I'll ever be."

They were at the training center, outside in one of the practice fields, with lots of open space, in case Kev's dragon decided to make an unscheduled appearance.

"Okay, Lucky?" Katrin asked.

In the twenty-four hours or so since Kev had asked for her help, Katrin and Zeke had taught Lucky to better understand and use her Gift. With his Gift of Knowledge and countless years of experience navigating minds to implant commands and information, Zeke gave Lucky a general sense of the mental terrain. Katrin helped her see her ability as something that could heal as well as destroy. Too bad neither of them could tell her what she had to do to help Kev and his dragon integrate. That she'd have to figure out on her own.

Lucky nodded. "Okay."

She and Kev knelt a few feet from Katrin.

"I will hold the energy field for healing," Katrin said. "Kevin, you need to open to Lucky. Let her in. *Invite* her in."

Kev took a deep breath, his gaze steady on Lucky's. "Okay."

Lucky opened her senses, and she felt Katrin's healing field take shape. Holding Kev's sunlight-flecked eyes with her own, she reached for his mind and that of the dragon.

Kev must have taken Katrin's words to heart. No sooner had Lucky reached out than his eyes faded from view behind the intricate pattern formed by the tendrils of his thoughts and emotions overlaying the equally complex pattern formed by those of his dragon. The colors were more vibrant, the patterns clearer, than they had appeared any of the previous times Lucky had viewed them. And she did feel invited in. His openness both awed and humbled her.

She let herself move beyond sight, sensing the shape, the texture, the temperature of Kev's and the dragon's mental landscapes. She took her time moving through them, learning how the threads and ribbons connected, noting how they shifted and changed.

She had been right when she had told Kev his mind and that of the dragon seemed to be integrating. The patterns were more similar now than they had been three days ago. And, though they still didn't match up, the grids of the two were closer to alignment.

She pushed her senses further and stepped into Kev's landscape. The threads and ribbons and tendrils now formed hills and valleys, caves and mountains, and rivers of light she could explore. She let herself touch, feel, learn, accept, know.

It was like resting her cheek on Kev's chest so she could feel his heartbeat or running her fingers through his hair. And at the same time it was even more intimate.

When she had learned which of Kev's thoughts and emotions were where and how they interconnected, she moved into the more alien realm of the dragon's mind. Here she felt the slightest resistance. Some part of him still didn't trust her.

The dragon's landscape held steeper mountains with more jagged ranges, and what had seemed rivers in Kev's mind here were waterfalls. The tendrils of thought were less developed, the ribbons of emotion more so. Again, she let herself wander, touch, know. She had to work a little to push through the dragon's resistance.

When that resistance fell away, she finally found the space where Kev was missing. Feeling that lack in the dragon, she remembered feeling the corresponding lack in Kev, a space that had somehow seemed empty.

Holding those spaces in her own mind, Lucky withdrew from the mental landscapes so she could see both patterns laid out before her. She reached out with her senses, felt for the two empty spots, and using her Gift, she shifted the patterns until each emptiness found its connection point.

As the pieces interlocked, Lucky released Kev's mind.

Then she heard him scream.

All the flames he had ever breathed in dragon form consumed him from the inside out. Kev's back arched, every muscle and tendon straining, and a cry ripped from his throat. Thoughts and emotions whipped through him, masses of tangled, sparking cords seeking connection in the swirling blast.

A shift took him, and the firestorm raged through the dragon's form. His huge body thrashed and twisted, his tail lashing. He burned. He roared.

The roar morphed into a human scream as he shifted again. And then the shifts came in such rapid succession, he no longer knew whether he was man or dragon, dragon or man.

He was fire. He was flame. He had no form, no name, no being, apart from the burning.

Then the gale stopped, the arcing currents from the sparking cords caught, held, and the roaring flames subsided to a slow burn, centered in his head, his heart, his belly. His body, human again and strained past endurance, dropped to the ground.

Just before consciousness faded, he whispered, "What have we done?"

Kev's stark whisper resounded through Lucky's head with all the intensity of the screams and roars that had come before. It echoed the cry that had threatened to escape her at each of his rapid-fire shifts, each of the agonized contortions of his body, both human and dragon. The words, in a feedback loop, rang above the pounding of her heart and the rushing of the blood through her veins, forming the soundtrack to the images that burned in her mind.

She raced to wrap her arms around his unconscious body, barely registering Katrin's instructions about getting him back to Zeke's. Kev's endlessly looping question and the remembered sounds of his screams drowned out everything else.

It took the touch of Katrin's hand on her shoulder to pull her back to the awareness necessary to concentrate on dematerializing herself and Kev. She had to focus. Zeke's brownstone, the upstairs hallway.

She closed her eyes, opened her senses. Holding the memory of her destination in mind, she also absorbed every sensation she could of the young man in her arms—his weight, his heat, his scent. She had to make sure she took him with her. She filled her senses with him. Then she swept them both away.

Katrin was right beside them when Lucky reformed in Zeke's upstairs hallway with Kev in her arms. As soon as she lay Kev's body on the bed in his room, Katrin started her examination.

Lucky stood, trembling, at the foot of the bed. She had seen Katrin at work with Josh and G-Ma, and in both cases an efficient compassion had colored her skill. She showed that same skillful economy now, but beneath it lay an emotional intensity missing from her interactions with the other two patients. Kev's belief in his mother's lack of feeling was mistaken. Watching Katrin's movements, Lucky saw more than a healer. She saw a mother caring for her son.

"Will he be all right?"

"I think so. I don't know. It is too soon to say."

Katrin's uncertainty shook Lucky more than she wanted to admit. "Did—did we do the right thing?" What if she had made everything worse? What if he didn't recover?

Katrin stopped fussing over Kev and directed her full attention toward Lucky. "What purpose does that question serve? We did what we did. Now we take care of him." She turned back to her son. "Go find Zeke. Tell him we've returned. I will let you know if there's any change—or if you are needed."

With a last look at Kev's still form, Lucky fled the room.

The sound of footsteps on the stairs interrupted Lucky's efforts to catch any noises coming from Kev's room. The steps seemed too heavy to be Bryn's, so Zeke must have returned from wherever he'd disappeared to. When she couldn't find him earlier and he hadn't answered his cell, she'd left him a message explaining what had happened.

The angel's wheat-blond head came into view as he mounted the stairs, and Lucky almost leapt from her seat on the hallway floor to run into his arms. The expression on his face stopped her. For someone who never slept, he sure looked like he could use a day-long nap.

"What's up?" she asked.

Zeke shook his head and lowered to the floor to sit beside her. "It will keep until we are all together." He sounded as weary as he looked.

He nodded toward the closed bedroom door. "Why are you out here?"

Lucky glanced down at the locket and dragon medallion she worried with one hand as she slid the chain through the other. "Aidan's in there right now, working with Katrin."

"I see. And where is Bryn?"

"In the gym. She invited me to come with her, but…" Rising tears closed Lucky's throat, stopping the words.

One of Zeke's big hands covered both of hers.

Lucky leaned her head back against the wall and closed her eyes. A few tears leaked from beneath her lashes and slid down her cheeks.

"I can't help thinking," she whispered, "that we shouldn't have done it, that I should have stayed out of his head." She opened her eyes and looked at Zeke, blinking back tears. "Zeke, what if he never wakes up?"

Zeke wrapped his arm around her shoulder and tucked her close to his side. He didn't offer any words of comfort. When Lucky turned to wrap her arms around him, she sensed the angel needed the embrace as much as she did.

Propped against the back of one of the leather chairs, Aidan scanned those gathered in Zeke's study. Josh and Ben, who occupied the chairs across from him, stared at each other, worried looks on their faces. Bryn perched on the edge of the chair Aidan leaned against, her eyes on the floor. Katrin sat next to them. Her hand gripped her cane so tightly her knuckles showed white. Zeke paced in front of his desk. Lucky fidgeted by the door, her desire to get out of the room and back upstairs to Kev evident in every tensed muscle. No one spoke.

When Malachi materialized a few feet from Zeke, Aidan imagined they all breathed a collective sigh of relief. With everyone present, maybe Zeke would tell them what had him acting like the whole world had crashed on his shoulders.

Malachi leaned back against the edge of the desk, his arms crossed over his chest.

Zeke stopped pacing and positioned himself beside the desk where he could see everyone. He looked at each of them in turn before he spoke, his voice like a contained storm.

"I am sure you all know by now that, after the procedure to unite him with his dragon, Kevin is unconscious and under his mother's care. I will make this as quick as possible, so Katrin—and Lucky—can return to him."

He paused, looking from face to face once more, lingering on Aidan's. Aidan shifted under his gaze until Zeke looked away.

"While Katrin, Lucky, and Kevin were at the training center, I received a summons from the Metatron, directing me to report to the Allied Council Hall immediately. There, I was greeted by Adrigon himself, accompanied by several members of the Dominion guard. He informed me that a contingent of the Forces of Light had invaded the Halls of Hell."

Aidan sucked in a breath and stood upright, muscles tensed and fists clenched. Zeke's gaze locked on his.

"They have imprisoned Lucifer in one of his own cells and installed a new Light-Bringer, a Virtue called Helel, in his place. For now, they have allowed Ba'al to retain the title of second, but that seems an empty gesture. They have locked down the Forces of Darkness as well and warded their barracks against escape."

"How did they breach Lucifer's wards?" Malachi asked.

"The same way the Wraiths did, I'd bet," Aidan answered. "At least one of the Dark had to have helped them."

Zeke nodded. "Agreed. And until we find out who that is—as well as who killed Jahoel—they have tied our hands."

"When Kev wakes up, I guess we can tell him he's out of a job," Aidan muttered.

"Which frees him up," Malachi added, "to rejoin the Forces."

"What do we do now?" Ben asked.

"We continue the investigation," Zeke said, "and we wait."

Kev lay, unmoving, on the bed, as he had for the last two days.

Lucky had dragged a chair close to the bed, and she sat there, turning the statue of Michael and the dragon over and over in her hands. The old lady with the spider brooch had said he would protect her—and she had never questioned the truth of those words. She had carried the statue the day Josh was attacked, and she had always wondered if he would have been safe if she had thought to let him carry it. When she had pulled it from the backpack she had retrieved from the cabin, she had thought of Kev. Maybe the statue could help protect him. Studying it now, though, she had second thoughts.

She couldn't explain why she had initially been drawn to the piece in the old woman's crowded little shop. Something about it had spoken to her, something the old woman recognized, something that prompted her to insist Lucky take the statue free of charge. "He will protect you," she had told Lucky, "from the Dark that is coming." Once Lucky had learned the truth about the Fallen and about Aidan, she had also associated the statue with him. He had been her protector.

But the sculpture portrayed the Archangel Michael, the one Archangel she'd never met, defeating a dragon. That dragon was Lucifer, the father of "her" dragon. Kev had spent a lifetime trying, if not to defeat, at least to subdue and control the dragon he'd inherited from his father, only to have those attempts backfire. He couldn't subdue the dragon; he had to befriend it. A statue that depicted the vanquishing of his father's dragon didn't seem like an appropriate symbol of protection for Kev. Especially now that the Metatron had invaded Lucifer's realm and locked him up for a crime he didn't commit. It made the statue seem almost a mockery.

With some surprise, Lucky realized the statue no longer seemed an appropriate symbol of protection for her either. Her fingers touched the dragon medallion she wore. Not only did she love Kev, but he was one of her Makers. The dragon was a part of her too. What she'd done with her Gift had not been intended to defeat or subdue the dragon, but to unite it to Kev, to make their minds one. Kev's dragon wasn't evil, and neither was her Gift of Madness. Both Gifts offered as great a capacity for creation as they did for destruction.

Lucky tucked the statue back inside her backpack and moved to the bed. She snuggled in next to Kev, her arm around his waist, her head on his chest. She could hear his heart beat, steady and strong.

If only he would wake up.

Something startled Lucky awake.

She hadn't meant to fall asleep curled against Kev, but weariness had overcome her.

She felt it again—a touch on her cheek.

She opened her eyes. Kev's hand rested on his chest, his fingertips just brushing her face.

"Kev?" she whispered.

She reached for his hand, and his fingers closed around hers.

Holding her breath, she raised her head from his chest, so she could see his face. His dark green eyes looked back at her.

"Hi," he said.

Half-sobbing, half-laughing, she wrapped him in her arms.

# ACKNOWLEDGEMENTS

Bringing a book to birth—and then getting the word out about it—requires more than an author. I'm grateful to everyone who helped make this book possible. I won't be able to name everyone here, because if you're part of my life, you were in some way part of this work. So, thank you, family and friends, one and all.

As for those who can be named:

To my beta readers, Bonnie Jean Feldkamp, Michaelangelo Allocca, Kathy Huffman, Traci Selvidge, Jim Sonday, Megan McFadden, and Dan Brogan, many thanks for the comments and suggestions. The book is stronger, tighter, more compelling because of you.

Thanks and admiration for my cover artist, Ravven, who created another stunning cover. Lucky lives not only within these pages, but also in the cover illustration. You rock!

Thanks to my brother Doug for telling me sound waves can extinguish fire. You didn't even know you had solved a plot problem for me, did you?

Thanks to Laurie Phelps for reading the first draft and providing a sounding board for plot ideas and character development.

Thanks to Annette Shutty for converting the medallion on the cover to a chapter head graphic, as well as for taking author photos and creating some fabulous business cards and book marks.

Thanks to the members of my book group for wanting to read my manuscript when you could have been reading something else. I'm grateful for your friendship and support—and, of course, for the food and wine!

Thanks to the members of my blogging group for support and inspiration.

Thanks to the bloggers/reviewers who have reviewed my books or interviewed me on their sites. You can find links to their posts on my website: www.stephanieastamm.com.

Thanks, finally, to my readers. I'm thrilled and humbled every time one of you tells me you loved *A Gift of Wings*. Your questions about when the next installment would be published kept me going when I struggled with plot problems and rewrote and reorganized, and rewrote and reorganized, and rewrote some more. I hope you enjoy reading *A Gift of Shadows* as much as I enjoyed writing it.

# ABOUT THE AUTHOR

Stephanie Stamm is the author of the Light-Bringer Series of NA/YA urban fantasy novels. She lives in Southwest Michigan, where she works as a technical writer, practices yoga and tai chi, and watches too much *Doctor Who*. You can visit her on her website at www.stephanieastamm.com or on Facebook at www.facebook.com/stephaniestammauthor.

www.ingramcontent.com/pod-product-compliance
Lightning Source LLC
Chambersburg PA
CBHW021434240626
47153CB00001B/147